W9-ACG-307

THE KNOCKOUT

THE KNOCKOUT

SAJNI PATEL

Mendota Heights, Minnesota

First Edition
First Printing, 2021

Book design by Jake Slavik
Cover and jacket design by Jake Slavik
Cover, jacket, and interior images by photolinc/Shutterstock

Flux, an imprint of North Star Editions, Inc.

Library of Congress Cataloging-in-Publication Data
Names: Patel, Sajni, 1981- author.
Title: The knockout / Sajni Patel.
Description: First edition. | Mendota Heights, Minnesota : Flux, 2021. | Audience: Grades 10-12. | Summary: When seventeen-year-old Kareena Thakkar finally admits she is a top-level Muay Thai fighter, knowing that might further alienate her from her Indian community, her classmates, especially handsome Amit, enthusiastically support her.
Identifiers: LCCN 2020008206 (print) | LCCN 2020008207 (ebook) | ISBN 9781635830590 (hardcover) | ISBN 9781635830606 (ebook)
Subjects: CYAC: Muay Thai—Fiction. | Dating (Social customs)—Fiction. | High schools—Fiction. | Schools—Fiction. | East Indian Americans—Fiction. | Family life—Texas—Fiction. | Texas—Fiction.
Classification: LCC PZ7.1.P37698 Kno 2021 (print) | LCC PZ7.1.P37698 (ebook) | DDC [Fic]—dc23
LC record available at https://lccn.loc.gov/2020008206
LC ebook record available at https://lccn.loc.gov/2020008207

Flux
North Star Editions, Inc.
2297 Waters Drive
Mendota Heights, MN 55120
www.fluxnow.com

Printed in Canada

To my husband, who has patiently been at my side through the roller-coaster journey that is known as publishing. To my brother and parents, who've helped me through all the good and bad times.

Dear Reader,

You. Yes, you. The very special person holding this book. First off—THANK YOU! Books are a reality because of readers, because of wanting to get lost in a story, because it creates a bond that allows us to share this experience together over a bridge of time.

I want to remind you that *The Knockout* is a work of fiction. Most of the characters are based on real people (yay for my high school peeps!), and many of the situations and emotions are rooted from personal experiences. This story most certainly stems from my perspective growing up disconnected from my Indian heritage, on the outskirts of an Indian community, raised in the South and as a mixed martial artist in high school exposed to female Muay Thai fighters in college. However, this book does not represent the entire Indian culture/community/diaspora and in no way attempts to. Also, please note that fictional liberties were taken with some aspects of USMTO and IFMA. I hope to have portrayed the Art of Eight Limbs to the best of my ability and with respect. Any errors were unintentional.

Would you like to know the story behind the story? Aside from *The Knockout* being based on real events and people, it's the book that saved me. Several years ago, something seemingly minor and accidental happened (just like the situation with Saanvi and Rayna). It shouldn't have mattered much, but it did. I'd stopped writing then. I went into a depression for ten months and no matter how much I tried to write I couldn't string one sentence. I'd given up on many things and battled some very dark thoughts. It just happened that my brother was getting married and I went along on a family trip to Dubai and India to shop for the wedding events. I spent three weeks with my family, and it was the best medicine. I returned renewed and determined to write this tiny nugget of a story that had tried so hard to come out over the past year.

I wrote furiously. My creativity returned in full force. My depression eased away. *The Knockout* was born! It was the end of 2017. 2018 began with a new literary agent, my brother's amazing big, fat, Indian wedding (move over Priyanka Chopra and Nick Jonas), and ended with a publishing offer. Through everything *The Knockout* had gone through, no one called it a niche book, or too brown, or too Indian, or too different. It was just a story about a girl. Her name is Kareena Thakkar. She's imperfect and has self-esteem and body issues, feels disconnected from her culture, suffers from the mental blows that gossip brings, and swims through teenage drama. But she's also an amazing Muay Thai fighter, has the best friends and family one could ask for, and is ready to take you along on an adventure through all the ups and downs of her last semester of high school.

I sincerely hope you enjoy!

Many thanks and so much love,
Sajni Patel

ONE

Pink was reserved for the most badass in the sport of Muay Thai. It was an unspoken rule. You had to *earn* it. I, Kareena Thakkar, was at the top of my game . . . at least when it came to my division and weight class in Texas, anyway. But that didn't give me the right to wear pink. Nuh-uh, not yet. I knew deep in my bones that one day I would rock the most coveted color in all the land, but for now, pink gloves sufficed.

Sweat poured in rivulets down my body like this was the fight of my life, and the aforementioned pink gloves got their licks in. My fists were up to protect my face and every muscle and nerve were lit. I ducked and dodged and hit and punched. My lungs pounded out breaths in controlled grunts. Adrenaline surged through my veins. My teammates called me "the girl on fire." I scorched the ring and this blonde chick had *nothing* on me.

At least, that was what I told myself during every fight. They were good, but I was better. They were tough, but I was fierce. They hit and punched hard, but I was stone. And what did stones do when they careened toward someone? Why, they knocked them out. And Mama said knock. You. *Out.*

In this very moment, the cheering crowd muffled into bleak silence, sending a ringing through my ears. Every face blurred into one long, ambiguous slate of heaving bodies.

I counted the milliseconds as everything went into slow-mo.

My breaths escaped hard, roaring in my chest. My skin tingled with excitement and anticipation. I bounced on the balls of my feet. My nails dug deep into the leather of my gloves.

I was fit from years of training, but parts of me would always be skinny. Peers ridiculed my tiny wrists with sharp, jutting bones. I had chicken calves and bony ankles. But the good thing about possessing all of that? I also had sharp, strong-as-hell elbows and those were fan-freaking-tastic for Sok Ngad. The Uppercut Elbow. In I went. Striking my opponent and bringing her to her knees.

Most people didn't get this, this whole Muay Thai business. Too much violence. Too much hatred. It was the sort of stuff left for boys. Cuz what? Boys would be boys? Boys could act rough and girls had to sit with ankles crossed in pristine dresses and keep their opinions to themselves?

Society said girls shouldn't be fighting. Indian girls *especially* shouldn't do these things, yaar! But right now? Whatever anyone else said or thought didn't matter. This was a sport of passion, of skill, of years and tears in the making.

I had a way of wiggling into my opponents' heads, knowing their fighting patterns and logic. The equally strong blonde had managed to kick me in the ribs in the first round and stepped in to go after my injured side. With moves faster than anyone in my local weight/age range, I shifted toward Jenny and went uppercut, slicing through the marginal space between her gloves and knocking her back. But ah nah, I wasn't done with her, following with a quick rear cut and taking. Her. Out.

Jenny hadn't even hit the floor when the crowd exploded, screaming, applauding, and chanting, "K.O.-K.O.! K.O.-K.O.!" Lyrical music to my pounding ears.

Yeah, she wasn't going to last an entire three rounds with me. I stepped back into my corner, bouncing and shaking off the adrenaline, and ignored the searing pain racing down my forearms while watching the girl on the floor. It took three tries for her to sit up and cup her bleeding face. Where did all that blood come from anyway? Her nose? Lips? Teeth?

Suck it up, Buttercup. This was Muay Thai.

The referee sliced down through the air with his hand, to make sure everyone was clear on the count, as he yelled, ". . . Eight! Nine! Ten! Fight over! Kareena Thakkar for the win!"

Everything else was nonconsequential. I extended my hand to Jenny. She glared up at me, holding her bleeding face in one hand as her instructor entered the ring to help her. She got up on her own, a bit woozy, and we made a short bow toward one another in respect.

During the fight, she was just the "other girl." One of the coolest things about the sport was how we could be competitors in the ring and friends (or *friendly*, in the case of Jenny) outside.

"I whipped your butt." I stuck out my tongue when my coach had turned away.

Jenny rolled her eyes and nursed her sprains and pains and let her instructor dab her bleeding face before she stained the entire mat. If she was anything like me, and I knew she was, she'd replay the match over and over in her head, wondering where she could've done better. And then actually do better next time.

"Good fight," she said, her voice nasally as she held her nose upward. "I won't be the one bleeding next time, though."

"Can't wait." I grinned.

Time to shower off the sweat and grime, slather on Icy Hot like a med addict, slip into baggy sweats, and call it a night. Coach and all of my teammates wanted to grab dinner, as was the custom after winning a big fight, but I didn't have it in me.

"Sorry!" I called back, slinging my old, trusty duffel bag

over a sore shoulder and brushing off the wave of light-hearted teasing.

The sky was already dark without a cloud in sight. Silver dusted stars and a waning moon shone bright. The Texas air had chilled considerably since afternoon and sent goosebumps up my still sweaty arms. I slipped into my beat-up, four-door sedan that only had three working doors, onto the towel that Mama insisted I sit on if I forewent showering before driving, and turned up the heat before leaving the now half-empty parking lot.

It was a quick drive home and I couldn't get out of the car fast enough. One would think there were puppies or imported chocolates waiting for me in my room, but there was something far more important.

I lugged the duffel bag past the foyer and through the long corridor, depositing it outside my bedroom, and continued down the hall to Mama's room.

The door was wide open, but I knocked anyway.

"Come in! How was the fight?" my mom asked, a smile on her face because she somehow always knew when I had won or lost without having seen the fight.

"I won. Knockout in round two!" I climbed into bed beside my father and hugged him. "Hi, Papa. Welcome home!"

He hugged me tight, wrapping me in an unforgettable smell of dad shampoo and soap. From the sight of his damp hair and barely wrinkled pajamas, it was safe to assume that he'd just showered, which meant he must've been home for less than an hour.

While Mama folded clothes at the foot of the bed, Papa kept an arm around my shoulder and I nestled into his side, careful to not aggravate my pains and bruises.

"Tell me all about the fight. She didn't hurt you, did she?"

"Naw. Can't punch stone that hard."

He chuckled and I smiled at Mama. Her smile slowly faded when Papa coughed and reached over me for a tissue. I sat up to give him room.

"Give us a few minutes, beta," Mama said with that sad but hopeful smile she'd perfected over the years. Seven years to be exact. Seven years since Papa first went to the doctor with stomach issues, dizzy spells, migraines, anxiety, inflammation, abnormal blood tests, and half a dozen other things that apparently didn't add up to a real diagnosis. Not until he kept getting hospitalized for high fevers and passing out.

Papa had diabetes. Then he got renal disease. It advanced. This time, he'd gone septic, which was scary as crap (imagine someone telling you that you had an actual *blood infection* that could lead to system failure and possible death), but the doctor had caught it in time.

I nodded and slipped from his arms, trying not to imagine how it would be to slip out of his hold for the last time. Renal disease didn't just go away, not at this stage.

They refused to say it, but Papa was basically inching toward multisystemic failure. Mama never told me as much. Just like our bank account, she offered partial disclosure according to what she felt I needed to know or could handle. But I was nosy, or as I called it—concerned. Enough to snoop through Papa's records and lab test results and bills. I had to know how to take care of him and what to look out for in case he relapsed.

Mama gave me a brief rub on the shoulder in passing and I hurried with a quick step to my room, dragging the duffel bag inside and then hopping into the shower.

A few minutes ended up being an hour and a half, in which time I'd showered in lava-hot water, washed my hair, shaved, hopped out, dressed, wrapped a towel around my damp head, and dutifully took my mind off Papa by diving neck deep into homework at my small corner desk.

Math. Ugh. The bane of my mortal existence. Contrary to the stereotype that Indians excelled in math, calculus jumbled into meaningless gibberish right before my very eyes. This unintelligible nonsense worked when Mr. Strothers explained it on the white board, but leave me to my own devices and I was ready to burn all the math books within five minutes of trying equations on my own.

I flipped through the pages, back and forth, and noticed scribblings in the first chapter. They were from Rayna, who had calligraphy-type handwriting compared to my chicken scratch. Last fall, when she used to help me study Calculus I, she'd drawn doodles to help me get math.

I traced my finger over them. Chapter one was a long time ago. Her sitting beside me, giggling at me falling asleep and Saanvi throwing tiny paper balls into my hair was eons ago. So much had happened since then.

Despite my gnawing emotions, I looked through more of her drawings. Some silly faces, some serious equations, but my fingers stopped at the hearts. Hearts that represented us in a sea of paisleys and coffee cups.

Friends forever, some said. The short dark hearts represented Saanvi, the taller ones Rayna, and the pink ones with boxing gloves were me.

Then there were some that read *R + D = Life*.

I groaned and erased them all. But no matter how hard I rubbed, faint outlines of those dumb hearts remained. Against better judgment, I roamed through my phone and stopped on the last group chat I had with Rayna and Saanvi. I didn't know why I'd kept the text chain. Maybe as evidence?

Slow scrolling and random words revealed the evolution of

that once innocent conversation gone horribly wrong. Rayna talking about how she was over Saanvi's brother, Dev. Saanvi being sad but okay with it. Me asking if I could talk with him. Rayna and Saanvi being okay with it.

And then suddenly they weren't. They'd thrown in exclamation marks and angry emojis. And you knew when someone was ready to go savage when the all-caps came on.

I closed out the text message.

Ugh. There was no better way to break a teenage heart than to relive the death of a friendship.

I went back to equations and eventually switched to comp-sci after a torturous—I glanced at the digital clock on the wall—after a torturous twenty-eight minutes. Well, I lasted as long as I could, didn't I?

True, computer science had its fair share of numbers and equations and symbols, but they were an entirely different language than calculus. Literally. And I could rattle off programs in four comp languages easily. I'd just finished the last chapter and the assigned study questions when Papa knocked a single rap on the door, walked in, and sat on the edge of my bed.

His once vibrant dark brown skin was pallid; his features sallow and hollow, but he always managed a genuine smile—one that made my heart forever melt.

"Are you okay, Papa?"

"*Hah*, beta. A little dizzy, but that's okay. Now, tell me all about your fight."

I beamed and went into detail, full of gestures met with excited high fives and air fists from Papa. There was absolutely nothing better than having him home again, seeing him up and walking and exuberant. On my insistence, he stayed up with me until one in the morning, until both of our eyelids fluttered heavy with sleep.

TWO

I slid into a chair in the back of AP Comp-Sci II class and blinked a good fifty times to ward off sleepiness. That didn't really help. Slowly, the weight of my body pulled me down and forward until I slumped in an oh-so unladylike way, although that alleviated the pain in my side. My left elbow, the non-bruised one, was propped on the desk, chin in hand.

Computer science was a good class, it really was, just not when I was the walking dead struggling to keep my eyes open. At my section of one of four long tables, the screen blinked at me mockingly, but I was too exhausted to fight with it.

"You win," I muttered. Knockout, round one. I sucked.

Lily, my best friend since freshman year, sat beside me and unloaded her books in the small space between our keyboards. We exchanged grins as she flipped her ponytail over her shoulder. Her hair was harder to control than mine, but she actually made an effort, so her ponytail was totally rocking. Lily was Filipina but her hair was thick, coarse, and dry, and no one knew where she'd inherited such tresses. Her parents had sleek, smooth hair, and her older brother used to joke that she was adopted. She once divulged that she spent an hour every other morning with conditioners, creams, hair straighteners, and blow-drying techniques that would probably break my wrists.

"You should go natural," I had said when I first saw her hair after a shower, air-dried and undone.

"Afro, curls, or waves are gorgeous natural. My hair is a horror show of spiderwebs making awful love to twigs," Lily had replied.

About accurate, actually.

"Freaking cute boots," I muttered, desperately willing my bleary eyes to focus on the ankle-high, black shoes over Lily's leggings.

"Thanks! They're the ones I bought last weekend." She side-kicked my sneakers. "Where are yours?"

"Enjoying the view of my bed from the closet. I wish I was there now." Plus, my boots were so old, they were starting to literally fall apart.

"Ooh, what were you doing so late last night?" she asked in a sing-song voice.

I rolled my eyes. "Fight club."

"Whatever. Fine. Don't tell me."

"You never believe me when I say fight club."

"You can't be doing Muay Thai stuff *every* night. What happened to student council and Spanish club and choir? And boys?"

"What boys?"

"Travis was totally asking about you."

I gently tapped the keyboard, my slump taking me ever closer to the smooth surface of the table, to the sweet call of sleep. There was no time to think about something as trivial as boys, especially Travis. The guy was the senior class flirt. We'd known each other for years, so if he was asking about me, he was just making his rounds.

Lily swallowed. "Really?"

"Hmm?"

"You really have been fighting every day?"

"Yeah."

"That's not good."

"I need something to distract myself, and unfortunately, all the clubs in the world don't help. Plus, I'm still pissed at . . . well, you know."

"Yeah."

"So I can release anger too. Win, win. People's faces feel better than punching bags anyway."

"I'm sorry."

Lily meant that, she really did, but words were just words. They could cut a person deep, but somehow they didn't always have the same impact when trying to console. Before we tumbled down a road filled with sympathy and questions, I said, "Wake me if Mrs. Callihan comes over."

"She's on crutches. She ain't coming over here. Get your sleep on."

I winked and almost slid into the perfect position to doze off when the last student walked toward the back of class. His dark hair floated over the top of the computers. I recognized that carefully combed hair anywhere. I'd seen it only twenty minutes ago at lunch.

Amit Patel didn't have an MO. He was enigmatic. Not bad boy, brooding enigmatic, but simply puzzling. His perfect hair and nice clothes were straight up out of GQ, but his selection of classes was nerd city (as if I could talk because we shared classes). He never sat in the same place, and sometimes slept more than I did behind a book. Sometimes he chatted up a storm with others and other times he hid in the library. He was both popular and unpopular, charismatic and shy, extroverted and introverted. *Enigmatic.*

Most times, Amit made eye contact once a day, preferably

in passing so he didn't walk into me. Today, we caught each other's eye as I straightened up and he happened to glance my way. He held my gaze this time, and not in an awkward oops-we-saw-one-another-and-it-would-be-rude-to-look-away-but-why-were-we-still-staring kind of awkwardness (usually our thing), but a steady stare. The way football players looked at girls as they rolled down the hall after a big win.

Most times, I didn't notice Amit. But then there were incomprehensible moments like this where my heart beat faster. Fight club kind of faster.

"Tension," Lily whispered, her head downturned at her notebook.

"Shut up," I mumbled and broke eye contact Did I forget to smile? I probably did. Great, now Amit would think I was being salty.

I tucked a few loose strands of hair behind my ear. Through the corner of one eye, I watched the movement of his feet as he took the empty seat to the left. The bottom of his dark-blue jeans folded over the tops of red and white sneakers.

My gaze wandered up.

The hem of a plaid green and black shirt wrinkled around his waist. The short sleeves tightened around his biceps and a muscle in his forearm constricted every time he wrote.

Amit cleared his throat.

My cheeks flared hot and I gaped at my screen, at the empty, taunting one that had already won our battle for the day.

Amit cleared his throat again.

I side-eyed him and he jerked his chin toward the front.

"What?" I mouthed, confused.

He tapped the eraser end of his pencil against his paper.

"Oh." Crap. I scrambled for a pencil and scribbled my name and date across the top of my paper.

Mrs. Callihan had been talking this entire time? I struggled to make sense of the first two questions she'd already asked. I looked to Lily, hoping to catch her attention. When she caught me trying to decipher her chicken scratch, she shrugged.

God. Lily sucked at computer science more than anyone. How'd she get into AP anyway?

Today's attendance quiz proved two things. One, I was present. Two, I didn't pay enough attention to figure out the primary algorithm. Fail.

As I tried one more time to glean answers from Lily, tilting toward her while checking for any sign of Mrs. Callihan, a slight cool swish of air hit my arm. An answer magically appeared on my pathetically vacant paper. In Amit's handwriting.

I gawked at him. He never did that. But he hunched over his desk and wrote, not paying any mind to my bemusement. I forced myself to forget it ever happened and finished the last question. We passed our papers to the right and then to the front. Mrs. Callihan went over the answers and thank goodness for Amit, because he had given me the right one, although when he passed his quiz over I saw that he had written something entirely different on his sheet. I was too exhausted to wonder why, or if my sight was too blurred to read straight.

With Amit right beside me, I could *not* fall asleep. Jerking awake, drooling, snoring, muttering in my sleep? I probably would do all of that. But my eyelids drooped and the next thing I knew, I woke up with my cheek hot, pressed against my short stack of books, an angry crick gnawing at my neck, and Amit shuffling out of his chair along with the rest of the class.

Lily giggled.

"Why didn't you wake me? Why did you let me fall asleep facing the other way?" I rubbed my eyes, my cheeks, my . . .

oh lord, was that drool on the corner of my mouth? Yep. It sure was.

Lily laughed. "Cuz you like him. Admit it." Then she quietly, somberly added, "And you need a little fun."

I stood, sucking in a breath when the pain in my ribs sprang back to life. Jenny might've gotten knocked out in round two, but she kicked harder than I did. "Shh. He's still here."

"Why don't you just talk to him?"

"I dunno. Maybe because most boys can't handle a girl who can kick their butt at any given moment. Seems to dissuade the majority."

In the near distance, at the front of the classroom, Amit nodded to Mrs. Callihan while she spoke to him. He caught my eye for a brief second before leaving.

"Well, this was too cute to wake you up for, but . . ." Lily swiped across her phone and turned the screen to my incredulous gaze.

My jaw dropped. Lily had, at some pro-level angle, snapped a picture of both Amit and myself asleep on our desks . . . facing one another. Like, two lovebirds or something. And in the background, Jared made kissy faces.

I hated cell phones, and this was why. We weren't allowed to have them for this very reason because kids took humiliating pictures of people without their permission. "Don't send that to anyone or show anyone."

"Ha!"

"Oh my freaking goodness. Please don't. That's embarrassing." I glared at the picture, hoping the annoyed part of me overpowered the amused part long enough to keep face.

"I think it's cute." Lily looked at the picture one last time before dropping the phone into her purse. "I'm keeping it."

"Are you sure it's not because you're crushing on Jared and you'll pretend that he's making kissy faces at *you*?"

She ignored me and said, "I wonder what kept Amit up so late last night for him to fall asleep in class."

"Studying? Video games? I don't know."

"Hmm." She fixed her ponytail. "Maybe he was at fight club too."

"Yeah, right. I cannot imagine Amit fighting."

"So what's his secret nightlife all about?"

I shrugged and headed for the door, hoping to evade Mrs. Callihan by hiding behind Lily. But nope. The teacher called me over to her desk.

I put on my best smile and said, "Hi, Mrs. Callihan. What's up?"

"Kareena, I wanted to ask a huge favor of you."

"Sure."

"I'd sincerely appreciate it if you could tutor Amit."

My heart skipped a beat and words tumbled over one another on my tongue like clumsy fools. "Um, what?"

"I know you're probably busy with your own classes and extracurricular activities, but Amit's grade is on the line and I'd hate to drop his average. You know, he's set to be valedictorian and I'd feel awful if this one slip-up ruined years of hard work."

"What . . . what about Mike or Angie? They've got straight As in your class. I mean, I'm honored that you think of me as someone capable of helping the valedictorian, but, yeah. What about them?"

"I'm afraid they're tutoring someone in another class, and I've asked a few students already."

"Oh." Well, maybe I wasn't that special after all.

"Any help is better than none, and I would give you extra credit." She pointedly looked at me as if to add: *And you sure could use it, missy*. I mean, I wasn't a perfect 4.0, so yeah, who couldn't use extra credit?

Which begged the question as to *why* ask me to tutor anyone unless Amit was actually about to lose out on his valedictorian status? But how could his grade be so bad? He knew all the answers all the time. He didn't always write them down, and he never showed the work. He was a freaking genius, for crying out loud. If anything, *he* should tutor *me*!

But . . . extra credit was extra credit. And if I'd learned anything from my parents, it was how to haggle.

"Well, I'm awfully busy, Mrs. Callihan. I have all AP classes and clubs and sports. Lots of cultural stuff to organize and participate in."

"Oh, I know and I'm so proud to see so many of my students involved in various activities and still do so well in school."

"Like a whole test grade impressed?"

"Kareena," she chided. "That's a lot to ask for."

"Tutoring takes a lot of time, especially with family obligations." I didn't mean to play that card, it wasn't there to help me get things, but it *was* the truth. Papa's health was deteriorating and tutoring someone who wasn't anyone to me took time away from being with him.

"I'll add ten points to your lowest test score."

"To my test average," I countered.

"All right."

Wait. What? Just like that? I eyed her suspiciously. This wasn't some ploy so she could give me sympathy points, was it?

Mrs. Callihan laced her fingers together on top of her desk. "Is everything okay at home?"

I shrugged and pressed my lips together in the universal

gesture for: *No, but I'm politely going to nonverbally ask you to stop this conversation.*

"Okay. I'm here if you need to talk. Thank you, Kareena."

"Sure." I left and turned the corner at the hallway, walking right into Amit, who'd been waiting for me.

We both stumbled away from the other, his cheeks red and mine hot. When he realized his hands had landed on my waist, he jerked back and scratched the back of his neck. "Sorry."

"So, Mrs. Callihan said you need a tutor?" I asked, trying to ignore the pleasant burn his touch had left through the fabric of my shirt.

"Yeah," he replied. His voice was deeper than most boys our age and always threw me off, but it sure was nice to listen to.

"How are you even near failing?"

He shrugged, like no biggie. I didn't get it. No MO. He was ridiculously smart, but he needed a tutor? *Me* of all people?

Oh, well. If nothing else, if I couldn't figure him out, we had a reason to talk. But I played it cool, as if the possibility of constant close proximity didn't rattle my insides or give me goosebumps.

Down the hall, beyond Amit, Lily peered at us from around her locker door, undoubtedly being nosy, when Travis strolled past and flicked her ponytail. He didn't stop to flirt with her, as he had the habit of doing with many, many girls, but instead slid to a stop beside me.

"What's going on, Kareena? You going to the party this weekend?" he asked me and then gave a nod to Amit.

"No," I replied. I didn't even know which party he was referring to. Parties weren't my thing. Then I froze, suddenly hyper aware of Amit. He was . . . to put it bluntly, the perfect Indian boy. He went to mandir and participated in all the religious stuff. He listened to his parents and got perfect grades.

He had a ton of Indian friends. No one at school hated him and all the Indians respected him. All the teachers loved him. He never got into trouble. He was . . . the opposite of me.

What did he think about this guy asking me about parties? Did he think I was a party girl? That I drank at those parties? Made out at those parties?

"I'll talk to you later, Kareena," Amit said and gave me a small smile before turning to leave, but I grabbed his wrist and pulled him back, stunning both myself and Amit. A shocking amount of electricity sparked beneath my fingers, the kind that could potentially stop a heart. If anyone watched us, I didn't notice.

I blinked back into the moment, realizing all too suddenly and powerfully that I was holding a boy's hand. There was no throwing it away or playing it off. Instead of continuing this awkward staring thing we seemed to be doing a lot of these days, I gulped, pulled out a pen, and wrote my number on his palm.

"Text me," I managed to say without sputtering. *Real smooth, Kareena.*

The corner of Amit's mouth curled up into a half smile, but the scruffy clearing of Travis's throat ruined whatever this was. Amit backed into the hallway and disappeared into the throng of students hurrying to their next class.

"I'm not going to any parties, Travis," I told him and walked away.

Plenty of students waved and said hi to me in the few minutes I had to get to my next class. I smiled at all of them. Kimmy gave a high five in passing, flipping her red curls over her shoulder. "I better see you on the bleachers this weekend!" she called back but didn't wait for an answer.

Tanya did a little dance move in the hall, probably pumped about her basketball win from last night.

"Nice game!" I shouted to her through the growing crowd.

Most students wore green and black on game day, so the soccer players, like Jared, walked around with pride colors on and smiles turned up. I glanced around looking for Lily to see if she was swooning yet. Yep. Right against the door to her next class before slipping inside. Staring hard and grinning like a fool, even though she'd just spent an entire hour and a half sitting ten feet away from him.

At my locker, I exchanged comp-sci books for bio and checked my phone out of habit. Mama had texted. I didn't want to know, not yet. I didn't want to hear in definite terms if Papa's condition had worsened overnight, or even that he hadn't improved, that maybe he had to get readmitted to the hospital. I just wanted to fight, to have a few hours a day where my focus honed in on kicking butt and my brain concentrated so hard on compartmentalizing techniques that I didn't have a second to think about all the crap going down.

I read it anyway.

Kick butt at school!

I grinned and shook my head. Okay. Those were the best texts.

My phone dinged before I tossed it back into the cavernous void known as my locker. Email. I thumbed through my inbox, opening a message from Coach.

I read it quickly. Then again. Slowly. Because I couldn't have read the elite invitation correctly the first time.

My heart palpitated so hard that I forgot to breathe, and wheezed for the next breath of air. Oh my freaking goodness! This was not happening. Like I was Cinderella finally being noticed by the prince, something she never thought could actually happen (because c'mon, the *prince*), but then one day! Bam! The seemingly impractical and improbable shoe fits!

Or in this case . . . the hot pink and black boxing gloves fit.

I scrolled to the very beginning of the email and read the opening lines another five times.

THE ART OF EIGHT LIMBS. Kareena Thakkar qualifies for this year's US Muay Thai Open: Class A Juniors Girls Lightweight Division. First place prize: $50,000.

THREE

I hugged the phone to my chest. My body pulsated with a jillion emotions and possibilities. They came crashing over my soul, dragging me down with an intense current, and throttling me back to the surface, only to repeat the pattern. There was so much to gain! Title, prestige, yeah, of course.

But the prize money. I needed that money. I needed it to help the family because ever since Papa fell sick, like beyond being able to keep up kinda sick, we'd spent most of our money on basic bills and the rest went to medical stuff.

"Don't worry, beta," he'd said when we had to sell our two-story, four-bedroom house and half the furniture two years ago, after the first five years of endless renal disease relapses sucked money out of the bank, on top of endless doctor visits, hospitalizations, tests, and medications. "We don't need such a big place for the three of us, and you'll be off to college in a few years and what will we be? Ghosts haunting a giant house all alone?"

I didn't care about the material things then. Not even when Mama decided to sell off a bunch of clothes and jewelry.

"It's fine," Mama had said with teary eyes as she stroked her necklace and gold bangles. "They're just things."

I had surprised both parents when I furrowed my brows, started up the computer, and replied, "Leave the selling to me. I'll research the best places that'll give us the biggest bucks."

The only reason I continued with Muay Thai with all its expenses was because a few local places were willing to sponsor me. When I couldn't buy anything during shopping trips with friends or eat out with teammates and go on club field trips, I rammed all my focus into three things: family, grades, and Muay Thai. Nothing else mattered.

Muay Thai was my passion and a release. I didn't know what I'd do without it. How many extra hours would I have to fret over my parents? I'd considered giving it up to work, but they wouldn't let me. Now, it could pay off in big, monetary ways.

Except there was a price tag attached to this invitation. My sponsors would only go so far. Maybe Coach would help. But what then? Spend a few grand in hopes of getting fifty in return?

Wow. What would fifty grand get us? Probably pay off some of Papa's debts. Catch up on bills, set some money aside for future bills, and oh yeah, this thing called college because there was no way I could help support myself and an ailing father with a minimum-wage job for the rest of my life.

Even before I put the phone away, Coach texted.

Did you get my email?

I giggled. *Yeah, Coach! I got it! Can we chat about it after school?*

Sure thing, kiddo. I can swing by and we can talk with your parents.

Sounds good. Let me ask them first and I'll let you know.

Then he shot a shaka emoji—Coach was Hawaiian. All right, so we could discuss the chances of me winning, the price tag of actually attending, and if everything fell into place, the rigorous training.

There went the weekend pizza sleepover with Lily. And tutoring Amit? Well, he could find an online tutor probably.

My next thought automatically turned to Rayna. I almost texted her the news, but my fingers hovered over the screen.

I bet she'd be ecstatic for me, despite what had happened. She knew what this meant.

My heart sort of plummeted into my stomach for a minute. It sucked really hard when one of the few people who knew about and excitedly accepted my passion didn't want to be my friend anymore.

Amit texted right after the final bell at the end of the day, before I had even reached my locker, before I had a chance to find Lily and tell her the good news in person.

When do you want to study? I can't tonight, maybe Thursday for an hour right after school?

I twisted my lips. For a guy who had a lot riding on this, he sure wasn't making the best effort. I'd think he'd want to study every night for as long as it took for him to get back to the top. Amy Smith and Daniel Ng were on his tail in this running, and they were freaking cutthroat.

But Amit bailing worked out for tonight anyway, and I was glad not to be the first to break our commitment.

Thurs right after school in the library.

Okay. Thanks!

NP. See ya then. TTYL

"Texting your boyfriend?" Lily sang as she slid into place against a locker, her side pressed to the cold metal surface.

"Which one?" I winked and she laughed.

"You look glowy. What's up?"

"I can't even!" I beamed.

"What? What!" She bounced up and down. "God, what happened that you're so excited?"

"Shh!" I took her hand to stop her jumping but found myself wanting to bounce too. "Don't tell a soul, okay?"

"Promise." She pretended to zip her lips.

"I just got invited to the Muay Thai Open." Then I slapped a hand over my mouth as if I'd just let out the world's biggest secret since smartphone tech, my eyes wide and glistening with unadulterated joy.

"Oh, my lord!" Lily threw her arms around me for a giant bear hug, which didn't go unnoticed by some. Some nosy bodies.

"Remember, don't tell a soul."

"When do you leave? When is it? Can you have cheerleaders? Screw this cheerleading team; even if I didn't make it freshman year, I totally rock as a cheerleader. I can make black shirts with hot pink skulls to match your badassery."

"I freaking love it! Okay. Calm down. I don't know the details yet. I don't even know if my parents will let me go, or how much it'll cost. I haven't told them yet, haven't told anyone."

"Well, you have to go. You've trained your entire life for this."

"I know. I know." I hugged my arms around my waist as tumultuous adrenaline coursed through me, like slowly easing backward on a roller-coaster and then dropping straight down at full speed. It was a dizzying, wonderful, infectious rapture mixed with unbridled fear.

"Whoa, what's going on? You okay?" Lily reached for my arm.

"Yeah. Just so much. It's a dream, a huge life accomplishment. Oh, man. What if I fail? What if I can't stand one round with national girls? What if I get knocked out so hard, my brain goes *kasplunk* and I'm a walking dead zombie forever and ever?"

Lily's grip tightened in a reassuring way. She anchored my worries to the ground, but I could feel them taking me higher and higher. "Girl, chill. I've never seen you get worked up. Let it sink in, enjoy the moment. Talk to your parents and let me know what happens. I will be by your side one hundred percent, okay?"

"K."

"Breathe."

"Yeah. I'm breathing."

Lily half waved at someone behind me, the someone who strolled by with her books hugged closely to her chest. Rayna.

Rayna made my heart ache. The back of her glorious, dark, hip-length hair swayed past and she didn't even say hi. I wanted so badly to tell her about the Open. She'd probably pull out a congratulatory cupcake from her locker, the flavor of the month from her dad's bakery, with pink sprinkles of course. She always saved the glittery ones for me. Or, at least she used to. She'd most likely force me to do that shoulder Bhangra-style dance right here in the middle of the student body and shout, "Hands up!" People wouldn't know what the heck was going on, but they'd join in anyway, and we'd have a party on our hands in zero-to-sixty.

"Don't worry about her," Lily muttered.

"Have you talked to her recently? Is she still mad at me?"

"We haven't been real friends since all that went down, but we keep it friendly enough. I'd rather not talk to her, cuz I might lose my crap, but if you want, I can casually bring it up. But don't let her and that dumb stuff get you down."

"It's hard to see her and not feel depressed again."

"I know, I know, but you've got bigger, better things

happening. What happened between you and Dev was last winter. I mean, seriously, she even told you to talk with Dev, that she was way over him. What are you supposed to do? Never talk to a boy that your friends have ever crushed on? That's not realistic. I mean, who *haven't* your friends crushed on? And as amazing as you think Rayna is, if she doesn't want to be your friend anymore, then that's on her. Give me a break. Treating you this way for a whole two months for trying to talk to a boy who she wasn't even dating, and who she gave you the green light to talk to? It's all *her* loss."

"And mine." Just thinking about the implosion of our friendship made my stomach tie into queasy knots. All I wanted was to crawl into myself and pretend none of this had happened.

"*Hers*," Lily reiterated before I tumbled down a rabbit hole of how perfect and lovable Rayna was. Uh, why did I try to talk with Dev in the first place? I should've known better. I really did miss Rayna, one of my closest friends, and seemingly the only Indian who didn't turn up their nose in disgust or quiet judgment at my extracurricular pursuits.

I shook it off and stretched my neck from one side to the other, eyes closed in meditation. Shake off the haters. Shake off the negativity.

When I arrived home, my parents were in the living room watching one of their prime-time dramas. Two mugs of chai steamed on the coffee table beside a plate of biscuits from the Indian grocery store. My mouth watered at the sight. Parle-G were my fave, rich and buttery and oh-so sweet . . . but nah,

I had to train hard now. That was, if the parental units even let me go.

I took in a few deep, calming breaths. I seemed to be doing a lot of that these days. After taking off my shoes in the foyer and setting my backpack down, I trotted to the living room, leaned down, and kissed both of them on the cheek.

"Well, you seem to be in a delightful mood," Papa said. He looked better, and hope swelled inside me. His eyes and cheeks weren't as hollow, and some color had returned to his face. He looked rested.

I sat on the edge of the couch, my fingers laced on my lap. "First of all, I want to thank you for letting me pursue Muay Thai."

Mama rolled her eyes. "Eck minute, beta. Are you starting this whole working a job instead of Muay Thai nonsense again?"

"Um, no. I am thanking you for letting me do this. I know it's unconventional and expensive."

Papa tsked. "Don't mention money or budget to us, beta. We want you to enjoy life, you know? And nothing brings such happiness to your eyes as Muay Thai. Except maybe chocolate cake and fried pickles."

I grinned sheepishly. Fried anything tasted really good. My smile faded, replaced by seriousness. "I appreciate everything you've given me, and also how you keep some of your struggles to yourself because yeah, I'm a kid. But I'm older now, and you can be frank with me."

"We appreciate this."

"Okay. Well, you know how I applied to USMTO and I've been winning all of my fights this year?"

They nodded, pride in their smiles. Yeah, they'd let me apply to USMTO, but we didn't expect anything to come of it. I surely didn't.

"Coach just told me that I qualify for the national level."

Mama clapped her hands together. "That's amazing news!"

Papa laughed and gently applauded, then pointed a finger up like his hand was chanting "We're number one! Way to go, beta! I knew the first moment you tried on gloves that you would be exceptional."

"Coach wants to come by and talk to you about me possibly going."

"Possibly?" Papa asked. "Why not definitely?"

I bit my tongue to keep from mentioning the budget. I had no idea of the costs. "Something can always come up. Anyway, he wants to talk to all of us. Is that okay? Can he come tomorrow after practice?"

"We'd love to talk to him, catch up, find out what to expect. This is so thrilling. Do you know that some cousins have played sports in high school, like wrestling or softball? But they were average. They only played to boost their college applications. No one has had your kind of talent."

My cheeks warmed. Being complimented as anything other than ordinary compared to my über-successful cousins made me feel more Indian somehow. "They've very prestigious careers, though. That has nothing to do with a random sport they played in school."

"True. However, they studied very hard and tried even harder to get to where they are. And so have you. No one in our family, in our social circle, can say their daughter is a national-level athlete. And she's smart and beautiful on top of that? No contest."

"Papa . . ." I rolled my eyes but smiled.

"It's true! And whatever you decide to pursue in college will only enhance your accomplishments. What did everyone else do by senior year? They were in the top ten percent, right? So what? That's nothing. You're in the top ten percent! *And* you've excelled in something as hard and rigorous as Muay Thai." He waved off the cousins. "You've surpassed them."

"Thank you, Papa. That means so much to me. I know others don't like it—"

"Forget the others," Mama spat. "Do you mean other Indians?"

"Yeah."

"Who are they, anyway? They can keep their unsolicited opinions to themselves."

Papa rubbed her shoulder to calm her down. Mama was a fierce tiger. Whatever had happened in the past that led her to walk away from the Indian social circle was something she wouldn't talk about in depth. I knew some basic stuff, like her pregnancy and dropping out of med school. But it seemed there was more, and as my elder, she didn't get that deep with me. It was the reason my parents didn't press me to go to mandir and festivities and get knee-deep involved with the Indian community.

"You are our daughter," Mama continued, "and we're proud of everything you've done. Can your coach come over today? Why wait?"

"Let me text him!" I sent out a quick text to Coach, who agreed to drop by in an hour.

I'm beyond excited for you, Kareena!

Thanks, Coach! You're behind this success too! But how much will it cost?

That was the burning question hot on the tip of my tongue when he finally arrived. He'd never texted me back.

I let Coach in the minute he rang the doorbell. Couldn't help but to pace the foyer in hopes of catching him first about expenses, but my parents were on my heels, and eagerly invited him to join them in the living room. There was, of course, a cup of hot chai waiting for him.

"Cost of admission into USMTO itself is less than a hundred dollars, which is not bad," Coach began as he sipped his drink on the end of the couch closest to Papa and his recliner.

My father leaned forward with keen interest, and I curled into myself to bear the brunt of disappointment.

"Cost of spectator admission is about forty dollars a person. The event is four days, but we want to get there at least one day early and check out one day later, so figure at least six days, seven preferably. Food for those days, plus transportation, which is airfare and cab rides."

Papa nodded, but I twitched as I did the math in my head.

"Kareena will have to get blood tests done. And, not to sound superficial, but this is a huge event and we want to look our best, plus all of her gear and clothing need approval from the Open. She'll need new Muay Thai shorts, a few high-quality tank tops, new gloves for training, shin guards, elbow pads, and helmet."

Crap. Crap. *Crap.* I needed everything new because all of my stuff was worn the heck down. I wasn't technically allowed to keep using some of my equipment as run down and wretched as it was.

"We're looking at nearly three grand to be safe."

I sank into my seat with a heaviness in my bones. That was . . . a lot. Maybe to some people it wasn't much, or maybe some parents could come up with the cash. But not us. And three grand was just for me. Plane tickets and admission for my parents and their food would be extra.

"It would be less except, well, as you know, Kareena hasn't kept up with replacing her equipment. It wouldn't be within regulations at USMTO, and she would be disqualified from fighting. Also, I highly encourage her to start seeing a chiropractor and getting regular deep-tissue massages. That's an additional few hundred a week."

Papa let out a long sigh and I barricaded my hopes. *Three* grand in five weeks. My parents didn't have that kind of money. Coach couldn't front that. My sponsors and teammates might offer a few hundred, but that was being very optimistic.

"However," Coach continued, "here's the thing. There is a substantial reward at the end." Now *he* scooted to the edge of his seat, leaned his elbows on his thighs just as Papa had. They were eye to eye and an explosive excitement wriggled off of him. He couldn't stop grinning and kept tapping his fingers together.

"Yes, there is a cash prize that will help Kareena out in many ways, but the best fighters at USMTO gain the recognition of the IFMA."

Dizziness hit hard. IF-freaking-MA? Holy crap. That was something I'd known about for years, but never in my wildest dreams had I thought it was a real, obtainable possibility to get noticed by them! Was I about to faint? I thought I just might!

Coach could tell from Mama's puzzled gaze that he had to clarify. "IFMA is the International Federation of Muaythai Associations. They're the governing body that determines the participating fighters for the US team in the World Championships."

Mama and Papa laughed wholeheartedly, startling me. They didn't laugh as if this was the most outlandish joke ever played on them. They laughed like this was the best thing to ever tickle their funny bones, with tears sparkling in their eyes. They were *proud*.

"Not only that, but there is serious talk of including Muay Thai in the next Olympics. And Kareena is so talented and skilled that I am unbiasedly telling you that your daughter has a realistic chance of getting on both teams."

"Holy crap!" I slapped a hand over my mouth, eyes wide behind my palm as my parents scowled. But their scowl was almost immediately replaced with earth-shattering grins.

"Are you for real?" I asked, my words mumbled behind my hand.

"Yes. As serious as the day I walked into this sport. I didn't want to inflate your ego or get your hopes too high, but things are happening now, things that solidify my gut feeling about you. Kareena, you have to go; you have to do this."

I held my breath and tried not to let Coach's words go to my head. There was nothing worse than a cocky, entitled fighter. Coach didn't let those types into his gym, so his meaning was way beyond superficial hype. So instead of my head getting big with pride, my heart swelled with gratitude. I was here because of my parents and Coach.

"I've trained you since you were eight. You went from cautious to fearless by the time you turned ten. Nothing should get in your way. You have major accomplishments about to be handed to you if only you train hard, bring your A game to USMTO, and keep your head on straight."

I nodded, getting more and more excited as Coach started getting into it, as he pulled my parents into how big of a deal this was with his ever-growing gestures.

"This is not a game. This is not a hobby or a pastime or something to add to your college application, Kareena. This is the big leagues, serious stuff, and a wide doorway to even greater things." He paused. Dramatic affect: *leveled up*. "You can make history."

"Oh my!" Mama fanned herself. "You could be the first

Indian girl in the USMTO. The first Indian on the US team for the World Championships."

"Part of the first Muay Thai Olympic team . . ." I breathed. My body heated to furnace levels, my head light and filled with swooshing. My skin prickled with a million fiery stabs.

"You could make history here," Coach repeated.

His words echoed through my brain all night.

FOUR

Well, that was quite the evening with some bombshells laid down like: no freaking big deal, y'all. All those many *huge* things kept me awake the entire night, tossing and turning and texting Lily until she stopped responding, at which point I assumed she'd fallen asleep.

Coach had given my parents a packet that he went over with us, plus the rules to USMTO, which alone was thirty pages. It was nothing new, mostly reiterating what I'd been doing for the majority of the past nine years. I had a stricter routine now, though, because I only had five weeks to get into Nationals shape.

I woke up when the alarm buzzed at six. I didn't have to wake up yet, as class didn't start until ten. The other nice thing about having pushed myself in school and getting ahead of the required credits was that not only did I need a measly three courses my senior year, but that meant I only had school on Tuesdays and Thursdays starting late but ending at three. Papa had encouraged me to graduate early and get a head start in college, but I knew we didn't have the funds last year for me to start at the community college this year.

Besides, I took all AP classes during junior and senior year, which meant I only had to pay a hundred bucks per AP test to get college credit. I'd enter ACC—Austin Community College—as a sophomore. We'd saved big bucks already. Then finishing up another year with whatever transferred to UT saved more still. ACC wasn't cheap for a community college, but UT? That place would break the bank. By then, I'd have some financial aid and hopefully scholarships, and maybe even a little of this prize money to help out.

And if I made it to the World Championships? I mentally whistled. That had to earn some dough. And the Olympics? Definitely some money and commercials and stuff? That could pay off a class or two.

Day one was not the day to get lazy. I managed to wake up with energy, and, as I had been doing most days, donned a pair of short, blue mesh running shorts, a green tank top, and ankle socks with my kicks. I gathered my mid-back-length hair and tied it into a bun on the top of my head to keep it from irritating my neck. My hair only found freedom at night and was bound by the law of hair ties at all other times.

From the sound of light snoring oozing from my parents' room, Mama napped in between her two jobs and Papa slept soundly at her side. The front door creaked on its hinges when I slipped out. Popping in my earbuds and turning on my "Run Jam" playlist, I jumped down the steps to get the blood going and bounded to the end of the driveway, working my calves and thighs before starting a two-mile run.

There was a time when I loathed running; the shin splints, the boringness, the effort, but Coach taught me to use running as a time for meditation and reflection. Which seemed to contradict the pulse-raging music screaming through my head, but it worked. I loosened my grip on all the worries and anxieties that weighed heavy on my shoulders. I concentrated instead on the feel of my legs pounding against the pavement, of the smell of dewy grass, the chill of morning air, the rush in my lungs, the stretch of my muscles, the sound of steady breaths, and the fog emitted from my lips.

It was all beautiful and harmonious and stuff. Better than calculus any day!

A few neighbors were out giving their dogs potty breaks or leaving early for work. A couple of guys jogged across the main street and I had the urge to pick up my pace, to run faster than them. One of the guys, twenty-something, noticed and grinned. He picked up his pace, leaving his friend behind.

Oh, it was *so* on! And thus, the quiet beauty of a morning run turned into competitiveness with random strangers. Those dudes had nothing on me. I'd been running five times a week since for as long as I could remember.

I crossed three streets and made it to the next main intersection, a minor highway, and came to an abrupt stop. I beat them, no contest. I waited patiently with hands on hips, my breathing easy.

The guys slowed to a stop on the other side of the street, winded and trying not to bend over. I waved and they smirked with a thumbs up. Then I turned around and sprinted home, knowing I'd left them in the suburban dust of my wake. Acorn and pecan trees lined the patchy grass section between the sidewalk and the crumbling subdivision stone walls. The whoosh of speeding cars over cracked pavement hurried by in the morning rush. School buses with peeling yellow paint appeared on the horizon, stopping by clusters of yawning, sleepy kids.

When I reached my street, the sprint slowed to a jog and then a quick stretch of the legs before doing lunges all the way to the cul-de-sac and back to the house. My thighs burned, but in a glorious, accomplished way. Kicking off my shoes in the foyer, I rolled out the yoga mat and stretched some more before lying down for crunches, bike abs, v-crunches, Thai sit-ups, and the dreaded Superman.

By the time I finished, Mama had awoken and moved about the bathroom getting ready for job numero dos and I headed for the kitchen, sweaty as always. I figured I went through Costco amounts of deodorant and body wash.

Second thing on the agenda was diet. Boo, no pizza gorging with Lily this weekend. After Coach left last night, Mama and I made a market run. We bought Papa's meds and with what we had left, we bought food. There would be no junk food, nothing processed, mostly no bad carbs (rice was a must, okay?), and nothing that would lag my digestive system and make me feel like crap. I had to cook everything that went into my mouth myself, but I was used to that anyway since Mama worked two jobs and Papa could only occasionally cook when he was up to it.

Thankfully, no one in the house was a vegetarian. There were no dietary restrictions except for Papa, who could not have too much sugar, junk food, and most carbs. Which worked out great! We were already on the same diet! I cooked for the entire family at once.

"Beautiful morning, beta." Papa hummed and took a seat at the table. He crossed his legs, ankle over knee, and opened the paper.

"Morning, Papa! You're in an awesome mood."

"Exceptionally good mood. I feel great. My daughter is about to make history. I have a beautiful family and a warm home. What isn't to love?"

"You don't love eggs, but you're getting them. Soft-boiled, yeah?"

"I'll love eggs, even."

I washed my hands and bobbed my head to some

imaginary beat in case I had to keep an ear out for the parental units needing something. Eggs sizzled in the pan and the last of the wheat bread toasted on the side while a pot of water boiled on the back burner. A small glass of orange juice for Mama, and lots of water for Papa and myself, waited on the table.

Mama swooped in like a hungry eagle, devoured her eggs over easy and buttered toast and downed her OJ with a quick "thanks." I poured mint chai into a thermos for her and off she went, with a quick kiss on my head and a gentle hug to Papa's back.

Papa liked his eggs on the softer side of hard boiled. Six and a half minutes to be exact once the water boiled. He preferred a shake of salt and chili powder while I opted for the traditional salt and pepper. He didn't eat much these days, or probably couldn't since he was used to eating little and filling his belly with meds instead. He had two eggs with his cup of chai.

"There's extra chai in the thermos on the counter if you want some at lunch," I mentioned.

"I will definitely drink the rest."

Plopping onto my seat, I dove into my four eggs, bacon, spinach, and chai. Then I proceeded to make lunch: cream cheese-stuffed celery for Papa and black forest ham and cheese roll-ups for me.

"What's that?" I asked him, nodding at the scribbled list beside his newspaper.

"Ah, this. This is a list of businesses that we can talk to about sponsorship for the Open."

"Really?"

"Yes. Places around here like to sponsor kids' events that

are this amazing. We just need an intro to pitch them and then reel them in."

"Like . . . door-to-door stuff?" I groaned, remembering how many times I'd bugged our neighbors to buy candy bars to raise money for stuff in school. There was nothing more awkward than knocking on people's doors on Saturday mornings and asking them to give me five dollars for a candy bar. Except maybe telling them why they should care enough to give me five dollars. A few bucks at a time meant a lot of doors to knock on. But maybe businesses did things by the hundreds of dollars?

There was no way Papa could drive around and talk to people, and no time for Mama to help. I smiled softly and took the list from him. "Thanks, Papa! I'll come up with a pitch and a game plan."

"Are you excited?"

"To talk strangers into giving me money?"

He chuckled. "About the Open?"

"Of course. I guess that'll make it easier to talk to people. I really want this."

He nodded. "That's my girl."

"Your lunch is on the top shelf in the fridge. I gotta go."

"Is it still cool to take your lunch from home?" Papa laughed.

"It's way undercool," I replied as I tucked plastic-wrapped roll-ups alongside sliced bell peppers and hummus into a beige and silver polka dot thermal lunch tote that looked more like a purse than those old aluminum lunch boxes from the nineties that Mama still used.

Leaving Papa at the table with his row of medications for the day, I quickly showered and dressed for school. Starting class late only sucked in terms of trying to find a parking spot for my beat-up sedan, but an extra-long walk didn't hurt. I even squeezed in some lunges.

The sun hit the sky high and warm for mid-February. There were two sayings about Texas weather: give it five minutes to change, and it only got cold every four years. This was not a fourth year, thank goodness.

A few seniors, who also skipped having a first period class, meandered up the sidewalk. So, who cared if I looked like a weirdo doing lunges through the parking lot with a heavy backpack on?

Ignoring any stares and giggles, and keeping my attention on alert for any revved-up cars, I went low for lunge after lunge, my bony knees almost touching the ground.

"Hi . . ." a quiet voice said, followed by the sound of a car door closing.

"Oh! Hi." I automatically stood like a normal person, suddenly self-conscious because Amit had noticed me being weird.

"What are you doing?" he asked.

I stared at him and he shifted from one foot to the other and scratched the back of his neck. He swallowed, the movement of his throat catching my attention and keeping it.

"Uh . . ." he added, snapping me out of this daze. What the heck was wrong with me?

Eyes popping wide for a split second, I half smiled and noted his crisp khakis and brand name dark-blue and red button-down shirt. "You look nice."

"Oh . . . thanks?"

"Is that a question?"

"No?"

I pinched my brows together then smiled. "Why do you dress so nice every day?"

"I just got off work."

"Really? Where do you work at so early in the morning?"

"I help my uncle out."

"Doing what?"

I expected something like a restaurant or a store. Instead, he answered, "Programming stuff."

I arched a brow. "You need tutoring in CS, though? And why are you programming so early?"

"His company creates medical programs. I have to go with him early mornings to collect data from hospitals." His gaze drifted to the car beside us, as if keeping eye contact might make him combust. He looked nice, but he also looked sleepy. Maybe that was why he fell asleep in class so often.

"That's nice of you."

He shrugged and dragged his gaze back to me. "Were you doing lunges?"

I nodded.

"That's cool."

Pause. Very awkward pause.

"So, this is like the most we've ever talked, isn't it?" I asked. "That's too bad, because we've had so many classes together."

The corner of his mouth twitched at this.

"Are you always so quiet?"

He looked me dead in the eye, as if he were about to say something profound and passionate. "No."

Oh . . . "Just with me, then?"

"I guess so."

"We're studying after school, right?"

"Yes, if you still want to . . . I mean if you still can."

"Yes. To both."

He smiled a smile that reached his eyes, creating little

wrinkles at the corners, which made him irresistibly adorable. "I better get to class. Have fun with your lunges." He waved and walked ahead so I could have the privacy of a spectator-free parking lot to finish my new routine.

I placed my hands on my hips and lunged forth, a smile on my face as Amit disappeared beyond the sea of cars.

Lunges plus a light jog down the steps into the atrium of the school and then up a flight of stairs to my locker pressed a nice soreness into my legs, taking some of the focus away from the ache in my side from Jenny's killer punches. I slipped into calculus just in time, sliding into the last corner chair in the very back, right behind Kimmy, as we'd been doing since eighth grade.

"Hey, girl. You gonna lift weights with me after school?" she asked, twisting in her chair to face me. Some things never changed. Hiding behind her during senior year was as natural as doing it in middle school.

"For sure. I need you to check my technique."

She gave a thumbs-up and asked, "When are you going to join the team?"

"I can only do so many weights. Can't figure out how none of y'all haven't broken your backs with dead lifts. Sheesh," I muttered.

Kimmy giggled and Tanya asked me, "Why don't you come back to softball? You played with us in middle school."

I chewed on the inside of my cheek. God, how badly I wanted to blurt out the news about USMTO. I'd never talked about it with most Indians, seeing there was a stigma about females in contact sports. But with friends like Kimmy and Tanya? The secret was to be friendly with everyone but keep my close friends to a select few. We weren't BFF close, but Tanya and Kimmy were the type to come over with one text.

"You know what? I've been busy with Muay Thai," I finally said. And it felt like a pressurized damn had been opened.

"What?" they said simultaneously.

"Since when?" Kimmy asked.

"Say that again? Like real Muay Thai?" Tanya said.

"Nah, like fake Muay Thai." I stuck out my tongue.

Tanya laughed. "Badass. Do you fight other people or just practice? Either way, I want to see what you got."

I grinned. "As a matter of fact, I do fight."

But before I could get into anything else, Mr. Strothers shuffled his papers noisily. His way of telling us to calm down and get quiet.

"Later," Kimmy mouthed and turned around.

The best thing about sitting behind Kimmy was that she completely blocked me from the teacher's view. Kimmy was tall and broad, both a softball player and on the weightlifting team. She had crazy-good posture, which seemed to make her much taller. Her shoulders were always back, which made her seem much broader. And she had this wild, red curly hair that totally blocked my view of the whiteboard, but also blocked the teacher from seeing me.

Tanya sat to the left, one chair down, right beside Kimmy. She was tall and had shoulders pulled back with great posture too. Sometimes she had braids and sometimes she rocked a natural 'fro. All that tallness and broadness and hair in front of my slumped posture and quietness nearly made me a ghost. I occasionally raised my hand toward the end to make my presence known, proof that I was indeed in class.

I yawned and slumped further and further into my seat. The excitement of USMTO finally wore off and I just about crashed.

The next thing I knew, the bell jolted me awake and I

groggily gathered my things in a hurry, as half the class had already left.

"I want to know more," Kimmy said as she walked partway down the hall with me.

"Definitely," I replied, happy to know some people were delighted about my passion. I didn't know why I even thought that Kimmy and Tanya wouldn't support me. I guessed a lifetime of having been scarred by others' opinions had illogically warped my presumptions. It was good to be cautious, but maybe not so much so that it forced me to close myself off instead of being more secure and confident. Still, old habits were hard to break.

Kimmy took a right at the next hallway and I went to my locker, where Lily waited.

We somehow managed to keep from screaming. Keeping this ginormous secret under wraps was as hard as acing calculus.

And Lily, without a single word uttered from my lips, knew. She saw it in my face. We couldn't scream, but we squealed like piglets. Bear hugs ensued.

"Oh my god!" Lily drawled. "It's fenna be on! I'm totally being your personal cheerleader. I don't care if it looks weird."

"I don't even care. We can match."

"Pink, right?"

I twisted my lips. "Pink is reserved for the best. I don't deserve it. I haven't earned the right to wear it."

"For real?"

"Mhmm."

"What's training going to be like now? I hardly see you as it is."

"I know, sucks on that account. Maybe you wanna come

with and ask businesses if they would sponsor me?" I gave her an over-the-top grin in lieu of begging.

"Definitely!"

"For real?"

"Of course. I'm going to support you any way I can."

I bit my lip and considered my nonexistent pitch. Maybe she could help me with it? Instead, I asked, "You wanna talk for me?"

She gave me some side-eye then shook my shoulders. "The words will be spilling out of your mouth once you see how excited businesses are to sponsor you!"

"I guess."

"Either way, I'm there to help."

"Cool. Thanks! Aside from that, for the next five weeks, it's all training and whatever I can do to squeeze in homework. Really, calculus is the only thing that will require time. I'm acing bio and my grade in computer science will go up because I'm tutoring Amit." I paused as realization hit me. I'd double-booked myself after school. "Oh, no. I have to take time out to tutor him. I forgot!"

"Can he find someone online?"

"But then my grade won't go up as much as I need it to. Catch twenty-two."

"Just study with him for a couple hours a week. Maybe even at lunch?"

"Hey, that's not a bad idea. I bring my own lunch anyway." I held up my thermal tote.

"You're the only senior who does."

"Judy from English does."

"Judy from English has a ton of food allergies."

"Well, I'm training. Do you know how bad cafeteria food is? And y'all race to the nearest fast food place for off-campus lunch, clogging your systems like y'all ready to die and don't even care."

"But you can sit in the car with me and eat your boring training food while I scarf some burgers?"

"I would love the chance to watch you eat your weight in fries, but I think it's a better idea to tutor Amit during lunch instead of wasting time after school."

"Well, there he is." She jerked her chin, indicating his presence behind me.

I glanced over my shoulder and sighed. "Let's get this over with."

FIVE

Even though it was less than five minutes, I soaked up what little time I had with Lily before she left for burgers, which sounded ridiculously delicious. By the time I turned to search for Amit, he had disappeared. I knew where to find him. He was bound to be in one of three places: the library, the courtyard, or the cafeteria. In that order.

Thankfully, he was already chilling out in the library. Mrs. Cartwright, the librarian, was pretty laidback with allowing us to use the library for lunch. She let us eat and read and study and do homework, as long as we were quiet and clean and took our trash to the bin in the hallway.

The guy sitting next to Amit did a double take when he noticed me cruise toward them. He elbowed Amit, who sat hunched over his notebook, his textbooks closed and off to the side. He eventually noticed me, too, and straightened his back as I sat beside him.

"Hi," I said, not understanding why my mouth wanted to clamp shut. I could talk to just about anyone if I wanted to, except certain girls who hated me at the moment, aka Rayna, and narrow-minded people who turned up their chins because I wasn't Indian enough, aka Saanvi, who was the epitome of a "temple-going, perfect example" for the rest of us. Amit didn't fall into either category. Or maybe he'd fall into the latter if he knew the truth about my fighting.

"Ha-hi," he stammered.

"Do you mind if we study now?"

"Uh, sure."

I didn't mind if the boy, Vinni, if I recalled, wanted to hang around or not, but he, without a word, zipped up his backpack, gave Amit a sidelong glance, and left.

"He didn't have to leave," I insisted.

"He doesn't know how to act around girls," Amit replied.

"Not suave like you, huh?"

A tinge of blush colored his cheeks, and realizing how I sounded, I was certain my cheeks turned a pretty unflattering shade of pink.

I grabbed his textbook and opened it to chapter twelve, our next chapter. "What exactly do you need help with?"

"All of it?"

I smirked, my focus skimming down the page. "You have a habit of answering with what sounds like a question."

"Sorry?"

"You're cute." I froze, and I was pretty sure he froze too. Crap.

"I didn't mean . . ." I didn't mean what? That he was cute? That was like implying he was the opposite of cute, which tended to be bad manners. I shook my head and asked again, "Where do you want to start?"

"It's all a little fuzzy around the edges."

I stared at him and he stared back. Our thing, remember? "You're going to be valedictorian. You're in AP Computer Science II. You wrote the correct answer on my quiz but wrote the wrong one on your paper. What gives?"

"Maybe I second-guess myself."

I sighed. "All right. I get that. That's me and calculus."

"You're bad in math?"

"Weird, right? Aren't all Indians math geniuses?"

"Uh, no. What I meant was, how are you bad in math but good with computer science?"

I shrugged. "I dunno. How are you so smart and making little mistakes in class?"

"Touché."

I couldn't help but smile a tad bit. "I can't believe I'm tutoring the valedictorian."

"You don't have to keep reminding me of that. Not the tutoring part. I'm not embarrassed."

"It's an awesome achievement. Should just call you Sir Valedictorian. That should be a mandate, actually. I'll bring it up with the principal."

He chuckled. I'd never heard him laugh before. It was nice.

"Your family must be ecstatic with you being Sir Valedictorian."

He shrugged.

"Don't tell me they're not."

"It's . . . expected."

"I get that high grades are, but top of the class? It's kinda cutthroat up there. It's a huge deal."

He nodded but didn't say anything else. There was a sort of sadness, or maybe stoicism, in him. Maybe he didn't care? Maybe he expected it from himself? Maybe he didn't like the pressure? Or did he want his family to be more excited? Getting the top spot wasn't easy, especially in this school. There were a lot of big brains and gifted students walking around. He deserved to get some praise.

Amit never gave a clear direction as to where to begin, so I just started at our last lesson in class and went from there: typeof operator and the six possible returns.

The best thing about Mrs. Callihan was that she didn't

believe in giving cumulative final exams. She gave weekly pop quizzes, daily homework, chapter tests, a midterm, a final exam based on the chapters post-midterm, and an extra credit project. Comp-sci was one of those classes where if you couldn't get one thing, you weren't going to be able to continue on to the next and she could tell when that happened, hence this need to tutor Amit, probably. Something must've happened between the first month of school and this week.

The nice thing about comp-sci was if Amit had a breakdown in understanding, I could figure out where as we maneuvered through programming.

The problem? He wrote programs beautifully, the way artists paint complex scenes. He wrote them fast and without glitches, and once he started, he just went on and on and on until he finished a perfect, fully functional masterpiece.

I stared at him as he grinned at his handiwork. His smile faded the moment he saw my look.

"Are you sure you need tutoring?" I eyed him skeptically.

"Yeah. I uh, get this stuff, okay? I bombed on my paper."

"Which one?"

"P versus NP."

"Oh. Well, lucky for you I'm good at theorems, you know, except in calculus."

"I think that's why Mrs. Callihan asked you."

No, actually she asked me because she'd asked all the smarter people in class and they didn't have time to help you. But I'd never say such a thing aloud.

He suggested, "Hey, how about if you help me with theorems, I'll help you in calculus? Free of charge."

"Free of charge?" I quirked a brow.

He laughed, which had me quietly rolling when Mrs. Cartwright shushed him.

We went over theorems, but he seemed to vaguely grasp the idea. It was very simple, actually, and I was dumbfounded that he couldn't get it. But who was I to judge? He'd most likely feel the same way when he pulls out his GQ hair trying to teach me basic calculus.

We eventually moved on to polynomial time and when P was unequal to NP and the potential consequences of those examples. We ate as we studied, and I found myself scooting closer and closer to him. Mainly because Mrs. Cartwright kept shushing us. What? Comp-sci could get exciting. Before I realized it, rolling my eyes at the final shush, I closed the last inches of space between us. Our arms squished together, and an electrifying spark went off.

We stilled. Did he feel that too? Or did I actually shock him with the constant moving of my feet on this old, decrepit carpet?

"Did I shock you?" I asked.

He nodded.

"Sorry."

"It's okay."

A literal spark. Whew! I was not, in any way, crushing on Amit. I didn't have time for that. He was already taking up too much time as it was.

"Is it okay if we study during lunch? I got a lot of stuff going on after school and on the weekends."

He frowned, looking genuinely disappointed. "Yeah. Sure."

"I'm not brushing you off," I said defensively. I was not a flake, but more importantly I didn't want him to feel that my aversion to time these days had anything against him personally.

"Yeah, no. I figured you would be busy."

"I have a lot going on," I said quietly. He didn't need to know what *all* I had going on. He didn't need to know that we were broke and my mom worked two jobs and I had to be home to cook and clean and take care of my sick dad. He didn't need to know that I was in Muay Thai and . . . maybe think I was too rough, too violent, too . . . not a girl. Too . . . not Indian enough. I didn't want him to look at me differently, to treat me differently. I didn't want him to think less of me. And yeah, that sounded stupid, but, well I guessed no one was logical and confident all the time. And if they were, then they for sure had a rare superpower.

He watched me thoughtfully, as if I would elaborate. He waved a hand for me to continue.

"That's all I can say." That was all I wanted to say, anyway.

"Why? Is it top secret?" he joked.

"No. I'm not that interesting."

"I bet you are way more interesting than top secret."

A smile tried really hard to curl my lips. "I mean, I barely know you."

"Then you should get to know me." He cleared his throat and scratched the back of his neck, looking as flustered as I felt. How was that like not the sexiest thing a guy had ever said to me? And coming from Amit Patel of all boys?

"I mean, you know? I'd like to be friends," he said. "We'd never really talked and now we have to, and why not get to know each other while we're studying?"

I smiled and hoped it looked as authentic as it truly was. "We're supposed to be keeping you on track for top spot. I don't want to mess that up."

That sounded much nicer than, "I don't have time to talk to dudes at the moment. Much more pressing things happening in my life."

Saved by the obnoxiously loud bell from getting mud-deep

into why we couldn't hang out, I closed my book. "Same time, same place Thursday?"

"Yeah. Hey, are you going to Holi?" he asked.

I stood and turned to look down at him. "Holi? At the mandir?"

"Yeah." He stood to meet my eye. Actually, he surpassed it. I was five-eight, but the boy was at least six-one. And now I stared at the smoothness of his throat.

"No." I snickered.

"What's that for?"

"I haven't been to mandir in years."

"You don't have to do anything, just go for the celebrations."

"I don't have time anyway."

"Oh. Well, if you change your mind, we could, you know, maybe go together."

I grinned, but only internally. "You can't go to Holi with a boy like it's a date."

"No! Of course not. I mean, as friends. My family is going, and it would be nice to see you and your family there." He put his hands behind his back and rocked on his feet.

Holi was a yearly thing that drew a butt-load of Indians to celebrate and throw brightly colored powder on each other to the rhythm of vibrant music well into the night. It was not a date thing. It was a family thing. A cultural thing. A community thing.

An Indian thing.

I frowned. "We never go to those."

"Let me know if you change your mind."

"Definitely. Thanks." As tempting as it was to go to something as energetic as Holi with Amit, feeling inferior in comparison to other Indians was not my idea of a good time. Of course, I'd never admit that to him.

It didn't take long to forget about Holi when the rest of the day zipped by and the next thing I knew, I was in the weight room looking for Kimmy. She wasn't hard to find, seeing that she was one of four girls on the coed team.

She was a beast. I could barely lift the bar at times and she had it loaded down with weights galore. She had great form, though. In all these years and through all of her competitions, she'd never hurt herself. Which amazed me. Dead lifts? I'd be dead for sure. With a broken back and cracked knees, probably.

She gave the best tips on posture and pose and technique. I'd been sopping up her advice since freshman year.

She spotted me first and asked, "So you gonna tell me more about Muay Thai?"

"Yeah." I helped her take most of the weights off the bar before I lay on the bench to lift. My arms got sore with each push. "It's this sport I'm in."

"I don't know anyone in Muay Thai, much less a girl. How could you keep that to yourself? I'm always talking about my games and competitions, and you just listen. You never once said, 'Hey, Kimmy. Wanna come see my match too?'"

"Having my friends there makes me nervous."

"Key word: *friends*. How do you not tell your friends about Muay Thai? It's not like you play something common or boring. Why didn't you ever mention this before?"

I caught my breath on the last push and we switched places, putting all of her weights back on the bar. "I dunno. I didn't want people to judge me or act stupid."

"Judge you? Like thinking you're a badass because you

are one?" She added more weights than before. Like I'd said: Kimmy was a beast.

I rubbed my forearm. "I dunno. I feel self-conscious, I guess. Like boys are intimidated and make dumb jokes. One girl asked if I was really a boy, as if being a fighter makes me less of a girl. Or wonder if that's why I don't wear makeup and dresses. Is that supposed to define what a girl is? Some guy actually asked why I don't do my hair and put on makeup during fights so I don't look so rough. I'm not there to worry about my looks, you know? It sounds dumb, I know."

"You're talking to a girl who turned the all-boys weightlifting team into a coed team." She grinned. "Are you scared of what people might think?"

"Yeah. Think your mom would like you hanging around a kid who might be out there doing drugs and beating up people because she's a fighter?"

"What the actual crap, Kareena?"

I shrugged as I studied her form. "Parents have said that to their kids, though."

"It's very stupid. Some people are ignorant and just threatened by things they don't know about, but times are changing. Also, my parents would think you were more of an anti-theft, anti-assault assurance masquerading as a teenager."

"Well, when you put it that way . . ."

"I mean, I'm not exactly doing a quote, unquote, *girly* thing, but do I care? Does anyone judge me? More importantly . . . why *should* I care?"

I gnawed on the inside of my cheek and mulled over her words. She was right, of course. Then again, I wasn't Kimmy. I wasn't that confident unless I was in the ring.

I wish I were though. I wish I could just not care what other people thought.

The beautiful thing about Muay Thai? We were in this together. We were a community and this gym was the only place where I felt whole and real and raw, and absolutely, one hundred percent myself. Being at home was a close second, but my parents kept me at a fair distance with their woes. I tried to be optimistic for the sake of our family's mental health, but I couldn't even begin to know their pain.

Coach came in at nine after dropping his kids off that Friday. He stayed near me the entire day, making sure my form and technique were at peak performance levels. The gym filled with sounds of punching gloves against bags and pads, of skin hitting skin, of grunts and war cries, of bells, clapping hands, and heaving breaths. Sweat and determination filled the air. There was a whole new level of resolve and purpose percolating through the gym.

"Do you feel that?" Coach asked, bearing the brunt of my kicks against his pads.

"Yes," I puffed, focused on removing the pain in my shins. They always hurt the worst.

"We've trained hard, but now we train our hardest alongside you. You are our heart right now."

I grunted with another kick and wiped the sweat from my neck.

"We are the body pumping lifeblood through you, and you will be our strength manifested at USMTO."

Yeah, no pressure.

I took a short break for lunch and then, while my stomach digested, I sat down for stretches and meditation. At some point, I even lay down on a mat. I didn't even care how dirty or sweaty it was. My body, my mind, my bones and muscles and thoughts all just had to go *bleh* for a quick minute.

We continued our day with warm-ups and sprints and drills and god-awful plyometric conditioning and ended with sparring matches. We always removed our shoes at the door, but we made sure our feet were clean before stepping onto the mat.

Coach began with wai khru, a sort of performance of respect for all the teachers and masters that came before him. I expected to perform this at USMTO in honor of him.

Coach sparred with me once, but I fought alongside others to increase my reactions to a number of variables. No one took it easy on me. No one treated me like the golden child, someone special just because I was going to USMTO.

Coach called me over for a weigh-in at the end of practice. I lifted the hem of my now-soaked tank top and wiped my face as I stepped onto the scale.

"You're tip-toeing at one-thirty."

I groaned. "I know. I'll pack on the calories."

"Make sure they're the right calories."

"Will do."

"Try to keep stress at a minimum, and don't change up anything sudden. No new restaurants or food brands or new vitamins or medicines, yeah?"

"Yes, sir."

Every day began at six in the morning and ended at eight, at which time I made dinner for my parents. Tonight, we ate green curry shrimp salad, which was quick and easy to make. Sauté shrimp in butter and olive oil, add garlic and green curry paste, and level it over mixed greens and my all-time favorite, feta cheese.

Mama leaned against me on the sofa as we ate because, honestly, we were just too beat to sit straight and proper at the dining table. We had our feet on the coffee table—forgive us etiquette gods—our plates balanced on our bellies, and the TV on but turned low.

"Have you put together a pitch for the business list?" Papa asked.

"Sort of. Lily is helping me, though, and she's going to go with me, so no worries."

"Such a good friend," Mama commented. I hoped she didn't go into a spiel about how much she wished she could help too. That she should be the one working on a pitch with me and going door-to-door. Usually, she wanted me to figure things out on my own, independence and self-sufficiency and all that, but this was one of those moments where she wanted to help. We all knew this was something a little beyond me.

She didn't go into her spiel, though. Which was good. She didn't need to feel bad or frustrated when she was doing everything she could already.

"How was practice? Ready to fight?" Papa coughed.

"Yeah," I muttered, unable to form cohesive thoughts much less verbalize them.

Mama's eyelids drooped over perpetual eye bags from her second job, and we were both content to let Papa talk. He didn't converse much when he was really sick, when he was just too tired and in pain and lethargic and didn't have the energy to sit and chat, not to mention the side effects of his many meds, so when he did talk up a storm, we welcomed it more than he would ever know. He talked about sports, politics, UT, and of course USMTO.

"I've been getting involved with the federation: phone calls, emails, research, that sort of thing." He grinned at my grin. "And we're making this happen. This will be an Olympic sport, just you watch."

"Y'all are awesome parents. I love you to death and back."

"Death can wait," Papa said pointedly. He slapped my knee. "Get your homework done."

"Okay." I struggled to get off the couch, my muscles über sore. "Coach wanted me to start with the chiropractor and massages . . ."

Mama nodded. "Already taken care of."

"Really?" I asked, surprised. I mean . . . how had my mom scraped money together for that already?

"Yes. After school tomorrow, before you go to the gym. You're going twice a week now."

"But isn't it—"

"*Choop*," Mama said bluntly, an Indian parent word/grunt for *quiet, I won't hear of it.*

"Thank you." I hugged them both tightly, knowing this was going to be another strain. I would work *extra* hard for this. There was no place to waste a single penny. I pulled away and went to the hallway, turning back before I forgot. "Are we doing Holi this year?"

Mama sat up. "No. We never go. Why do you ask? Do you want to go?"

I shrugged. "I dunno. Just wondering."

"We can go if you'd like, but there is no obligation to go."

"Okay."

"And I got the email from school about Cultural Heritage Day next week. Do you want to wear something Indian?"

I rubbed my arm. "I don't think so. But I have an old salwar kameez if I change my mind."

Not that I especially wanted to go to school wearing one. It wasn't a big deal, but I was way more comfortable in sneakers, shorts, and a tee. Could I wear kicks with the long tunic and leggings? Probably looked weird. And the dupatta? What was the point of an extra-long shawl hanging over one shoulder?

Nah. Shorts for the win.

Mama nodded knowingly, and I turned the corner into the dark corridor. We saved on electricity by walking in the dark and leaving the AC off. I pulled up my window halfway to cool off my room, making sure the screen was secure. As the thought of jumping into bed overtook me, I remembered needing to talk to my parents about shopping for new gear. So I made my way quietly, apprehensively, with a heaviness in my gut for even thinking about asking them for more money. I stepped back out into the hallway to ask, but accidentally eavesdropped on them instead.

"I feel bad now," Mama said quietly. The walls were super thin.

"It's fine," Papa insisted. I couldn't see them, but his habit was to rub her lower back when she fretted.

"Do you think we're the reason why she isn't . . ."

Indian enough, I finished in my head.

Papa said, "No. She is everything we want her to be and everything she needs to be."

"She should have that tie with our culture. She shouldn't be left out because of me. She is not me."

"I know, I know. You can't beat yourself for it."

"Maybe I should've sucked up my pride and swallowed my words so she could be at mandir and have friends there and fit in."

"Don't dwell on the past."

"She should go, huh? She should go and have fun and explore her culture without feeling like an outsider."

"She can go if she wants. We never said she couldn't."

"Maybe if she had some Indian friends, she would be more

comfortable. I'm not exactly the comforting type when it comes to them. And you can't be around so many people."

"What ever happened to Rayna? They're not friends anymore?"

Mama replied, "She hasn't talked about her in a while."

"Are you sad that she doesn't go?"

A long, deep sigh filled the room. How could an unspoken response be so very clear?

SIX

I'd braided Lily's hair during our sleepover at her house that Saturday, but only with the stipulation that it be natural. The thick, coarse hair grabbed onto the style of double braids beautifully. Afterward, she kept my feet in place while I did crunches. I had to build up resistance in my core after Jenny's brutal hits.

"Sorry I couldn't go with you this morning. Did you get any more sponsors today?" she asked.

We'd gone to what felt like a million businesses over the past week. We got the runaround and disinterested faces and folks who were like, "Are you for real?"

"I'm definitely not a salesman. I feel like I'd buy anything a sales guy told me to, but I can't get someone dying of thirst in the desert to buy a bottle of water from me. I don't have those haggling skills that my mom has. She's hardcore."

"So's mine. I think first-gen Asians are like that, though."

I laughed. "I feel like a little kid hiding behind my mom so she can negotiate stuff for me." To be honest, I wished that she really did have time to go with me. She would've persuaded more than the few sponsors and extra five hundred bucks that I'd gotten.

"Maybe the 'I need money for something that you don't benefit from, but can you go fund me, anyway?' approach isn't working."

"We'll keep trying. Gotta do something new."

"Like what?" she asked.

"Let me think. Um. I mean . . . I'm going to USMTO. The nation watches it. I can boost their names. Isn't that enough? They can hang a picture of me in their business and proudly declare they supported a local, national athlete. It'd be easier if I could throw in the words: *Olympic team*. They'd scramble for that."

"Duh! Why the crap weren't we saying that?"

"There is no Olympic team."

"No. But we should be saying that USMTO leads to the World Championships that could lead to the Olympics."

I face palmed. "We gotta go back to those guys then."

"Square one tomorrow."

"Ugh. Thanks." I switched up my sit-ups with side ones, touching my left elbow to my right knee and vice versa.

"How can you work out after so much Filipino food?"

"That's exactly why I gotta work out . . ." There was no saying "no" to Lily's mom's Filipino cooking. One: Filipina moms were as notorious as Indian moms in making guests eat. It was loving Asian hospitality at its most aggressive. Two: it was rude not to eat. Three: Filipino food was delicious. Tonight, she'd made shrimp lumpia (I only ate three, I swear!), which almost always led to pancit, as well as healthy and hearty chicken afritada over rice.

"My mom made extra for you to take home. Don't forget."

"I never leave your house empty-handed. Unspoken rule."

"So your parents want you to go to Holi?" she asked.

"Yeah, I'm pretty sure they want me to get in touch with my Indianness."

"So go."

"You don't understand how uncomfortable and—"

"Lily!" her mom called from downstairs. "Your friend is here!"

"Okay!" she yelled back.

I propped myself on my elbows as Lily kept a death grip on my feet. I could still kick her or, even better, punch her. Not that I would. "Which friend? Oh my god, did you invite Rayna?"

"No. You'd be super pissed if that went down."

"Then who?" I inquired as Lily's mom asked the surprise guest if they wanted to eat.

A throaty laugh ensued, followed by a deep voice responding, "Not right now. Thank you, ma'am."

Oh, god, don't tell me it was who I thought it was!

A knock rapped on the door, followed by Lily's enthusiastic, "Come in!" right as she jumped back and scuttled into the corner, a giant grin on her face.

Yep. It was Amit. I hadn't moved a muscle when he walked in with a sheepish but awkward smile and a backpack hanging in his hand. He waved as Lily invited him to sit at her desk.

Not wanting him to feel any weirdness or out of place, I smiled as naturally as I could. He pressed his lips together and concentrated on emptying his books from his pack. I shot Lily an annoyed look.

She shrugged and said, "So, I figured that we could all study together since we have this big test in computer science coming up."

"That's a good idea," I begrudgingly admitted, pulling my knees to my chest and blindly searching the bed beside me for my notebook. Grabbing the slender one with the metal spine, I dragged it down. "We can do prime and integer factorization?"

"Yeah. Next logical step from our session Thursday," Amit said.

"Sounds about right," I added, seeing that he had two days to let that info sink in.

We should've read the chapter aloud to fill the void, but I for one had to read silently, taking in every word and maybe rereading a dozen times before getting it. For the first ten minutes, having Amit around was no different than not having him here. Except, ya know, being hyper-aware that there was a very cute boy in our presence.

Until Lily broke the peace and asked again, "So, are you going to the celebration or not?"

I froze, panic-stricken. *Please, lord, do not let Amit venture into this conversation.*

He glanced up from his textbook. At this angle, I noticed that a thin notebook was splayed open in front of it, as if he tried to hide it by pretending he was studying the chapter.

"Um, maybe. I don't know."

"I'll go with you," she offered and bit into a Twinkie. God, that junk food looked so good, like it could be the last Twinkie in the world.

"Stop coveting my food. You can't eat it," Lily added and, worse than an enemy, slowly finished the rest in front of me and licked her fingers.

I threw a pillow at her face. "You're so wrong."

She laughed.

"Why can't you eat Twinkies?" Amit asked.

"I'm cutting back on sugar."

"Why?"

I shrugged. "It's the healthy thing to do."

"That's cool. I don't think about food that much. I probably should."

"Lily needs to. Eating burgers and Twinkies every day."

She stuck out her tongue and rummaged through her

drawer for another. She didn't eat just junk food, obviously. Her mom made delicious, healthy Filipino food and her dad was a salad connoisseur, but it was fun messing with her when she taunted me.

"I can't stand you," I joked.

"Tell me what to wear and I'll go," she repeated.

"I don't know if I want to go."

"Where?" Amit asked.

"Holi," I muttered.

He perked up, extending his neck so that half his face could be seen from behind his pseudo studying. My face warmed as our eyes locked. We slowly moved past the silent, accidental stares to something a little more meaningful, like I could interpret his thoughts.

He beamed. I couldn't see his smile, but it reached his eyes and made them crinkle at the edges.

Lily watched all of this quietly. With her here, there was no pressure to be cool around Amit.

"If you want someone to go with, you can come with me, I mean, with us. My parents and uncle and me," he stuttered with a croak.

"I don't know. What if your parents . . ." How to put this? "Do your parents know my parents?"

"Yeah."

I frowned, my heart heavy and sinking like a rock stuck in a well of mud.

"I asked them if they would mind. They'd love to see you again, um, that is, to have you join our family. We could pick you up."

"See me again?"

"Guess we all knew each other when we were kids. Anyway, they remember you, and you know how desi parents are, all wanting to meet every friend and every Indian their child goes to school with."

The sinking sensation halted. "Yeah?"

He lowered his book, revealing the extent of his bright smile. "Yeah."

The years of heavily guarding myself from other Indians sprouted up, as aggressive as ever. I tried to reason with my brain that there was no justification to distrust Amit. He'd never once been mean to me or ignored me or turned up his chin. He knew I wasn't into attending mandir or doing anything religious or ever showing my face within the Indian community. And he was okay with that. He never made me feel less than.

Then again, he didn't know about Muay Thai. He didn't know how other Indian parents looked at me like I was some abnormality for fighting, how they took away my friends because they thought I was a bad influence.

I played it off and nodded, my gaze flitting back to my textbook. "I'll think about it."

Through the next hour, Lily managed to stay quiet in her corner, leaning against a stack of pillows and a throw blanket tossed over her legs. My legs and back started to cramp and forced me onto the soft bed. Lily had a memory foam mattress and it was like lying on a giant marshmallow.

Amit moved on to proofs of P being unequal to NP theorem. When he answered questions aloud and engaged in conversation about the chapter, he didn't have any issues.

"You understand this," I stated.

"Yeah, when you explain it like that." He grinned. And something stirred in my gut. "Do you want to work on calculus?"

"Sure." We switched up books.

Amit pushed out of the chair, the seat pivoting in

momentum, and came to stand beside me. He bent at the waist to flip through the chapters to my most basic of grievances.

He chuckled. "All the way to the beginning, huh?"

"Yep."

"You can sit on my bed, you know?" Lily said from her nest.

"Thanks." He carefully sat beside me, as if I would spit poison. He kept half an arm's length from me and explained calculus equations simply (math for dummies, remember?) but passionately. The way his lips assembled strings of derivatives was mesmerizing. I couldn't stop fixating on his mouth. Why had I never noticed it before?

Maybe because we'd never been this close, nearly alone in a bedroom? Maybe because he actually conversed with me in more than four-word increments?

Amit looked a little like he could have a side modeling gig. He had that tall height, dark skin, broad chest and shoulders, chiseled cheeks and jaw, curly modelish hair, and full lips that stretched perfectly when he smiled or twisted his mouth. Wait, twisted?

I dragged my eyes back up and yep, he only curled the corner of his mouth when we were staring at one another. I grinned and squeaked a lame, "*Hee.*"

Oh, god! *What* was that!

He tried not to laugh, but utterly failed and I lightly punched his arm. "Ow. What was that for?" He rubbed the spot, feigning injury.

"Continue," I said instead. "Please?"

He nodded and started speaking again. He'd mastered math. It bowed so obediently and willfully to his command, displaying its inner depths for someone as mathematically challenged as myself to comprehend.

"Does that make sense?" he whispered.

"Yes. Why are you whispering?"

"Why are you whispering?"

"Am I? Cuz you are."

He cocked his chin at Lily and her fluffy nest. She had her knees to her chest, body slanted, and slept on her pile of plaid pillows.

"She's faking it," I muttered.

"Are you willing to test that theory?" he asked, a devious glint in his eyes.

My eyebrow quirked up. "You're asking for trouble."

"Well, it's rude to invite me over and then fall asleep."

"True. Seeing that she offended you, how shall we proceed?"

"Take her Twinkies."

"Ooh, yes. If she's faking she'll never stand for that." I tiptoed toward Lily on the plush, gray carpet and eased open the drawer where her secret stash lay hidden beneath empty, multicolored folders.

She didn't twitch.

I reached in and rescued a Twinkie, the wrapper crinkling as loud as a blaring TV. I froze. She didn't stir. I stood up and shrugged at Amit. She really was asleep. How rude of her.

I tossed him the Twinkie and snatched his textbook off the desk, opening it immediately to the chapter he pretended to have read. My eyes skimmed over the detailed program in his flat notebook, the one he'd written and was looking at rather than paying attention to what I'd been going over this entire time.

"What's this?"

"Nothing," he said, suddenly at my ear, and grabbed the notebook from my grasp.

"What is it?" I repeated, trying to take it back.

Amit was about half a foot taller than me, and his arms

were extremely long. So when he held the notebook behind his back, I couldn't reach around his slight turns.

"Why are you so interested?" he jested.

"Why are you so secretive?" I countered and stopped, my hands on my hips. "You know? I could beat you up and take that."

"Probably. But you have to respect my boundaries."

"You were pretending to study with me but writing this. I deserve an answer."

He smirked and held the notebook above his head. "I guess punch me if you must, but—"

Enough talking. I went straight for his armpits. No, not a punch, although getting punched in the armpits sounded like a bad way to go down. I tickled hard and he succumbed in half a millisecond, trapping his laughter behind clamped lips so he didn't wake up Lily.

He blocked the assault by turning or swiping his arm down, but never tickling back.

"You're going to regret this, Kareena Thakkar," he promised.

"No, *you* are for working on something else when you were supposed to be studying with me."

"Don't tickle unless you're prepared to be tickled."

"That's not fair," I hissed when he did a surprise maneuver and ducked under my arms, lifted me off the freaking floor, and dropped me on the bed like a puppy. I glared at him, baffled.

"See, don't mess—" he began, turning from me to slip the notebook back into his backpack. But I was faster than him, and nimble. He didn't stand a chance.

I snatched the notebook and scurried into the corner of the bed before he turned and said, "Hey!"

"Shhh . . ." I held a finger to my lips and tilted my head toward Lily.

But Amit couldn't take a hint. He slid across the bed just as I twisted away. How did we get in this position? The position of us on a bed. The position of his chest against my back, his arm around my waist trying to weasel through my hold where I kept the notebook tight against my chest.

"What are you two doing?" Lily asked, an impish smirk glowing against her tan skin.

I froze, wide-eyed. Amit eased away from me and we sat up, our backs hitting the wall behind us.

"I'm not moving," he declared, holding out his hand.

"If you don't tell me what this is, I'm going to assume you *don't* need tutoring," I said firmly.

He dropped his head, his knees bent and his hands dangling over them in defeat. He grunted, "It's a program."

"Duh." I flipped through the dozens of pages, noting where the writings were scribbled junctions when he must've hurried and the areas that were marred by gray where he must've erased over and over. This was, by far, the lengthiest and most detailed coding I'd ever seen.

"What is this?" I asked, wondering if he actually needed tutoring. Then again, just because he wrote a freaking long program didn't mean it worked or even made much sense. Also, who wrote programs on paper?

"A project I'm working on."

"For class?"

"No. For work and for myself. I have to work out these things in my head by writing them out."

"I don't understand. I thought you did data collection for work."

He gently took the notebook back. "It's like there's a furious accumulation of coding pieces that appears in my head and gets stuck there. I used to think it was residual things I'd learned in school, but new things appeared, and it started to drive me nuts. So I wrote them out to get them out of my brain and after a few months, I realized they fit together."

"Like a puzzle?"

"Yeah." He flushed.

"And it makes sense?"

"They turn into unfinished, complicated programs. From there, I figure out the missing pieces and when it's all complete and functional, I feel as if the giant ball of pressurized code leaks out."

"Is this the one?"

"The one? No. There's been others before and I'm sure many more after this one is done."

"What will this program do?"

He shrugged, but by the way his jaw clenched, something told me he knew. Which begged the question: "So, why are you slipping in comp-sci?"

He quickly replied, "Uh. It's the basic stuff. My brain only has so much room." He jumped to his feet, the bed depressing then rising back up. "I should go."

"Why?" I asked, not wanting him to leave.

"You should stay," Lily added as she stretched and yawned.

"You're clearly in need of sleep," Amit stated.

She shrugged. "Kareena will be up. She always ends up staying awake after I fall asleep. You're welcome to stay. You can sleep over, if you want."

"What?" we both exclaimed.

"My parents don't care."

"My parents do," I refuted, then looked at Amit. "No offense."

"None taken. My parents would be mad if I stayed over."

"You guys talk like your parents have to know."

"I'm sure my mom will eventually talk to your mom and something like . . . 'How Amit doing?'" I imitated Lily's mom's slight Filipina accent and then my mother's more Southern drawl, "Who's Amit?" And going back and forth, added, "That boy from school who came over to study. He end up spending the night with your daughter in my daughter's bedroom."

"Well, first of all." Lily held up a finger. "My mom's accent is way thicker. And second, she's asleep by now. She knows we're not doing anything. You guys are gross. Get your heads out of the gutter."

"Thanks for the invitation, but I should go. I have work in the morning," Amit quickly said and rushed out.

I jogged after him and held the front door open. "Are you mad at me?"

"No. No," he breathed out. "I'd never be mad at you. Why would you think that?"

"Because I read your program."

"No. It's fine. I just have to go."

"Oh. Okay."

"You sound disappointed."

"I just don't want you to be mad is all."

"Are you sure it's not because you want me to spend the night?" He flashed that eye-reaching, soul-piercing smile.

I swallowed in spite of myself. "No."

He laughed. "I'll see you Tuesday. Lunch study session."

"Yeah, right. You don't need my help."

"It's like how you get the complexity of physics and differentials but can't get a grip on derivatives."

"All right. See you in the library at lunch."

"And Tuesday is Cultural Heritage Day."

"So?" I feigned disinterest.

"Are you wearing something Indian?"

"Are you?"

"Yes."

"Hmm . . ." I huffed indifferently.

He scratched the back of his neck. "Well, maybe you'll change your mind."

"Why? Because I should be more Indian?"

"I don't understand that question. I only meant, I bet that a bright salwar kameez would look amazing on you."

Oh . . .

"Not that you have to wear a dress. Technically, you'd be wearing pants . . . and now I'm babbling . . . okay. I'm going to go. I had fun, though. Goodnight, Kareena."

My heart sort of tumbled around in my chest. "Me too. Bye, Amit."

I locked the door behind him and found Lily in bed, on her side, waiting for me. "So . . . you two would make an adorable couple."

I threw a pillow at her face.

···< SEVEN >···

The occasional TV shows I watched with Papa were a blur. The music raging through my earbuds during runs and shadowboxing was a blur. Spending hours trying to convince people to sponsor me was a blur. Shopping for new gear and cringing at the accumulating prices was a blur. Even homework and school were a blur. Training was not, and never had been. It couldn't be. I had to be alert and I had to remember everything. My body, my muscles, had memory and they knew how to react and take hits before my brain registered the situation.

Whatever tiredness I felt, whatever stress, anxiety, worry, what-if's, low self-esteem, nervousness, fears . . . it all joined together during practice. These small and large flames of personal issues swarmed through my brain and collided into one, gigantic ball of fire. I used it like a laser beam, extremely potent power on a very narrow and straight path, and aimed it all into Muay Thai. The sport of my heart enabled me to vent. The drive and strength I needed came together with every punch and kick.

Most people saw violence, anger. I saw passion, skill, relief.

"It's because Muay Thai is your calling," Mama said over a quick breakfast.

"No. My calling is computer science. That's going to be my major."

"Why?" She looked at me with a very calm, interested look.

I stumbled over my thoughts. "What do you mean, why?"

"Why major in that?"

"I can't major in Muay Thai, Mama."

"But you can go to the Olympics."

"That's a dream, a possibility. The statistics of probability lie in computer science, in programming. I can train as hard as I can in Muay Thai, doesn't mean it'll go anywhere."

"Except USMTO," she corrected.

"Yes, that."

"And maybe the World Championships."

"Okay, that too."

"And maybe the Olympics after that."

"Mama," I groaned. "That's still a possibility. I'm not saying it's not going to happen. But if I major in programming, then I will get a degree and find a job. I can support us."

She reached over the counter and touched my hand. "How did I get a child like you?"

"I'm pretty sure I gave her to you," Papa chimed in.

Mama laughed and waved off his remark. "You have to follow your passion, to try to make it into a lifelong thing, not a temporary hobby."

"I won't give up Muay Thai. I can go to college and train. And if the Olympics happen, then that's even better. But my eggs are dispersed in different baskets."

She didn't listen to me; I could tell from the way her daze took over. "I was a natural in biology. I loved dissecting and working on cadavers. Molecular biology came to me with ease. Everyone knew I'd be a surgeon," she said softly, sadly.

But she wasn't a surgeon. She'd gotten pregnant with me and had complications and she had never pursued med school. Her hand tightened over mine. "Pursue your dreams, no matter the variables, no matter the chances, just try. Okay? I didn't try hard enough, and I regret it to this day."

"You had a baby and got sick, then Papa got sick. It was circumstantial."

"It was never because of *you* or *Papa*, beta. Don't ever say that or think it. It was because I went easy on myself and made some mistakes in school and gave up." She took in a huge breath and released it, her chest deflating. "Indians tend to push their kids, huh? I push you, not to be perfect or do exactly as I say, but I will always push you to be your best. As long as I live, I will not shut my mouth on the subject. Now get your homework done and don't forget, you have a chiropractor appointment today after school."

"Thank you."

"Oof. I left my purse in my room. Can you bring it for me?"

"Yes!" I called back and jogged to their bedroom at the end of the hall.

"And my compression socks?"

I rummaged through the left side of my parents' dresser, Mama's side, and found a pair of her black compression socks that she'd started using a few months ago to help with the circulation she needed while standing up during both her jobs. I grabbed her one and only purse from the nightstand, accidentally catching one loop instead of both. It fell sideways and the contents spilled out.

I dropped to my knees and quickly scooped everything back inside and checked beneath the bed to make sure nothing had slid into the darkness. Something had. Mama's checkbook. It burned in my hand, a fire of information.

My parents kept insisting that I needed to know only so much, but truly, I needed to know if we could afford this. This

USMTO thing, this pursuing passion over practicality, even pursuing college.

I knew I shouldn't. Mama would be pissed. But I had to know how much of a strain I was.

So I glanced over my shoulder to check the doorway and then flipped open the checkbook. My new gear had made a large, one-time dent that made my heart drop into my stomach, but my chiropractic and massage appointments pounded out a hundred bucks each. They weren't covered by insurance. Papa's consolidated medical bills were spun out in payments of four hundred each, going as far back as this checkbook. His meds were another thing, and food, and electricity, and water, and phone.

Tears stung my eyes as I skimmed down the numbers to the last one, the current balance of only eighty-three dollars and nine cents. Payday was next Friday, an entire eleven days away.

Crap.

My heart cracked and sank into the pit of my being. How did Mama keep everything together? She didn't even have money for today's appointment.

"Kareena?" she called from the foyer.

I sniffled and blinked away tears, hurrying to Mama and handing her the socks and purse.

"Thank you." She sat on a chair and tugged on the tight, restrictive socks. "Are you all right?"

"Yeah. I don't think I need to go to the chiropractor today. I've been doing Muay Thai all these years and never needed one."

"No, you go. Coach has a valid point. You can't take these beatings and not take care of yourself better. Besides, you're training extra hard now."

"I just had one last week. Maybe once a month is okay? And massages, too, at the most, once a month?"

She gave me that don't-argue-with-me-look that all mothers magically develop the moment their child comes into the world. "They charge thirty dollars for cancellations within twenty-four hours. I'm not wasting thirty dollars. We'll discuss having less appointments later on."

"It'll get expensive," I pushed out the words, little devilish paper cuts all over my tongue.

"I've worked something out with the offices. Don't worry." She touched my cheek. "That's not your job, huh?"

Then why did my body feel numb and empty?

I wasn't into doing lunges across the school parking lot and avoided Lily in between classes. I didn't even have it in me to brush off Travis when he purposely walked into me just to put his hand on my back. I mindlessly walked toward the library where Amit waited.

His hair was done in its typical modelish fashion, but instead of the usual nice work clothes, he wore a classy, semi-shiny dark-blue kurta pajama. My breath stopped dead in my throat. His smile was brilliant as ever, but it quickly faded when the crowd thinned. His eyes darted to Travis . . . and the arm that snaked behind my back.

I shrugged out of the hold. How did I not notice that?

I slowed down before we came across Amit, who nodded and walked into the library.

"What?" Travis asked.

"Don't put your arm around me."

"What? You walked with my arm around you for an entire minute."

"I honestly didn't even know you were still here."

"Well, damn."

"I mean, you can't just go around touching whoever."

He held his hands up and backed away. The notorious high school flirt . . . he wasn't really after me. I could tell by how he brushed off the rejection and started flirting with another girl in about two seconds flat.

"Bye," I said bluntly and walked away.

Entering the library was like entering another dimension. The hallway was warm with crowds and noise, boisterous laughing, and the smell of cafeteria food. The library, exceptionally quiet with only a handful of studious souls, had me shivering in the cold.

I dragged my nails down my arm, not understanding why I felt as if I'd been caught red-handed doing something illegal.

My legs got weak. They didn't want to move toward Amit, didn't want to take me to face his opinion.

Amit didn't look up when I sat down. He read his textbook.

"Hi," I said.

"Hey," he muttered.

I swallowed, my throat dry. A shaky breath escaped. Why did I even care so much?

"You didn't wear a salwar kameez?" he asked.

"I forgot Cultural Heritage Day was today. You look nice." "Nice" wasn't the perfect word. "Perfect" was the perfect word.

It would be impossible not to notice how the lushly colored, long-sleeved tunic fit against Amit's torso, showing off the slight curve of his biceps and V-shape. The navy blue with gold design was an excellent contrast against his dark-brown skin and brought out the honey specks in his eyes.

Was I staring? Yeah, just like old times.

My chest tingled, and not in a good way. A whole lot of anxiety squeezed my ribs and the pustules of nasty agitation that sprouted everywhere popped.

I clenched and unclenched my hands and then wiped my sweaty palms against the desk. Mistake. They left gross streaks that didn't go unnoticed by Amit.

"Are you all right?" he asked.

"Are you judging me?"

"What?" he asked, seemingly shocked.

I swallowed hard, my spit sliding down jagged edges inside my throat. I was so tired of this, of being judged. "Were you judging me because of Travis?"

"That's not my business."

"Then why did you look at me like that?"

He carefully looked around, pointedly, to tell me to lower my voice. "Like what?" he whispered.

"Like . . . like . . . how old-school traditional, fresh-off-the-boat Indians look at an *Americanized desi* who let a boy touch her?" I bit my lip the second those words tumbled out.

His confused, worried expression fell to stoicism. "That's not what I was thinking."

"Really? Because it sure looked like it. Listen, I didn't even notice his arm there."

"You didn't notice someone touch you? That a guy was walking you down the hall with his arm around you?" His voice went low, seasoned with annoyance.

"My mind has been somewhere else. I don't even know what happened between driving to school and getting to the library."

He stretched his neck left and then right, slight popping sounds relieving the pressure. "Do you like him?"

"Travis? God, no. He's a douche."

He bit back a laugh. "I looked at you like that because . . ."

"Because *what*?"

"Never mind," he finally said.

"Whatever."

"It had nothing to do with judging you, okay? I promise. Can we just study?"

"Why don't we read the next chapter and you ask me your questions."

"Fine."

But there were no questions. Not a sound came from either of us other than shuffling pages and scribbling pencils. The bell rang forty minutes later and we wordlessly packed our stuff, walked out the double doors, and strolled down the hallway. It was very difficult to stomp away from Amit when he had to follow me to the same classroom, but at least he stayed a few feet behind.

I went to the back row of computers, as usual, and he stationed himself up front. That was fine by me.

"Why do you look so pissed?" Lily asked. Had she always been sitting there, or was she a ninja slipping into class?

"Bad day."

"Does it have to do with Travis?"

"How'd you guess?"

"I saw you two walking. I thought . . . wait, don't you like Amit?"

"I don't like either of them. I don't have time for boys, remember?"

"All right then." She rolled her eyes and tapped her books.

"Sorry. It's just . . . Amit saw that too, and I swear I didn't even notice Travis. I was totally thinking about other stuff. And Amit looked at me like I was despicable. He's just as bad as all those people judging me for not being Indian enough, or in this case, wild with some American guy."

"Uh, I think if Amit gave you a disapproving look, it's more likely that he's jealous."

"What for?"

"Obvs, woman. He likes you. He doesn't want to see another dude's arm around you, especially Travis's."

"He doesn't like me."

She leaned in and whispered, "Were you or were you not flirting in my room?"

"What flirting?"

She had a big ole wild smile when she said, "Trying to get his notebook, tickling, sitting on my bed?"

"I *knew* you weren't sleeping."

EIGHT

A few more sponsorships came through, plus my regulars, amounting to just over a grand. Still had two grand left to go in three weeks. Ugh. Money was definitely on the brain during Tuesday training.

I didn't have the heart . . . okay, I didn't have the girl balls to tell Coach the truth. It would break his heart. I just couldn't look into his determined, excited face and those of my fellow fighters and say, "Hey, sorry guys! You put a lot of work and faith into me, but I'm not going."

Maybe it wasn't a lot of money to some people. But money had a different meaning when you were already broke *and* taking care of a sick parent whose medical bills never went down. Finances were a conniving, maniacal vortex. If it meant putting money toward Papa and bills, then so be it. I had to be okay with that.

So, I did what any scared teenage girl would do in this situation. I went to the gym and practiced as scheduled, pretending that I had nothing to confess. Mama was already spending money we didn't have on appointments. I couldn't waste it . . . no matter how bleak the idea of scraping another couple of grand together seemed.

Anger riled my insides and aggression spewed through my kicks and punches. I went through sparring and pad partners faster than usual until Coach told me to hit core and circuit training. My teammates called me the girl on fire because I scorched in the ring, but right now? I felt like I was just burning myself. My skin was on fire. My blood boiled. My heart wouldn't calm down. I wanted to crawl into myself and at the same time, out of myself. I just felt a mess.

Anger was not usually my thing. I felt like I was a pretty chill, nonviolent person. But when you had all sorts of anxieties building up, you had to let them out. I mean . . . was this anger clawing through me like a hundred nightmares, or was this an anxiety attack?

Well, might as well utilize it. Might as well unleash the fury of having no control over my life by channeling all this unfurling chaos into practice. Made sense.

When not fighting, I had plentiful time to cogitate over the truth. The longer I kept my mouth shut, the more the fear built up.

Tuesday practice came and went, alongside the chiropractic appointment that we couldn't afford. Wednesday pushed back harder than ever. Natalia, one of the best fighters we had, nearly knocked me out. Her fist came fast and strong but hit the side of my helmet instead of my face. I tumbled back and she took me out at the legs with a swipe.

Natalia gave me a hand, pulling me up from the floor with disbelief. We retreated to our corners until the bell rang. I sprang to my feet, bounced back and forth, and let the sport flow through me. It took only seconds for the rest of the world to fade out of existence, to forget woes and stress when I channeled my frustrations right. I only felt the pressure in the balls of my feet, the thrum of my nerves where I'd been hit, the swoosh of blood behind my ears, the trickle of sweat down my jaw, the demands of my heart as it urged me forward.

No matter how Muay Thai soothed my soul, the connection

to peace crackled all around me. There was no fight that could evade the fact that we were too poor to go to the Open.

Natalia swung left and I ducked. It took longer and longer for me to rebound, to regroup. Natalia had no mercy on me. Her knee shot up and that was that.

I was done. I was out, and Coach yelled across the mat, "Get up!"

I didn't want to get up. My body hurt in all the wrong places. My heart hurt the worst, and at this point I couldn't tell if it was physical or emotional or a rigid mix of both. My head wasn't in the fight today. I'd barely kept myself sane yesterday.

"Get out of your head!" Coach yelled.

Natalia offered a hand and pulled me up, yet again, asking, "You okay?"

"Don't give yourself that much credit," I joked and then wheezed to catch my breath. Beating each other up didn't mean we didn't love our teammates. Natalia had a lot to teach me, but that didn't mean I should've gotten knocked down. Ugh. Frustration rattled my insides, and Coach was for sure going to rip me a new one.

Natalia nodded and readjusted her gloves as I followed Coach's irritated finger, wagging and ordering me to get off the mat.

"Do you want this or not?" he asked, hands on his hips, neck craned to the side as if he needed to press his ear against my mouth to hear my response.

"I want this," I replied in truth. I wanted this so badly.

"Then get in the fight."

"Yes, Coach."

"Look at your posture. You're stiffer than usual. Have you been going to your appointments?"

"Yes."

"All right." He gently slapped my damp shoulder over my tank top strap. "Go, uh, hit the rowing machines for the next hour."

I did as he asked and popped in my earbuds to heavy rock, not normally my thing but the blood in my veins required it.

I checked my phone after a brutal and disappointing practice. Amit had texted. I read it in a hurry on my way to the car.

Sorry about yesterday. It wasn't what you think.

I scoffed but replied.

Ok.

He immediately responded.

TBH? I can't stand that guy. Was that harsh? Nah. I mean it.

I smiled at the brightly lit screen.

Same here.

He sent a smiley face and a peace sign and that was the end of that. If only he could make it rain money the same way he patched things up between us.

The house was eerily quiet when I got home, but I kicked off my shoes in the foyer and they thudded against the wall.

"Papa?"

Dishes fell in the kitchen. Without wasting a second, my feet moved faster than my whirling thoughts. An intruder didn't cross my mind. Papa having fallen and passing out did.

I skidded to a stop, my socks absorbing the veggie soup that quickly covered the laminate floor, prowling toward the living room carpet. A bowl had smashed into a hundred pieces alongside spoons and the soup container.

Papa hissed and grabbed his head, pushing himself against the fridge door. I hurried to his side, tossing the towel from the counter onto the sopping wet floor. I squatted beside him and checked for any visible injuries.

"What happened, Papa? Are you okay?"

"I just got light-headed, that's all."

"Are you lying to me?"

"No. I would tell you if I didn't feel right, if we needed to go to the ER. I was hungry and got off the couch too quickly to make soup. I was excited for soup." He gurgled out a laugh.

"Not floor soup, though."

"No."

I wrapped an arm below his shoulders and helped him to the living room, my heart clamoring through my ears. He eased down into the recliner that pushed back so he was semi-sitting. After bringing him a glass of cool water, which he slowly sipped, and his nightly meds, I cleaned the floor and tamped down the cavernous rise of fear.

"Have you been dizzy since you returned home?" I asked, hoping that keeping my lips moving would stop bad thoughts from careening out of control.

"No. Just tonight."

"Did you skip any medicines?"

"I don't think so." He groaned. "Maybe."

After cleaning and mopping and drying the floor with paper towels, I made Top Ramen soup on the stove for him, throwing in some frozen veggies. While we waited for the three-minute cook time, I checked Papa's meds, counting all the pills in each bottle and hoping he'd missed something, that there was a simple answer.

I prayed for an extra pill.

And there was. I counted the pills in the red top bottle five times and closed my eyes. I brought Papa his soup and helped him bring the recliner back to a sitting position.

"Thank you." He blew on his soup and took timid slurps. "You forgot a pill."

"Oh. Good. It was user error." The worry melted off his face, but it stayed solidified in my thoughts.

"Are you going to Holi?" Amit asked on Thursday during our lunch study session. He'd returned to his old self, with that billion-dollar smile and warmness. That smile was hard not to stare at. Wait . . . was he saying something?

"Hello? You there or did you check out on me?" He snapped his fingers above my textbook.

"I can't." Couldn't he ask me to do something else? Like the movies or dinner or the park or even a study date outside of the library? Stuff that didn't revolve around religion? Not that it mattered much. Anything outside of school was on restricted time.

I'd be perfectly content staring at his beautiful teeth, but nope. He had to press on. He had to know *why* I wouldn't be interested in something like Holi. Like there was something wrong with me for not caring to go.

"Oh," he breathed, sounding disappointed, and slouched. "Why not?"

"I just can't." I slammed my books shut, shoved them into my backpack, and knocked back my chair getting up.

"What's wrong?" he asked, going for my chair while I went straight for the doors. He scrambled for his stuff.

Look, dude. You don't really want to know how I really feel about the Indian community that you love so much. The community that shoved my mom aside. The one that pushed me away. The one that had taught their kids I was a bad influence because of what? My sport? My mom?

Not to mention that I had so much stuff piling up in my head that I could explode any second. Screaming sounded nice right about now. Screaming about nothing and everything at once.

Despite walking fast, he caught up with me in the hallway. I ducked into the nearest girls' restroom, locked the stall door shut, and sat on a closed toilet seat.

I breathed hard and steady, but my body shook and goosebumps ran up and down my arms. I closed in on myself as tears stung my eyes, making everything blurry.

Papa was so sick. He was home but he wasn't better. We had no money for his bills, for us, much less for USMTO. Everything was like sand escaping from a broken bottle that I was desperately trying to keep together, but the sand kept slipping through my fingers. And without money, my one refuge, my outlet for stress, had become the most painful dream vanishing before my eyes. I almost wished that I'd never been invited to the Open.

Three girls came and went without a word. Then two more walked in.

"Did you see Travis all over her the other day?" That high-pitched voice reverberated off the walls, bullets of deadly words.

"Shh," the other girl said, then muttered something.

"I know," Saanvi replied. "First she goes after your crush, *my* brother, while she was talking to Reg? Of course Travis wants to mess around with her. He probably heard about her hooking up with guys. There's no way she dated Reg and didn't do stuff. She probably *would* fool around with Travis. Why else would he bother flirting with her? Travis is ever only after one thing, we all know that. And he only goes after girls who he thinks he can get."

I rolled my eyes. That frosty snitch. But my throat was

dry and aching from keeping it in. Stupid high school gossip shouldn't bother me. Way more pressing matters in my life right now.

"It was a long time ago." Great. Saanvi talked crap about me with Rayna. With her still bringing the past up, Rayna would never forgive me.

"No wonder she doesn't show her face at mandir. She wants to be American, let her mess with American boys and leave my brother out of her nastiness."

"Okay. Let's go," Rayna insisted, her voice small.

"Of course I'd never say that to her face. She'd probably hit me."

"Saanvi," Rayna pleaded.

"She still does that stupid boxing thing. I'm embarrassed for her parents."

I rolled my eyes. What even? My parents were my biggest motha-freaking fans.

"She's way far gone. She doesn't fit in with our community. A freakish liar and a slut. She'd taint the mandir if she ever came. But now we gotta have a chat with Amit. Warn him."

"Okay, I'm leaving. This is out of hand; you don't have to be that mean to her." The door opened and closed.

Saanvi at least assumed one thing correctly: I *was* about to punch her.

She muttered something in Gujarati, what sounded like a nasty little word that conveyed filth and disgust to the highest degree. Then she kicked my stall.

I jumped out of my skin, and she walked out. They knew I was in here?

I seethed, my body on fire. Part of me wanted to punch her face to a bloody pulp and the other part struggled to reason with the wrath. I was so pissed I could kill her. My knuckles turned white. My nostrils flared. I shook with anger.

Saanvi was talking so much crap about me, filling Rayna with malicious gossip to keep her from wanting to be friends again. If she could say those things knowing I'd hear, then how much worse was her crap-talk when I wasn't around? How freaking dare she.

Oh, she wanted to say that I'd probably hit her? Yeah. I was about ready to show her what I'd learned in my "*stupid boxing thing*."

Breathe. Just breathe.

If I punched her I would get expelled. I'd mar my record and college applications. I'd disappointment my parents. I'd let down my sport. I'd be disqualified from entering USMTO. If I didn't go to the Open, it would not be because of her.

I pushed all the hate and anger out and meditated on peace and harmony, imagining my mind and body and soul aligned instead of ripped apart just as Muay Thai had taught me. It made me rise above the stupidity and ignorance and hostility. Muay Thai wasn't about violence. I had to honor that.

That wasn't easy, though, and tears slid down my cheeks. I wiped them away as fast as I could and slammed opened the door. If I so much as saw a glimpse of Saanvi's stupid face, I was going to break.

I startled the moment I walked out of the restroom, coming face to face with Amit. He had a beckoning half smile waiting for me, but it slipped away. Was it because of the anger in my eyes or the pain? I retreated into the restroom. He followed me in. Did he, like, not realize where he was?

"What happened?" he demanded, firmer than any question he'd ever asked, one laced with concern and rolled with a hint of his own anger.

When I didn't respond, frozen into place beside the sinks near the far wall, beneath a window that was too small to crawl out of, he asked, "Did Saanvi and Rayna say something to you?"

I shook my head like it was the truth. They did not speak directly to me. But had they spoken to him? Had Saanvi infiltrated his kindness toward me with vicious lies?

"Was it Travis?" he asked, his voice low, his hands inching toward fists. "Did he do something?"

I shook my head again.

We were at a stand-off. He couldn't make me talk. He didn't have the right to know.

I stomped toward him and reached for the door handle. He didn't stop me from taking hold, but he stayed in place. I tugged. Hard.

"God, are you made of concrete?" I muttered. I wanted to still be angry, but Amit made things a little less red.

"Well, my dad says I'm hardheaded, so . . ."

I couldn't look him in the eye but asked sternly, "Can you just get out of my way?"

He looked around, seeming suddenly surprised when he realized where he was and what he was doing when he said, "Oh . . . no. I probably shouldn't be in here." Amit stepped aside and added, "I'm sorry. That was way out of line."

I sighed. If I'd felt threatened, I would've made sure he knew how out of line he was. But honestly? I kind of wanted to tell him. Instead, I muttered, "We're late for class."

"Maybe, we can skip one class?"

My eyes went wide. "I have perfect attendance."

"*Nerd*," he fake coughed.

I scoffed. How did he do that? How did he make a hurricane of life's crap simmer into a light rain . . . of life's crap?

"You're one to talk. So what? Because we've hung out for a couple of weeks we're best friends? We're just study partners."

"I thought we were *dating*," he said in all seriousness.

"Are you joking?"

He laughed. "Yes. Now, doesn't being friends sound conceivable?"

I took a moment to breathe, to calm down, to consider his words. "You want to be friends?"

"Like chana needs masala."

"What? That's stupid."

"But you're smiling."

"Am I though?"

His laugh died down, his gaze dropping to my mouth. "You're very pretty when you smile."

"As opposed to . . . being ugly when I frown?"

"No. As opposed to . . ." He swallowed. "Being exceptionally pretty no matter what."

"Oh . . ."

He scratched the back of his neck. "So, yeah, we're late to class and people might wonder if we walk in together."

"True."

"I vote that we get out of here."

"Where is this streak of rebellion coming from?"

"From seeing you miserable. And you won't talk to me. You'll just brood in class and glare at the computer screen, which by the way didn't do anything to you."

I crossed my arms. "And where do you suppose we go?"

He cocked his chin toward the door and eased away, sticking his head out for a sneak peek. "Coast is clear."

I could've made a run for it as soon as we slipped out of the girls' restroom, but I didn't mind when Amit brushed the back of my hand and jerked his chin toward the back halls. I nodded. He gently took my wrist and led me toward my first absence. His touch electrified, a burn that branched up my arm in lightning patterns, crackling and sizzling and splitting my nerves.

We walked in rushed steps, ducking around corridors and pretending to be opening lockers if someone appeared in the desolate hallways. We trotted down the steps and slid out the side doors to the back of campus. The courtyard to the cafeteria loomed to the right and slowly filled with students from Lunch B.

Amit released my wrist and my skin immediately missed the warmth. I stuffed my hands into my pockets and watched my steps across the trimmed lawn, to the higher grass, and along a dirt path through the preserved forest around a babbling creek.

"Where are you taking me? You're not a demented, knife-wielding killer, are you?"

He ducked beneath limbs and held back a branch for me. "You already warned me that you could beat me up. I'm not testing that."

Fallen leaves crunched beneath our feet and birds chirped above us. The sights and sounds of campus faded beyond the curtain of trees at our backs. At night, this would've totally creeped me out.

Amit searched for something and it didn't take long to realize it wasn't a particular spot. Finally, he crouched by the stream where large rocks created tiny pools and small waterfalls. Pink thistle flowers dotted the other side against a canvas of browns and greens and a moving mass of gray and white.

"What is that?" I whispered, crouching beside Amit, the toes of my shoes barely out of the water's reach.

He pointed to the moving creatures. A duck, a mama duck, quacked and waddled out of the brush. She was beautiful in her dark colors speckled with brown and gray around the face. Her beak curved upward like a perpetual smile that made her look happy and carefree and like she was absolutely loving the crap out of life.

"She's gorgeous."

"Wait until you see the brood."

She quacked again, her webbed feet splashing against wet rocks and moss. Tiny noises emerged from the brush, followed by tiny, freaking adorable webbed feet. Ducklings. They were dark gray with white fluffy heads and a streak of black around their eyes that extended all the way to their backs, making their eyes look like ancient Egyptians had painted them with eyeliner.

Their beaks also curved upward, and they joyfully, awkwardly ran after their mama. There were so many. First three, then six, then a total of eleven.

"It's a horde of ducklings," I gasped.

"A horde of cuteness coming straight at us."

"I can't even . . ." I grinned, my lips stretching far and wide. I wanted to die from cuteness overload!

One of the ducklings walked right into the one in front of it and fell flat on its bottom.

"I want one so bad."

"Yeah?" Amit stood and we followed the family down the way until mama duck slipped into the water and all the ducklings followed.

He traipsed over exposed rocks dug into the creek bed and scooped up a duckling.

"What are you doing? You're going to traumatize it! And mama duck is going to rip you a new one."

He chuckled and brought over the most gorgeous little bird that ever lived. It sat pacified in his cupped hands, water dribbling down his wrists and arms.

"I thought they fought back?" I asked, amazed and mesmerized by the fluff ball.

"I come out here all the time and feed the mama duck, and after a while she let me get close to the babies to feed. Here." He offered the baby to me.

"It's going to bite me."

He laughed. "She won't."

"How do you know it's a girl? Are you looking at their cloacas?"

He laughed even harder, startling the duckling, who squirmed. Amit wrapped his fingers over her wings. "I don't know. I guessed. Don't be scared. She won't bite."

"How do I?"

"Like this. Cup your hands like mine, and when I slide her into your palms, gently close your hands over her body, keeping her wings down, but yeah, avoid her beak."

I trembled as the little ball nestled into my hands.

"Just like that."

Her feet were cold, and I wanted to cuddle her and take her home. "What do they eat?"

He scooped up a string of algae growing over the water and laid it over my hand. The duckling pecked at the food, trying to gobble the string, tickling me in the process. She squeak-quacked and mama duck shook her little tail feathers to swim toward us.

"Oh, she looks mad." Even with her perpetually grinning beak.

"Carefully set her into the water. But, ya know, over there away from mama duck."

I trudged over the rocks and mud and deposited the duckling in the stream, near the edge so the current didn't sweep her away. She shook her wings and met her siblings and mama, and together they swam farther downstream. We followed quietly, wandering farther and farther away from campus. I didn't mind.

For a good half hour, we watched them until they gathered in their nest. If you didn't think ducklings could get cuter, then you'd never seen them lean their heads against their downy siblings and fall asleep.

We watched over them from across the creek, planted on a cleanish, flat boulder, our sides touching, our arms pressed against one another. I could've easily laid my head against Amit's shoulder and fallen asleep.

He cleared his throat. Oh! My head had a mind of its own then, already resting on the tip of his shoulder. His fingers twitched beside mine. I didn't move. Neither did he. His fingers lifted off his lap and floated over to my hand.

I tamped down a smile.

His fingers, larger than my own, fell in between mine. He swallowed hard beside me. The muscles of his neck and chest constricted, filling my ears with an audible gulp that resonated along with the sound of rushing water, the wind, the call of the wild.

"Friends don't hold hands, you know?" I said softly.

"Hmm, they don't, huh?" The warmth of his body encompassed mine, making me forget that I wore shorts beneath the chilly shade of the canopy.

After another bout of silence, he sighed. And I knew what was about to come next. "You don't have to tell me what's wrong."

Oh. Not that.

He went on, "I won't keep asking because that would be bugging you, and I don't want you to tickle me to death again."

"Don't forget what you just said."

"But I hate to see you down. Just know that you can always talk to me."

"Okay. But I won't."

"I understand. We're not even best friends."

"No. We're not."

"And you don't know me that well."

"Nope. Hardly."

"But we can get to know each other."

"I think you're all-consumed by the magic of the forest."

"You're going to avoid me once we leave, then?"

"No." There was no way in this world I'd want to avoid Amit Patel.

"Just know that whatever's got you down has a silver lining."

"No, it really doesn't." Besides, silver linings aren't enough to diminish the problems.

"Then it can be fixed."

"No, it really can't." I exhaled and sat up straight but didn't break our interlocked fingers.

"You're smart. I'm smart. We can figure something out."

"You're sweet for trying. You wouldn't understand."

"I'm not sure why you think I'm a certain way."

"I don't."

"Yeah, you obviously do. You thought I was judgmental of you because of Travis. Now you assume I'd never get a clue about what's going on with you. I mean, is it a girl thing?"

My left eyebrow shot up fast and sharp.

"If you're pregnant—"

"Oh, god no. Why would you even think that?" I tensed, wondering if he'd heard the rumors, if he thought I was easy or had been sleeping with a boy.

"I didn't think so. Okay, in relative comparison, how much worse or better is it than being pregnant?"

I stifled a sigh. Oh, was that all? "I've never been pregnant so I wouldn't know. Look, I mean you wouldn't understand because I honestly don't think you have a problem, or problems, plural, as significant and devastating as mine."

"Are you sure? Because we've already established that you hardly know me."

"Touché. Tell me your biggest grief in life then, and maybe we'll compare."

His expression squirmed. "I can't."

"Wow. You want me to open my woes to you and you can't tell me the one problem you have?"

"My one problem is pretty huge."

"Yet I somehow doubt it stacks up to my many."

"I do want to tell you my problem. I haven't been able to talk to anyone about it because I'm not allowed to."

"Some cosmic secret?"

"Close."

I rolled my eyes. "Sure."

"It's a problem that only I can solve. At least that's how my brain sees it. So there's an entire world's pressure to solve it. Alone. And I feel that I'm a giant, incendiary pile of nothing if I can't fix it fast enough. The guilt crushes me. It keeps me up all night, working on it."

"Is that why you fall asleep in class?"

"Yeah. I'm up all night either trying to fix it or worrying about it."

"And your parents don't know?"

"They know."

"They don't help?"

"They can't. No one can help me."

That was hard to believe. Especially when he had such a

large community supporting him. "I'm sure someone can. If you tell them what it is."

"Look who's talking."

"Is it . . . personal? Like, a problem at home? Parents beat you?"

"What? No!"

"Parents beat each other?"

He made a weird face that spoke of incredulity.

"Well, it happens. So, is it a relationship problem?" I held my breath. Did he have a girl?

"Nope."

"No clues, huh?"

He smiled. "Maybe one day you'll tell me what's got you so down and then I'll tell you."

I scraped the mud on my shoe against a rock. "We're at an impasse, then. You won't tell me; I won't tell you."

"But we know the other person feels the same way, maybe not about the same thing."

"I feel like it's going to destroy me. I don't see any of my problems getting better, much less working out. One is a disappointment. The other is losing something that can't be replaced."

"I wish that you'd share."

"Same here. We should get back."

He checked his watch. "It's partway through last period. Might as well finish being rebels."

"So . . ." I rubbed my palms against my shorts. "What exactly do you do at work?"

"Part of my cosmic secret."

"You actually work in fast food, huh?"

He tilted his head down and laughed.

···❮ NINE ❯···

I kept all of Amit's random proverbial texts that he'd sent. *Laughter is the remedy for a 1001 illnesses* followed by a dozen GIFs and social media links to things ranging from baby monkeys to people tripping over things.

Alas, laughter did not make it rain money to pay for Papa's medical bills and enable me to go to USMTO.

He who undertakes too many things at once seldom does them well. One step at a time, Kareena. Followed by videos of stumbling animals learning how to walk.

Don't fall into a fire in order to avoid the smoke.

At that one I responded, *How does that cryptic one even apply?*

Smoke = problems; fire = depression.

No. Send more funny ones.

Fall 7 times, stand up 8.

That's not a funny one.

But it was one I'd known for years. It was an old Japanese proverb that I'd learn in Muay Thai. In the beginning, I sucked hard. I fell a lot and had little coordination. I was always getting hurt and losing matches. I used to think about giving up or stepping back because it was too difficult, and I never saw myself getting anywhere near being decent.

Coach had said, "You're going to fall many times, but if

you don't try at least one more time, then you won't know how it feels to stand."

I took in a long breath and closed my eyes, pretending to be standing in the ring with the weight of the world lost on me. That was how it felt almost every time. Nerves? Sure. Scared? Sometimes. Hurt? Probably. But other problems vanished. Maybe that was why I lost myself in the sport just to deal with reality. Maybe that was why I kept going even though I wasn't sure if my parents could scrape up the rest of the money. Maybe that was why I hadn't told Coach the possibility of not going. I needed the ring the way a bird needed the sky. It was freedom, even if temporarily.

Are you going to Holi tonight?

I lay flat on my stomach in bed and dangled my arms over the edge so that the phone grazed the floor. Parties made my skin crawl, especially festivities involving large numbers of people. Mama had brought out *the* suitcase, the one filled to the brim with kurta pajamas and salwar kameez with a few saris and chaniya cholis. In case I wanted to go.

I chewed on my lip and shut my eyes. I'd thrown my entire soul into the gym yesterday and today, and it took more of a beating than my shins (poor, bruised shins).

My parents would love to see you, Amit texted.

Yeah, right.

Serious. They said they hadn't seen you since you were a kid and went to mandir with your parents. I don't remember you. Do you remember me?

No. I didn't remember much about mandir, if anything, except dance classes with Rayna and Saanvi. I did have fun with them.

How long ago were you last at mandir, anyway?

God, think when I was 9 maybe. Yeah, about 8 yrs ago.

You haven't gone in that long?

You think everyone goes to church??

After a long pause that consisted of me restlessly tapping my fingers on the screen without the bubble with the dot, dot, dot popping up to indicate that I was typing, he texted.

I'm wearing all white.

That's dumb, I replied quickly, unable to help myself.

Genius, really.

It'll get wasted with color.

That's what bleach is for. Can't use bleach on a colored shirt to get the rang out.

Rang?

Rang. Rung. Gulal. Whatever the colored powders are called. I dunno. I just throw them.

LOL.

Most people wear old jeans and a shirt they don't mind tossing away. But wear whatever you have that you don't mind getting color wasted.

I giggled, imagining my shirt getting wasted off variously bright colored powders, and dragged my feet to *the* suitcase. I figured it might be fun to get dressed up a little, and maybe an old kurti or salwar kameez wasn't what most people considered getting dressed up, but it was for me. A short burst of giddiness hit me as I rummaged through the suitcase, but I didn't find anything white. There was an abundance of red, wine, gold, yellow, green, blue, purple, and pink. No black. No white.

"Are you going to Holi?" Mama asked from the doorway, her expression pleasantly surprised.

"I think so. Do you remember . . . hold on." I text-asked Amit what his parents' names were. "Do you remember Raju Uncle and Manesha Auntie? They have a son in my grade, Amit."

She looked off into the corner as she mulled over the names. "It's been so long. Are they from mandir?"

"They go to mandir. He says that his parents remember us."

"Oh. Too bad I don't remember them. Are you texting boys, Kareena?"

I tucked my phone into my pocket and tried to evade her question. How did I tattle on myself just now? "So not the point."

"Hmm, I think it is. That phone isn't for you to text boys with."

"I know. My teacher assigned me to tutor him for class. We had to exchange numbers. He's texting because he and his parents invited us to Holi and he wants to know if we're going."

"As you know, Papa can't be around large crowds, plus all the music and dance, it's too much for him."

"I know," I said in a small, sad voice. "What about you?"

"I'm just too tired from working. What little time I have, I want to spend with you and Papa."

"I won't go then."

"No, no. I mean, I'd rather stay home with my family. But you should go. I want you to experience our culture." She sat on the bed and bent down to run her fingers over the silks and metallic threads. "I feel awful that we didn't expose you more to other Indians."

"I know why and it's fine. I don't want to be around judgy people. Too much negativity."

She studied the fabrics with a sort of fondness, longing even. I wondered if, aside from the gossip and ridicule, she missed the Indian community. "Not all Indians are the same. I don't want you to view them so negatively. Maybe things at mandir are different these days. Does Amit know about the Muay Thai?"

"No."

"Oh?"

"We're not that close. We just started studying a couple of weeks ago. We don't hang out outside of school . . . actually, just lunch. That's when we do our study sessions and we focus on classwork."

"I see."

"He said most people wear old jeans and shirts they don't mind throwing away." Which was basically almost everything I owned. I mean, everything was old, but we took really good care of our clothes. No throwing anything away.

She picked through the worn clothes and pulled out a dark-blue salwar kameez with matching dupatta. "This is plain, but it will work perfectly for Holi. We won't worry about any stains. Color your heart out."

"Thank you." I took the knee-length tunic, leggings, and shawl from her.

"You know? Holi is about color and celebration, but also thanksgiving, gratefulness, forgiveness."

"Really? I thought it was just another religious thing."

"Not at all. Some of its roots goes back to religion, but it's mostly about new beginnings. You should have new beginnings. With our culture, our people."

"What if they ostracize me for being a fighter? They did that before." Or worse, what if they said or even implied crap about my parents? There was no returning from that, no redemption.

She rolled her neck the way Indian moms did, all sass and attitude and a moment of, "Let me tell you something, child . . ."

"You didn't need to be friends with girls whose parents stripped away your friendship. How dare they. Who do they think they are, huh? So special?"

"Mama . . ." I cringed, hating to hear her relive the past. Sure, she had her very strong opinions about my confidence outshining any haters, but maybe she hurt too. Maybe she hurt knowing that others thought less of me. I knew that I hurt, for sure, realizing that those same people disliked her for stupid reasons such as marrying for love, not finishing college, and having a "lesser career" as a secretary opposed to being a doctor.

"Did I ever try to make those girls think they were any less because they secretly ate meat when their parents wanted them to be religiously vegetarian? Did I end your friendships with them because they were little liars? Or shun their parents for raising something 'less' than perfect?"

"I mean, I did accidentally punch one of them."

"An accident, hah. Kids will be kids. It happens. It was because you are supposed to be a lady, reserved, a dancer on the team."

"Not a fighter," I muttered.

"Don't let that get to you. You're a great fighter."

"I can take a punch, Mama, and even a beating. But mentally, emotionally? I wish I was that strong."

She took my hands in hers, the salwar kameez falling limp beneath our hold. "You're better than any preconceived prejudice. Holi is a time and event for everyone, and you deserve to be there if you want. You have the right to attend mandir if you want. If they don't like it, then they can sit in the corner and shut their roti holes," she snapped. "And if you want to go to festivities and mandir for *anything* and they try to scare you or run you off, then *I* will go with you and they can deal with *me*."

"Wow, Mama. It's okay."

"It is not okay. If they want to talk rubbish about me, then let them. Not everyone who has higher degrees is a good person, and not everyone who has less is unworthy. And, no, I have never and will never regret marrying your Papa. They say the term 'love marriage' like we're living last century in India, as if it's a crime to marry someone because you're in love.

"If they turn that against you, then I won't stand for it. You are a child. You are *my* child. I've tried to protect you from what I experienced with them, by keeping you away. But what I should've done was expose you to them and shown you how to stand up to them, verbally, mentally, emotionally. Not cower or avoid them as if you are doing anything wrong. Do you understand? If you want to go to Holi, then pack your water gun and shoot them all in the faces."

I laughed. "You're so crazy, sometimes, Mama. Oh, my lord."

"You know they use water guns, don't you?"

"I did not know that."

"Challo. Go play Holi, beta, and demolish them."

"Water guns, huh?" I muttered as I took the outfit and changed.

I texted Amit. *I'll be ready in ten minutes.*

Oh, good! I'm already outside your house.

What the frick? I pulled the curtain aside and peered through the slit where the edge of the fabric barely touched the window frame. Outside my house, on the street adjacent to the short driveway, perched Amit's dark-green Corolla. His shadow waved. I jammed the curtain back into place and heaved. Could he see me? Did he see me change? Nah. The curtains weren't that flimsy.

I rushed into the bathroom and checked out my reflection. The top fit my body just right, not too snug or baggy, and I had room to raise my arms. I smeared on tinted BB cream with my fingers and added a little eyeliner and rose-tinted Chapstick.

Mama appeared at the doorway with a knock, her hands already moving through my hair. "Do you want me to fix your hair?"

"It's fine."

"A French braid with a bun at the end? Not fancy but very nice."

"Hah," I agreed.

As she effortlessly braided my hair from my temple to the shoulder and wrapped the rest into a loose bun, she commented, "He's very nice."

"He's inside already? I told him ten minutes."

"He's eager. Very cute too. But absolutely no dating."

I rolled my eyes.

"Where are his parents?"

"Maybe they'll meet us there."

Mama walked me to the living room where Amit and Papa chatted in the foyer. Amit wore a white kurta pajama as advertised, with the sleeves rolled to his elbows. The look was incomprehensibly attractive, the way his forearm bulged with every gesture of the hand. Although his clothes were simple, it had fresh creases, the kind that came from brand new clothes from India when they'd been pressed and folded a certain way and inserted into plastic packaging.

He laughed with Papa, ending, "They hope to see you soon, Uncle."

Papa nodded and both turned to me with grins, their faces lit as if this were some bizarre parallel universe and I had just walked down idyllic steps in a fluffy gown for prom.

"That's a nice color on you," Amit commented.

"You look nice too. Is your outfit new? Or does your mom have super bleach?"

"It's new. We always get new clothes for all the celebrations."

I subconsciously folded my hands in front of my lap, hiding the faded color and frayed dupatta. "You must have a lot of clothes stacking up in your closet."

"No. Most of us at mandir send back suitcases of old clothes to India every year for donation."

"Every year? You just wear them once or what?"

"Usually. You know how Indian style changes fast."

Yep. And that made my threads *extra* old. Must've been nice to buy new clothes every month. I'd been wearing the same ones for years.

"My dad should be around, but it gets packed and dads seem to go off and do their own thing. My mom went early to help with the food. She made barfi." Which happened to be my all-time favorite sweet. He turned to Mama. "Would you like us to bring you back a plate?"

"That's very nice of you. That would be lovely. Thank you."

"Of course."

"We better get going," I said, trying to push Amit out the door without actually touching him.

"Nice meeting you," he called over his shoulder.

I ignored my parents' hopeful, hinting faces as they closed the front door behind us. Seriously, *were* we in an alternate dimension where my parents liked a boy for me? Or were they hopeful about me fitting into the mandir community?

Amit's car beeped as he unlocked it with a handheld key. Fancy. His scent of light cologne swooshed past me as I reached for the door. He grabbed the door handle before I could and opened it for me.

"I have hands, you know?"

"It's not you. I do this for everyone," he said in all seriousness and with a straight face. He was a Southern gentleman, then.

I slipped in and he closed the door before jumping into

the driver's seat. The car smelled just like him; a light scent of cinnamon and shampoo and soap and paper. His back seat was covered with notebooks and binders and textbooks.

"Don't you have a bedroom for all this stuff?"

"I believe in osmosis. It makes me smarter," he replied.

"Do you have calculus back there? Maybe I'll get smarter too."

He grinned really hard and peeled onto the street. My house and neighborhood disappeared in the sideview mirror.

"Thanks for coming," he said.

I twiddled my thumbs in my lap, hoping really hard that this wasn't a mistake. I swore that in the movies this sort of thing almost always led to some huge public fiasco and sent the main character running home crying. "Thanks for nagging me."

"What! I did no such thing."

"Do they have water guns?" A girl had to protect herself.

"Yes. Usually the kids use them." He glanced at me. "Why the sinister look? Are you planning on destroying me with a water gun? Because that means retaliation and I'll have to snatch one too."

"No, no, not you. Okay, well, maybe you too."

"What are you plotting?"

"Oh, don't worry your pretty little head, darlin'." This event was hosted by mandir. Which meant Saanvi would probably be there. And while it was a bad idea to punch her in her smug face, ending her with a water gun, and on her turf, nonetheless, was just the sort of thing she deserved.

"No, seriously. Should I be worried? Are you hatching an evil plan to get back at me for something?"

"No. I might get you, but I won't drown you."

He side-eyed me at the stoplight. "Are you going after a certain person?"

"Yes. Saanvi. Are you going to stop me?"

"Well, this is a celebration, one about new beginnings and forgiveness. Not an opportunity for vengeance."

"Yeah, yeah." I waved off his words. He wasn't in that restroom with me when Saanvi pushed me over the edge. And he probably wouldn't even get it. To anyone else, her words weren't that sharp. But to me, they were devastating. She was . . . oh my god . . . she was my bully. I had a freaking bully. Oh, heck no. Girls in Muay Thai didn't stand bullies. I crossed my arms and huffed, even more determined to put her in her place.

"It's also a festival of love," he added, cutting through my thoughts.

"Say what?"

"Love of neighbor and family that is. What did Saanvi do to get on your hit list?"

I glared out the window.

"Come on, you can tell me."

"What if you're a spy?"

"For Saanvi?" He laughed. "First of all, I'd already know the story then, at least her side. Second, Saanvi and I are as close as snails and rats."

"Which one are you? The snail or the rat?"

"Now you're just being mean. You do understand that I can't allow you to run around with a target on her back, right? This is *Holi*, not paintball."

"How many people will be there?"

"A few hundred. Why?"

I grinned. Let him try to stop me in a crowd that big.

Amit's guesstimate was not far off. A substantial crowd gathered on the grounds of the mandir with a sprinkling of Americans here and there. Strings of fairy lights were strewn around the temple and trees and bushes. Heart-pounding, upbeat music thrummed through the ground, snaking its way to my soles and seeping into my bones. Extreme, romantic, powerful, exotic, and easily becoming a part of me. It was hard not to be drawn to my culture, to not appreciate the majesty of it.

There were a lot of people dressed in old jeans and T-shirts, but some were dressed in bright clothes and clouds of rainbow-colored mist sprinkled down from thrown puffs of powder. Two tables at opposite sides of the lawn were covered in steel platters. Each platter held a pile of colored powder: sun yellow, mustard yellow, light orange, burnt orange, bright red, blood red, fuchsia, violet, purple, and midnight blue.

Where were those water guns, though?

"My mom wants to say hi." Amit broke my concentration and led me into the mandir where a smaller crowd stood around centrally located life-size idols clad in silk garments and adorned with marigold strands. Most of the inside group were older: parents and grandparents.

I followed Amit, although not too closely, to the food tables. An assortment of fried and saucy dishes lined the tables with uncles standing behind them, armed with spoons. At the far end were pots of basmati rice, roti, and parathas. Still, past that, drinks, and at the very end, a smaller table completely covered in plates stacked high with sweets.

Amit greeted a woman in a glittering pink and gold sari with a hug. Her hair was pulled back in an elegant bun. Chandelier earrings danced from her ears. Ornate necklaces and bangles shimmered with every movement.

"Ma, this is Kareena. Her parents couldn't come, but they said hello."

"Nice to meet you, Auntie," I said.

"Lovely to see you." She beamed and I saw where Amit had inherited his billion-dollar smile. His mom was stunning, with big brown eyes lined with thick lashes, a narrow nose with a diamond stud, and full, red painted lips. "I've not seen you since you were knee high. You had short curls back then."

"You remember me?"

"Who could forget you? You were the prettiest little girl, so much life when you walked into a room. You were so talkative."

"Social butterfly?" Amit asked aloud.

I shrugged. I guessed? Dunno. I didn't really remember.

"We've missed you. We should get together with your parents. How are they?"

"They're good. I'll let them know," I replied with a hint of excitement. Maybe my reaction was as fake as hers? It would've been really cool if she meant that, but based on the facts that I'd never heard my parents talk about her or remembered her, she was probably just making small talk and hitting all the polite buttons.

"Namaste, Auntie," Saanvi said in a sickeningly sweet voice, appearing beside me with her hands clasped together.

"Oh, Saanvi. How are you, beta?" Amit's mom lit up on seeing the devil in disguise. When she walked around the table to hug her, Saanvi immediately bent to touch her feet, then pressed her fingers to her chest and clasped her hands together in front of her. Amit's mom touched her head in response. A greeting of deep respect and tradition between child and elder, and here I was acting like a Westernized heathen.

She spewed into pontificating jargon about mandir stuff,

mainly dance and puja, and honestly, most of it flew over my head.

Amit touched my elbow as the two spiraled into an animated conversation about the festival. "Bye, Ma."

"Hah, bye, beta."

We backed away and disappeared out the door.

"Sorry about that," he muttered into the collar of his kurta, his hands in his shirt pockets low on the waist.

"I'm used to that."

"Being ignored?"

"Ignored and replaced when it comes to aunties."

"Ah, nah. My mom isn't like that. She's the dance teacher and Saanvi is one of the older students, so she takes the lead in organizing and helping the younger girls."

"Okay." I crossed my arms and walked toward the colored powders.

"She didn't mean to drop the conversation. When those two get together, it's all dance talk all the time." He rolled his eyes in exasperation, cuter than ever.

He took my elbow and reigned me back toward him. "But hey, what do you mean you're used to that?"

"I'm used to Indians ignoring me or—"

"Hi, Amit!" Saanvi bounded up to him and deliberately stepped in between us.

"Uh, hi, Saanvi."

"Hey, Saanvi," I groaned with a sarcastic wave.

She ignored me and Amit frowned. She edged closer to him and placed a hand on his arm, opening her hate-spewing mouth before he said a word, filling the white noise with her stupid giggles.

"We were talking," I said.

"And now you're not," she snapped.

"Saanvi," Amit hissed. "Why are you being so rude?"

"Why are you talking to her? Don't you know her reputation?"

"Which is what, exactly?" I asked.

"Travis," she sang without looking at me. "Went the wrong direction after my brother."

I cowered into myself when Amit shot a curious glance at me. *Please don't listen to her. Please let someone smack her in the back of the head with a water balloon and end this before she says anything else.* Ugh! Why couldn't *I* just say something? Why couldn't I just shut her mouth for her? But it was too late. Give the devil a second, and she'll pounce without deliberation. Should have gotten that water gun first.

"What happened with Dev?" he asked.

"Oh you don't know? Rayna had a crush on him and Kareena swooped in like a vulture and tried to . . . I dunno, he wouldn't say."

"*Talk* to him," I said, but my words came out softer than I intended, as if I had done something much worse. Talking to a boy was not the same as sleeping with him! Talking to a boy after talking with another boy was not the same thing as cheating! But Saanvi didn't care. She wanted drama, and she wanted a reason to drag my name any way she could. And even though I should've just voiced my thoughts aloud, as pointed and annoyed as the words appeared in my head, my lips couldn't manage to move.

"Right. Dev and Travis are friends and word got around. Which is the only reason Travis hangs around you. But, I guess you know that," she added with a sharp tongue.

Heat struck my face like an angry viper. I didn't know which I wanted more: to hide from Amit before the look of judgment crested his features or to punch Saanvi in her stupid, fake face.

She turned and scowled at me, at which point an irate Amit mouthed, "Water guns," and cocked his chin toward the barrels behind the tables.

I quirked an eyebrow at Ms. Stank and walked away. As I approached the water guns, a newfound level of vengeance surged through my veins. Holi was about forgiveness, yeah, yeah.

I loaded the water gun with the darker blue powder and shook the liquid mixture.

In a way, I had forgiven her. I didn't hate Saanvi anymore and I sure as heck wasn't going to feel small every time she threw an accusatory glance at me.

I pumped the gun a dozen times and walked back toward them.

After so long—and seeing how she couldn't fool Amit—the fear of what I'd done dissolved. She wanted drama? She wanted something to really complain about?

I pumped until the water gun could take no more. It sat rigid in my hands, ready to burst from the pressure. Amit had his arms crossed over his chest, arguing with Saanvi, when he looked up and I caught him.

Blue water sprayed across his face. His eyes were clenched shut, his mouth open in shock. Colored liquid dripped down his handsome lips and splattered on his white shirt, staining it cobalt.

Saanvi scrunched her shoulders up and spun toward me. Before she sprouted any more idiotic words, I unleashed the fury of a pent-up water gun, one hit after another right into her pretty, craptastic face. She fought the air but I stepped closer and closer.

Amit wiped off the liquid from his face and burst into laughter and so did I. Saanvi fell back on the grass, gathering stares and becoming the spectacle that I'd always felt I was. I pumped to re-amp the gun, leaned toward her, and said, "Happy Holi!" *Muahahaa.*

"Come on!" Amit said, taking my elbow and leading me back to the tables as a pack of water gun-wielding, maniacal little kids descended on Saanvi. Fair game.

"You're not mad?" I asked, turning from her and facing Amit.

He grabbed two fistfuls of colors, one gold and the other pink, and tilted his head, his brows most definitely raised with mischief.

I aimed the gun at him. "I dare you."

And then it rained colored powder everywhere, from all directions, as everyone threw fistfuls into the air. I slowly turned in a semicircle, taking in the beauty that descended all around. Colors sprinkled down and were swept away by winds. A rainbow fog glimmered as far as the eye could see.

Amit gently grabbed me by the waist and held my arms down with his, pinning the gun to my leg. His fists were still full as I struggled and squealed. One hand came up and I slowly stilled, my back melting against his chest, as gold fluttered down and over my head, covering us both.

His hold loosened and I turned into him. There was something undeniably magical about the colors and vibrations that surrounded us in the night. His eyes foretold a million incredible fortunes and that smile did funny, amazing things to my stomach.

He swallowed, like he could lean down and kiss me. Had he lost his mind? Had he forgotten where we were?

I smirked and pressed the barrel end of the gun into his gut. His serious expression turned devastatingly romantic as he smeared powder across my cheek and dragged a pink trail down my lips with his thumb.

Holi? More like ho-ly crap. What was this guy doing to me?

My heart actually exploded. Like *kapow*! A jillion pieces floated chaotically in my chest. But he couldn't do this. Amit could not kiss me. Especially not here.

I did the only thing I could possibly do.

I fired the water gun and let out an avalanche of bellowing laughter.

And Amit got soaked.

TEN

The great thing about Holi was how the colorful haze made equals of all. No one knew or cared if the man beside you was a world-famous surgeon or Bollywood A-list actor or a housekeeper. The high-born rubbed elbows with the forgotten, aka me. Amit turned out to be one of those guys who could befriend anyone and everyone. Nearly all three hundred people present made a point to say hello to him. And about three hundred times he turned to me and said, "Have you met Kareena?"

Talk about being under a spotlight, but with the ever-genuine Amit at my side, the spotlight didn't sear the flesh off my bones. Nope. No smell of crackling skin.

They didn't probe into my mandir and/or festivity absence. They didn't pry about my parents. Which, combined with school, were the only things they asked about. I appreciated keeping conversations superficial and light.

The cranking gears of Amit's car jostled the silence. We sat, parked, on the street at the end of my driveway. The front porch lights shone dimly.

Heat sprang from the vents. The night had chilled considerably and Amit, thanks to my eagerness and the call of the little ones to back me up, was soaked clean through. Good thing he wore an undershirt beneath his white kurta or the aunties might've chided him for indecent exposure.

"Did you have fun?" he asked.

I beamed from ear to ear. Fun didn't begin to describe demolishing Saanvi and then enjoying myself with Amit the rest of the time. "You know I did."

He grinned. "Looked like it, especially when you took out Saanvi."

My face lit up. He knew me so well already.

"Are your parents up? They might like the plates my mom made."

"That was nice of her to hook them up, but they're asleep."

"It's only ten."

"My dad doesn't feel well, so he goes to bed early. And my mom's tired from work, so she goes to bed early too."

"And what about you?"

I looked over at him. "I stay up until midnight most nights."

"Is that why you sleep through class?"

My skin turned hot, remembering not too long ago when I fell asleep facing him and ended up drooling a river down my face. "Part of the reason."

I searched his profile for any thoughts. He watched the clock on his dashboard turn to 10:04 p.m. The darkness tried to swallow him, but the streetlight one house over kept the edge of his silhouette illuminated.

"What do you want to do for the next hour and fifty-six minutes?" he asked.

"That's assuming I want to spend any more time around you."

The corner of his lips curled up. "I know you do."

My heart did a funky dance in my chest, pounding to a new, intriguing beat. The funny thing was that Amit was right. "There's a neighborhood park around the corner. It's just a small jungle gym and benches and swings. It's dark and creepy, and probably a place insomniacs like us would hang out."

He chuckled. "Probably."

We stepped out of the car. He opened his trunk and pulled out a jacket.

"Are you cold?" he asked, the jacket welcoming in his hand.

"I can grab something from inside. You should wear it. You're drenched."

"Yeah, thanks to your trigger finger. Here." He laid the jacket over my shoulders.

"What about you?"

He tugged out a gray wool blanket.

"You just keep blankets in your car?"

He wrapped it around himself and closed the trunk. "It's for emergencies. Got food and water and flashlights and all kinds of stuff in there. You hungry?"

"Nah." We'd eaten plenty in between water gun fights. I'd tried my best to eat healthy when we were faced with so many delicious sweets. Had to keep my training front and center.

"Lead the way."

He walked beside me in the dim illumination of the streetlight as I stuffed my fists into the large pockets of his jacket. The leather smelled just like him, all boy with hints of faded cologne and guy body wash. He might never get this thing back.

We didn't speak during the walk. Leaves crunched beneath our shoes. Small rocks slid across the pavement. Damp soil flattened beneath our weight. Crickets sang their songs in the distance.

The suburban scene of cement and brick and metal and glass dissolved behind us in the night. A path appeared in the moonlight, guiding us through a thicket of oak and pecan trees. Shells crunched under us as loudly as wailing cats. The air was crisp and clean, with traces of grass and early spring flowers. Soon, bluebonnets, pink thistle, and red paintbrushes would sprout up, bringing in hordes of people sitting in the tall wildflowers for yearly pictures.

We didn't need to bring Amit's emergency flashlight or use our cell phone lights. The brightly lit stars and moon worked just fine, as did the busy, flashing fireflies that looked more like fairy lights strung across the trees.

We approached the makeshift baseball field with its semi-built fence and headed toward two benches that appeared before the kiddy playground.

I led Amit to the bench, but he veered off course to an oddly bent tree. I'd never figured out what sort of tree it was, but the split trunk attracted all the tree climbers. The leaning left side of the trunk partition grew at a gradual slope, but the right side did its own funky thing and curled down and over like the back of a hissing cat.

Amit swung on the trunk so that his feet dangled a good foot off the ground. Then he hoisted himself up and sat with both legs over one side. He offered a hand to pull me up, but he knew so little of me.

I went to the partition where crooked steps grew out of the trunk and crawled up the right side. I stood up straight, perfectly balanced, and walked toward an impressed Amit. Or at least, he looked impressed in the dark.

I carefully squatted, pressing my palms into the rough bark, and sat beside him. He scooted over, closing the few inches between us. His blanket-covered arm pressed into my jacket-covered one. I stared at our swinging feet, noticing for the first time his fancy sandals next to my worn-in flip-flops.

"This is cool," he said, breaking the silence.

"I like it. Sometimes they set up a sheet screen and play

old movies, and people from the neighborhood bring blankets to sit on and watch."

"That sounds like fun. Maybe we can catch the next movie?" His voice cracked.

I bit the inside of my lip to keep from smiling.

"Cuz, you know? That sounds pretty cool. Sitting on the grass with a bunch of random people and watching a black and white movie."

"I don't like old movies, so I never went." I stared at the bark beside my hand and flicked off little rough pieces, trying not to get swallowed whole by the moment. I couldn't like a boy. I didn't have time for this. Yet, here I was. Not trying to leave.

"What kind of movies do you like?" he asked.

"I'm into superhero movies, especially ones with kick-butt girls."

"I totally see that. I like superhero movies too. Well, much of anything sci-fi and fantasy and comedy. Not into romance or artsy."

"Me, either."

We dangled our feet some more before he asked the inevitable, "Why don't you go to stuff more often?"

"What stuff?" I asked and tensed. I already knew what he meant. Indians should do "Indian things." Hang around other Indians. Be more Indian.

"Our kind of stuff. Diwali and Navratri and things that the mandir puts on."

"I just don't."

He said lightly, "Ah, come on. There's a better excuse than that. And if there isn't, then there's no excuse not to go."

"I'm not religious. So, don't think one fun night at Holi will turn me around."

"I didn't mean that," he said softly. "It's cultural and social."

I replied dryly, "Well, I'm neither. Sorry to disappoint."

"That's not disappointing. Just wondering why."

"Honestly?" I bit out, getting a little heated. He kept asking and probing. Why couldn't he just accept that I didn't like that stuff? Did he want me to change? Be more cookie-cutter? More . . . I dunno . . . acceptable? Part of me was getting annoyed, but another part of me just wanted to tell him the entire truth and let him decide if this friendship was going to continue before I got too attached.

"Yes. I'd like to know."

A hot rush of emotion flooded through me and my mouth didn't stop. "Because I don't feel comfortable. I don't conform to Indian ways. I'm not *Indian enough* and that's how they see me and treat me. So, no. I don't go to mandir or get involved in festivities. And no, I won't be going back."

"Whoa." He raised his hands in defense. "I wasn't trying to insinuate anything or attack you. You're no less Indian for not doing all this stuff. And what do you mean you're not Indian enough? Is that even a thing?"

"Yes. Take for example Saanvi. She observes all the holidays and fasts and prays every morning. We used to do sleepovers at Rayna's, and she'd bring this portable prayer kit. You know? With a prayer towel, pictures, prayer book, and beaded necklace thing, I don't know what that's called. She'd wake up at dawn and face the south of the house, or something, and pray. She used to get mad when I walked in on her, even if we were quiet.

"She's active in mandir and goes to all the weddings and parties and is devout and just perfect in every way to every auntie and uncle I know. They light up when they speak about her; they've never done that when they speak about me. They don't even say more than two words if they see me.

"I don't pray. I don't like going to festivals. I don't even like curry. I can only eat so much roti and rice. I eat meat. And I like things that most other Indian girls here don't, so I don't conform to their view and they make me feel like I'm less of an Indian, an outsider, too Western. I've always been on the fringe of social things. Most people have never said, hey come on over or we'll see you at whatever. When I got close to being friends with other little Indian girls, their moms pulled them away."

I paused long enough to drag in another breath, but I didn't look at Amit. I didn't want to see how weirded out he was or even, maybe, how upset he might be. And since I was on a rant, might as well get it all out. Might as well completely push the boy away.

"My grades are okay. My Gujarati is embarrassing, and my understanding of Hindi is laughable. I don't get Bollywood movies. I can't do a single Indian-style dance, including Garba, the easiest of them all. I can't figure out how to wear a sari properly. I can't grasp the spices to know what to put into Indian food. My rotis come out square and uneven, and my barfi comes out bumpy and not at all square.

"I'm not saying that's all an Indian is. You can't quantify an entire race by a few abstract things. And I'm not saying all Indians view me that way, it can't be. But I'm saying there are enough Indians in *this* community to make me sorely aware that I'm not . . . what . . . good enough? Americans have no issue in reminding me that I'm brown by saying crap like I must be good at math and know computers and must want to be a doctor and obviously eat curry every day, but Indians have no regard to remind me that I'm not brown *enough*."

There. It was all out in the open like a shredded trash bag with its innards of rubbish flapping in the wind. All ugly and smelly.

I braced my hands against the trunk, readying myself to

push off and go home once Amit realized I was not the sort of Indian girl he could take home to hang with his parents. I was a blimp passing through his life, which was fine because no girl needed to be around a guy who thought less of her. Especially based on stupidity.

When he didn't speak, I did. "Yeah. You can judge me just like the rest of them do. It's expected."

"Wait." He took my wrist as I shifted to jump off. "I'm sorry that you feel that way, but you shouldn't. No one has the right to tell you that you're anything less. I've never felt that way from anyone at mandir."

"That's because you're perfect."

"I'm-I'm not," he stammered and cleared his throat. "I'm pretty sure we established that I'm definitely not perfect."

"You are everything they expect you to be. I'm not."

"Did you feel out of place or judged tonight?"

"Only with Saanvi."

I could feel him rolling his eyes. "She's a whole other entity. She does not represent the entire community, by the way."

"You're not in the least bit curious to know about the whole Dev fiasco?"

"It's not my business. Except . . ."

Now *I* rolled *my* eyes. Here it came. Get on with it.

"It sort of pissed me off. That she would say that about you."

"Are you more upset that it could be true or that she fabricated some giant story?" I spoke tentatively, my stomach clenching with anticipation.

"The latter."

"What if Dev and I had done something?" I asked, my head whirling from relief but bitterness still biting my tongue.

"I'd be a little mad."

"Exactly."

He explained, "Not at you, but the . . . um . . . the idea of someone all up on you. I'd get over it, definitely wouldn't judge you or view you differently or think any less of you." He went silent for a minute. "So did you—"

"No!"

"What happened, then?"

"Why?"

"Because I'd like to know the truth instead of whatever Saanvi said. Not that I believe her."

"If you don't believe her, then that's all that matters," I said, waiting for his response.

He didn't say anything for a good minute, and finally relented. "Okay."

"Just like that? You're not going to probe later on?"

"No. If you don't want to share, I have no right to push you. I'm sorry."

I sighed. Part of me wanted to tell him, to get it out, to move past this, to vindicate myself. I tempered my words so I didn't sound defensive. I didn't owe him an explanation. I did, however, want him to know the real story because once I said it aloud, it wouldn't sound like such a monstrous deal.

"Rayna, Saanvi, and I were squad-level friends."

He sat up and watched me, but I kept my focus ahead or on our feet. "During last semester, I was talking with this boy, Reg. Nothing serious, nothing physical. Rayna was talking with Dev. Also nothing serious. Then one day I asked about Dev and she said she didn't care. So Dev and I started talking for about a week. I'd never told the other boy that we were done, seeing that we weren't serious. It should've obviously faded away when I stopped texting. Saanvi found out and told Dev and they were super mad, like I'd cheated on my boyfriend while testing the waters for a new boyfriend.

"Rayna was upset, too, because she thought the same thing and also because she still liked Dev. Anyway. It all sounds inconsequential and trivial now, but at the time it was enough for them to defriend me. Broke my heart, actually."

"Doesn't . . . sound like that big of a deal. I mean, not to diminish your feelings, but why is Saanvi acting this way?"

I shrugged. Cuz she spawned from hell?

"Maybe she didn't want you in her clique and just, I dunno, latched onto some small mistake and blew it up."

"Probably." It would explain why she kept shoving it in Rayna's face. Maybe Saanvi wanted me out of the group, and this was her way of making it happen. "It really hurt, to know they thought I was shady or would betray them. And I told Rayna play by play what was happening. But, whatever."

"Their loss. They lost a good friend, but guess you dodged some shady ones."

"Better way to look at it. Maybe it wouldn't be so bad if I didn't miss Rayna so much. And if Saanvi wasn't telling everyone I was easy, which probably is why Travis tries to flirt with me."

"I'm sure there are a hundred other reasons he tries."

Wait. Was he saying that I was flirt-worthy? Good thing there was a breeze to cool off my face.

"So, um, are you dating anyone now?" he asked and scratched the back of his neck.

"Why? Are you even allowed to date?" I tried not to smile, but my stupid lips went up anyway.

"Not exactly, but there are extenuating circumstances that allow rule-breaking."

"Like what?"

"Like you."

Flustered, I jumped off the trunk. My brain couldn't come up with anything witty or smooth to say. So it rattled off the first thing that came to mind. "I'm in a monogamous relationship, to be honest."

Amit followed suit, hurrying to walk alongside me back to the street.

"Oh, really? What's his name?"

"Um, MT. We don't flaunt us."

"Some guy at school that I know?"

"No, definitely not at school."

"Ah. How long have you been together?" he asked, his mouth near my ear, his hands beneath the blanket cloak.

I smiled unwillingly. "Since forever."

"What are we talking? Forever in high school?"

"Since fourth grade?"

"Are you asking or telling?"

"Telling."

"What! That's insane. Do your parents know you've been involved with someone for that long?"

"Yes. And they're cool with it."

"You're playing me."

"No. Ask them yourself if you want. It's all true. MT is my first love."

"Hmm," he said suspiciously.

We stopped at the end of the driveway to my house, at the hood of his car. "I should go and clean up. I really did have fun though."

He raised both eyebrows high, as if to challenge my admittance.

"Don't you have some cosmic secret to work out? That multifarious program growing like a tumor in your brain?"

"Multifarious!" he choked out. "What does that even mean?"

"Look it up when you get home."

"All right, Kareena. Thank you for coming tonight. I had a great time too."

"I didn't say I had a great time. Just fun."

"Okay. Now you're just flirting with me."

"You should look up that word when you get home too." I went to shrug out of the jacket.

"Nah, keep it."

"Give it back to you Tuesday?"

He tugged on the collar, pulling me toward him. "I think it looks better on you."

My heart pounded like an 808 against my chest. I was pretty sure he could feel it thumping against his wrists. What if he pulled me another few inches into him? What prevented my lips from touching his lips?

But then he *actually*, slowly, deliberately, pulled me into him. My hands crashed against his side to prevent full frontal contact, because who in the world knew if I could handle such a thing.

I gulped, hard, possibly audibly. My palms sweated against his kurta, or maybe that was just the dampness of his shirt.

His warm breath, laced with cardamom and cinnamon from the sweets, hit my lips. His gaze wandered to my mouth and mine dropped to his.

Boy, he sure was tall. He'd have to lean all the way down because my body seemed to freeze up.

His lips twitched before he grinned. "I better go."

"Yeah," I breathed, my tongue unable to form coherent words.

"Wouldn't want this *MT* to beat my butt."

"MT definitely is known for fighting, yup."

He swallowed and leaned down, moving his head to the side, and kissed me ever so gently on my left cheek. On the far corner of my lips. And I was so very inclined to turn my head into his, but my entire body froze with the exception of the mass of butterflies mauling my insides.

ELEVEN

"No burger-flipping way," Lily said, her back against my locker.

I nodded, trying not to cheese. "True story."

"He kissed you? Your first kiss. Aw. You're growing up."

My skin turned warm just thinking about it. "It was sort of a kiss. On the cheek."

"Did his lips or did his lips not touch yours?"

"Just the tiny corners."

"Lip on lip action. *Dang*."

I giggled, tickled by the fact that Lily didn't care if most kids in our grade had already done the big deed and then there was me . . . romantically challenged and unable to date and did not care to date.

"It just happened."

Lily nodded. She also didn't try to convince me that a corner kiss was nothing to get worked up about because that was so fifth grade. A first kind of kiss was still a first kind of kiss.

"It's a huge freaking deal," she stated. "So you had the whole 'low self-esteem/poor self-worth in comparison to what you *think* other Indians think of you' talk?"

"It was more of a blurted ramble."

"And in this blurting and rambling, did you mention your deepest passion in life?"

"We're not that close."

"You locked lips. *We* haven't locked lips and *I* know."

"I want to tell him."

"You'll have to eventually," she stated with a wave of her hand.

"That's assuming this will turn into a thing." I chewed on the inside of my lip. It could be, or it wouldn't be. But who had time to worry? Especially when we couldn't date anyway.

"Even if it doesn't work out but you want to be friends, because he seems like a cool dude to be friends with, you might want to tell him. It's a huge part of who you are."

"So's my dad's health, but no one needs to know that much."

"But Muay Thai is your passion. Shoot, you are going places with it. I think . . . now correct me if I'm wrong . . . but if you make it to the World Championships or I dunno . . . the *Olympics* . . . people might notice. Besides, you want to tell him. What's the holdup?"

"That I'm afraid of him judging me."

"He didn't think any less of you when you told him about not feeling Indian enough. I don't get why you're so concerned with what others think of you."

"It makes me feel disconnected from my people." And also . . . low self-esteem issues? Hello? I knew that much. But no one wanted to admit that aloud.

"They're no one to you. You're not friends with them. They're not family. You never see them except the few who go to school here, and even then, it's in passing."

"Insecurity isn't logical."

She hugged her books to her chest and shook her head. "Here's how I see it: If someone doesn't like you, then that's their problem. Not yours. You keep doing your thing and not give them a minute of your time. Whatever narrow-minded, inferior judgment others pass is a cloud of negativity living in their head. Meanwhile, you're living your best, most positive and happy life. Eventually, their heads will explode from the pessimism while you're frolicking in a field of joy."

"Am I high in this scenario?"

"Might as well be, since that's what happiness from not stressing over others' opinions of you feels like. How can someone as confident and badass as you be so insecure with strangers?"

"How can someone as kind as you be crude with my feelings?"

She smiled. "Sorry."

"We all have our thing. You're not perfect."

"I never brought perfection into this conversation."

"Let me break the complexity of my thought pattern for you: You don't care what anyone thinks of you, but you feel very self-conscious if you were to leave your house with natural hair. How about, if I can learn to not care about what someone may or may not think, because honestly, I know I'm speculating sometimes, you come to school with that glorious Filipina 'fro."

She eyed me warily. "Have you at some point mastered your issues and are pulling the long con?"

I crossed my arms, did that sassy neck roll thing, and pursed my lips. "Deal or no deal?"

She spent whatever time we had left before the warning bell sounded to consider. "Start with him?"

"I will." Eventually. Maybe when I left for USMTO . . . if he asked where I was.

"C'mon. I know he's going to react well. You don't give him enough credit. He's already proved himself worthy."

I huffed out a breath. "Fine, I'll tell him."

She grinned. "Nice! Maybe we can all go door-to-door together to get more sponsors. Put him to work. Gonna let him see you fight?"

I cringed but bit out, "Sure."

"When are you going to tell him?"

"Why so pushy?" I asked nervously. Why were my palms sweating?

"Because it would be awesome if he supported you for the Open. It's only two weeks away!"

Oh, lord. Only two weeks to practice my butt off and get the rest of the two grand? "And it would suck hard if he didn't like it and I got distracted."

"Trust him. It won't be that way."

I mulled over her words. "Maybe you're right. Okay. I should tell him. And then you radiate the same level of confidence with your hair."

Huffing and walking off to class, she called over shoulder, "Deal!"

Amit's thoughtful gaze burned a hole the size of the sun into my side. He tapped the eraser end of his pencil against his notebook, his cheek resting in his hand and his elbow propped on the desk.

"What?" I finally asked, watching him through the corner of my eye and pretending he wasn't adorable.

"Do you want to come over for dinner?"

Like a date? Or like, to chill with his parents? "What makes you think I eat?"

"I've seen you eat. I know."

I scoffed. "Why?"

"Why eat?" He shrugged and straightened up. "Sort of vital to this whole living thing we got going on."

"You know what I mean. Why are you asking me over for dinner? Is this a trick?"

He sat upright and swiveled a pencil between his fingers. He asked gently, "Why do you think everyone is against you? Is there a master plot that you've deciphered? Because I must be behind."

"Seriously. What's up?"

"My mom asked about you."

"Your *mom*. Right." That was hard to believe. I was a fleeting blip on her radar from Holi.

"Honest. You can ask her, if you want."

"Hmmm." Or had Saanvi mentioned something insidious to her and she wanted to gather intel and weed me out of Amit's life?

He released the pencil and looked directly at me. He waited until I slowly dragged my gaze over to his before he started. "So, yeah. She asked about you and wants to invite your family over. I mean . . ." He shuffled through his pages. "Don't think you're special or anything. My parents weed out bad influences this way."

My heart constricted. I knew it! "Well, I am a bad influence."

"How so?"

"We can start with the fact that we're not religious or involved in any way with the Indian community."

"You kind of assume people judge you. You don't want anyone making assumptions about you, but you're pre-judging everyone else."

"You're going to end up in these study sessions alone."

"I'm not saying it to be mean."

"Just up front."

"Exactly."

I narrowed my eyes and he nervously smiled.

"Think about it: You loathe the fact that you've been judged, so you assume that others will judge you the same way. You were hurt. But, imagine how I feel because you assumed I would be judgmental of you before you even knew me. That hurts. I'm not like that. My parents are not like that. And before you say they're Indian, etc., etc., so what? I'm Indian. I don't think you're anything less than—"

He stopped and I waited for him to continue. "Less than what?" I pressed.

"Uh . . . adequate."

"*Adequate*? What the heck? I'm not sure if I want to dine with you in the first place."

"Will you please think about it? It's a standing offer. My mom's a good cook. My dad's nice. My house is warm."

"Anything else?" I glanced at my phone as Lily's text came through.

Did you tell him?

I replied without thinking. *Sure!*

"The dining room chairs are soft. Your butt may never want to leave," Amit continued.

I put my elbow on the desk and rested my chin in my hand. "You've been thinking about my butt?"

He flushed. "Um . . ."

I waggled my eyebrows. Messing with Amit was fun.

...⟨ TWELVE ⟩...

Sweat gleamed on my skin. Adrenaline surged through every inch of every vein and took me into a druggy high. I loved this feeling. I wasn't addicted to it by any means, and definitely didn't consider myself an adrenaline junkie. Although, I could see why people went after this kind of high.

For some people, adrenaline rushes felt insanely good: a roller-coaster sensation in their gut, a light-headedness, a near literal feeling of floating off the ground. As for me? Well, it made me weightless, nimble on my feet. It was a wave of ice and fire washing through my soul. I could do anything, be anyone. Clarity sharpened my vision and thoughts, my logic and maneuvers.

Nothing could touch me.

With each punch, kick, and strike, I imagined my body as concrete crashing into mortal flesh. Pulverizing my opponent. Shattering her bones.

I hadn't figured out how to tell Coach, or anyone, for that matter, about scraping the sewers for USMTO money. So, naturally, I took it out on Natalia.

One distraction was all it took to take a fighter down. One weakness, one gap. My problems and anger would not be that sliver in my armor. Nuh-uh.

Natalia came in for a hook, her strength above all else

because the girl had steel fists. Steel could go up against concrete. But it had to make contact.

I ducked and immediately rose to a fighting stance a foot to the left, behind where her fist had been. She lost a fraction of her balance with the miss, enough for me to come at her with a knee. Once an opponent crouched that close to the floor, it was easy killings after that.

Coach called the fight before Natalia ended up on my long list of beatdowns. The gym roared, giving props to us both.

As the adrenaline rage subsided, leaving goosebumps and dizziness in its wake, I reached down and offered Natalia a hand. Pulling her up, she nearly stumbled into me and wheezed out, "Awesome fight."

Catching my own breath, I huffed out an offbeat laugh but stopped short. My heart stopped too. At least for a long, lonely second as my vision blurred and then came back into focus.

There, in the small crowd of fighters and spectators, stood Lily. She hadn't come by the gym for a practice fight in a while. Her presence wasn't what reaped my thoughts like a scythe.

It was definitely the boy standing beside her, the one with the "Oh, holy hell" glazed-over eyes, the one with the dropped mouth like a giant donut.

My feet melted on the spot, cementing my legs into place. What the heck was Amit doing here? How could Lily bring him? Oh my freaking goodness, I was going to kill her!

The next breath was a deep burn all the way down my throat and chest. It could've been from the chest hit Natalia got in, or the fact that I had to talk to Amit, to face whatever he thought of me now. A girl fighter. An Indian girl fighter. One with huge arm and thigh muscles that were now on display in these short, ratty Muay Thai shorts and snug tank top. Would he think I was gross? Too manly for him to stomach?

Ugh! Why did I care so much? Why did those stupid questions even cross my mind?

Forget that. Muscles were sexy and healthy. They weren't a bad thing. We all had muscles all the time, under skin and fat layers. They allowed movement and strength, for goodness sake. I was pretty proud of them, especially seeing where they were taking me. But my self-esteem was not as bulletproof as my strikes.

So I braced myself. I would not let his opinion bother me. I was not any less Indian or any less of a girl because I was a fighter.

Several people patted my shoulder and hollered their appreciation of one thing or another, but my thoughts careened toward mental mantras.

I did not need others to validate myself.

I did not care about what others thought of me.

I was Indian enough.

I was girl enough.

I was motha-freaking awesome.

"Hi," I blurted, glaring at Lily who shrugged apologetically. Her smile faded. "What are you guys doing here?" Crap, my voice cracked like a boy going through puberty.

"Came to rally you on. Yay . . . ?" She pumped her fist slowly into the air and grinned sheepishly. "I asked if you told him, you texted back yes."

Oh, crap. I had, hadn't I?

She looked to Amit. "What did you think I was talking about when I asked if you wanted to see Kareena practice tonight?"

"All I heard was, 'Do you wanna see Kareena tonight?'"

Lily's face turned as red as mine felt. She mouthed an

apology, but honestly, it wasn't her fault, and this was for the best. It needed to happen.

"So . . . you're a boxer?" Amit asked, forcing me to meet his still wide eyes.

"Muay Thai fighter," I corrected and stood straighter. What? If he was going to give me nonsense then I was going to look as intimidating as heck. Why was I acting ashamed?

Lily slinked away and talked to a water guzzling Natalia. I'd deal with her later.

Well, let's get this over with. I put my hands on my hips and lifted my chin. "So, what?" My voice came out bitter and angry.

"Is this why you feel uncomfortable around mandir? Why you feel less Indian?"

"Part of it. It doesn't conform to perfect desi girl standards."

"Wow." He rubbed his chin and glanced away for a minute. "Why didn't you ever say anything? I thought you knew by now that I'm not judgy."

"Most boys are intimated that I can knock them out with a flick of my wrist."

"I am not most boys, Kareena."

"Really?"

"You don't see me running from you or making excuses to get away."

I narrowed my eyes.

He stepped closer, the tips of his toes almost touching mine. The heat from his body clashed against the dampness of my clothes and skin. He stood unwavering, unyielding, but so was I.

"I'm not running," he said firmly.

"Why not?"

"Why would I? Do I assume you have a bad temper? Nope. I know you. Are you into drugs? Probably not with your grades.

Do you beat up random people in the halls? No. You would've knocked out Saanvi by now."

I smirked.

"Am I afraid that you'll kick my butt? Am I scared that you're more man than I am?"

That was the million-dollar question. "Are you afraid of me now?"

"Yeah. I'm shaking in my socks. Can't you tell?"

"You're barefoot."

"I'm shaking so hard, they must've run off screaming."

I stifled a smile. "So? You still like me. But do you want to take me around your parents?"

He stuffed his hands into his pockets and nodded. "Wait until they hear what an amazing fighter you are!"

"No!" I gasped. "That's the thing I was trying to tell you after Holi. When my parents put me in Muay Thai, the other Indian parents couldn't handle me being around their kids."

"What even?"

"Exactly."

The small crowd had thinned to a few, and Lily was nowhere in sight. Crafty. The lights in the back dimmed, cue for us to leave or get locked in.

"We need to disperse," I muttered, aware more than ever of how sweaty and stinky I was.

He glanced around. "Oh, okay. I'll walk you out."

I packed my stuff into my duffel bag and fished out the keys to my car, meeting Amit by the door where we slipped into our respective flip-flops.

At my car, where a decent breeze picked up away from me and sprinkled my stink elsewhere, thank goodness, Amit asked, "How long have you been doing this?"

"Fourth grade."

He smirked. "So then is this the MT stud that you're monogamously into?"

I bit my lower lip and nodded.

"You're amazing," he said.

It took a few seconds for the words to sink in. "Thanks. A lot of years of hard work went into my skills."

He swallowed. "I mean, *you're* amazing. You're like this package of awesomeness that gets better and better the more I get to know you. Everything about you blows me away. Smart, kick-butt, pretty. You're like Black Widow. But Indian, and not a spy. I don't think."

My breath hitched.

He scratched the back of his neck. "You should come over for dinner."

"You know, it's strange for an Indian boy to have a girl over for dinner."

"Like I mentioned before, my parents like to meet my friends."

"Friends, huh?"

"Unless . . ."

Heat prickled my face. "I can't date . . . not that I'm saying you want to or that I want to . . . or . . . whatever . . . but my parents would lose it if they knew I was at a boy's house."

"That's the thing. My parents want to have your parents over. My parents are strict too. Can't date, either. But the idea was to get to know your family again."

"Oh, yeah, of course! That makes sense. But, they're really busy and my dad doesn't feel well."

"Then just you."

"That's not how things happen."

"They'll understand. It'll be simple. You wanted to come over, your parents couldn't, but you felt bad that my mom made dinner so there you are. All considerate and everything, despite social taboos."

"Okay," I found myself saying, despite knowing this was a bad idea. "On two conditions."

"Okay."

"I'm on a strict diet for Muay Thai. I have to log in all my calories and macros, so don't let your parents cook a lot on my account. I'll only eat a few vegetables, preferably not soaked in ghee or oils. And two, don't mention my fighting to your parents."

He frowned. "But it's a huge part of who you are."

A subtle pain shredded my throat. "They might not want us being friends."

"I'm trying not to be offended here."

"All right." I sighed. "Tell them if you want. But don't blame me if it goes south. It'll make Saanvi look like a saint."

He laughed. "Saanvi, I think, is actually a devil in disguise."

I shivered. It had gotten colder in the dark, the breeze gaining speed.

"You probably want to get into a warm car. I'll let you go." He searched the near-empty parking lot. "Where's Lily? She gave me a ride."

I tried not to groan. She was in so much trouble because she now for sure did this on purpose to make this conversation happen. Although, she was right, I admitted happily. "I'll give you a ride home. Hop in. But don't expect me to open the door for you."

He laughed and slid into the passenger seat. I turned up the heat and shimmied onto my towel-draped seat, turned the radio off, and eased out of the parking lot.

In between conversation, Amit gave directions to his house, which, as it turned out, wasn't far from my neighborhood. We could potentially do many family dinners all the time if his parents liked me enough.

"Is this where you live?" I asked, parking between his driveway and the next. I craned my neck to look out his window at the tall two-story brick house with white trim, large porch, and fancy bay windows. The yard, though dark, was immaculate, with two giant oak trees and a border of yellow rose bushes. Everything about Amit's home was so upper-middle-class Texan hill country.

"Yep. Been here my entire life."

"It's nice." I turned to him. "Well, you know my secret. You know what that means?"

He grimaced.

"Nuh-uh. We had a deal. What's your secret? Your big problem that you couldn't tell me?"

He scratched his forehead. "Can we talk about it later?"

"Speaking from experience, this feels like a giant, soul-crushing weight taken off me for you to know," I said, feeling a wonderful sort of high. Heck, maybe I might even get the girl balls to tell his parents too.

"It's just . . ." He bit his lip and looked down at me for a quick second in a way that totally blew my mind. It didn't really matter what his next words were if he kept that look going. "I'm not supposed to tell anyone."

"Am I just anyone?"

"No. You're definitely not."

I gulped and took his hand. We both glanced at our fingers as they interlocked and spread warmth between our touch. Maybe I was just overjoyed with his reaction, that he had proven to be as real and amazing as I knew he was. Or maybe it was because there was something more going on. Whatever the case, all that mattered was that he made me feel invincible and able to stand up to anything. I wanted him to feel the same way too.

He leaned in and whispered in my ear, "I might be delirious."

"You're ruining a moment," I whispered back.

"It's the job I'm doing. It's top secret and only a few people know about it."

"What kind of job?"

"I'm coding something that will . . . change everything."

"That's pretty awesome, not delirious."

"There's a lot of pressure to finish it fast. There's glitches and holes and I can't figure them out and it drives me up the wall. On one hand, this is a major project and my work will make or break the success of it. That's a lot for a seventeen-year-old kid. And it's not a new video game or phone tech. It'll change everything. On the other hand, part of my brain is practically a computer. It's coding so fast, the rest of my brain can't keep up. It's all I can think about. Well . . . almost all that I think about."

I swallowed, aware of how close his mouth was to mine and the fact that his parents could probably see us under the streetlight. "I thought for a serious second that you were going to tell me something really *weird*."

"I feel like I am weird, not quite right. I see numbers and equations everywhere. There are pages of coding all over my car and on dry-erase boards covering my bedroom walls. I can't sleep half the time. I just work through the night. My parents tried to calm me down from it, but they can't. They know finishing it is the only way to get my calm back."

"So they let you go to work all night and to school during the day?"

"We don't have a choice. I started scribbling equations on the actual wall when they tried to keep me home at night."

"Dang. That is intense."

He sat back and glared at the console between us. "You think I'm strange, don't you?"

I squeezed his hand and said, "It's more that you're a genius. I think, anyway. What's the project for?"

"I'm legally obligated to keep that to myself."

"Seriously?"

"Yes. Giant corporation business."

"Oh."

"But you'll be the first to know when I can tell someone."

"I'll hold you to that. Your parents must be so proud."

He released an agitated grunt. "They put on a lot of pressure for me to be . . ."

"Perfect?"

He sort of snorted and glanced away, his brows knitted in annoyance. "Yeah. Perfect grades. Perfect at mandir. Doing plays and traveling and teaching the kids in classes and making sure I talk to everyone and am always smiling. Making sure all the teachers like me, that I have a lot of friends, that I don't make mistakes or bring reproach to the family."

"I thought it was natural for you."

His face hardened, the already angular lines of his jaw tensed. "I want to do those things, but at some point, it became an expectation and anything less isn't right."

"Oh," I breathed, recalling how he'd mentioned that his parents weren't excited about his valedictorian status. This was why. It was expected.

"My parents are great, don't get me wrong. I love them and I know they love me, and I owe everything to them. I am me because of them. I like that they push me to be my best. It would just be nice if they told me I'm doing a great job instead of simply nodding because I'm just doing what I'm supposed to be doing. Or if I miss any number of high marks, that they don't look at me all disappointed. If I was salutatorian, they would be disappointed. If I was just top ten, they'd be disappointed. Not to mention passing all the mandir tests. It's never-ending." He hit his head against the headrest and stared out the window straight ahead.

I watched him for a few seconds more, taking in his waning emotions and gently said, "Maybe I was so engrossed in my own stuff that I didn't think you had any problems. Guess we all have different pressures weighing down on us."

"You're right, though. Telling someone is like a weight lifted off my shoulders. Keeping that in for so long . . . sometimes I can't handle it."

"I know exactly what you mean. But you once said you'd be here for me whenever I need someone to talk to, and that goes the same for you."

He nodded thoughtfully but didn't make a move to unbuckle his seatbelt. "Are you scared when you go into a fight?"

"Sometimes," I replied carefully. "I try to be confident and focused, but sometimes nerves get to me and, if the opponent is especially intimidating or has a fierce track record, I'm pretty much scared crapless."

His face lit up when he said, "You didn't look nervous up there tonight."

"I've fought Natalia a hundred times. It was a practice fight."

"Wow. That's intense. I can't imagine what a real fight must be like. Do you do competitions?"

"Yep."

He turned toward me, all excited. "Oh, yeah? Can I see your next fight? You know, if my presence doesn't make you nervous."

"You give yourself way too much credit, dude."

He laughed. "Then, I'd love to go."

I smiled shyly, although my insides were exploding with giddiness. A boy who wasn't intimidated by my sport? "I have one coming up in a few weeks, but it's in Arizona."

He scowled. "That's far. Are they all that far?"

"No. Maybe in the summer you can come to some home fights?" I asked, hopeful.

"Okay. That sounds like a lot of fun, to see you in action. I'm pretty stoked, actually." He beamed that killer smile.

I mentally sighed in relief. Amit being at USMTO would make me more nervous . . . that was, if I managed to get there.

"So . . . does anyone know about Muay Thai? Or am I among the few and privileged?"

I laughed. "You know the answer to that."

"Why not tell people? Okay, so I get not wanting everyone at mandir knowing because I do see your hesitation. It's unorthodox to the traditional. But what about at school? Americans are more open to female athletes. The school has them in droves. It's not a big deal."

"Isn't it though? A Muay Thai competitive fighter against a basketball player. Tennis. Softball. Soccer. It's not as common, and it's definitely a lot more brutal."

"Martial arts," he added. "Martial artists can be competition-level fighters."

"We don't have a martial arts team."

"But there are girls at school who do martial arts outside of school. Like . . . hmmm . . . MaryAnn, Jamice, Tanya, to name a few. You should talk to them."

"Why?"

"Because you feel that you're alone. But you're not."

"They're not Indian. That makes me alone."

"But they're girls. Bad mofos who can throw down in a ring. Just like you. It's support, understanding."

I gritted out, "Because it sounds stupid when I say it aloud. Yeah, it's a real fear that mutates into a devouring emotional monster, but imagine saying, in actual words, 'I don't tell people because Indians won't like me.' Sounds stupid, right? But it's real. Guess that makes me stupid too."

"It's not stupid, and you're not stupid."

"I guess."

"You're friends with women like Natalia, right? And other Muay Thai fighters. They're not Indian, but you feel that connection with them, support, insight."

I mulled over his words quietly.

"You have different journeys and different struggles. Why go at things alone when you have a network of friends to back you up?"

"Amit Patel?"

"Hmm?"

"Stop making so much sense."

THIRTEEN

Weights clanked against one another. Metal bars hit metal holders in the school's weight room. The scent of sweat perforated the air, but thankfully the thermostat kept it below freezing in every corner of the school.

I immediately went to Kimmy and asked, "Are you going to keep this up in college?"

"Yes! Didn't you hear? I got a scholarship for soccer to UT."

"No freaking way!"

Kimmy beamed. She had trifecta status, starring in soccer, softball, and weights. "Yep. Four years. I found out last week. Shoot, I thought I mentioned it during calculus."

"Oh, well then that explains it. Was I asleep?"

She pursed her lips. "Probably."

"But you're going to finish the weightlifting team?"

"Oh, yeah. Can't let the team down. I'm top spot for state."

"That's awesome! You're teeming with amazing news."

She shrugged, like no big deal. "Gotta help these boys out."

"Like you don't already intimidate boys enough."

"Who, me?"

"Girl, please. You're pretty, athletic MVP of everything, and in top ten. Triple threat."

"Who wants a boy who's intimidated by what? Success? That's lame and insecure."

I twisted my lips, thinking back to Amit and how he totally

inhaled my fighting prowess with awe. It was super hot, to be honest. He could handle me and my skills along with my insecurities. But Kimmy had a point. No one wanted to be with a person who was insecure.

We switched places. Kimmy spotted me while I bench pressed.

"Whoa, check you out. Seriously, you got the guns of someone who's been training. Is this from Muay Thai? Can we talk more about that now?"

I grunted out the last set and she took the bar from my shaking arms before it dropped and guillotined my neck. She could lay on the bench and converse, but not I. Not with the looming fear of having the bar break and letting loose crushing weights. I sat up and straddled the bench.

Saanvi and two others happened to walk through the weight room, a shortcut from the auditorium to the art and drama corridor. She eyed us and muttered something to her friends. They responded with boisterous laughter.

"What's that cackling?" Kimmy asked loudly, drawing the attention of the entire weight room.

Saanvi sneered.

"I thought it was only me she disliked," I said.

"She does that every time she comes through here. Why bother walking past us if she tries to mock us? I don't even get her issue."

"Ah . . ." I said, realization dawning on me.

"She hates on every girl athlete I know. Not the boys, mind you, she's in love with all of them."

"She hates girls who are athletes?"

"You didn't know?"

"I just thought she personally disliked me super bad. Guess I'm not that special. She's in dance, so she's also an athlete, and therefore her attitude makes no sense. Unless you consider the fact that she almost failed gym." Oops. Had I said that aloud?

"Say what?" Kimmy asked even louder.

I grinned, and repeated myself over the noise of the room, "Saanvi almost failed gym."

"Who in the history of this school almost fails gym!" Kimmy blurted and guffawed, mimicking Saanvi's irritating laugh.

Saanvi turned bright red and stomped her last steps on the way out.

I giggled. "Seriously. The coaches are super supportive of even the most athletically challenged. Still boggles the mind. Dancing means coordination. I can run and lift weights, but I cannot, to save my throat, swing my hips to a beat. A few years back Saanvi coaxed me into joining her dance troupe at the temple, and it was an epic fail."

"Hey, listen. You still got social?" she asked.

"Yeah, but I'm not on it much. Why?"

She dug into her backpack and roamed through her phone. "Check it. Welcome to the sisterhood. I wanted to tell you way sooner, but it's hard catching a minute with you."

I reluctantly clicked through my cell and logged onto Facebook, where an invitation from Connally Girls Athletics awaited. "What's this for?" My fingertip hovered over the "accept" icon.

"The school has a private page for all the girl athletes. It's monitored by the coaches. They have a few others: for boys, of course, and other groups. I don't know about the rest, but we post news about games and encouragement and questions and issues and sometimes silly pics or videos. We got the weightlifting team, basketball, softball, track and field, tennis, golf, swim, dance, cheerleading, marching band, and I know I'm forgetting someone but you get the idea. It's pretty cool."

"That *is* way awesome. But I'm not involved in a school sport."

"Doesn't have to be in school. Hillary and Tanya are in martial arts at a dojang up north. Clarissa is in a cultural dance group at her church. Miranda is on a bowling team. Literally half the girls at school are athletes."

"Wow. I didn't realize there were so many."

"What? You thought you were the only one?" She sucked her teeth. "You're not that special."

I laughed, nodding my head. Okay. Yeah. Fair enough. "So, Saanvi could also be invited, then?"

Kimmy pressed her lips together. "Yes. By the rules of her being a girl attending this school and involved in something athletic. I wish she *would* come into this group and throw that attitude around. Anyway. Think about it. If nothing else, be a lurker. See what's going on and what others are going through to keep in their game. Might be inspiring or encouraging. Sometimes it's just a good laugh because those girls can crack you up. Just join the group. Bold font, boxing glove emoji the crap out of your introductory line. Text me when you accept and want to say something, and I'll log on. I'll be right there."

Gratitude swelled in my heart and I nearly hugged her but seeing that Kimmy and I had never hugged before, it might've been awkward. So I grinned instead and tried to keep my happy tears from spilling over.

No need to get so emotional in front of the weightlifting team.

···< FOURTEEN >···

I wrung my hands together in front of me, tying and untying my threadbare cardigan edges in front of Amit's pristine Texan home with its absurd amount of new paint and uncracked cement. How old was this baby house, anyway?

Since barely a sweat bead formed during the minimal amount of weightlifting, seeing that Kimmy and I had gabbed in the corner more than anything, I hadn't changed from my school clothes. Suddenly, my shorts were too short, my top too low, my cardigan too dull, and my kicks way old.

Why was I even here? I had way too much to do to get ready for USMTO. I had to focus on practice and spending extra time looking for more money. While some businesses had added to the pot, the costs kept growing because of chiropractor appointments. I was still eighteen hundred dollars away. By the looks of this house and yard and cars, I bet Amit didn't have to worry about money.

Someone lifted the edge of the sheer lace curtain in the window adjacent to the front door with its diamond-shaped pieces of opaque glass. That same door opened wide enough for Amit to step out. He approached with a welcoming smile, but my dumb legs wouldn't move, and my trembling hands wouldn't stop fussing with this fabric.

He slowed his roll real quick and cocked his head to the side, eying me warily. "You okay?"

"Sure."

"You've been standing out here for a good five minutes. At least. Do you want to come in?"

"No, not really."

"My parents are nice, promise. They really want to spend time with you."

"In my head, they want to meet me to find a reason to forbid us from being friends."

Amit arched a questioning brow and jammed his hands into his pockets. He looked a little annoyed. "So, I'm getting more and more offended by your assumptions of the evilness of my parents."

"Sorry. They must be nice, I'm sure, because they raised a nice kid."

He tilted his head and hiked up his lips in a crooked smile. "Okay, so breathe and be yourself. And if anything else, be proud of who you are."

"Are you giving me life lessons?" I asked him but looked at the house, at the windows where his parents were surely watching and scrutinizing.

"It's what I tell myself when I get nervous."

"When are you ever nervous?"

"Are you kidding? Who doesn't get nervous? First day of school? Class presentations? Contact sports in gym class, especially dodgeball. I *hate* dodgeball."

I cracked a measly smile.

"Meeting my parents' guru. Visiting the giant mandirs in Houston or Jersey. Doing plays there . . . and in Gujarati mind you. In front of thousands of people. Did I mention it's all in Gujarati?"

My smile widened. "Okay, okay."

"My parents are just people, and there's only two of them!

I'll be there. I'm not going to turn on you." He offered his hand and I glared at it.

"Are you joking? Your parents are probably watching."

He retracted his hand and scratched the back of his neck. "Oh, right. Come on."

We walked alongside one another to the front porch. "Have you ever brought a girl to dinner like this?"

"We have families over all the time. But just a girl? No. On the other hand, don't forget your parents were invited." He opened the door to let me through first.

Amit beamed when we passed the modest foyer, leaving our shoes by the door, and entered an opulent dining room with its crystal chandelier hanging low over a cherry wood oval table set for six. Everything was so bright and clean and new.

His parents stood on the other side of the table pouring water into glasses and arranging silverware.

My stomach growled at the delicious-smelling food. His mother smiled warmly, just as she had at Holi, and walked around the table to hug me. At first I froze, not expecting such physical hospitality, but then I lightly, awkwardly, hugged her back.

Amit stifled a laugh, unseen by either parents, and I mouthed, "I don't know what to do."

"Thank you for coming, Kareena. Are your parents joining us?" his mom asked.

"Thank you for inviting us. No, they aren't feeling well, but we hope to get together soon."

"Oh, no! Hope they feel better. But hah, we will need to get together another time. Please. Sit."

But I couldn't stop looking at her face. She was pretty, and she had great facial expressions, totally committed to each emotion behind her words. Happiness seeing me, gratitude that

I came by, hopeful to see my parents, sympathy, hope again, eagerness to chat and eat. My face was probably on the verge of stoicism most times compared to hers. According to Lily, I had a great RBF game.

Amit's father nodded with a short smile and sat across from Amit, who sat beside me. His mom ladled out food for us before taking her seat beside Amit's father. I'd barely touched my fork when all three bowed their heads and clasped their hands together. I froze, still grasping the utensil, and looked at the food on my plate, focusing on what I could eat and how much. The broccoli and cabbage were great, even if that meant gas in the middle of the night. A small fraction of dhal would work, rice was okay. The veggies were soaked in spices and oils, and puri was fried alongside pappadum. And no meat.

Amit subtly cleared his throat, his hand touching my knee clandestinely beneath the tablecloth. I startled and looked up. Oh, they were done with prayer.

"This is delicious," I said after the first bite. The seasoning was light with a mixture of spices, not all Indian.

His mom beamed and pushed a bowl of food toward me. "Thank you. Have some more."

I waved my hand. "This is plenty. I don't eat much."

"Nonsense. You're a growing girl."

"How was school?" Amit's father asked, his voice deep and gruff.

Amit looked to me, allowing me to go first. "It was fine. Nothing extraordinary happened."

Then Amit spoke, "My day was the same. Class, lecture, quiz."

"Are your grades staying top level?" his dad asked.

Amit glanced at his plate and slumped the slightest. He looked like a deflating balloon. "Yes, Papa. The teachers will turn in our grades early, for the top five percent, to calculate valedictorian. But I think I will keep the title."

"Not think. Know. You are very smart. Your grades are perfect. And you?" He looked to me, dismissing his son's amazing achievement as if being Sir Valedictorian was as expected and easy as breathing air.

"My grades are good too. I'm not in the running to take Amit's spot."

"So you are in the same classes?" He studied me with a . . . yep . . . a very scrutinizing glare.

"We've shared most core classes together over the years."

"And you are just now friends?"

"I think I was too focused on my grades and my family to spend much time talking to a lot of people outside of school. But this semester, we worked on . . ."

Amit's face twitched.

"A project for computer science." Amit didn't have to worry. I had his back.

"Lucky for you, Amit is a genius in computer science."

"Yeah, I'm starting to see that," I gritted out.

"Uh, you know, Papa? Kareena is really good in computer science too. She explains theorems in a way that's easy to understand. I'm all technical and boring, she makes the project easy to relay."

His parents nodded, and we continued to eat with intermittent questions about school. During the entire dinner, my posture remained straight and rigid, my bites small and exclusive, and my answers as polite and friendly as possible. Hopefully the sweat seeping out of my pores didn't blind them.

"Have you any college plans?" his father asked me.

"I want to get my BS in computer science from UT."

"Just like Amit. He might go for master's or PhD."

Amit groaned. "Maybe. We'll see how much studying I can take."

"No 'we'll see.' Why not go all the way?" his dad chided.

Amit clamped his mouth around a bite of food.

Then his dad said to me, "We knew your parents when you were little. We miss them."

"Well, they're only a phone call away," I replied, perhaps more bitterly than intended. It wasn't that hard to pick up a phone or drive to a house these days. If they were that inclined to see my parents.

"This is very true. What a shame we let our friendship wither. We'll get back on track. They're very nice people. Seems they raised a likewise daughter."

"I'll let them know you said this."

"It was nice to see you at Holi," Amit's mother commented. "Did you have fun?"

I grinned. "It was very fun."

"Hope to see you at more functions." She rattled off a few upcoming events that sounded like lectures and puja.

"Mandir is open every day," his father added. "You should come by."

I nodded.

"This Sunday?"

"I have a lot of homework and finals around the corner, plus sports and . . ." Crap. It slipped out. Where was that high I had before with Amit, when I could tell everyone anything and take on the world?

"Oh, yeah? What do you play?" Amit's mother asked. She laughed, motioning to Amit, "Your cousin was good in . . . what did she play?"

"Volleyball."

"Brutal sport, nai?" She clucked her tongue. "She always

had bruises on her legs and arms. But she liked it, so who could dissuade her?"

I admitted, "I was never good in volleyball. I was always afraid of getting hit by the ball."

"Seriously?" Amit asked, his right eyebrow quirked.

"Yes. Balls hurt and you don't see them coming."

"But . . ." He shook his head and clamped his lips.

"So what do you play?" his mom asked me.

"Nothing with balls." I laughed awkwardly.

They smiled and waited. In the corner of my peripheral vision, Amit pushed around his food and said, "You know why I hate balls? They hurt, and people use them like weapons. Take for example: dodgeball. Why? Why do we have that sport? It's just mean. There's no sportsmanship in the game. Just a bunch of people racing to get to a line of balls before their opponents and then brutally hitting them to take them out."

"What sport is this that you're playing, beta?" His mother shook her head ruefully.

"That's the thing! It's not a sport. And they make us play this in gym. I'd rather do basketball or run the track or football. Anyway. That's why I'm against dodgeball. It has no place in our society. Speaking of society . . ." he went on and I bit back a smile. "The honor society is doing a group picture for the yearbook and I need my one and only suit dry-cleaned."

"Why do they make you wear a suit for this picture, huh?"

"It's prestigious. Plus, I need it anyway for graduation. I'm giving the speech."

"But you're wearing a graduation gown over your suit. Who will know if it's just a shirt and slacks? Won't you be hot up there?"

"Also my thoughts, Ma, but the principal told us today. Please? Can you have my suit dry-cleaned?"

"Hah," she agreed.

"Oh, my mom made a dessert too," Amit said, turning to me with such enthusiasm that he could've burst.

"Is it edible gold?" I joked.

"You mean varak? It's edible silver foil."

"Close enough."

"Gold and silver are not close." He laughed as his mother excused herself, disappearing into the kitchen, and returning with an uncovered plate filled with long, green, diamond-shaped sweets with a shimmering layer of thin foil.

"Oooh, pista barfi," I said.

She passed around the plate and I grabbed two, yep. They were a smidge warm and nutty with texture. She had only a saucer-size plate, and that was as close to remembering my diet as possible. I'd never known an Indian mom not to offer sweets to her guests, and since it would be rude of me to object . . . well . . .

I took a small bite. "This is amazing."

"Thank you. It's my Masi's recipe. It's adaptable to kaju and badam. Take the rest home. Your parents will like too."

"These might not make it home."

Amit purposefully held up his wrist to glance at his watch. "It's getting late and it's a school night."

"Amit! Don't be rude," his mother chided.

I grinned. "It's true. I have to get going."

Amit's father walked us to the door while his mother wrapped the sweets and handed them to me. Shoes on, sweets in hand, I was happy to leave. It wasn't so bad after all, and they seemed to like me. Well, they seemed to like the impression I gave.

Yeah. They liked the *impression*.

They didn't know the real me. I was putting up a front and

that was no way to live. Besides, Amit had said his parents were cool. So they should be able to handle the truth, which wasn't so bad. I mean, why was I still doing this to myself? Why was I always so afraid of what others thought of me? Who were they anyway? If they didn't like me, oh well. I'd rather be true to myself and not liked for ignorant reasons than to hide myself from people who were, essentially, no one to me. They shouldn't have that power. I had to stop giving this control to others.

My insides burned up. You know what? I had nothing to be ashamed of. Their judgment shouldn't mold my behavior. Instead, my steadfast truths should barricade their judgments. I was a good kid. Freaking phenomenal, if you asked me.

Part of my brain told my mouth to zip it. It wasn't their business. They didn't have the right to be so inside my life. But the other part, the part amped up by Amit's claims that his parents weren't like the others I'd encountered, that I should own it and not hold back and not let anyone make me feel bad about myself, revved up.

Amit held the doorknob between us and smiled, pleased.

I dragged in a long, deep breath, and his smile faltered. But then something truly amazing happened. He retracted his hand, seeming to know full well what was about to go down. He stood beside me and we faced his parents together. It wasn't the three of them against me. It was the two of us against everyone else. And that made the excruciating burn in my chest turn into devastating flutters.

"There's something you should know, if you're allowing Amit and me to be friends. Things you'll hear anyway, but it's the real me and the real me is perfectly fine, and a perfectly good friend for your son."

"Oh?" his mother asked in her soft voice.

"I'm not top of my class, and that isn't for lack of trying.

We have some very smart people in school, but that's okay. I'm not going straight to UT, I'm going straight to ACC, and that's not a bad thing. I don't pray and don't go to mandir because people have been mercilessly harsh against me and my mom. That's why you haven't seen me in nearly eight years. That doesn't make us bad people, and I hope that you're more open-minded than others have been."

Amit nodded to me reassuringly. His parents, on the other hand, stared at me wide-eyed in an awkward, frozen state. But I kept going, because, heck, why not? If I'd vomited words all over Amit about how I truly felt, then maybe that was just the only way I could manage the courage to do this whole confrontation thing. And word vomiting was better than holding it in and slowly dying from the inside.

"The sport that I play is Muay Thai. It's like kickboxing. Yes, I fight, but only in practice and with other Muay Thai fighters in regulated fights. That doesn't make me violent or a bad association for your son."

"Oh . . ." His mother frowned as if trying to piece it all together.

The bile in my stomach crawled up my raw throat. "I'm not perfect, and neither are my parents. But no one is the *perfect Indian*. Okay, your son is pretty close, but the best thing about him is that he doesn't judge. He accepts. And it would be great if you allowed us to be friends."

I rolled on my heels and looked off into the distance, quietly adding, "That's all."

Amit gave a sweet smile and commented, "I think it takes a strong person to want you to know deeper things about her, and not just what you want to hear on the first impression. All the good and bad, although it's not really bad at all. She's honest and open. Great qualities, huh?"

"Hah," his mother replied. The simple word (grunt?) had neither derision nor approval, and I couldn't decipher if we'd be friends come morning. But then both of his parents gave a closed-lip smile and I knew our friendship was burnt.

Ah, well. It sadly proved my point, but at least they knew the real me and not the presented superficial layer. They couldn't say Kareena Thakkar tried to pull one over them.

With my best pleasantries and heartfelt words, I ended with, "Thank you again for dinner and the delicious sweets, Uncle and Auntie. I had a good time, and I hope we'll do this again."

"Yes." Amit's father nodded, his closed-lip smile widening, but still no teeth. Never had exposing teeth been so freaking important.

"Goodnight," they both said.

Amit opened the door for me and I walked out into the chilly night air, relief cooling my perspiration and anxiety floating away with the breeze. The door closed behind me and my shoulders relaxed.

"Well, that was awesome," Amit muttered beside me.

I groaned but then asked, "Where are you going?"

"You think I wouldn't walk you to your car?"

"You had to get out of there for a minute, huh?" I asked, waiting for my heart to calm down.

"Yeah."

"I couldn't help it. I'm tired of hiding or acting like I can't be my true self around people."

He laughed into the darkness. "Finally! You don't care about others' opinions."

"Sucks that it had to start with your parents. I actually do really care about what they think of me because they're *your* parents. I want them to like me, to let us be friends."

"What teenager wants to be friends with the kids their parents approve of? We're going to be rebels raging against parental wishes."

My heart warmed. "You'll be my friend even if they don't approve?"

"Yep. But don't give up on them yet. They're not like this. You caught them off guard. You did sort of spew words at them."

My face turned hot. Oops.

I unlocked my door and reached for the handle at the same time Amit did. His hand covered mine and I froze. The butterflies in my belly went agonizingly mad as his fingers curled over mine and held our hold against the cold metal. Good thing the driver's side faced the street and not his house, so his parents couldn't see all this teenage touching.

As if that wasn't enough, his thumb grazed over the side of my hand and I just about exploded. I pulled the door open and retracted my hand. All right. *Calm down.* I wanted to be friends with Amit Patel, but nothing more. Too many things took up too much time, and anything beyond a casual friendship threatened to unhinge the delicate balancing act.

"Thanks for coming over," he said.

"Thanks for making me."

"Admit it, you liked it."

···❮ FIFTEEN ❯···

I glared at my phone. The screen was cracked in the corner and sometimes missed calls and usually skipped the letter "B" when texting. But the words strung together from Coach were clear.

Don't forget the money.

My heart sank. Time to pull up my big girl undies and just ask. Straight out ask. It would be worse to tell Coach I didn't have the funds later, and it was already getting pretty late. His hopes were high. So were mine. Time for a definite answer.

"Mama?" I asked, swinging around the corner of the hall to her room, where she lay in bed beside my sleeping father.

"Hah, beta?"

My throat dried up. I twisted the edge of my shirt around my finger, dreading this. "I hate to ask, but . . . Coach was wondering when we'd have the rest of the money for the hotel and stuff."

"It's coming," she said with a faint smile. She knew how hard I'd been working to get funds, and I knew how hard she was working to save money.

"Are you sure? Because I don't have to go. It's fine if we don't have—"

"*Beta?*"

"Yes?" I gulped.

"It will be fine." Her words broke my heart. She said that

exact phrase every time things *weren't* fine. When Papa first got really sick. When he kept getting worse. When we had to sell the house and some of our stuff.

"I know we don't have money," I said as patiently and understandingly as possible.

"We will find a way."

I tried to reason with her, because what we really needed was a miracle. We weren't going to go into more debt for me, not for something that was a luxury when we had so many necessities. "It's less than two weeks from now."

"Two weeks is nothing," she said with an upbeat tone but shaky lips. And I knew.

I smiled reassuringly. "It's good either way, Mama. No worries."

"In this house, Kareena Thakkar, we do not quit. We do not give up or give in." She got out of bed and touched my cheek. "Didn't we teach you that?"

I blinked away stupid tears. I breathed through a burning chest. And I nodded.

"Besides. Your coach has already bought admission and plane tickets and a hotel room. I gave him the money you raised from sponsors, said the rest was coming soon. And it will be here soon."

"You did?" I asked, surprised.

"Yes. He needed that money a while ago. We couldn't keep him waiting. So now . . . you're stuck. You have to go. You want to go. You will go."

Yeah. I had to find a way to get the rest of the money. I owed Coach a lot.

"We're almost there, beta. Don't worry, huh?" She kissed my forehead and crawled back into bed.

I retreated to my room before she insisted that things were

fine. I scratched my arm hard to keep the stings of failure from overtaking me. It was okay. I could try next year. And now that I knew I could get in, I had an entire year to come up with funds and to practice harder. Win. Win.

Really.

Things were okay.

My phone buzzed with a dozen text messages. The first few from Lily asking about Amit, and of course squealing with emoji joy for his perfect reaction. The next few from Amit, which went unread because my self-esteem wasn't ready for the hit of knowing his parents forbade our friendship. The last came from Kimmy.

You accepted or what?

I dragged in a super-long breath and released. The computer screen glowed in front of me in my dimly lit bedroom. The social media home page blinked back with its blues and grays. The clock at the bottom of the screen changed to 11:20 p.m. The arrow cursor waited patiently over the "accept" icon.

I dragged my fingers through my damp hair, dropped my elbows onto the desk, and glared ever harder. Part of me wondered what the point was now. There wasn't enough dough to get to the Open. But the other part knew I'd have support and happiness and understanding. That half of me needed this.

Kimmy repeat texted me.

Oh, freaking fine!

Hit.

Connally Girls Athletics private group invitation accepted.

I see you, girl! Kimmy texted.

Maybe at this time on a school night, no one would notice me slipping into their space, but then the typing indicator bubble popped up at the top of the group page.

Hey, y'all! Let's give a big ole shout-out to Kareena Thakkar. Girlfriend finally joined us!

Agh! Kimmy!

I bit my lip and watched in horror as a million, okay not literally a million, but darn near close to a million little typing bubbles with their dot dot dots popped up, followed by an avalanche of comments and greetings.

What were these girls doing up so late, anyway?

I read through each comment, and compelled by common courtesy, replied to and liked every single mention. Then the inevitable question sprang up:

Please introduce yourself, even if we all know you. What's your superpower sport?

Another long breath before my fingers typed:

Hi! I'm Kareena, senior, starting ACC as a sophomore this summer right after graduation, just two more months, then transferring to UT for comp-sci. My sport is Muay Thai.

I paused. Well, why not spill the whole truth? My journey was about to get epic, and that was something to be proud of.

I've been in Muay Thai since I was eight and competitive fights since twelve. Found out a few weeks ago from my coach that I qualify for USMTO (United States Muay Thai Open). I might even be the first Indian girl in USMTO history. If I compete well, the IFMA (International Federation of Muaythai Associations) might like me enough to invite me to the US team for the World Championships. And if that didn't already rock my world, Muay Thai is on the verge of becoming an Olympic sport and I could have the chance of getting on the first Olympics team.

And. Post!

Ah! Why was I so nervous? Would I ever *not* be nervous telling people about myself like this? I resisted the temptation to bite my nails. Instead, I sat on my hands and gently kicked the floor in anticipation, my socked feet rubbing the worn carpet.

A barrage of comments and an ever-climbing number of likes, hearts, and surprise emojis racked up the tally. There was so much outpouring of love and respect and praise that my heart swelled.

Amid the sea of awesomeness, many of the commenters wondered why I had never said a word. So I explained, and another outpouring of support flooded my screen.

My chest tingled all over and a calm warmth unfolded throughout my entire body. I wasn't alone. I'd *never* been alone. I was too caught up in my own insecurities to find more girls like me.

Some girls wear tights and glittering makeup, skirts and pompoms, ribbons in their hair, balance marching band hats, cowgirl hats to accessorize with rodeo ropes and spurs, baggy shorts and loose jerseys, tall socks and cleats, shin pads, mouth guards, karate gi and black belts, boxing gloves . . . the list goes on and on. But we're all here and beautiful and strong and frankly (please don't kick me out coaches) severely BADASS, y'all. Welcome to the group!

Oh man, had to love Kimmy. Her optimism poured into the others, and another deluge of comments and likes bombarded the screen.

My fingers trembled as I profusely thanked the group. They asked for all the deets to the upcoming USMTO and I obliged, my heart revving up again. This time, not from nerves, but with undiluted excitement. I gave all the info, ending with:

Why do you ask?

I don't know about everyone else, but I want to be there!

Followed by a dozen more volunteers.

My heart ached as I confessed:

That's so amazing and y'all are full of awesomeness that I can't even begin to describe. But the sad truth is that I don't even know if I can go.

What?! Why not!

You have to go!

Don't miss this opportunity!

World Championships and the Olympics are at stake!

Of course, I already knew all this, but when several demanded a reason as to what held me back, I confided:

Money. It's expensive to go with the traveling and hotel and food, plus I had to buy all new gear and chiropractor treatments. It's already adding up. I tried to get sponsors from businesses, but it's not enough.

There was a short pause in responses. I rhythmically tapped my keyboard, wondering how the group would respond. There went my excitement. Here came reality. Here came the "keep your chin up, there's always next year" comments.

I almost logged off. The heartbreak physically hurt; heavy, harsh stones dragging my stomach down.

We'll have to raise money.

Definitely.

Huh? Wait a minute.

What can we do real fast with a little amount of expenses/ time and can be offered to the masses?

For sure! Can't let this slip away without trying something!

Car washes?

Bake sales?

Movie night? Admittance plus concessions.

Oh my god. Was this even real? Were these girls, some friends, but most of whom I wasn't even that close with, brainstorming to help me? I drew in a deep, shuddering breath and blinked away tears. When had I become so emotional?

Raffle? We can do neat giveaways.

Auction? We can pool some money together and auction something off.

Bet some local businesses will get in on that.

Maybe even the athletic department has some school funds that can be parted with? Don't know how that works.

Prom's coming up, we can sell flowers and chocolates.

That surge of adrenaline and excitement came rushing through me again. I sat on my hands and tapped my toes against the floor in rapid beats. I clamped down on a squeal. I had to text Lily and tell her what was happening! Well, as soon as I stopped shaking.

Riya and I did a henna booth at the school carnival in Oct. Henna cones are cheap and we can do half a hand in thirty seconds. Raised a lot of money.

Spring carnival is next Saturday! Let's do all of these booths and movie night Friday night AND Sunday night. We can do the prom flowers and chocolates during the week.

Who do we get into contact with to get approved?

Student council?

Nah, should be the events committee.

Maybe we can have booths up at all the sports games too?

Think we have to ask the coaches about that one.

All right then, let's get on it.

And from there, I hunched over my desk and read every comment within comment as the thread got longer and longer. In fact, it had gotten so long that someone had to sever it into sections: prom committee events, carnival booths, game booths, and freestyle, meaning additional raffles and auctions held at random during the week.

After a while, my eyes were too blurry to keep reading, and once the tears fell, they wouldn't stop. I hiccupped and blubbered as love and support and amazing ideas and efficient strategies trickled out of my classmates.

No one organized fundraisers better and faster than a throng of high school girls.

The comments died down around one in the morning. I logged off and crawled into bed. Snuggled beneath the covers, I set my alarm and noticed six messages from Amit. Click off. His parents' verdict could wait until later.

My eyelids closed for literally half a minute when someone knocked . . . on my freaking window!

I warily turned my head as my phone beeped again. I grabbed it, ready to call the police and beat the intruder at the same time. As I quietly crawled out of bed and crept toward the side of the window, my eyes caught the beginning of Amit's latest message.

Hey, I'm at your house.

I groaned as the adrenaline eased away. Fight mode off.

You better be the stalker at my window . . . or someone is about to get their butt whipped.

He replied with a flushed face emoji followed by a grimacing one with the toothy grin.

You're about to get it . . .

Nevertheless, I carefully lifted the edge of the curtain. When I couldn't see him, I yanked the curtain back all the way, ready to attack whoever it was.

Amit, with one hand in his pocket, the other holding his lit cell, grinned and waved.

I glanced back at the bedroom door. The lights were out and not a sound rose from my parents. With a groan, I pulled up the window and stood with arms crossed.

"Are you stalking me because I didn't answer your texts?"

He scratched the back of his neck. "Nah. I was on my way

home from work and was in the neighborhood. Saw that your light was on."

"Really? Cuz my house is two streets from the main road. And in a cul-de-sac."

"Might have taken a detour," he admitted sheepishly.

"Are you still working long nights? The project hasn't improved?"

"Still driving me up the wall and keeping me up all night."

"You know what would make it less irritating is if you told me all the details."

"And risk ruining everything for my company?"

I glanced over my shoulder and low-key listened for my parents. "You know, if my dad finds out you're here, he's going to beat you with his nine iron."

"Your dad plays golf? Cool!"

"Shh!" Oh! This boy was gonna end me!

"Can you come out?"

I bit my lower lip. I really wanted to. But things were getting too . . . intense. I liked Amit more and more every day, but I couldn't spend any more time on him. "No."

"Can I come in?"

"Definitely no."

He shrugged. "Can we talk through the window?"

I glanced at the bedroom door again. The walls inside were thin and Papa and Mama might actually lose their crap. With a sigh, I pulled out the screen, and now he knew how flimsy our house was and how to break in.

I grabbed the edge and crawled out, not expecting him to help by taking my waist and picking me up so effortlessly and powerfully. The movement of being swept off my feet took me by surprise, and I faltered like a combative baby monkey, accidentally shoving off from the windowsill and toppling

Amit over. So much for his valiant display of lending a hand as I totally fell on him and crushed him in the dirt beneath my window. Although his body was a nice cushion for my fall.

He leaned his head back into the ground and laughed, his hands firm on my waist, never having left.

"Shh!" I said and ducked my face against his chest, embarrassment taking over. I didn't even know what to do now. Getting up and sitting beside him seemed preferable, but my body had turned into lead, like how my legs felt right before a huge fight.

His arms wrapped around my waist and my breath hitched as he spoke into my hair, "Is this part of the 'sneaking around to be friends rebellion' we're plotting?"

"Shut up," I muttered into his shirt.

"Because I really like it."

I pushed myself up, my hands planting themselves on either side of his head as my damp, and now probably filthy hair, spilled over him. His constant, light laughter faded. And so did his smile. The usual cordial, approachable expressions he sported turned dead sexy.

My brain screamed to my body to move and get out of the strike zone before something hit me. My thoughts shrieked a jillion reasons why this moment couldn't evolve, all logical and true and consequential.

But my body didn't listen. It was immobile and in shock and my elbows even locked.

We both swallowed. Hard. He reached up and stretched his fingers into my hair at the nape of my neck and lifted his head as he gently pulled mine down.

Oh, lord. It was happening. Commence freak-out.

Our lips touched with an explosion of senses that I didn't even know existed. His cologne hit my nose, mingled with the smell of dirt and grass. His warmth against my skin, the softness of his mouth against mine, the taste of cardamom and pista on his tongue.

I gasped and pulled back, my heart racing and a horde of butterflies raging in my belly.

"I think I came here to do that," he breathed.

"Amit, we can't do this."

"Why not?"

"I can't date. I don't even have time for a boyfriend. You have ridiculous work projects and grades to keep up. Your parents probably don't even like me. After graduation, we'll be in different colleges. The list goes on."

"I can't date either. I don't need much time; what I get from you right now is more than what I can ask for. My parents actually really liked you. And I'm going to UT-Austin, so we'll still both be at our parents' houses and end up at the same college."

"I can't have any distractions with my big fight coming up."

"I'll wait."

"It could be months—" I paused. "Wait. Did you say that your parents like me?"

"Yep. Told you. You're not easy to dislike, by the way. I've tried."

I scoffed. "You didn't try hard enough."

"It's *really* not easy to dislike you when you're still lying on top of me."

"Oh!" My cheeks turned fiery hot as I shifted to move away, but his arms held me in place.

"I kinda like it, though. Kinda really, really like it."

I quietly laughed and pushed away. "My dad will kinda really, really beat you if he saw this."

We sat on a patch of grass and brushed off the dirt. I helped dust off Amit's back and picked little leaves out of his hair.

"What did your parents say?" I asked softly.

"Didn't you read any of my texts?"

"No. I got busy. What did they say?"

"They said they liked you. That you're smart and polite and pretty."

"I don't fall short of their expectations for friends?"

"Nah. You exceed them."

"That's hard to believe."

"Why do you doubt yourself so much?"

"Because Indian parents have high standards for Indian kids. I know. I have Indian parents in my family. Lots of them. They're mainly about high grades and prestigious degrees, impressive careers and income, nice houses and cars, and it all starts with training and expectations from day one. My parents may not push me to want a bigger house or be the foremost surgeon in the world, but they push for my best efforts, which turns out can lead to high standards."

"Well, they're impressed by all of you. They said you're well-rounded and hardworking, and that's admirable."

"What about Muay Thai? That didn't freak them out?"

"At first they were baffled, like why would a girl get involved in a sport where she has to fight? They don't know much about it, but then I explained the basics to them and showed them some videos of girls in training and how rigorous and disciplined they are. My parents respect dedication."

"Oh . . . well, guess you were right about them not judging."

He nudged my shoulder with his. "Told you so."

I nudged him back harder. He almost fell over. "Muh-muh-muh," I muttered mockingly. "How do you know so much about Muay Thai?"

"I didn't know anything about it before, but after that night at the gym, I researched it. Training is wildly intense, and those fights . . . how do you do that?"

"Which part?"

"All of it. The training, the discipline, fighting, getting hit, not crapping your pants."

I crushed my hand over my mouth to stop from laughing.

"It's amazing. I can't wait to see you fight."

"Really? You're not going to be scared of me?"

"I've always been scared of you."

"Shut up. So we're allowed to be friends?"

"Yep."

"My parents liked you too."

"Enough to date?"

I nudged him, but not as harshly. "No. And even if they did, seriously, I have a lot riding on Muay Thai."

"Oh, yeah? Like what? Trophies? Scholarships?"

I bit my lower lip, which tasted of Amit and cardamom and pista.

"Something bigger? Now you gotta tell me."

Well, the secret was out. Come tomorrow morning at school, everyone and their mama would know. It wasn't every day, much less every generation, that our school had a possible Olympian walking through the halls.

"So, my next fight that's in Arizona?"

"Yeah?"

"It's the US Muay Thai Open."

"No way! That's awesome."

"You know about it?"

"Came up in my research." He then, to my utter disbelief, went on to nerd-splain Muay Thai and USMTO to me. With full-on excited gestures and exuberant explanations.

As I watched Amit, this boy who totally blew my mind the more and more I got to know him, my heart swelled something big and fierce and overflowing. He was *so* into everything. He was impressed, elated, baffled, in awe . . . the entire gamut of positive responses. None of which included disgust or ignorance or assumptions or judgment.

I grinned hard at him.

"What?" he asked, suddenly pausing his wild gesticulations.

"You really got into it, huh?"

"It's incredibly interesting. And if you're doing it, if you're passionate about it, then yeah. I'm one hundred percent into it."

"So you know it's a huge freaking deal."

"Yeah. Wow. I can't believe you're going. No wonder you don't have time for me . . ." he ended sorrowfully.

"You said you'd wait," I reminded softly.

"I will."

"How long?"

"What do you mean? It's only a couple weeks away, right?"

I pulled my knees to my chest and hugged them. "The thing is, if I do well enough, I could get picked for the US World Championships team. And who knows how long that could go on."

"Dang," he said, the word heavy with equal amounts of awe and disappointment.

"And then . . ."

"There's more?"

"Muay Thai is on the verge of becoming an Olympic sport. I could be on that first team."

"You're way out of my league, Kareena Thakkar."

I smiled to myself. A boy had never said that to me. I had never even considered myself to ever be out of someone else's league, especially a guy as remarkable as Amit. "It's just that . . ."

"What?"

"Ugh. It costs a lot of money. I have to raise funds and you'd think asking sponsors for money to support a possible future Olympic athlete would be a great sales pitch, but no."

He mulled over my words for a bit. "Everything will work out," he said finally.

I chewed on the inside of my cheek and rested my chin on my knees. "We're talking a few weeks if I suck and a few years if I'm top level."

"I'd never get in your way or be the distraction that keeps you from being your best."

My heart broke, but at least one of us said it.

"Although part of me is convinced that we could date as our schedules permitted. You'll have Muay Thai and college. I'll have my job and college. We both have to make time for family. What else is there? In between classes and family dinners and sports-slash-work. We could do it."

Ugh! We were almost there! "You and your logic." I pushed around some dirt with my toe. "I have to focus."

"Okay," he replied without hesitation.

He stood and offered his hand, pulling me up and into him. My body would definitely miss his. "How'd you get into Muay Thai, by the way?"

I hit my forehead against his chest. It seemed to love it there. His warm hands wrapped around my waist and for a few minutes, we just stood this way. Then my arms found their way around his back as I told him my story.

"I like that story."

We embraced for another moment before I finally pulled back and saw the turmoil on his face. "What?"

"Huh?"

"You look like you have something to say."

He shook his head. "Just don't want this to be over."

"It's not over. We hit *pause*." I slipped out of his arms, my body suddenly cold as I crawled back inside.

Amit braced the edges of the window and leaned in. "Can we hit *replay*?"

I crossed my arms. "You're postponing the inevitable."

"Seems like it, huh?"

Stepping closer made things worse. The presence of him hit all too strongly. At this angle, his mouth aligned with my jaw, and he did not waste time. Gentle lips brushed against my jawline with the ability to move any direction they wanted.

If he moved to my throat, I was done for.

If he moved to my ear, I was done for.

If he moved to my mouth, I was done for.

I cupped his face, bent down, and muttered against his lips, "You're asking for trouble."

"Don't think there's anyone else I'd rather be in trouble with." His gaze dropped to my mouth. "Don't do that."

"Do what?"

"Bite your lip like that."

"Was I?" I hadn't noticed.

"You always bite your lip when I say something that gets you flustered. That makes me want to look at your mouth. Which then makes me want to kiss you, and maybe . . ."

"Maybe what?"

"See what biting that lip is like."

I tilted to kiss him. He didn't relinquish his white-knuckled hold on the edges of the window, but he leaned in as far as he could. It was safer that way.

The kiss was soft and perfect. Until he gently bit my lower lip and I moaned.

Heat and mortification surged through me, lighting my skin on fire. I released him and shuddered. “You should go.”

He smirked something knowing and wicked and all-consuming. “Okay. But now I know how much you like me, Kareena.”

I flushed. There was no point in trying to hide what Amit did to me. “You’re just now figuring that out? I thought you were supposed to be a genius.”

SIXTEEN

By the time Thursday lunch came around, I had cooled off. Yeah, I had it like that. It was pretty bad but thank the lord that Amit and I hadn't seen one another since that smoking-hot Tuesday night. And also, thanks to Coach, my training session all day yesterday had been brutal. I could barely walk right, much less concentrate on Amit and his sexy-as-heck kiss.

Unfortunately, the principal waited at the entrance to the school and called me into her office. I nervously followed, although she'd greeted me in her usual warm way.

I sat in the small office, stiff and not knowing what I'd done.

Principal Sanchez sat on her side of the room in a big leather swivel chair, laced her fingers together on the desk, and smiled.

"So nice to see you, Kareena," she started.

"What's up Principal Sanchez?"

"I understand that you joined the online social group for Connally girl's athletics."

I nodded.

"And as you know, the page is monitored by the coaches."

"Yes. Did I say or do something wrong?" I didn't think I had.

"No, no, not at all. They did however bring to my attention the amazing opportunity that you have ahead of you. I am so thrilled and proud of you. I had no idea. And it seemed that most people didn't. I'm now also aware of the roadblock with funds."

"Oh. Were some of the suggestions too much?"

"No. The coaches called me yesterday morning. I chatted with them and some of the teachers. I later sent emails to the entire staff as well as the PTO."

"Uh, huh . . ."

"And we'd be honored if we could raise some funds to help you get to USMTO . . . and quite possibly lead the way to the World Championships and the Olympics." She squealed out the last word.

I laughed. A new burst of love and warmth for my school sent tingles all over my skin.

"We'll get you there. Why didn't you come to me before?"

"I didn't even think about it, to be honest. And I didn't want to be a charity case or make my parents feel bad that I went to other people. Some students are in worse situations than me with more important things. Why help me and not them?"

"We can only help if we know, and how we help is usually kept under wraps for student privacy."

"Oh. Yeah, that makes sense."

"You're okay with this being public?"

Was I? I mean, it was already public in the forum. Half the school knew about it or would know about it soon enough. It was time to own up. I didn't have anything to hide. I was a female fighter. A pretty freaking good one.

After a long pause, I exhaled a sharp breath and replied, "I guess so."

"I think it's important to make this a community effort. This would end up bringing a lot of publicity to the school, and it's a wonderful way of getting people together to help.

We do it for all of our sports and arts, so why wouldn't we do it for a student who has a shot at the Olympics?"

"Thank you so much," I replied, but the impact her declaration had didn't sink in just yet.

"How is everything else?"

"It's fine."

She tilted her head with her let's-be-real look.

I swallowed and rubbed my arm, lowering my gaze to her desk as I started. "Papa is really sick, Principal Sanchez."

"I know. We've kept in contact with your parents." She sighed and gave me that pity look, the look I hated seeing. She stood and walked around her desk to sit next to me, and gently patted my shoulder. I leaned back. Not because the touch made me uncomfortable, but because any more sympathy and I'd lose it.

"Do you want to talk about it?" The way she asked, totally sincere and nice, made my lips quiver and my vision blur behind a screen of tears.

Yeah. Actually. For the first time in a long time, I did want to talk about it. So I told her all about Papa's advancing renal disease and his constant septicemia bouts, ending with, "Muay Thai keeps me balanced and afloat. It makes me forget everything for a while and helps me to focus on positive energy."

It seemed like maybe she wanted to chat longer, but I also had to get to class, and she knew. I'd taken a deep sigh and walked out of her office after the tears evaporated. Maneuvering into a river of students, the tall, open hallways filled with laughter and conversations and yells and rustling paper and bumping backpacks was a surreal way of rerouting my thoughts.

I was in school. And I was happy to be here. So I put on my "nothing's got me down" game face.

Kimmy, breaking through a crowd, locked arms with mine on the way to class. "Quick question!"

"Shoot." I smiled faintly. No matter what, it was hard not to smile around Kimmy.

"You're okay with us fundraising, right?"

"Totally. I appreciate any and all help."

"So, going public is a must, right?"

I shrugged. "I can't keep it hidden, don't want to."

"Awesome!"

"But what's going on?"

"You'll see at lunch."

"Am I going to regret anything?" I side-eyed her suspiciously.

"No regrets. We're going to go all out, if you don't mind some attention."

I wasn't quite sure how to react as she slipped away and walked into the classroom first.

Normally, I'd get to calculus early enough to get a seat in the back, preferably behind Kimmy or Tanya, and try not to fall asleep.

Today? Walking into calculus was like being a pop diva walking into a club. Everyone threw their hands up and hollered, welcoming me as if the party could now get started. Even the teacher offered a high five.

What even?

Bizarre, but okay. I didn't mind this kind of attention and support, if that's what Kimmy was talking about.

Apparently, word had spread beyond the female athletes to most of the student body, and of course the teachers were in on this madness too. Was this how it felt to be a star quarterback at UT? Everyone wanted to talk to him when he walked into class, sit beside him, get selfies with him, slather said pics across social?

Probably.

The downside? Man, I had to sit near the front because everyone wanted to hear my story. Still, this was hands down the best calculus period ever. In the history of all time.

SEVENTEEN

"So, prom's coming up," Travis announced as he leaned a hand against the locker next to mine.

I shoved my books inside the metal box the way I wanted to shove his head inside. How could someone be so irritating so fast? World record fast. I thought he'd gotten the hint that I was not interested in him. Flirting? Sure, whatever, fine. It didn't bother me too much so long as it was light and respectful, and he didn't touch me. But a prom invite? No freaking way. Not with his prom stats.

"Yep," I muttered.

"You want to go with me?"

I made a face. In my head, I imagined it was a concoction of "You for real?", "What the heck are you smoking, dude?", and "Nothing would disgust me more."

Travis had gone to senior prom since he was a freshman. Yep. He was that good-looking and that smooth. Also that gross, because every prom he'd get that senior girl to rent a hotel room upstairs, get lucky, and then blab about it the next week to all of his buds.

I slammed my locker, absolutely livid that he'd try to pull that crap on me. "Oh, hell no. Get away from me."

"What's your problem?" he asked, pissed and very loud.

"You are. Isn't that obvious? You think I'm like those other girls who took you to prom? What? You gonna get me to front for a hotel room, think that I would get into bed with you, and think that I don't know you'd spill every lewd detail to the entire school?"

"What are you talking about?"

"You've noticed me this year. You never realized I stood behind some of those crowds where you told your disgusting tales. I'm actually quite offended that you think I'm that stupid, seeing that I've had four years to get to know your tricks. I'm not interested."

"Saanvi must be right. You like girls, don't you?"

"Just because I'm not buying your trash? Get out of my face."

"Or what? You gonna punch me? I heard about your boxing."

Irate and having waited far too long for a boy to make all these assumptions that I knew a guy like Travis would make, all sorts of words and emotions sprang to mind. Because one, I'd had a lot of time to think about what I'd say and do in the many, many scenarios that I'd created in my head as an excuse to keep my opinion and my sport to myself. And two, because I was just not in the mood to be Travis's next conquest.

I straightened up and stepped forward so that his face was a literal four inches from mine, even if I had to look up at him. "Then you've heard how many people I've knocked out. And yes, I sure will punch you in your face if you keep harassing me."

I wouldn't ever hit someone outside of the ring or because they made me mad, of course. I wasn't stupid or short-tempered or violent by any means. I wasn't even mad enough to lift a finger, but if he wanted to play this game and get his ego handed to him by a girl in the middle of a packed hallway full of kids who now watched our interaction, then so freaking be it.

"You gonna hit back?" I asked, my eyebrows high and mighty. "You want to *try* to hit a girl or get your butt knocked out by one?"

He shook his head and awkwardly laughed. "Pretty sure you're into girls anyway."

A whoosh of air hit the back of my neck. Amit had his forearm casually leaned against the locker behind me, rattling my brains with a whole new level of what the hell. Because seriously, the boy made the air itself change from annoying Travis-infested to floaty-hearts infected.

"I'm pretty sure whoever she's into isn't your business," Amit said in a level tone.

"So the nerd has balls, huh?" Travis shot back.

"Pretty sure they're bigger than yours."

I giggled. Ew. That was so gross but strangely kind of hilarious.

"You can try to hit me, too, if you want."

"Maybe I will," Travis snapped.

"Just remember who *you* are and who you're hitting."

"What's that supposed to mean?"

"I may get hit and laughed at, but you'll get expelled and then won't graduate, making you like the oldest high school senior in Texas history."

"Damn . . ." one of the guys across the hall muttered. Yep, about two dozen students watched us.

There was no secret about Travis's age. Dude was old. He had flunked a grade in elementary school for being way behind and held back in seventh grade for behavior. By the time he hit eighth grade, finally, he actually excelled in something: basketball. So the view of the school system shifted in his favor because he had great potential to go somewhere and also because they were just tired of him still being here.

Basketball skills aside, one more misdemeanor from Travis and even the school board couldn't help him.

"You just have to ask yourself if *I'm* worth it," Amit added. "You know, if you want to be twenty and still in high school."

"You can't hide forever."

"Who's hiding? I'm right here."

"Hiding behind the boxer." He sneered, looking around to get a few chuckles.

Amit surprised both of us by stepping beside me and, somehow, discreetly moving me behind him. How did this even happen?

"It's called Muay Thai. And now she's behind me."

"Sounds like you want to get hit," Travis snarled.

"Sounds like I'm baiting you."

Travis scoffed. "Whatever. I'm graduating this year and you will not be the reason I'm stuck in this place." He stomped away in the wake of immature ridicule. My, my, how the fates of high school could suddenly change.

Amit turned to me and grinned but faltered when he saw that I was not amused. "What?"

"You think I'm a damsel and needed you to step in?" I scowled.

"Well a damsel is a young, unmarried woman by definition."

"You know what I mean. A damsel in distress who needs a guy to save her."

"I actually tripped trying to walk past you and played it off like I meant to lean against the locker."

My lips betrayed me and twitched.

"You can handle your own. But does that mean you'd be offended if someone stood up beside you? Although technically, I was behind you."

I cracked a smile. "I'm kidding. I know why you did what you did."

"Seriously. I tripped."

"He did actually trip. I saw the whole thing," Lily said as she strode across the hallway to join us. "It was a very smooth play-off, if you ask me."

"Mhmm . . ." I muttered.

"Are you coming to lunch with me today?" she asked me. "No fast food."

"I'm eating in the cafeteria today cuz I miss you."

"Cafeteria food is also bad plus gross."

"But you brought your own lunch and we can eat together." She pouted. "Unless you're tutoring?"

"Ah, no. We can skip today," Amit insisted.

"Are you sure? You got theorems down?" I felt like we'd been stuck on the same thing forever.

"Yep." A shadow of something crossed his features, just as it had Tuesday night. He had something on his mind.

"Is everything okay?"

"What?" he asked, distracted.

"You look like something's on your mind."

"Same old, you know the deal."

I watched him for another second as he shrugged. "All right. Well, do you want to join us?"

He looked at Lily for approval and she hooked arms with his. "Be our date, Amit!"

"You're so weird," I told her, but went along for the ride as she practically skipped down the hallway with him.

He glanced over his shoulder at me and mouthed, "I don't know what's happening." Then cocked his chin toward her.

I giggled and walked a few paces behind them as he escorted Lily into the cafeteria.

Rayna was the first person I saw, lingering at the end of a table and talking with another student. She glanced at us and offered a closed-lip smile.

"You should talk to her," Amit said.

"Closure, then be done with it," Lily added.

They went ahead to a depressing line of cafeteria food while I wandered toward Rayna. She stepped back from the student as I asked, "Can we talk?"

"We should chat," she said at the same time and then smiled. Her dimples deepened in her cheeks. We used to joke that she could fill them with water to store for later they were so deep.

"What's up?" I asked instead.

"This whole thing got out of hand, right?" She played with her fingernails like a kid who had gotten caught, the way she had made me feel for so long.

"Let's sit?"

She nodded and followed me to a corner table where I snagged three seats. Rayna sat beside me. My heart no longer hurt as much when I saw her, but there was always an ember of hope on the outskirts of this burnt friendship.

I turned to her, empowered by having stood up to Saanvi, of letting the truth out with Amit's parents, of finding solace and comfort with my fellow female athletes. It was easy to speak to her now. She had words to say, but so did I. So I went first.

"Look, I've apologized before for what I did. I wasn't being shady. I asked you about Dev and you said you were over him. I even told you everything I was doing. I honestly did not think the other guy and I were still talking, much less dating. We were never dating. I get why you were mad, but I don't get why you hated me. Especially for this long. I especially don't get why you let Saanvi talk so much malicious crap about me.

We both know those things aren't true, and you're way too nice to let that slide. So why would you rather be friends with her and not me? Or friends with her at all, even if not with me?"

She sighed. It was hard to ignore Saanvi's behavior, to pretend she hadn't changed. Even Rayna couldn't possibly see the better side of Saanvi right now.

"I'm not going to beg for our friendship back. I'm over that. I've apologized and given you space and waited patiently for almost half a year. If you don't think I'm friend material, then that's too bad for you because I'm still an amazing person. It hurt to lose you. But I didn't deserve to feel that way for this long. I don't have time to waste on negativity. It was all a snafu and I did my part to try to make up for it."

"I know," she said and chewed on the inside of her cheek like someone who knew they were guilty. Finally!

"Sometimes friendships need time and space to heal. That would be awesome. And maybe the fact that it hasn't bounced back by now means that it never would've lasted in the first place. And that's too bad. But that's all I have to say. I'll always wave and smile at you in passing, okay? No more awkward glances or looking away like I'm dirt."

"I'm not mad at you anymore," she said after a moment of silence. "*You* should be mad at me. I don't know why it took me so long, but maybe because it felt weird to be the first one to say something. I thought we were over. And what's the point of saying anything if we were?"

I replied, a bit annoyed, "The point would've been to let me know so I didn't feel like crap for so long. Also for closure. We'd know for sure, no guessing, no assuming."

"I was pretty mean to you."

"Petty as hell," I muttered.

"Deserved. I felt used, to be honest."

"Huh?"

She shrugged and looked off into the distance when she said, "You used to ask me about Dev all the time when we were talking. Then I wondered if you'd only been asking because you'd liked him all that time. I got self-conscious."

"So you assumed crap about me and never bothered to clear it up? Were we even friends at all?" I asked curtly, crossing my arms and scowling.

"Yes! Of course we were." She heaved out a breath and went quiet, as if she tried to summon the right words. "I missed talking to you about everything under the sun. All the weird stuff that happens at work. Boys. College picks. Recipes."

"New ones?" I asked. Her dessert recipes *were* the best.

"Yep. I made one for you."

"What is it?"

"It's a pink lemonade cupcake." She slowly smiled, her grin getting wider until I got it.

"That sounds good. Oh, wait. Did you make it up?"

"Yes! Pink. Get it?"

"Oh!" I laughed. "For Muay Thai?"

"Yes! I know it's your favorite color and it always reminds you of Muay Thai."

"That's super cool." And that meant that she'd been thinking of me all this time, enough to create a delicious concoction in my honor.

"I miss how easily we talked to one another. I was a brat."

"You wanna use a stronger word?" I arched a brow.

She laughed. "Yeah, I know."

She lurched forward and hugged me. "I'm so sorry! It wasn't as big of a deal as we made it out to be! And not for this stupid long! I was pissed at first, but I didn't want to accept that you were right about how it all went down."

She pulled back, and added, "Life is too short for this. Can we be friends?"

"It really messed me up."

"I'll do anything. This friendship can't die."

"Rayna. I want to, but it's hard to trust you after leaving me like that, siding with Saanvi, letting her talk crap about me. In the restroom? Remember that?"

Her eyes glistened. "Yeah. I don't deserve your forgiveness, but I'll earn it. I saw you at Holi. I wanted to say hi, and it killed me that I didn't."

"That was your own fault."

"Yeah."

"Why are you friends with Saanvi? She's the not the same person anymore. You've got to see that. She's not the girl we played dolls with and practiced dance with and did sleepovers with. She used to smother us with hospitality, and now she wouldn't give me a sip of water if I were dying at her feet."

"She has some good qualities."

I raised a sharp eyebrow. "Enough to be friends? Toxicity poisons everything it touches. She does that crap on purpose and there's no reason to be a vindictive person."

"Let me talk to her. Maybe she'll put it behind her and apologize and we can all be friends. I think that's better than brushing her aside and letting her poison herself more."

And if only I'd gotten that sort of response and consideration from Rayna, but bygones were bygones. "I would never be friends with her again. And honestly, I can't be friends with you again if you don't see the truth here."

"Is that an ultimatum?" she asked.

"Nope. Just telling you how it is. I can't be friends with someone who is friends with a person as vindictive and cruel as her, or with someone who wouldn't stand up for me if I were wronged. We can be friendly, but real friends are better than that. Whatever decision you make is up to you."

"I understand. I will talk to her, though. She at least owes you an apology."

I nodded, but I didn't have any craps left to give for Saanvi.

Rayna left for her table, where Saanvi sat, having watched the entire encounter with darkness in her eyes. Some people couldn't be redeemed.

Ignoring her, I opened my lunch tote and chowed down.

A buzz filled the room, something more than the usual clamor of goofing around and stuffing hungry French fry holes. Amit had offered Lily to jump ahead of him in line, which meant she walked across all three tiers of the cafeteria before he finished paying for his meal. That left ample room for Saanvi to hop over to him. They exchanged a few words. He shook his head and glanced at me, then smiled big.

"Ooh, are you two making googly eyes at each other from across the room?" Lily asked as she plopped down across from me.

"No. And why are you sitting over there?" I asked.

"Saving that spot for your boyfriend."

My cheeks turned hot. "He's not my boyfriend."

"Did you or did you not lock lips with him?"

I flushed. How did she know! Oh . . . wait . . . "That was a peck on the corner of my lips over a week ago. Let it go."

She'd kill me later for keeping the juicy bits from her, but all this boyfriend talk had to wait an entire two weeks, until after USMTO . . . if I made it there.

I looked around, curious from the noise and energy.

Ah. Now it all came together. The table on the far side had turned into a booth, and a bake sale was going on. What a perfect place for it. Kimmy and three other girls from the soccer team waved excitedly at me. Kimmy walked onto the stage with a microphone and I froze. I sure hoped she wasn't about to announce anything about my prospects.

Amit sat down beside me with a sad tray of cheese fries.

"Is that all you're eating?" I asked.

"Not much to choose from today."

I slid my lunch container over to him. "Have some."

He eyed my lunch skeptically. "Looks like slim pickings."

"It's plenty for me. But I'm not that hungry. Eat."

He picked up one of the lettuce wraps and examined it with scrutiny.

"It's a bean sprout wrap." And it was freaking delicious.

He turned it one way then another, as if something would magically appear. "Where's the tortilla?"

"No bad complex carbs, and those tortillas are full of the wrong kind of calories."

He took a bite and said, "Not bad."

"I still deserve to enjoy my food, even if it's healthy," I said to him but eyed Kimmy as a line of girls stood behind her to the left and a line of boys to the right. They were all on stage.

"What are they up to?" Amit asked.

I narrowed my eyes and munched on my apple slices.

EIGHTEEN

"Hey, hey, hey!" Kimmy boomed, stopping conversations across the cafeteria dead in their tracks. "You've heard the buzz since yesterday morning. We're going to be doing a lot of stuff in the next couple of weeks, so don't miss out! We've got a Friday night movie bash on the football field with lots of goodies to eat. Prom committee is selling flowers, corsages, and chocolates with special pop-the-question cues. We'll be having bake sales at lunch every day and at all the games, so don't walk right by us! Heard someone's mama made mini buttermilk pies, y'all!"

That earned a huge hoot because we all knew Lizzy Stanley's parents owned a delicious bakery and her mom was citywide famous for the best pies this side of Texas.

"Twice a week, we'll be doing either an auction or raffling off some majorly cool things. Today's auction is probably the reason why most of you opted out of off-campus lunch."

I glared at Lily, who shrugged guiltily but turned her full attention to the stage.

"We're auctioning off dates to prom!"

What the crap? Was this even legal?

"Speaking of prom dates . . ." Amit winked at me.

"Oh, no. Dances are not my thing. I can't dance to save my life, remember?"

"It's a rite of passage. Get to dress up, eat fancy food, hang with your friends who are also dressed up and eating fancy food."

"I've never been to a dance and don't intend on starting with prom."

"Just breaking my heart all over the place, Kareena."

"Wait. Are you asking me to prom?"

His cheeks flushed. "Guess so."

"Is that how you ask a girl to prom? I was expecting a little romance or doves or something."

He grinned. "I don't think you could handle me getting romantic."

Did someone turn up the heater in here? Thank goodness for Kimmy's auctioning because that was the only thing that pried Amit's eyes off me.

"Now, the rules are each person pays for their own ticket and meals unless anyone is inclined to do more. Don't expect them to otherwise. No hanky-panky. Don't expect to get to any bases. They don't owe you anything more than a friendly prom and dancing and eating with you at your table of friends. But you know these guys, and they love to dance and take pictures and are always the life of school parties. Be nice to them because they're volunteering to do this. You can make arrangements after the auction.

"Auction starts in five minutes, so get your giant green auction hand from our table if you haven't already. Then please return them when the auction is over. You have twenty-four hours to pay in full or you lose your claim and the student date goes to the next highest bidder for up to three bidders. So don't make these awesome dates feel bad!"

The guys made broken hearts on their chests, and some of the girls, including Lily, went wild. She had the hugest crush on Jared up there. And she had a giant green hand ready to go. Girl meant business.

"This auction was approved by the PTO and the principal, but if we have problems, they'll never let the student body do this again. However, we need everyone to be safe and respectful, so if any of the participants have an issue, bring it to me ASAP. Bidding begins at ten bucks. That seems like a great price for a great date, but I know we can do better! All proceeds go toward a great cause!"

My cheeks flushed. Oh, boy. Here it came . . .

"Did you know that one of our very own athletes is going to the US Open?"

The crowd gasped and excitedly looked around.

"Which athlete could it be?" Kimmy asked.

Amit grinned at me. I wanted to hide. So much attention . . .

"Hint: She's a girl. A very badass girl." Then she mouthed to the teachers and coaches watching from the door, "Sorry!"

The crowd laughed.

"Any guesses? Well, her sport is . . . get this . . . Muay Thai!"

More gasps. More fervor.

"A female, national-level fighter right among us! You might've never known. She kept this awesomeness to herself for a long time, but we found out! Okay, she finally *told* us! She doesn't play any school sports. She's a senior. She's sitting on the top tier right now."

I groaned. That narrowed it down to about thirty girls. Some eyes landed on me and they guessed correctly. Maybe it was my slumped, please-don't-look-at-me posture, or Amit grinning like a fool beside me, or Lily bouncing in her seat.

Travis had heard. Surely they'd heard too.

"Even more exciting, if you're wondering why we're raising money for her to go to the Open, aside from it being a fabulous, rare opportunity that she worked very hard for and will be the first student at Connally to go. If she does well at the Open, she has a real shot at trying out for the US World Championships team."

An applause.

"And finally, a shot at the Olympics."

An all-out explosion of applause and chatter and cheers broke through the cafeteria. A myriad of hands came at me, some to pat my back, others to hug, some to high five. A tangle of students amassed in our little corner with me at the center.

It was a lot. Like hyperventilating a lot. I grabbed Amit's hand beneath the table, which he then squeezed and held.

I was about to lose it. *God, Kareena, don't cry in public.*

"All right! All right!" Kimmy reeled everyone back to the auction. "Make sure you show your support whenever you see our fighter; in the halls, in class, in the car, walking down the street, at the store! Make sure you help make history by showing support at all the fundraisers, which we guarantee you'll enjoy and get something out of too. You're not paying for just her. Eat some pie, watch a movie with your sweetheart, surprise your prom date, and right now, raise those green hands as we start the bidding. First up! Jared!"

The girls went wild, leaving me alone to go after him auction-style, including Lily.

"Jared is soccer royalty, a straight-A senior giving his prom night to a special young lady."

Jared walked to the front of the stage in his soccer jersey and jeans, flashed a dimpled smile, kissed two fingers and then raised them toward me with a wink. Jared was a hot commodity and he went quickly. To Lily. She had the biggest smile on her face, and no one could say others didn't get something from helping me get to USMTO.

"You okay?" Amit asked, glancing down at my white-knuckled hold suffocating the blood flow to his fingers.

I released the death grip. "Sorry. Yeah. It's all so much. I wish Kimmy would've told me about this beforehand. I mean, it's amazing and I'm blown away, but a better hint would've been nice to brace myself with."

"It's awesome."

"It is, no doubt, but so much at once. Look at them. They're popular, gorgeous, accomplished athletes sacrificing something as special as prom with their girlfriends and boyfriends for me." I blinked back tears. Dang it!

Most of the volunteers were my friends, but we weren't that close. They hadn't known about Muay Thai before. We never hung out outside of school.

My entire body flared hot as I fought back tears. "I need to go to the restroom."

"You can't leave. This is all for you!" Lily said.

Jared shot her a wink and she just about crumpled.

She was right, though. This was all for me and it would be rude to leave.

I took my hand from Amit and wiped the clamminess against my jeans. I kept my hands there and his hand landed on top of mine, warm and secure, an anchor.

My brain struggled to find something to distract myself with. Thinking of Papa only made me sad because he hadn't gotten any better. Thinking of Mama made me emotional because she would cry when she found out about this. Thinking of anything Muay Thai made me want to happy cry because it was within real reach. Thinking of Amit and how wonderful he was made me want to sob. What else was there?

Saanvi, with her gaping mouth and incredulous, confused gaze helped. Could we actually be friends again? Would the winter fairies hovering over her head stop sprinkling so much frostiness?

For the next thirty minutes or so, my thoughts honed in on Saanvi. The auction ended on prom queen nominee and star track and fielder, Amanda. The props came and went, and I happily thanked everyone, but I could not get out of there fast enough. As soon as the bell rang, I sprang out of my seat and nearly jogged to class, leaving Amit and Lily behind.

The halls filled with an upheaval of congrats and even when I walked into class after managing to grab my books and maneuver through the adoring crowds, everyone in comp-sci applauded when I arrived, startling me. Even though Kimmy told them to do this, it wasn't something I'd get used to.

My steps faltered and I was pretty sure I looked like a deer in headlights. Being in Texas, I'd seen them plenty of times. They froze in the middle of the road as a racing car approached. Their mouths dropped and their eyes went wide and glazed over. It was an "oh, crap" moment. Very much like this one.

Except I wasn't getting rammed by a deadly car. Just thrown into another "don't-cry-in-front-of-people" moment.

I put on a shy, shaky smile, my pulse spewing blood through my veins, and hurried to my seat.

I'd turned into a celebrity overnight.

···❮ NINETEEN ❯···

Really good things were almost always counterbalanced with really sucky things. Some called it karma, kismet, cosmic balance, luck, what have you. I would do anything to have it transform into a literal being so it could suffer my sentient wrath.

I'd skipped up the driveway, bubbling with all the feels. I'd barely made it to the porch when Mama ripped back the door. We startled one another, our eyes wide, our bodies still for a split second.

Her frazzled hair and red-streaked eyes and dilated pupils were enough to tell the same old story again.

"What happened to Papa?" I asked.

"Get in the car. He passed out again. His blood sugar dropped. He has pain in his stomach and head and back," she said.

I didn't peep another word and didn't realize Papa had been sitting in the car on the street all this time. He slumped against the passenger side window, his eyelids halfway closed in what one might've thought was a drug-induced haze. Drool shone on the corner of his mouth. The bones of his face protruded beneath pale skin.

I gulped, my throat raw and dry, as I quietly slid into the back seat with my backpack. I placed my hand on his shoulder and kept it there until we arrived at the hospital.

Mama pulled up to the ER where Papa's doctor and a nurse waited with a wheelchair. She must've called ahead of time, like before. Everything happened in a blur. They helped Papa out of the car and into the wheelchair.

The nurse immediately bent down and took his vitals. When she said something to the doctor, he allowed the nurse to go ahead of us.

Dr. Khan spoke in a hushed tone with Mama, who hurriedly walked alongside him.

"Mama," I interrupted. "I'll park the car."

She looked at me, confused, before nodding with realization. "I'll text you the room and floor."

"K . . ."

She, with the doctor, walked through the sliding glass double doors of the ER and turned the corner. I followed their ambiguous shapes as the wall changed from clear glass to opaque squares to cement.

I slipped into the driver's seat, closed the door, and gripped the steering wheel so hard it could've broken. No matter how many times we'd been in this exact same situation, the intensity never dulled. The struggle to keep hope alive was harder than any fight in all the world. The surge of anger and disparity drove mercilessly into my soul, a jagged sword being thrust in and out until I was left in shreds.

But the ER curbside was not the place to break down.

A parking stall on Level Two of Parking Garage N, facing the highway in the distance with a security camera just behind me, seemed like a much better place.

A fraught mess of good and bad things were happening, an affair of optimism and despondency. Instead of letting go, because crying in this moment felt like forfeiting hope, a severing betrayal that my fragility couldn't take, I let only the buildup of tears slip. But not one more. One more tear would lead to a million, uncontrolled ones. One hiccup would lead to relentless sobbing. Even the thought of giving in made the frayed tips of hope brush against my soul, threatening to drain away.

Papa would not die. Not this day. Not this year.

With shaky hands, I texted Lily and told her the situation. She responded the same way she had every time I'd sent a text like this.

I'm on my way!

I swung my backpack over one shoulder, locked the car, and followed Mama's instructions to the ICU on the fourth floor, room 460. She stood at the nurses' station with three doctors in white coats and two nurses. I clenched and unclenched my hands, wanting to stand with her and hear every word, but instead, I went to Papa's room.

A dozen tubes and wires snaked from beneath his sheets to machines on the walls. They glowed with numbers and words and symbols.

"Papa?" I asked and stood over his bed.

He didn't move, didn't blink, didn't twitch. He was asleep. Which was good, I supposed. He needed rest and peace and maybe sleeping made him forget the pain.

I dropped my backpack to the bench and lifted the open blinds to let in more light. They said sunlight was good for the body, mind, and soul.

I picked up a chair and set it beside the bed facing the window, sat down, and said, "You're going to be okay, Papa. We're going to be okay. This is just a setback, like the time I fractured my shin and couldn't fight for six months. We've had a lot of setbacks, but that's fine because we always get back to where we were. This is another one of those times.

"Not sure what happened, and not sure what the docs are telling Mama. Doesn't matter, because we're ready for anything. We'll fight through anything, right? Y'all taught me that we don't give up. We always fight. And that's what we're going to do."

The machines' beeping and IV bags' dripping haunted the silence. My heart skipped around in my chest and a hundred awful thoughts careened through my brain. Research said positivity did miraculous things for people. And that's where I had to go. If not for me, then for Papa.

The adrenaline of the school's support still stuck with me, so I pulled at it and tried my best to put on a happy voice.

"So, something super amazing happened. Maybe that would help? Some good news? You always said a little goodness goes a long way, how we have to be kind to people so we can be a powerful force for good in the world. You said it comes back to us in unsuspecting forms. I finally told people at school about Muay Thai. Did you know there's a social group page run by the coaches for girl athletes at Connally? Even if it's not a school sport, you can join.

"They accepted me with gigantic, open arms. I could've had a lot of back and forth support over the years, a lot more girls for me to talk to about wins and fails and the horrible and funny stuff that comes along with being an athlete.

"But then they really stepped up, without me even having to ask, to help raise the rest of the money for USMTO. I know you and Mama tell me over and over not to worry about expenses and money, but I've known for a long time that our bank account has been drained. I was okay with not going, I really was. I'd get the chance another time."

I took his hand in mine, remembering times when I'd been sick with a cold or the flu, and yeah it was nothing like what

Papa went through, but him holding my hand always made me feel better. It made me feel safer. His warm hand on mine, almost twice the size, made the aches and pains and fevers shuffle away. There was absolutely no comparable feeling to having a father care for his little girl.

Back then, I didn't know how sick he really was. He was just Papa. He was the one who protected me and raised me and played with me and tried to help me with math and then laughed alongside me because neither of us got it.

So, I imagined that holding his hand . . . maybe it would make him feel the way he had made me feel. Or maybe it would make him feel the way he'd felt holding my hand. That he was always there, always my shelter, always the stronger one.

He didn't respond, but I knew he could hear me. And he needed to hear all the good words right now.

"No one at school knows *why* we don't have money, but the moment I mentioned the costs being beyond my reach, the girls took it from there. They came up with all sorts of cool and fast and effective ways to raise money. I'm like a celebrity now."

I sniffled, all too and unfortunately aware of how the excitement took a dropkick in the gut and dragged me back to the reality of everything. "You'd be proud, Papa."

I looked over my shoulder, wondering what kept Mama so long, and startled to find her standing at the door, mute, and teary-eyed. Those sliding glass doors sure were silent.

I stood and met her halfway, hugging her. "What's wrong? What did they say?"

She shook her head and wiped her cheeks. "Same as before. They'll run tests and scans."

Which meant any minute, someone from X-ray would come up and scan his chest. Then someone from lab would come up and, I kid you not, drain his blood into two containers that looked like glass soda bottles for a blood culture. Then every few hours, someone would draw his blood. And every few hours, nurses would check his vitals and give him medicine through his IV and change his IV bags often so he stayed hydrated. And then the doctors would consult with specialists for other tests and more invasive steps and yadda yadda yadda.

As was the deal with Papa's relapses. It was a giant crap circle.

"It'll be okay, Mama."

"Is all that true?" she asked.

"What?"

"Papa *is* proud. We *both* are. I heard what you said. All that about your classmates and fundraising."

"Yeah. I was going to tell you when I got home. We'll get the money now, for me to go if . . ."

She turned my chin away from Papa to face her. "You're going to USMTO. No matter what happens here, you're going. Papa wants it that way, and so do I."

"How could I even?"

"Because you're strong and worked hard for this and because you'll fight in remembrance of Papa if the worst comes." She pressed her lips together, as if wanting to take back those last few words.

"How could I possibly fight in that state of mind?"

"Your focus. Muay Thai has always been your focus for hard times. Whatever sadness or anger or loneliness you might face, harness it. If nothing else, remember that Papa wants it that way. To try your best, not hold back, huh?"

I nodded but forced myself to imagine that Papa would be in the audience at USMTO watching every hit and cheering me on. He hadn't been able to travel far or go into crowds, but in my dream, he was always right there beside the action.

"There's nothing more we can do until the test results come in. There will be more in the morning," she said.

"He has to stay overnight?"

"He has to stay until further notice. Take the car home. Do your training and chiropractor and massage appointments, study. I'll update you."

"No. I'll stay here with you."

"Kareena—"

"I'm not going anywhere."

"This is not going to interrupt your routine."

"*This* is my family, the most important thing to me. And it's not an interruption." I cocked my chin at the backpack slumped over the bench. "I can study there, do lunges in the halls, weights and treadmill in the PT room like last time, and pick up on my appointments as usual."

"You're stubborn."

I dropped my head back for a second and stared at the weird ceiling tiles before saying, "We go through this every time, Mama. This is not an interruption." My hands landed on my hips, my tone getting a little sharper. "Just like a surprise punch or kick in a fight, a fighter must modify and redirect while staying on point. This is a surprise swing in life, and we are adaptable."

She shook her head. "When did you stop listening to me?"

"Are you upset?"

She placed an arm around my shoulder, gently squeezed, and plopped a little kiss on my head. "I'll never be upset with you wanting to take care of our family, beta."

TWENTY

The doctor gestured for Mama to sit on the chair beside Papa's bed and said, "We'd like to discuss the results of your husband's tests."

She nodded but looked to me when she said, "Kareena, can you give us a minute?"

My legs turned to stone and my tongue itched with the desire to deny her. I wanted to hear what the results were, straight from the doctor's mouth, not sugarcoated for what Mama thought was best for me.

Her sunken, red-streaked eyes and droopy expression were the only things that made me leave. She thought I was fragile, but she was wrong. Maybe I was wrong to think she was fragile too. But today was not the day to test her.

I walked into the hallway and gently closed the door almost all the way, keeping my hand on the door latch, and quietly listened.

"Because he'd gone septic last time, we immediately started a twenty-four-hour blood culture to rule out another blood infection," the doctor said. "His kidney specialist will be in later. We're checking all that as well. We're concerned he may have hyperkalemia, so we're testing his potassium levels. Several IV bags to flush out his system. Blood sugars, X-rays, CT scan to come shortly."

Then he went over Papa's most recent results. We didn't know anything definitive yet.

I sighed and quietly closed the door all the way.

The halls were barren without a soul in sight, until the nurses' station came into view. The desk bustled with scrub-clad nurses and doctors and secretaries. One of the doctors, whom I recognized as part of the team working on Papa, spoke with a man in a gray suit. Beside him stood Amit.

The doctor handed the suited man a flash drive. The man turned to Amit and said a few words, handing him the information. Amit deposited it into his backpack. He was as focused on the conversation as the other two men. No wonder he dressed so nice when he was around similarly dressed people.

Amit glanced over and saw me. We both froze. I didn't really want him to know why we were here. It just seemed all too personal to tell someone outside of the select few who knew. But then his expression turned almost painful when he looked down at the papers on the counter in front of him, as if he had connected the dots and knew. But no way could he know. There was a law that protected patient confidentiality.

A nurse approached me and asked, "Do you need any help?"

"Sort of. I was wondering how much this visit will cost."

She watched me more empathetically than pitifully. "It depends on a lot of factors, including insurance. I'm sure your mother—"

"She won't tell me. Maybe you can't, either, but I need a ballpark figure," I said dryly, annoyed that every adult around here tried to protect me by evading facts. "Not even for my dad personally. Just a person in ICU who needs this much attention and treatment and tests."

She sighed, as if she understood that my quiet demand

meant more than just numbers. "About five thousand a day. Less with insurance, of course."

Not if you have a bad premium and a cap on payout, lady. That much, I did know. Whatever little money Mama had in the bank had to go here.

"You know, we also do write-offs for certain cases. I can have a financial adviser speak with your parents," she added.

"Total write-off?"

"Not likely, but maybe."

"Covering meds and return visits?"

She shook her head.

"Thanks. Any help is a lot of help."

"Okay. Let me know if you need anything else."

"Kareena?" Amit asked, coming to stand in front of me as the nurse returned to the station.

"Hi. What are you doing here?" I inquired, hoping to sound chill.

"Helping my uncle with some work stuff. Are you all right?" he asked quickly, panicked.

I tried to relax, tried to ease the tension out of my face and fists. "For the most part. Are you here for your mystery work project?"

"Yeah."

"Wonder if I ask him what you're working on, if he'd tell me." I cocked my chin at the man in the nice suit.

"No. But I'd get into a lot of trouble if you did that."

I eyed the man, his head bowed over a tablet as doctors spoke to him. "He looks important."

He glanced back at him. "My uncle is CEO."

"That's cool that you're working with fam." Not to mention fam who was way up on the pay grade.

"It's not a hand-out, though. I got something he needs."

He turned to me again and changed the subject. "What are you doing here? Is everything okay?"

"Visiting someone." He didn't need to know. As much as I liked Amit, really, *really* liked him . . . he was new. Maybe fleeting. In any case, he wasn't Lily level.

"Hope they're all right. Not your parents?"

"Kareena," Mama called from the edge of the corridor, signaling me over.

"My mom and I are visiting someone. I have to go. See you at school?"

"Yeah. See ya." He gave a worried half smile, as if he knew. Maybe. Maybe my face gave it all away.

I turned and headed straight for Mama. Her attention fell away to the doctor who had been conversing with Amit's uncle. He called her over to the station and I froze, realizing that both men spoke to Mama and Amit stood between me and them with a worried frown.

He didn't pry but awkwardly stayed in place while Mama nodded and shook hands with Amit's uncle before taking a packet from him. She returned without giving Amit another glance. She probably didn't recognize him.

"What was that about?" I asked when we closed the door to Papa's room behind us.

"Census survey." She stuffed the packet into her purse.

"What did the doctor say about the results?"

"Still to come."

I side-hugged her and she patted my head. "He's stable. Why don't you go home and shower and get some sleep? I'll stay here."

She flipped through the packet and sternly replied, "No."

"Please?"

She mulled over the practicality of resting versus pacing a

hospital room dead tired. Finally, she agreed, "Hah. Call me if anything happens. If the doctor says anything, if Papa wakes up, if he gets worse."

Just like that? She never left him except to actually go to work. But as she pretended to focus on the packet, her lips quivered and her hands shook. Maybe she just needed a moment to herself. Maybe she just needed to vent. Alone. I totally got that. I had Muay Thai that helped me to channel my emotions. Mama was so busy . . . I didn't know what she had.

"Nothing will happen tonight," I promised.

Mama nodded and I followed her out to make sure she got to her car safely and that she actually left.

"Text me when you get home," I told her.

Mama closed her door, started up the car, and off she went.

My phone beeped with a message.

I'm here! And my brother dropped me off, so I have no way of getting home. You're stuck with me.

I smiled and met Lily in the front lobby. She didn't spring in with her brilliance and cheer, but solemnly wrapped an arm around my shoulder.

"Do you want me in the room, or shall I stalk the waiting room?"

"You can come inside the room, but guess who's here? Or was here." I pressed the button in the elevator for the fourth floor.

"Family?"

"Keep guessing."

"Ugh. Saanvi? Want me to kick her butt? I can do that, you know. With no formal training."

I giggled, picturing Lily taking Saanvi out with one slap. Don't get me wrong, I didn't underestimate Lily's ability to punch like a fighter if she wanted to, but I liked to imagine that Saanvi couldn't take a hit and a slap was all it took to take her out.

The doors opened and we stepped out into the all-too familiar wing of the hospital where everyone probably knew me by now. Turning the corner, Lily guessed, "Amit?"

"Yeah. How'd you—?"

"Hey," he said, suddenly in front of us.

"You look nice. Hope you're not here because of bad news," Lily commented.

He shook his head, keeping eyes on her and away from me. "No. Helping my uncle with some work."

"Cool. Is he a doctor?"

"Medical stuff, but not a doctor."

Lily quickly, albeit politely, added, "We better get going. See you at school."

"See you in class." He faced me, his expression serious. "Is your dad okay?"

A panic surged through me with a dozen questions. Was he that nosy? Did the staff not uphold privacy law? Or did his job allow him to dig into whichever patient file he wanted? In any and all cases, it was a vehement betrayal of privacy. I was not ready for him to know this part of my life. It was not for anyone to know. "What the hell?"

"What?" he asked, taken aback.

With gritted teeth, I asked, "How did you know?"

"Um, the packet that the doctor gave your mom. I know that packet. It's for seriously sick patients."

Hot breath escaped my lips in a guttural noise. "That is not your business."

I stomped past him, but he caught up, explaining, "I'm sorry. I didn't pry, but I was standing right there and noticed."

"Still not your business," I snapped, stopping dead in my tracks and pivoting on my heels so that he walked into me.

His hands landed on my waist and kept me from tumbling backward. I wanted to smack them away, but he had me against his chest, releasing me the moment he saw my anger.

He backed away. "I'm not trying to wriggle into your personal life, but I wouldn't notice someone I know at the hospital and not ask if they're doing okay. I'm not asking because I'm nosy. I'm asking because I care."

I scoffed and turned from him, because seriously, how else could I react? Papa's health wasn't something that I wanted to discuss with others. I didn't know how else to handle someone getting this close to the truth. How did one tell their friend that their father could die any day now?

Amit took my elbow and drew me close, speaking into my ear, "You don't have to walk away from me."

"You act like you have the right to know it all. You don't."

"I know that I don't, and you don't have to tell me. But you don't have to stomp away, either. Friends can be silent, in the dark, but still supportive."

I cocked an eyebrow.

"I can sit with you, wait with you, and you don't have to say a word."

I gulped as everything and everyone around us disintegrated.

"That's what friends are for," he gently added.

Except Amit Patel wasn't *just* a friend. He had been at some point, for a short time, and quickly evolved into much more. But my brain cells couldn't handle anything else that scared me. Just like computer programming, too many unknown variables created a glitch. One glitch could easily lead to another and bring everything down.

"Okay," he replied softly. "I'll go. But you can text or call anytime. And I will be right there."

He turned and walked away. I clenched my eyes shut for a few seconds. So much of me told myself to let him go and keep things bottled in this corner of my world. The fewer people who knew, the fewer who reminded me of Papa when I saw them. On the other hand, when I saw Mama and Lily, I didn't think of only the bad things. I thought of a lot of amazing things and they made the situation better.

"Wait," I croaked, unsure if he could even hear me as he made his way down the hallway. But Amit had superpower hearing and turned back.

We stood toe-to-toe, and for some reason, adding him to the select few who knew these deepest troubles calmed my derailing emotions. That was too important to dismiss.

I rubbed my arm and forced the conversation. "My mom and dad think they're protecting me by not telling me what the doctor tells them. And the doctors won't talk to me because I'm a minor and she told them not to." My voice cracked and I hated myself for that.

He pressed his lips together. His fingers twitched and his hand made the slightest move, as if he were naturally inclined to touch me but held back.

I let out a rough, irritated sigh. Not at him, but at this whole thing. How did people do this? Deal open heartedly and lean on others to take the brunt of some of their burdens? I bit my lip to keep from getting emotional, but then Amit touched my cheek and I almost lost my crap.

"It's coming," I said, my voice weak and trembling.

"Not today, though, okay?" he said. "Where'd your mom go?"

"She went home for a bit. She usually never goes home."

"Are you two staying all night?"

I shook my head and sighed. "No. They don't let us stay all night, but my mom will probably try to sleep in the visitor's room."

"I can give you a ride later, if you need. I can stay. If you want."

"Lily's here, so . . ."

He didn't look over my shoulder at Lily, who waited at a nearby corner. "I'd like to stay and be here for you."

I opened my mouth to tell him "no," but the way he looked, his focus still on our hands, all innocent and kind, made me crack. He really did care. How could I not lean on him for some extra support? "For a little while."

A little while turned into a few hours.

"You should go home, Lily," I told her after the sun set.

"I don't have a car, remember?" she said.

"Maybe Amit can take you home?" I was tired and wanted to sleep, even if only for a few minutes.

"I'll just sit here," she insisted.

"I want to stay too," Amit added.

"No. I appreciate it, I really do. But they have different rules for ICU. Can't have too many people here, and they ask us to leave at ten."

"Amit and I can walk the hall and get anything you or your parents need."

"That's super sweet, but—"

"But what?"

"It's Thursday. You got school tomorrow."

"We get kicked out at ten anyway. That's not late for a school night. Besides, forget class. You need us. We're best friends. You're stuck with me."

"And this is what friends do," Amit added.

Lily purposefully nodded once, a final, *There ya go. We're staying. Deal with it.*

I sighed, hoping it was more begrudging than not so they would give us this moment as a family without outside eyes. But nope. They were true-blue friends, and I couldn't hate them for that.

Lily swiped in for a sneak hug, extracting a laugh, one filled with gratitude.

"Do you want to talk?" she muttered in my ear.

I hugged her back and whispered, "No."

"Do you want something to eat or drink?" Amit asked after we pulled away and Lily went back to the chair.

"Nah."

"Quiet?" he asked.

"Yeah."

"Gotcha," Lily said with a wink.

Amit sat beside me on the bench seat in Papa's room, and Lily took the chair. The nurse brought extra blankets and pillows and it was just like any other sleepover. Or it would have been if Papa's life didn't hang in the balance.

We kept quiet most of the evening to keep the atmosphere calm and peaceful for him. Eventually, Amit and Lily went to the cafeteria for food, but my stomach couldn't take anything in. Amit brought back a slice of pecan pie anyway.

Lily plopped down beside me and tucked her legs beneath her. Amit sat on the chair, his elbows on the table, and slid the small plate toward me. I eyed the slice.

"You know you want some."

I gave in with a roll of my eyes. "How'd you know?"

"What are the chances of being Southern and not liking pecan pie?"

The first bite was always the best: sticky, thick, sweet filling with a giant pecan crunch on top and near soggy crust on the bottom. "Whenever we would fill up gas or take a break on long rides, Papa always bought me those little packaged pecan pies from the convenience store. I loved them so much that my mom started to buy them from the grocery store whenever they were in season. Once we'd tried to make one from scratch. Was a total disaster. The bag of leftover pecans was good, though."

"Yeah, I know."

I quirked an eyebrow and he indicated Lily, who shrugged and said, "I gave him the honor of bringing back a slice."

"It's good," I admitted. "Did you guys get a piece?"

The slice wasn't huge and dwindled down to a corner. I stuffed the last bite into my mouth when Amit replied, "It was the last slice they had."

Our eyes made contact and he smiled warmly as I gulped down the last piece.

We read and checked social media on our phones to pass the time. Lily swaddled herself in a green blanket and fell asleep for a good minute. She was the type of person who could sleep anywhere, anytime, and in any position. I was sort of envious, to be honest.

Amit sat beside me on the bench and tossed a blanket over us and pressed his arm against mine as we watched silly videos on his phone with the sound turned low. As sleep prowled closer and closer, my head fell against his shoulder but it was too heavy to move. He rested his head over mine and we sank into the bench.

I must've dozed off at some point because when I came to, my head was snug against the pillow at the end of the bench, my legs stretched to the other side, and a blanket was over me. Lily quietly played on her phone from the chair. The still mass of blankets beside me on the floor must've been Amit.

TWENTY-ONE

"Kareena, beta?" Mama gently shook my shoulder, rousing me from a groggy, heavy sleep.

I groaned and pried my eyelids open. They were so heavy and sticky, the eyelashes kissing each other like tomorrow would never come. Yawning, I sat up and contorted my face. It hurt. Sleeping on my side on a barely cushioned bench left a crick in my neck and a deep soreness in my right cheek and jaw.

"What's wrong?"

"Nothing," Mama replied and handed me a cup of orange cinnamon tea. It smelled like autumn.

I took a sip as she explained, "Everything is stable. I had a nice shower but could not sleep at home, not without your Papa. You go home and shower and sleep in your bed."

"No—"

"*Choop*," she softly chided. "Go home. Everything will be fine, hah?"

I nodded, although I was fairly certain neither one of us believed her.

She rubbed my shoulder. "We've discussed this before. No matter what, you concentrate on your grades, your mentality, and your sport. Use them as an outlet. We move forward, always. We do not wallow or feel sorry for ourselves."

I nodded mechanically.

"And take them with you." She jerked her chin first at Lily, who gave a slight wave from the door. Then Mama cocked her chin at the lightly snoring mass between a pile of hospital blankets beside me. "He's tired. Poor child. Let him take you home. He's a very nice boy."

I didn't respond, but instead pulled down the green blanket. Beneath, Amit slept in a scrunched position with an arm dangling off the side. He looked so sweet and utterly close to creeping all the way into my heart.

"Amit," I said louder than how Mama had spoken to me. When he didn't move, I carefully tugged his shoulder back. His dark-brown eyes flickered open, streaked red with sleep.

He offered a tired smile and asked, "Are you okay?"

"Yeah. My mom wants us to go home."

He sat up and asked her, "Are you sure, Auntie? We can—"

"Go home, beta. Your parents will be worried and there's no need for you to sleep here, on the floor of all places."

"Can you take me and Lily home?" I asked him.

He cleared the sleep out of his throat. "Yeah, of course."

We folded the blankets and set them in the corner with the pillows on top. Amit and Lily thanked Mama for the tea she'd given them and off we went, ever so slowly. Mama sat beside Papa on the bed and squeezed his hand as the door to his room gently closed behind us.

"Are you all right?" Amit asked inside the elevator.

I sipped the tea. Mama made it extra sweet, just the way I liked it. "No."

The quiet clenched around us.

"I wish I could help," he muttered.

"There's nothing we can do. Medicine can only do so much, only work so fast." The best we could hope for was that Papa hadn't slipped into total renal failure or, if he'd gone septic again, that we caught it in time before system failure.

"How long has this been going on?"

"The last few years. Worse over time. The end is inevitable. We all end up the same, you know? We know it's coming soon, and we're prepared," I croaked, but clenched my jaw to harden myself.

"Doesn't make it any easier."

"You have us," Lily said, her voice as smooth as velvet and just as soft.

Tears burned in my eyes. They couldn't fall because once they did, they might never stop. I glared at the screen above the buttons on the elevator wall as the numbers went down to G level.

In the moderately lit parking garage, Amit unlocked his car and opened the doors for both Lily and me. She sat in the back while I sat in the front. I could barely keep my eyes open, but we managed to get home safely and stumbled into the house.

"Y'all can sleep in my room if you want, or in the living room," I offered.

"Let me call my mom and ask. I'm pretty sure she's okay with it," Lily replied and slid to the couch with her phone to her ear. Her parents usually let her spend the night when they knew my dad was in the hospital. As long as she checked in and had her homework and verified with my mom. They were pretty awesome that way, and I didn't know what I'd do without Lily.

"It's okay if your parents won't let you stay here," I told Amit, although I wished he could.

He shrugged and looked off into the corner for a second, like oh, well. "They think I'm working."

Lily hopped off the couch. "My mom said yes once she

called your mom to ask if it's okay. Wherever you want us. Are you going to bed?" She yawned.

All this yawning was making me yawn. "I'm going to clean and do laundry and then shower."

"How about you eat and shower and we clean?" Amit suggested, casting a hopeful glance at Lily.

"Tell us what needs to be done," she said. "I know your laundry room. Just the clothes there?"

"Y'all don't have to—"

"Nah, but we want to," she intervened.

"That's so nice of you."

"What else?" Amit asked. On his way to the kitchen, he tidied up the throw blankets and pillows on the couch. "Kitchen cleanup?"

"Okay. Let me get some clothes from my parents' room and towels, and I'll throw them in the hamper." I jogged through the rooms and returned to the middle room with arms full of used towels and random pieces of clothing that Mama had probably tossed in a hurry.

The laundry room smelled of lavender fields before I even reached Lily. She had one load going and offered, "I'll vacuum the house and sweep and mop. Amit can go through the fridge for outdated food. Anything he should definitely keep?"

I shook my head. "There's not much in there anyway. The house isn't that bad, guys."

"It'll keep us busy, and your mom can come home to a sparkling clean house. I know that makes my mom feel better when she's running around or stressed. We can do a grocery run in the morning too. Go take a shower. He'll have something ready for you to eat."

I couldn't help it and sprang myself into Lily, muffling her laughter with a bear hug. "Thank you."

"Attack hugs are the best."

Grabbing sweatpants and a decent shirt and bra, I headed for the bathroom. The hum of the vacuum faded behind the closed door. Hot water steamed the mirror before my clothes were off. I couldn't scrub hard enough or keep tears from streaming down my face.

Alone and with time to think, to take it all in, to confront reality and envision Papa passing, of trying to console Mama, of never seeing his face again or hearing his voice was more than my heart could bear. It broke.

I slid down into the corner of the tub and crouched below the cascading water, my hands on top of my head, my fingers laced.

It took ten minutes to shower and about another ten just to cry it out. Water muffled the sobs and disguised the tears, but nothing repaired breaking hearts.

After what seemed like forever, I turned the faucet off, letting the steam dissipate. I dried off, dressed, blow-dried my hair, and then slipped into warm, comfy sweats—the same shade of dark-green as the school colors. My top was thick but worn, faded pink. My socks were striped red and white. Who cared if my outfit was mismatched?

The vacuum had been turned off and put back into the utility closet beside the laundry room. The gentle thrum of the washer played and so did the dryer from an earlier load left in the wash.

I walked through my parents' room, now spotless, and even my own room had been tidied. The living room was pristine and the kitchen shinier than my best cleaning days.

I took in a deep breath filled with something mouthwatering. Amit and Lily sat at the small dining table, hunched over food.

"There you are!" Lily exclaimed. "I'm starving here."

I slipped into a chair in between them. "You should've eaten. What is this?"

"Chef Amit insisted that we wait. I guess . . ."

Amit grinned. "It's nothing special, just soup."

"We had stuff for this?"

"Yeah. Some broth, noodles, and frozen veggies. Hope it's not too bland."

I blew on a spoonful and chewed on a piece of spinach. "Nah, this is amazing. Simple but perfect." Nothing like comfort food.

"Yeah, thanks," Lily muttered around her bite. She inhaled the contents and went for seconds, but Amit and I stopped when we finished and watched her.

"What?" she asked. "You're not hungry?"

"Good for now," I replied.

When she finished, Amit packed the leftovers and washed dishes while Lily and I started the second dryer load and folded laundry from the load Mama must've started earlier today.

"He's amazing," she said.

I side-eyed her.

"And totally into you."

"Now's not the best time to get googly over a boy, ya know?"

"Just saying. More support doesn't hurt. Distractions don't hurt."

"I don't want to associate either of you with what might be the worst time of my life."

"You got it wrong. You'll see us and find both happiness and sadness, support and relief. We're the shoulders you cry on so your mom can cry on yours. You got that?"

"You're demanding, aren't you?"

"Like you didn't know that." She winked. "Don't even try to push us away. We're on you like white on rice."

I laughed. "Original."

"Like Amit on Kareena?"

My face burned. "Shh. If he's a good friend, he won't use this situation to his advantage. In fact, if I feel like he's even leaning that way, I'll push him out of my life like that."

"It would be horrible if he did that, but he doesn't seem like that sort of guy."

"You never know these days. Dev didn't seem like the type of guy to sit around and let his sister rip me apart, but here we are."

She scowled. "You should've punched both of them."

"I will not use my power for evil."

"Did Amit tell you that he's been going with me to find sponsors to raise money for the Open?"

I stared so hard at her as the words realigned themselves in my brain. They still didn't make sense. I shook my head and stuttered, "Wait, what? You've been going out sponsor-hunting without me? And with Amit?"

She smiled a little shadily. "He asked me about it a while back. You'd mentioned it to him."

Had I? Oh! That night when we first kissed. Was that why he said things would work out? Because he had planned on helping out?

I could not stop from smiling as Lily nudged me. "See?" she said. "He's a good guy. Not many boys out there willing to make time and actually walk business to business asking random and total strangers to give up some money."

My chest fluttered. God. I wanted to . . . I wanted to march into the kitchen and just kiss him for this. "I don't even know what to say."

"Nothing. You don't have to say anything. This is what friends do."

I pressed my lips together, almost biting them. Wow. I had some freaking amazing friends then, didn't I?

"You don't need to worry about fundraising right now. It's not the type of distraction you need."

I groaned. "There is nothing that could distract me right now."

"You know what is a distraction? Prom."

Ugh. Really? That thing was coming up. Dances weren't for me. One, I couldn't dance well. Two, it was weird trying to find a date. Three, it was weird showing up without a date. Four, I'd rather just go to the movies or a friend's house. Five, the list could literally go on and on. "Never."

"You've never been to a school dance."

"I don't feel comfortable dancing in front of other people. And dates. My mom wouldn't let me have a date, and you're going with Jared."

"Jared can go solo, then."

"You won him in the auction. And if memory serves correctly, you've had a thing for him since last summer."

"Which is why me cutting him loose should prompt you to go, if nothing else, rather than feeling bad for me."

"I'll think about it. It's not on my mind at the moment."

"That's the point. The Open is stressful. Your dad, your grades, college, all that is stress. Plan for something that has no meaning to you, like prom, and let that fill your head."

"Maybe."

We each took stacks of laundry and put away the clothes into their respective places. The three of us met in the living room where Amit patted wet hands against his jeans.

"Thanks for everything," I told him.

"No worries. You should get some sleep, though? It's almost midnight."

"Yeah. I don't sleep much, but I should try anyway."

He rubbed his palms together but kept his distance. He looked to Lily. "You're staying over, right?"

"Yes."

"Good. Okay. I'll let you get some rest." He walked past me and into the foyer. "Please, please, call or text if either of you need anything. Even if it's five in the morning and you want milk and cereal."

I leaned against the wall beside the front door, my arms crossed at my chest. "Thanks. Um. You know, you can sleep over. If you want."

His cheeks turned a rosy shade of pink. "I think our parents would flip."

"Lily's here."

He checked his watch, one of those smart watches that connected to his phone and updated him on texts, emails, phone calls, steps, and probably the current temperature of the moon. "I'm supposed to be working. That's the whole arrangement with my parents. They don't bother me about being home late or out all night because they know it's how I work."

"Oh! Oh my god, are you going to get in trouble?"

He shook his head vigorously. "My uncle knows. I told him I needed to drive around to think for a bit."

"Go. Lily's here. It's all good."

"Okay. But seriously, let me know if you need anything."

"We will."

He slipped on his shoes and I locked the door after him, watching him through the slit in the blinds as he walked to his car. The headlights blinked and the alarm beeped. The blinds sprang back together and I met Lily on the couch.

"We can put on a movie and make popcorn until we fall asleep?" she suggested.

"That sounds nice."

Before we set out to look for a movie, we dragged blankets and pillows into the living room for our sleepover nest. We'd had lots of sleepovers when Papa was in the hospital, but we'd had even more for the fun of it. Lily had been right. I didn't associate everything with Papa's health negatively. Getting comfy in pajamas, building a blanket nest in the living room, and staying up all night with a movie was nostalgic and warm—all the good feels and none of the bad ones.

Someone knocked on the door. We shot into battle mode. Even though Amit had left not even two minutes ago, one never knew.

We crept to the foyer, where Lily grabbed the baseball bat from the coat closet beside the front door. I snuck a peak through the blinds and slouched. "It's Amit."

"Still . . ." she joked, her grip rubbing around the handle of the bat like she was preparing to swing in a softball game.

"Girl, put that away."

She groaned and lowered the bat. "Right, because you can defend us without a bat. I forgot."

She dragged the bat back to the closet and I opened the door.

Amit, flushed and adjusting the backpack strap on his shoulder, said, "Hi."

"Hi. Did you forget something?" I looked behind me. I didn't remember him bringing much inside.

He replied in a rush, "I can do my work from my computer. You know, that is, if you want me to stay."

Lily grinned in my periphery.

My heart palpitated. Of course I wanted him to stay.

"I'll leave before your mom gets home so she doesn't freak. My parents think I'm at work. There will be no leakage of info for anyone to speculate or gossip, promise."

"What if they ask your uncle if you're really there?"

He shrugged. "I'll deal with that if they ask."

"I don't want you to get into trouble."

"It's not a problem. Your name will never come up."

"I can't believe your parents let you stay out all night."

"What am I doing? Wreaking havoc? Valedictorian while working? There's no time to get into trouble. Is it okay with you if I stay too?"

Lily pulled the door back as I said, "Okay, but only if you're sure that you won't get into trouble."

"Nah." He stepped inside, locked the door, and promptly removed his shoes.

"We were going to fall asleep watching a movie," Lily said as she dug through the DVDs.

"Will you be able to concentrate on work?" I asked, becoming more and more aware that an actual, factual boy was about to spend the night in my house.

"Yeah. I can always go to the kitchen, but noise doesn't bother me."

Lily held up a few DVDs, at which I nodded to the last one, a ridiculous comedy that made me laugh even on the worst days.

Lily went to the kitchen and Amit dropped his bag beside the recliner.

I jerked forward to stop him. "Wait. Don't sit there."

"Oh, okay." He moved to the couch beside me. "Sorry."

"That's fine. It's my dad's chair," I said softly, my gaze lingering on the recliner. It was just the right level of firmness, the right height, the most comfortable, and it let Papa lean back to nap so he didn't have to go all the way to the bedroom. It was also situated perfectly in the living room where the glare of the sun couldn't quite reach if the curtains were left open, where the vent wouldn't push dust directly on him, where the breeze of the fan would still reach him, where he had a good view of the TV and easiest access to the kitchen and bathroom.

Amit offered a sympathetic smile. "No worries."

Lily returned with two bowls of popcorn. She set the larger one on the coffee table and proceeded to plop down on the floor with a pillow and a throw blanket.

"Do you want to sit on the couch? I can go to the table," Amit said to her.

"Nah. I like the floor for movies. I can't stretch out up there."

While the movie played, Lily covered her mouth to keep from cackling. Maybe she did that because Amit was here or maybe because she didn't want to laugh so hard under the circumstances. I kept my laughter down too. In part because Amit was sitting so close to me and working, but mainly because it felt wrong to laugh, all things considered.

I pulled my legs to my chest, curled up beneath a comforter, and nonchalantly peered over at the computer screen. "What are you doing for work?"

"The program," he replied.

"Says the guy who needed tutoring for computer science."

He kept his eyes downcast and forced a half smile. Interesting. Maybe he never needed tutoring, but was purposely failing? Or maybe he was embarrassed about the small things he didn't understand in comp-sci when he was obviously so smart.

He popped in a flash drive and worked some magic, then popped in a new one.

The first movie ended and Lily had long since fallen asleep

on the floor. Amit continued to work, quiet and in the zone as he fiercely typed and scribbled stuff into his notebook. I put in another DVD, the sequel and equally hilarious, and went to Papa's chair. I reclined it and pulled the throw blanket to my chin. No one sat here except Papa. We bought this chair specifically for him. But sitting here made me feel like a little girl on his lap. It smelled like him, part dad smell and part medicine cabinet smell, combined and oddly comforting.

I glanced at Amit to see if he was still fiercely working but caught him watching me thoughtfully. The corner of his mouth curled up, crooked and cute. I turned away from him, toward the TV, buried the lower part of my face under the blanket, and closed my eyes.

I tried to sleep. I really did. My thoughts wandered but I forced them to follow along with the movie behind dark lids. Epic fail.

Irritated, I decided to sit up and stretch, maybe go to my room and do some exercises.

Lily had stretched out on the floor, no longer on her side. Amit had fallen asleep too. He lay on the couch, facing me, with the comforter to his waist. His laptop and notebook sat on the coffee table.

It would be a gross invasion of privacy to log on, but I'd seen the notebook before. It was the same one from our first evening study session at Lily's house.

Carefully taking the notebook, I sank back into the recliner and read through the programming. It was massive, countless pages. They were the same scribbles I'd seen last time, but now there were also newer fragments and erased sections that had been scribbled over with different segments. I couldn't figure out what the program was for unless I started from the beginning, and that was assuming this was the entire thing. It wasn't. It was written in scraps, in either nonconsecutive intervals or portions that didn't go to the same program. Maybe that was why he wrote it on paper.

It took me the rest of the night to read through and piece it together, flipping back and forth. I watched Amit from over the ruffled lip of pages as it dawned on me. Amit wasn't losing it or weirdly consumed by this ever-growing accumulation of coding fragments. He was a freaking genius. All these parts that had appeared in his head from thin air formed a cohesive program, one that could actually work if he knew how to align them. A long, winding, artistic compilation of strands and loops and variables led to a brilliant culmination that even I didn't see coming. It was as if someone had written an intricate story in nonlinear fragments that was so comprehensive, they themselves didn't know how to glue it together correctly.

Morning light crested over the bent blind slats and soaked the room in warm light. Something about morning made everything better. A new day, a new hope, the fact that we made it through another night was nothing short of a miracle these days.

Amit stirred, shifting onto his back and raising his hand above his head. His eyes opened into slits and our gazes met. His lowered to the notebook in my hand and he lurched up.

"Are you reading that again?" he asked, panicked.

I quickly placed it onto the coffee table. "I couldn't sleep."

"I don't want anyone seeing that." He stared at the notebook like he wanted to snatch it.

"Is this about the work project that you said you'd tell me about?"

If Amit had ever looked upset, now was definitely it. Those slightly furrowed brows and flaring nostrils and pressed lips.

He was cute even when mad. But I didn't want him to be mad, least of all at me. I swallowed hard and braced for his anger.

He stuffed the notebook and laptop into his bag and muttered, "I better get going."

I hurried off the recliner and sat beside him, trapping him against the couch arm. "Not before you tell me about work."

He paused.

"Because one, you told me you'd tell me. Two, I need to know why you were at the hospital and how you knew about my dad. You know so much about me, all these ups and downs, and I want to know what this huge thing is. You can't tell me about it because you'll get into trouble? Your parents let you stay out all night? Your uncle looks like he runs some major corp. And you're a key component?"

He sighed and thought for a moment, but I wasn't going anywhere. "Promise you won't tell anyone?"

I nodded.

"I'm working on coding something that several big companies are trying to break into. They're trying to finish a similar program first, and there's rumor that they would steal ours if they could. Most people at the company don't know that I'm actually coding. They think it's an internship. My parents think that too. I always had trouble sleeping at night, and my uncle offered to let me work behind the scenes at his company. My parents knew I wasn't making a mess or slipping with my grades, so they agreed.

"Actually, they pushed me into it. They thought it would make my college application look even better, and then my actual resume when I start working. My uncle realized I'm better at programming than his top people, and he asked me to write some things. But I kept writing. I couldn't stop writing. And the project is so huge and life-changing, that it makes me feel like I'm losing my mind not figuring out the lost pieces." He clenched his jaw.

"Are you mad at me for reading it?"

"Sort of. Partially mad at you, but mainly with myself. It's frustrating being so close and not fixing it."

"It's a program for a major company. You can't expect to finish the entire thing."

He scoffed. "When your family and your community hammers it into your head that you're perfect and can do everything and should do everything, it's hard to accept something that isn't working out."

"Oh . . ."

He sucked in a breath and dragged his hand down his face, glaring at his backpack. "It's hard to fail when everyone expects so much from you. *Failure* takes on a whole new meaning. It's like . . . my parents just expect that I can do it all and if I don't, then it basically erases everything I've ever done. I hate that word."

Didn't I know it? Failure didn't come in the form of grades or college rejection letters. It came in missing out on the Open. On losing a chance to fund Papa's bills. Failure was . . . systematic organ failure. Total renal failure. Failure was my dad not getting medical treatment because we couldn't afford it. Failure was my dad dying.

I dragged my thoughts away from Papa and asked, "Why don't you want me to see the program?"

"It's not finished. It's all the chaos in my head."

"It's brilliant."

He froze. His big brown eyes twinkled with irritation and another wave of panic. "You understand it?"

I nodded.

"How? It's not complete; it's not even in order."

He may be a genius in coding, but I wasn't dumb when it came to programming. It was going to be my college major. He might've seen the world as coding fragments, but I understood them. "I see the gaps; I see how it should fit together. May I?"

"Now you ask?" he asked a little curtly.

"You gonna make me feel bad forever?" I shot back.

"At least more than five minutes." But he handed the notebook to me anyway.

I flipped it open to the third page and drew a circle around the center segment with my finger. "Typeof operate, third class of returns."

He initially shook his head and scoffed. "That's too simple—" But then he stared at my finger and the equations surrounding it. "It's simple," he repeated.

I rolled my eyes. "It's like you're calling me simplistic. I know I'm not the genius in pulling programs out of the air like you are, but dang, dude. Don't patronize me."

"No. No. I mean . . . you're right. That *does* work and it's so simple. I've been racking my head and digging into deep stuff to fix the gap. You just look at it once and know. You're the genius."

"Genius when it comes to simple fixes."

"It's medical programming. It's why I know about your dad."

"I don't want to talk about that."

There was a silent void that we'd suddenly fallen into. I chewed on the inside of my cheek and mindlessly flicked my fingernails. My brain wasn't working. I had questions, but I didn't care. Maybe it could be a distraction from Papa, but very few things could be *that* distracting.

"It really hurts me to know that you're in pain."

My lips trembled. Why did he have to say that? Why couldn't he just not talk about it like I'd asked?

"And I might get into a crapload of trouble for telling you, but I can't keep it all from you. I can't tell you exactly what this is, but if it works, it'll help sick people all over the world."

"Will it help my dad?"

He made a tormented wince and looked down at the notebook in my hands. "It's not done. It doesn't work yet." He clenched his eyes, as if "failing" to help with this project truly pained him. But I got it. He had to see sick people all the time. He knew how much more help they needed than what they were getting. He was going to be a part of something huge, of something way bigger than himself. And all he cared about was fixing it so it could hurry up and help people.

I sighed, annoyed with myself for even hoping a little extra. A thing like that would not be ready soon enough. "You know what? I'm tired and have to train while waiting to find out if my dad will recover." As soon as those words hit the air, my lips trembled.

Amit took the notebook away and hugged me.

Freaking frick. Because now the tears fell. I ugly cried so hard. I'd probably woken up Lily. And I might've accidentally bit Amit's shoulder to muffle my sobs.

···❮ TWENTY-TWO ❯···

Amit left the house before any signs of Mama's return with the understanding that we'd give each other some space unless I needed him. He had work and valedictorian status to lock down, and I had to focus on the big fights coming up. The living room was back to normal and there was no trace of a boy ever having spent the night.

"I can stay," Lily offered.

"And skip all the fun at school?"

She stuck out her tongue and crossed her eyes. "Can't wait to graduate."

"You'll be fine."

"But will you?" She crossed her arms and tapped a foot where we stood in the small foyer.

"Yeah. This isn't anything new."

"Doesn't mean it's anything easy."

"I have training and stuff to keep my mind off things. It's always been there to distract me. Thanks to the awesomeness of everyone at school, I know where I'll be two weeks from now."

"No matter what happens?"

"Nothing's going to happen." But if that optimism was more for her benefit or mine was uncertain.

"Can I do anything for you or your mom?"

"Nah. We got this."

"Anything I can do for your training? Pick up some groceries? Time you? Watch you do pull-ups while I sip on tea?"

"Sounds like fun, but I've got my playlist and earbuds and I'm ready to go. Thanks for everything, though. I really appreciate it."

Lily hugged me and then left.

I had plans. A long run, core workout, shadowboxing, hit the gym for more workouts and sparring exercises, and homework.

Yep. A long, fruitful, packed day.

I went to the bedroom to change, but the bed looked so inviting, all made-up with freshly laundered sheets and seductive whispers of slumber. Sitting for a second while changing into shorts wouldn't hurt.

Okay. Lying down for a minute to shimmy out of my sweats wouldn't hurt. But the bed was warm and soft, and I hadn't slept all night.

Just five minutes.

Five minutes, that was all.

My phone rang in my ear, muffled underneath a layer of pillow. Drowsily, I groaned. My eyelids fluttered open. The day was bright beyond the closed curtains, and the sunlight trickled through tiny spaces between the fabric.

Oh, lord. What time was it?

I shot up and snatched the phone. "Hello?" I rasped.

"Kareena? Why haven't you returned my messages?"

"Mama. I fell asleep. What's wrong? Is everything okay?" I asked in a panic.

"Yes. That's to say that nothing has changed."

I sighed, knowing this was the best we could hope for. Papa had only been admitted yesterday. The longest he'd ever stayed in the hospital was three weeks when he'd been septic and was on the verge of kidney failure. The shortest had been four days, but that was during his first bout years ago.

When Mama spoke, she was calm and collected. She didn't always keep it perfectly together. I could always tell when she was hiding bad news. But this time, the situation didn't seem too awful. Yet. "I don't expect him to be out for a few weeks, if he's worse than before."

"A few weeks, Mama? USMTO is in two weekends."

"I know. You'll go, remember, no matter what's happening here."

"But he's supposed to be there, he's supposed to watch."

"Beta, you know he was never going to be able to go. The traveling, the crowds."

"We could've driven there in a car. He could've watched from a private room, or on the TV in a hotel room."

"You know he can't go far from his doctors and hospital."

I crushed down despair. "I just hoped."

"We try for the best and do our best, and that's what you'll do. Why are you sleeping in the middle of the day? Shouldn't you be finishing up at the gym and going to your appointment?"

"Yeah. I didn't sleep last night."

"Kareena, this is not what we discussed."

"I'm sorry. I'm getting ready for my appointment now." I crawled out of bed and hurried to find my clothes still on the floor.

"Good."

"Are you going to work?" I asked as I changed into shorts.

"Yes. The hospital will call me if anything changes. I still have to pay bills."

I pressed my eyes together. Suck it up, buttercup. Time to get out of this daze and make ends meet. I needed first place, and I was going to get it. I needed to make it to the World Championships and the Olympics, and I would get there. I had to make them proud, especially Papa, to show that all these years had been fruitful and worthwhile. That they'd allowed me my passion and to excel. When the news broadcasters told my story, this would be a part of it. Adversity in its many forms. Mental setbacks, financial ones, physical ones, and emotional ones.

"You're going to stay here with Papa during USMTO?"

"Hah, beta," she replied.

I nodded once. "Good. We can't both be away. That's important."

"You're so understanding, my sweet girl, always have been. I'm leaving now. I'll be home in thirty minutes, enough time to change and go to work. Don't delay in your appointments, training, and studies," she said firmly.

"Yes, Mama. Your lunch and dinner will be in the fridge. The house is cleaned."

"You're much too good. Didn't know you were thirty already, taking care of a house and your mother at the same time."

I smiled. "Love you, Mama."

"Love you, too, beta. Now get going!"

"*Hah*," I grunted, mimicking her.

There was nothing better to keep the darkness away than filling my days with determination and hard work, blinders to block out distraction and rotting thoughts.

The next five days blended into one another. I trained more than ever, studied, took care of the house and Mama, making sure she had everything she needed without looking twice. Lily and I texted throughout the day and evening when we couldn't chat. Amit checked in on me and asked about Papa.

Same, I texted back.

Since you were busy, Lily filled me in on the sponsorships. We went out and got more. I know some guys.

I laughed. *What?*

Yeah. Turns out I have a good sales pitch. Throw in the Olympics and everyone wants a piece.

I grinned hard. That was *my* sales pitch. My heart grew bigger with an explosion of excitement and hope when he replied.

Does another two grand help?

I squeezed my eyes tight and chanted to myself: *Don't cry. Don't . . . like this dude even more than is logically possible.*

I shuddered out a breath and, with trembling fingers, managed to text back emojis only. Prayer hands. Cheesy smiley faces. And even . . . dare to do it . . . a smiley face with heart eyes.

Amit and Lily kept it up, dragging in sponsors to inch closer and closer to the final tally while I went to all the games and events where the school held fundraisers for me to get to USMTO. Anxiety was no joke. I was so close, and still so far. I didn't want to vent to Lily every time, and Mama had a lot going on. I needed to talk to Amit, but he gradually stopped returning texts and phone calls. Guessed he was busy too.

But I had to march on. This was crunch time.

We sold concessions and face painting and some girls did a henna booth. Even I'd gotten into it and had henna done on both hands. We had raffle tickets with big ole prizes that had been donated by the school. At the end of each event, the girls gave me the money. I counted and recounted and gave every dollar to Mama.

Last night's soccer game was the last fundraiser. Most of the money had come from the prom date auction . . . had to love hotties for sale. The rest came from bake sales, movie drives, and straight-up donations. But Kimmy had taken the announcer's microphone after her winning score and announced it was the last night for a formal donation.

"Bam," Kimmy said as she stood from the donation table and handed me the final two hundred dollars from the night.

I did the math in my head. Of course, I knew how much I needed. I needed a hundred more dollars to cover USMTO, including chiropractor appointments. But I didn't want to get too excited until I redid the numbers. I'd needed four grand, which was almost twice as much as we'd initially expected.

"We got it," I said, shocked. "We did it. We made all the money I need!" With Amit's unexpected two grand thrown in, we'd actually toppled way over. We had a nice cushion for surprise expenses.

Kimmy screamed and gave me a big ole hug. Once the girls around us caught on, everyone started cheering. It was bigger than any game. It was definitely a moment. A moment of pride and joy and relief and support and teamwork and utter emotional chaos. Girls. We could do anything we put our minds to.

I was going to USMTO.

Lily and Amit had tirelessly worked the city for sponsors.

My girls had done the impossible for me.

This school had my back.

I had an honest chance of winning the Open.

And I was now on my way to USMTO, on my way to a prize to help pay off Papa's debts, and on my way to the

Olympics because there was no stopping. There was no time to cry from gratitude or emotion. I had to work. I had to keep hustling. I had to keep the positive vibes going for the whole family.

I'd bounced into the hospital room and announced to my parents that we'd surpassed the goal. I gave Mama the rest of the money and hugged her so tight. "Thank you, Mama."

"Oh, beta. You did this. I just wish we could've helped more."

"Are you kidding me?" I asked and pulled back. "No parent has ever done more than you guys."

Before her eyes started to glisten, which would make mine fill up, I sat beside Papa and went into detail, even though he was sleepy from his meds. He managed to smile and pat my head.

I dutifully visited Papa every evening after training and told him about my day. I visited him every morning before school, or before hitting the gym, to gab about his favorite shows.

One thing that hadn't crossed my path of a blurry, fast-paced schedule as much as I'd liked was Amit. There were times when I couldn't sleep and I wanted to hear his voice or get his silly proverbs or cat videos. But he stopped responding. His calls gradually stopped, and his texts dwindled. Maybe he didn't want to crowd me, or figured I'd let him know if anything changed. I tried not to think about him, seeing that we'd already had the whole no-time-for-a-boyfriend-right-now talk. It wasn't until lunch on Tuesday that I'd realized he hadn't been around. No phone calls, no texts, no emails, no late-night drop-ins. He wasn't at lunch for our study session, but he was in class.

I walked over to Amit's seat in comp-sci. "Hi."

"Hey," he said, standing to hug me and asking close to my ear, "Your parents all right?"

"Sure," I replied. As fine as they could be. I'd been waiting all this time to tell him about the fundraising goal being met. I could've texted, but I wanted to tell him in person and give him a big hug for being a part of this. Now should've been the time, seeing that we were mid-hug. But the embrace was a little off and abrupt. He was quick to pull away.

"I have some food to bring over."

"That's nice. From your mom?" I smiled.

He didn't smile back. "Yeah."

"Does she know?"

"No."

"But she's making food for us?"

"Yeah."

"I'm confused. Does she know it's for me specifically?" I asked pointedly.

He glanced down at my scuffed sneakers and I hoped he couldn't see the small holes on the side. I needed to go to the thrift store to replace them soon.

"Does your mom know you stayed over?" I muttered so no one overheard.

"Not exactly," he replied distantly.

"Um. *Okay*. Well, I wanted to tell you in person since you stopped texting me. I got the money for the Open, more than I needed actually. Thanks for helping."

He smiled. Finally. "That's great, Kareena."

Um, was that all? No super hug? No blinding billion-dollar smile? No witty anecdote about how he knew I'd make it all along? What the crap was wrong with him?

Well, fine. I'd needed someone to talk to, about all this stuff building up and the anxiety that came with it. I needed someone to lean on about Papa because I didn't want to burden Mama or Lily every time.

But, whatever.

The bell rang and cut off the conversation. Whatever distracted him or had him down would have to wait. Not that I meant to be insensitive, but I had too much on my toppling plate to take on more.

Whatever was going on could hopefully wait to be dealt with after USMTO when I had one less thing on my shoulders. As the saying went: Boy, I got ninety-nine problems, and this ain't one of them.

…❮ TWENTY-THREE ❯…

Restrooms grossed me out. Thanks to biology and the project on bacteria cultures in petri dishes (because guess who did theirs on the germs in the girls' restroom?), the "ick" factor went through the roof. Since that fateful project, I always washed my hands before and after, turning the faucet on and off with a paper towel. My butt cheeks never hit the seat and preferred squats over sitting. But today, I had to pee before heading to my chiropractor appointment. The entire idea felt like an epic mistake in the making.

So when Saanvi waltzed in with her flowery perfume, I nearly barfed. The memory of petri cultures plus her face equated to some serious nausea. Rayna walked in behind her with a nod in my direction. They must've had a chat.

I washed my hands in my usual germophobic manner but eyed Saanvi.

She released a pent-up breath and looked at our reflection in the mirror as she said, "Listen. Rayna told me about what happened, that you guys patched things up and maybe it's best if we did too."

I carefully dried my hands, warily listening for the giant "*but*."

"We probably overreacted."

I scoffed. "Overreacted? You basically spread rumors that

I was sleeping around *and* dragged that mess into the mandir *and* strung it out for almost four months."

She nonchalantly twirled her hair, as if her actions had been validated by adding, "Things did involve my brother."

"You should've been annoyed, mad even, but malicious for so long?" I rolled my eyes and pushed past her. "Rayna, I don't know how someone as positive as you can stand the toxicity of Saanvi."

"Hey, wait a minute," Saanvi said.

"What?" I blurted louder than I'd intended and pivoted on my heels to face her.

She stuttered, "I'm not-not trying to go back, just forward, okay? Can we put it behind us?"

"With a neat little bow?"

"Why are you being so mean?"

Now it was *I* who was at a loss for intelligent words. "*Okay . . .*"

She quickly added, "Can we just put it behind us? Rayna had a really long, hard talk with me. I mean, I cried."

Rayna solemnly nodded. I had to roll my eyes at that. Were they for real?

"She told the truth and I had to face it."

"I'm waiting to hear an apology," I said, not caring.

"We were both wrong."

"The difference is that I apologized right away, and I didn't try to tear up your rep in my vortex of anger."

"I'm sorry. Can we put it behind us and be cool?"

"We can start with you stopping the mean talk. As far as putting it behind us? Now's not the time to ask."

"Oh, sure. Hey, it's pretty cool about your boxing stuff. You're going places." She smiled, bright and dazzling.

"Are you suddenly accepting it because I'm going somewhere

with it or because you genuinely don't care that I'm a female fighter?"

"Both. I didn't care before, did I?"

"You were passive aggressive about your stand on it. I honestly don't know how we were friends in the first place."

"Probably because of Rayna," she said frankly.

"Probably is right."

"But they were good times."

Not knowing how to handle her words, which were delivered with a suspicious mix of irony and enthusiasm, I walked to the door.

"There is one thing that I do need to tell you."

I gripped the handle and glared at the metal bar. Here it came. What diabolical crap had she conjured? It didn't even matter. It wouldn't affect me. I had very few hot buttons left for her.

"It's about Amit," Rayna said, which was the only reason I stayed long enough to listen. Rayna may have been mad with me. She may have overexaggerated the situation between us and allowed it to linger to epic proportions. Granted, she never stopped the aftermath with much effort . . . but she'd never lied to me, either. She told things the way she felt they were.

"I know you're tutoring him," Saanvi said, which was enough cause for pause seeing that Amit didn't want anyone to know and the only people who did know were Mrs. Callihan and Lily.

"Which is absurd, because he's legit a genius. Anyway, I know because he told me. Which means we talk. As in more than friends. Our parents want to arrange us, like nakhye."

Nakhye? As in, the arrangement was already determined and approved by all parties? What the hell?

"What?" Rayna asked. "You said you liked each other, and your parents and his parents wanted you guys to date."

"Why would I believe you, Saanvi? And why would I care? We're not dating. As you know, we're assigned to study," I said.

"You wouldn't believe me, but you'd believe Rayna."

Rayna chewed on her lip. "I mean, it's true that Saanvi's mom talks about arranging them all the time."

"We're doing the gor dhana ceremony after graduation," she added.

"I didn't know that, either," Rayna said.

"Mhmm. We haven't told anyone yet. Supposed to be our parents' privilege or whatever to officially tell people."

"Okay. Congrats," I bit out, tamping down the bile in my throat. Oh, I shouldn't believe her, but if there was one speck of truth to her words, then my poor heart would break into a thousand pieces for sure.

"I hope that you weren't into him like that. Didn't figure you were, especially when studying with him is such a bore. You're not upset, are you?"

I faced her, smoothing my expression over with stoicism. "Other than the fact that he's nice but gets stuck with you?" Ouch. Did those words spew venom on the way out, because it sure felt that way.

She cringed, even if momentarily. "Oh . . . you do like him like that?"

"As a friend. We're friends and nothing more. And he seems like a very good person. Pairing him up with someone as malicious as you? Don't get me wrong, we can put the past behind us, but that doesn't suddenly erase your personality."

Rayna bit her lip as her eyes rolled over to the corner to sneak a peek at Saanvi's reaction.

Saanvi always played her A-game, and it didn't surprise me

when she retorted, "You're barely friends. His parents have a strong say in who he can associate with, and he does listen to them."

"His parents don't have anything against me."

"Are you sure? Because I literally heard our moms talking about you."

The sheath around my hot buttons split open. She could be lying, as was her inherently insidious nature.

"Saanvi," Rayna hissed.

But she didn't stop. "His mom told my mom about you going over to dinner. Like, why did you set yourself up for that? Going over by yourself? Or don't you know the rules? Indian girls never go to an Indian boy's house alone. And spilling the beans about your parents and your boxing? Bad move. Should've kept that to yourself."

"And be shady? That makes it worse, as if I have something to hide. Look, his parents wanted to get to know me. And that is me. I don't care if they don't approve. There is not a single thing wrong with my life."

Saanvi solemnly nodded. "You're right. You deserved to know, though."

"Saanvi, stop," Rayna snapped, taking her aback.

"It's the truth."

"This is not what you told me. Look, we had a talk. You asked me to be here so you can apologize to Kareena and tell her something about Amit, not all this."

"Has to be said."

Rayna shook her head. "I totally see it now."

"You hadn't before?" I asked.

"I couldn't admit how bad it had gotten."

"What are you talking about?" Saanvi asked.

"You're heartless," Rayna replied. "The three of us used to be friends. We used to be there for each other when we knew others wouldn't understand. You know why we were really friends? Because it was convenient. Mandir, our parents being friends, dance team, classes. That's not enough to be friends, though."

Saanvi didn't respond.

"Come on, Kareena. I'm sorry this ended up being an ambush." She walked out of the bathroom ahead of me.

I scoffed and walked out as coolly as possible, even though my fists were on fire.

"Do you want to talk about it? Get a load off?" Rayna asked at the fork in the hallway.

"Nah. Not worth my breath."

"I honestly didn't know she would say all of that."

"Is it true about her and Amit being promised to each other?"

"I mean, their parents talk about it all the time. I have heard them say that, my parents even join in. But . . . they're parents. Who knows if they're serious? Amit and Saanvi are way too young!"

I shook my head. "It's fine."

"It's not. You like him and that was hurtful. I can ask Amit, if you want me to get accurate info."

"No. I'll ask him myself. I'll talk to you later."

She bit her lip with worry as I took the left corridor.

I snatched my books out of my locker, jammed them into my backpack, and slammed my locker door shut, mumbling all the while. Saanvi figured out a new hot button, but what infuriated me the most? The fact that she picked at something that she knew was a trigger? That Amit being involved with anyone else was actually a trigger? Or that I allowed either one to get to me?

Practicing meditation techniques and anger harnessing (save

it for the fights, girl), I'd cooled down between storming down the hall and strolling through the parking lot to reach my car.

"Kareena?"

I spun around to the sound of Amit's voice, my heart automatically racing no matter how much my brain cells rebuked the instinctive reaction. "What?" I gritted out.

He held his hands up. "You're pissed, and I get it."

I crossed my arms. "Do you though?"

"Yes."

"What exactly am I pissed about, Amit?"

He blew out a breath, his cheeks tinged with red. "The way I acted weird. The truth is . . . I really like you and I keep thinking about you. But you made it clear that you want space and maybe I need a little, too, at least until graduation and to finish this work thing. Which works out, right? USMTO will be done by then."

"That's all? The real reason you were acting a little shady? Because there were several times I knew you weren't saying something, but I didn't want to press."

"The truth?"

"Yeah, Amit. All of it."

He gulped and looked away for a brief moment before returning to me with careful words. "I lied."

"No crap," I seethed, allowing the anger of wanting to be mad overpower the inclination to feel hurt.

"You know?"

"I do now. I'll give you the next few minutes to tell me and then I'll decide if I want your type around."

He sucked his teeth, as if my words were too harsh to hear. "My parents didn't say they wanted us to be friends after dinner that night you came over. My mom did make food, but I asked her to. For a friend. She doesn't know it's for you."

Although I knew his parents' attitude toward me, thanks to Saanvi, my heart sank. There was no easy way to hear that someone didn't like me, much less the parents of a guy I was really into. "They're no different, then?"

He took a step closer. "In that regard? No. I don't get it and I tried to explain to them how Muay Thai was like any other sport. But they don't feel it's good karma, or kismet, or whatever they called it. They don't think girls should fight. They're all for female athletes, or so they say, but more feminine stuff?"

"What the heck does that mean?"

He slouched. "You know what that means. Rough sports, fighting, boxing, those are for boys. Less-contact sports are for girls." Then he quickly added, his hands up in defense, "I totally disagree. I think you're a complete Black Widow. She's super badass. She's smart and pretty and friendly and strategic, and very likable. You're the same way: strong, powerful, and ridiculously attractive."

I let out a sigh and tried to remain angry. Being genuinely compared to Black Widow, or any Marvel superhero, was truly cool. I'd never thought of myself that way, that interesting, that kick-butt. The fact that someone honestly thought of me that way made the pissed-off meter dwindle down a bit. And did he just say I was attractive?

Still. I was not so easily swayed by a few sexy words, even when compared to a Marvel character.

"I lied because I didn't want that to ruin our friendship, or make you feel bad, or make you think my parents are bad. Misguided and passively misogynistic, yeah, but not deliberately bad. And I didn't want you to feel bad if you knew I was going to be your friend anyway. Or maybe more. If you let me. After USMTO, maybe?" he asked, miserably hopeful.

"What about being nakhye to Saanvi? When were you going to tell me that you're getting engaged to someone!"

His eyes grew lemon-wedge wide. "*Nakhye*? To Saanvi? Uh, you do realize that we're only seventeen and this isn't India. We can't be promised to each other. That's absurd!"

"Then what is she talking about? I'd get that she can lie to my face, but Rayna is a bad liar and she conceded. Why would she back Saanvi up?"

"What *exactly* did she say?"

"What does it matter?"

"It matters a heck of a lot."

"There's only the truth and the lie. Which is which? Are you or are you not promised to Saanvi?"

"No," he growled, his deep voice dropping ever deeper. "I would never, ever in a million years make a life-altering and eternal decision like marriage before high school graduation. I don't even expect to be capable of making that sort of commitment until at least college graduation. I barely like her, especially now that I've seen her darker side. And I would never in my entire life cheat on someone. If Saanvi and I were promised, we'd be a thing and all this talking to you and flirting with you and kissing you is cheating. I am not a cheater.

"What I think she's talking about, what Rayna probably acknowledged, was the fact that our parents have discussed us being a compatible marriage couple. *In the future*. You know desi parents. They're thinking ahead to possible marriage potentials way in advance, but our parents haven't arranged anything. And no matter who they think is good for me, or which daughter-in-law candidates they toy around with, I have final say. I've never agreed to Saanvi. I never will. And if they press the idea of us even being remotely a good match, I'll let them know how intolerable she really is, all this malicious crap she does.

They don't want someone like that for me. They wouldn't want someone like that in our family."

"She said you're doing gor dhana after graduation."

He choked out a laugh. "Well, that's the first I've heard of it. Usually they tell the would-be-groom ahead of making a date."

I narrowed my eyes.

"I can't believe Rayna would back that story up. Are you sure she's a bad liar?"

"Well, no. She didn't know about that part until Saanvi told me."

"Mhmm . . . And she actually said that Saanvi and I were getting engaged?"

"Well, no. She said that Saanvi's mom is always talking about it."

He chuckled. "That part is true, unfortunately. Indian moms . . ."

"Yeah, your mom who hates me and loves her." I fumed and went for my keys, to get the door or to cut him, I didn't know which yet. He took my hand and I yanked it back.

Amit took a step toward me, but I crossed my arms and he crossed his arms too. All those arms now touched, and not a light graze, but full on skin-pressed-up-against-skin contact. When he looked at me with those intense brown eyes and playful, pleading smile, when he was anywhere close enough for me to smell his light-scented cologne and feel his body heat, adrenaline raged through me. Fight club sort of adrenaline. The kind that had me feeling high and euphoric, the kind that lifted my feet off the ground. Ugh. And I hated it because I wanted to be stupid mad right now.

I huffed. "What?"

"Are you pissed because you thought I'd actually do something like get engaged to your mortal enemy and hang out like this with you? Or are you pissed because you like me and the mere idea of me being with someone else tears apart your soul?"

"The former, obviously. No one wants to be played."

With crossed arms still the only thing between us, he stepped forward and forced me to step back against my car. How dare he!

"I think you really like me," he stated.

"I think you're full of yourself," I shot back.

"Then why so mad?"

"Because if a boy played me like that, he'd get it."

"The only part there is any truth to is that our parents might've joked, maybe even fleetingly considered, the possibility of Saanvi and me. She's not into me. Pretty sure she doesn't even tolerate me."

"Really? She's always all over you."

"Pretty sure she does that when she thinks you're watching. Which has literally been four times. She's never been that way around me before, and she doesn't even talk to me when you're not around. At mandir? Completely ignores me. In the halls? She doesn't even look at me. She's trying to get a rise out of you. This started after you came to Holi. Saanvi has no interest in marrying me. She's just trying to rile you up. Do you believe me? Because if you don't, we'll go talk to my parents and you can ask them."

I chewed on the inside of my cheek.

"And while we're there, we can ask what the heck their deal is with not approving you."

"No," I groaned. As much as I had begun embracing this whole confrontation and trying not to give a crap about what others thought of me, calling his parents out was a bad idea.

"Now what?"

"I'm going to punch her in her face."

He chuckled. "No, you're not. You're not losing your temper over her. You never have, right? Why start now? Why give that to her?"

"If you can't stand her, then how does she know all this stuff about us?"

"If she knows anything about my personal life, it's because she talks to my mom during dance practice. And our moms are best friends, so she probably eavesdrops on their conversations. And I'm so, so sorry that my mom even talks about you, especially in a way that isn't true. I'll talk to both of them about that," he gritted past clenched teeth.

"Don't bother."

"Don't say that." His voice rose. "They shouldn't be talking about you. Saanvi shouldn't be twisting stuff to get to you, and my mom shouldn't be talking about anyone behind their backs. It's a matter of principal, but also because it enrages me that anyone is doing this to you. My mom of all people!"

"Don't get into it with your parents over me. It'll make her like me less and I don't want to be the rift in your perfect relationship."

"Why do you think I'm so perfect?"

"Because you are. Model student. Model son. Model Indian."

"I'm not. And you're talking as if you're anything less. You're not. I'm no better than you. You're no worse than I am. We're both perfectly fine. And we can be perfectly fine together."

I twisted around, forcing him to step back. I totally understood his viewpoint. I even appreciated parts of it, of wanting to spare my feelings and not distract me or make me feel weird or awkward hanging with him knowing his parents disapproved.

But then, there was still the fact that he lied. To. My. Face.

"You're still mad," he stated.

"Amit. I needed you. All this time, you kept trying to get me to open up to you, to let you in. You kept saying that you'd be here for anything I needed. I don't just talk to people that easily about my problems. You got me to lean on you, but you weren't there."

"I'm sorry."

"I have an appointment."

He stuffed his hands into his pockets and watched as I got into my car and drove off. And every half hour for the rest of the evening, he texted. I bit my lip and glanced over his messages. Not all of me was mad, to be honest. And more than ever, I really missed him. I didn't want to lose him or let this one act ruin everything between us. Amit Patel was not perfect. Not by far.

But a girl couldn't just forgive and forget that easily. He had to work for it, to show that he wouldn't intentionally hurt me or lie to me again. There was a reason why I was friendly with everyone. It was best for my soul. And there was a reason why I only had a few intimate friends. I hated being lied to, being hurt.

All of his messages went unanswered. I did *not* have time for this.

···< TWENTY-FOUR >···

Coach hit hard. Not because he was a man or twice my age, but because he'd been doing this forever. Coach went all in. His hit to my jaw screamed, a pain so rattling that it shook the skin from my bones. But did he let up or back down or ask if I was okay?

Heck no.

He came down with an elbow followed by a knee. My entire body raged war with my brain, telling me to get out of there. But my brain said *we got this*, even though my thoughts weaved in and out. Images blurred and clarified.

It was the moment. The second when all the nerves and pain and *oh crap* instances tore themselves apart in the chaos of a fight and realigned.

One of Papa's doctors said something similar that surgeons did to their patients when patching them up. They took all the swollen, cut, frayed edges of tissue and sewed them back together nearly seamlessly. He called it reapproximating.

That's what this moment felt like. All the shredded puzzle pieces of my life, from Papa's illness to Mama's financial woes to Amit's stupid lying face to USMTO to the pain of the here and now as Coach whipped my butt . . . it all exploded.

Then the pieces all came together. Lucid coherence. Anything could be overcome with strategy and determination.

When the proverbial dust of my life settled, my muscles

struck faster than my thoughts. I ducked and weaved and punched and spun around Coach to hit him from the shoulder.

Coach was a big man. Like Jason Momoa big. But a precise hit could take down the best.

When practice ended at seven, my body still aching, I drove home and showered.

The house was eerily quiet when one knew they were totally alone. My phone beeped off and on from the usual suspects plus Rayna.

Are you all right? Did you find out about Amit? Rayna asked.

I rolled my eyes. The last thing I wanted was to talk about him. *I can't deal with that right now.*

Can you tell me details about the Open?

Like . . .?

Date, place, time?

Why?

I want to be there.

I sat up and smiled. *Really?*

Of course. It's one of the coolest things about you. I really missed out. Wish I'd been there to celebrate with you when you got the news. I'd have a cupcake.

I grinned. Called it!

I told her the details but added, *Don't go all that way for me.*

I have to go. I want to go.

All the warm fuzzies filled my soul. Could Rayna and I actually get our friendship back together? Could we be like old times? Better without Saanvi? I replied, *I'd get distracted, though . . .*

What if I hide?

I shook my head and ended the convo there, responding to texts from Lily.

So, prom and Jared huh? I asked.

Yes! Squeal! Want to double with Amit?

I ended that convo real quick. I had never wanted to go to a school dance, much less prom. I checked social instead to see what was going on with everyone else. There was major talk about prom, as the committee was mainly made up of athletes, but there were some threads about USMTO because people actually wanted to go.

But getting there and staying there wasn't cheap, especially since they wanted to rent a party bus with driver.

Although a Par-tay Bus sounds way cool! I typed, earning a bunch of likes, hearts, and agreeing comments.

Amit had texted at least a dozen times. Every time I saw his name, my eyes glazed right over the rest of his words on my home screen. I didn't even bother opening his messages. He was bringing a lot more drama and mess than I cared to handle today.

After a snack and making lunches and dinners for the week for me and Mama, I headed to the hospital to see Papa. He was so much better. He didn't have this abnormal bowing-over pain in his stomach anymore. He had been weaned off his pain meds, moved to a regular room, and took several walks around the floor every day.

He had gone septic again but doing that twenty-four-hour blood culture the second he was in a bed caught it right off the bat. Broad antibiotics and flushing his system out with a dozen IV bags had helped. He'd had a weird UTI and a kidney infection, but no renal failure.

I really hoped to hear good news today, that Papa could go home because everything was under control. When I turned the corner out of the elevator, I saw Amit's uncle. I looked around for Amit because *of course* he would be here right after we had a fight. But he wasn't.

Amit's uncle walked into Papa's room, and I followed, letting myself in. My parents were all smiles. They apparently knew who this guy was. He glanced back at me when my parents waved me in. I sat beside Mama on the bench. She placed a hand on my knee and beamed. "This is my daughter, Kareena."

"Hi," I said.

"Nice to finally meet you, Kareena. I've heard exemplary things about you," he said, his voice warm, and a smile on his face. He'd looked all business the other day.

"Cool," was all I managed to say. I just wanted to know why he was here.

But Mama went on, "She's getting ready to go to the Open in a few short days. Maybe the Olympics after that."

The man nodded like he was extremely impressed. "I've heard. But wow, the impact doesn't lessen. That is an amazing feat."

"Thank you," I said with a big ole grin. But still. Why was he here talking to my parents? And had been, apparently, chatting with them before?

He looked down at his tablet and said, "Ah. So, the reason I'm here again so soon after our last visit. Thank you for filling out the packet we gave you last week. Thank you, again, for letting me interview you."

"For what?" I asked. I couldn't help but wonder if Amit had told his uncle about my family and getting all up in our business when he was supposed to keep this to himself. If he'd done that, then our little fight was about to explode.

"Oh! I haven't had time to tell you," Mama said. "But you're here and it's good to know we might have another option. After you helped me fill out all that paperwork for the hospital to try to write off some of Papa's bills, Ankit Uncle—" she nodded toward the man "—gave us a packet."

Ah. The packet from the day Amit was here.

"It was a survey type thing."

Yeah, because Amit and Uncle worked for some medical programming company.

"But it also put us on a list for a foundation."

"Huh?" I asked, perplexed.

The uncle explained, "My company works with improving healthcare through various means, one of which is a foundation that helps deserving and underfunded families. The survey portion is for the improvement side. But when I came across your father's case, I had to personally interview him to see if he qualified."

"Does he?"

"He most certainly does. From a financial standpoint. I interview because I have to make the difficult decision of who may deserve it most at the moment. We only have so much."

"Do you interview everyone personally?"

"At the higher stages, I do. But I took a personal interest here."

"Why?"

"Well, to be honest. I have an assistant who sorts through cases for me. Sometimes that requires more attention than I'm able to thoroughly give."

I pushed out a harsh breath through my nostrils. Amit. I knew it. He was all up in my dad's personal business!

"My assistant pulls up the most pressing cases for me to follow through with. Normally, he compiles a spreadsheet with detailed information. This time . . . I don't know. He was very passionate about your case, Mr. Thakkar."

I blinked. Passionate?

"He truly cares for all patients, but your case spoke to him on a deeper level. And I'm glad. It means he has a big heart and it means he takes his job seriously. With that, I wanted to stop by and let you know that you've been moved to the top of the list."

Mama clasped her hands to her mouth while Papa gave a cautious nod.

"Now, it doesn't guarantee anything. The board makes the final decision."

It was indeed something. Something that could help, but also something that might not happen. It didn't mean we'd stop submitting paperwork for a hospital write-off or payment plan.

My parents thanked him profusely when he left, and chattered on about what tests they were waiting for and which meds Papa had to get to join his ever-growing pack at home.

"I'll be right back," I said and went to the hallway, but the uncle was gone. I went to the nurses' station and spoke to someone who had been working regularly with Papa.

"Hi, Cynthia," I said.

"Oh, hi, Kareena. Anything I can help with?"

"Actually, I was wondering about this whole foundation deal. A man was just talking to my parents about it."

"Oh, that's great news! Definitely a good sign. He should've explained it to you."

"I just caught the end of it. How do they pick the, I dunno what they're called, *winners*?"

"They're called recipients. He and his assistant go through cases by the numbers, the finances. If there are any patients with larger debts, they ask the family to read some material and sign a release form for the company to be able to go through their situation. The assistant does most of the sorting. He's always here."

"Amit?"

"Yes. That's him. Do you know each other?"

"Turns out, we go to the same school."

"What a small world! Well, Amit has been doing this for a couple of years. He jokes that he just crunches numbers, but I heard the CEO of the foundation company telling the doctors how his assistant was so intense about your father's case that he kept insisting the CEO take a better look. Usually he's not that vocal. I'm glad something caught his eye because that was a good call. He fought very hard for your dad, made the CEO himself interview your dad right away."

"Oh. Wow." There were no words. That was the absolute truth: there were no words to describe Amit Patel.

He had never mentioned his company funding a foundation, much less that he was part of the process. I couldn't believe Amit had done that. He hadn't been prying into our business at all. He was just doing his job. And apparently, very passionately advocating for my dad.

I clenched and unclenched my fists on the way back to Papa's room. We couldn't hold our breaths, despite how excited Mama was over Papa's new candidate position. We knew a little too well how badly false hope hurt. At the same time, it could be something really huge. And it was all thanks to Amit.

Amit who had never said a word.

Amit who had fought for my dad from behind the scenes and never used it for his advantage. Even when we just had our first fight, he didn't bring it up to win.

All I knew was that he gave my dad a fighting chance. Catching up on these bills didn't just mean being medical-bill debt free. It meant that if Papa needed invasive treatments, then we could go for them without the collections company coming after us. It meant we could breathe. It meant a whole lot of possibly good stuff.

It meant Amit hadn't truly ghosted me. He may not have been there for me to talk to, but he had been busy doing a whole lot more. He did something no one else could have. Maybe something no one else would have.

I exhaled through shuddering lips while I watched my parents laugh for the first time in days. The paperwork for a hospital write-off stayed in a pile on the counter behind the bench. We were, had always been, a proactive family. We never relied on others to help us, much less save us. I was ready to go all *Breaking Bad* so my father could get the treatment he needed.

Then came along Amit Patel.

He'd compared *me*, of all people, to a Marvel character. He knew that I did not need saving.

But I knew a superhero when I saw one.

···< TWENTY-FIVE >···

I'd finished stupid calculus, wondering if Mr. Strothers would give me a free pass for making history at school, and was walking to bed when someone rang the doorbell.

It was ten at night and every hair on my neck stood up. A burglar or attacker wouldn't give fair notice, but that didn't mean I was about to waltz to the front door and naively open it. I skimmed through my missed texts, all from Amit, starting with the most recent.

You still awake? I'm outside.

I sighed. Yeah. I was still awake and happy that he dropped by, even though he wasn't supposed to. I needed to know why he did what he did. I needed to hear it from him.

I dragged the baseball bat from the hallway closet behind me and checked the front porch through the peephole. The motion-activated sensors illuminated Amit in a bright, fluorescent glow.

I cracked the door open about five inches, my foot secure on the interior side of the door so he couldn't push through, my grip firm on the handle of the bat. I didn't honestly think I needed such precautions, but a girl couldn't be safe enough. Especially when she had been annoyed at a certain boy's behavior.

"What?" I asked sharply.

"I've been texting you. You haven't responded."

"Hmm. Somehow I know that feeling."

He blew out a breath. "I'm a prick. I get it."

"What are you doing here?"

"I have to explain myself."

"You already did."

"You're still mad at me."

"I didn't expect those things from you. The narrow-minded parents, the drama from my arch nemesis who happens to be BFFs with your momma. But the worst part is—"

"Is the lying."

I clamped my mouth. Bingo.

"But I couldn't stand the idea of seeing your face if I told you the truth, of knowing how much that would hurt, of the risk of losing you just because of them. And on top of that, I was consumed by this infuriating project, and my parents. Ugh. Always with the pressure and hating how they reacted to you. I can't talk to them about anything outside of being picture perfect. And I realized the more time I spend with you, the less I put into school and work."

"Oh, so now *I'm* the distraction?"

"That's my fault, getting distracted, but there's no way I can be around you and concentrate on anything else. I can't handle you."

"So you're using the fact that you can't handle a girl as an excuse to walk away when she needed you? No. Never mind. I *don't* need you."

"You're right. You don't need me. But that doesn't mean I should've ghosted you with the truth. There should've been a balance. Being there for you without distracting you, being there for you without getting distracted. But things got intense and I didn't know how to act."

We paused and just looked at each other. I couldn't even be mad, really, but I waited for him to 'fess up.

Instead, he said, "I can't stand the idea of being away from you, of having walked off when you needed me, of having you pissed at me. I can't stand the idea of not having you near me, Kareena. I'm sorry. I'm sorry that I wasn't there most of all. I won't ever do that again."

"I get why you did it. It's just hard to open up about very personal things, to trust people, and when they let you down, it's not easy to completely erase that. Maybe if we'd been casual friends, but—" I stopped myself.

"But what?"

I froze. I couldn't handle how intensely he watched me. I couldn't handle how my chest ached from him going to bat for Papa. "But we both know where things were heading and how we feel about each other."

"I still feel that way. I can't get you out of my head."

"Apparently there's not enough room in there for both me and work, though, right?" I probed, trying to get him to admit what he'd done.

He pulled his notebook from the backpack dangling off his shoulder. "You gave me everything about you. Your passion, your problems, your past, and I barely gave you anything."

"So you're offering your journal of fledgling program chunks?"

"I'm offering you the thing that no one knows about me."

I slowly took the book, not quite understanding. "So what? This is part of your work project. You're smart with programming. I'm sure every comp-sci teacher you've ever had knows, not to mention your parents."

"I'm not just smart. I'm a genius."

"Uh, okay ego-inflated boy with his foot in my door."

"My uncle is CEO of his company, true, but he's also a programmer for medical stuff for the government. He noticed some of my program fragments and asked me to take an IQ test administered by his department. My score is one hundred and sixty. That's what Stephen Hawking was, and Einstein. Then they gave me all these programs to decode and had me write the most complex thing I could think of. It was more complex and efficient than their top programmers."

"So why is a genius struggling to keep valedictorian status with simplistic theorems?"

"Because . . . I did it on purpose."

"What?" I fumed. I'd really, really hoped that Amit had gotten tripped up by small stuff instead of having lied about needing a tutor.

He replied slowly, like he was tired and winded, "All the pressure and expectations of being the best, doing the best. And anything less is unforgiveable. You keep thinking I'm some perfect guy, when I'm only running a race to keep up with what everyone wants me to be. I gotta get top grades, be friends with everyone, have everyone's respect, never make a mistake, be dependable, be devout, do all the things at mandir, do all the things at school, do all the things at home, do all the things at work.

"Anything less is unacceptable. You're so lucky to have the support that you get. My parents never once congratulated me on valedictorian status. They never once helped with homework. They thought everything should be natural if I worked hard enough. Which is contradictory, I know. I know they're proud, but they don't show it."

He scratched the back of his head. "That's dumb, right? Here you are dealing with your dad's health and helping your mom and going to the Open and raising funds, being totally badass and independent and just hustling to do whatever it takes. I'm feeling sorry for myself because of parental pressure. Then this job came along and my parents don't know what the program does. They're just . . . annoyed that I'm not good enough to fix it. I just need to know if you believe me when I say that I'm sorry for freaking out and being a dick and hurting you."

I twisted my lips. I didn't want to forgive that easily, just because a boy batted his pretty eyelashes and said stuff like how much he needed me in his life.

I flipped through the journal instead, noting where he'd taken my simplistic advice. "You fail quizzes in class on purpose, don't you?"

"Yeah. But they didn't add up to enough to lose my spot as valedictorian. Mrs. Callihan thought they might, but I knew exactly what I was doing. Just enough to not feel the pressure of having to be perfect. I tried to argue with her about needing a tutor, but she insisted, or she'd talk to my parents to make me see reason."

"You didn't need a tutor, did you?"

"No."

"You wasted my time," I bit out.

"I know. If you're mad at me for that—"

"I am."

"Then it was worth it."

"I could've been spending time with friends during my last semester in high school."

"But you *were* spending time with a friend."

"That's not what I meant."

"If I hadn't gone along with the tutoring, we probably would've never talked to each other more than we had to. And now look at us." He leaned against the doorframe, taking up the entire space.

"Yeah, look at us. A nonsensical dude who almost reached Travis-level doucheness by lying to me several times."

"And a girl who wants to be mad at him but isn't."

I took a few deep breaths and exhaled. In and out. In and out. "I can't hold on to any excess negativity."

"And I don't want to be the source of negativity. Ever." He reached out and took my hand. I didn't pull away. Not even when he stroked the back of my hand, sending butterflies through my belly and melting my anger.

I had the right to be upset with him, even though I understood why he did what he did. Even though not being there these past few days wasn't a regular thing for him. Even though he lied about his parents to spare my feelings. Even though his problems affected him the way my problems affected me. They weren't any less. Even though his messing up in comp-sci on purpose wasted my time but led to there being an us.

Because there was an *us*. And that was worth more than any residual anger. I had to let it go. There could be no room for negativity. Karma and all . . .

I sternly warned, "Then don't bring that crap around me again."

"Promise."

I leaned my right shoulder against the wall, touching his shoulder against the doorframe. He still held my hand in a way that I never wanted him to let go. "Now what, strange boy at my house at ten o'clock at night? Anything else you wanna confess?"

He glanced down at me. "Are you still mad at me?"

I shook my head. "Not really."

"Okay. Well, then . . ." He snatched me up by the waist

into a giant bear hug. I yelped and caught my breath. "First of all, I really missed you," he said into my hair.

I hugged him back, my arms around his shoulders and my forehead pressed into his chest. Being this close to Amit was really amazing. And I had missed him too. So much.

"Second, I'm truly sorry for hurting you. For lying. Third, I'm so proud of you for hustling and getting the funds you needed."

"You helped a lot. Thanks for going out of your way without me ever having to ask."

"It's what I do." Apparently!

I laughed. And I loved him for it. Wait . . . I didn't mean it like that. Did I?

Amit let me go and I instantly missed him. "Are you tired?" he asked, pulling me out of my thoughts.

"I don't sleep much these days. I honestly can't do another kick or math problem. My head might actually implode."

He grinned. "I got something to take your mind off the regular."

I narrowed my eyes. "Like what?"

He tapped the top of his notebook. "Maybe you can help me while I provide the shoulder that should've been here the past few days."

"Sounds like you're getting me to do homework for you."

"I'll tell Mrs. Callihan you tutored me the rest of the semester and prove it by acing all my quizzes and tests."

"You, friend, were going to do that anyway." I poked his chest.

He kept my hand there. "True," he said and bent down to pick something up from beyond my sight of the front porch.

I gasped and took the bouquet of dark red roses. They

smelled like Mama, like the rose-based perfumes she loved so much. "Are these for me?"

"No," he said. "They're for your dad. There's a card in there. And a gift certificate for your mom."

"Oh," I breathed, and realized how big my smile had grown. "That's very sweet."

Then he pulled a single yellow rose from behind his back and tapped it against my forehead. "This is for you."

I took the flower and smelled it. "I haven't seen a yellow rose in forever."

He dragged in a long breath. "Will you help me get the chaos out of my head?"

"What's in it for me?"

"Aside from getting your mind off all the things that need to get done and filling time until you fall asleep, it might actually put you to sleep."

"Try harder."

"I'd be in your debt."

"How much debt?"

He pressed my palm flat against his chest. "You'd have the keys to my soul."

"That's so corny, it hurt my stomach."

His hand fell to my stomach as he took a step inside and closed the door. Yep. The butterfly horde exploded. As soon as he realized how he'd touched me, he backed away and scratched his neck. "Maybe you can tell me about your dad."

"He's better."

"Is that all?"

I quirked a brow as I slid the roses into a water-filled vase and placed it on the table. We took a seat on the couch. Was he trying to get me to tell him about the foundation when I was trying to get *him* to tell *me* about it?

I let out a deep breath and flipped through the notebook. His intense stare bore a hole right through the side of my face. "What are you looking at?"

"Watching that beautiful brain work its magic. Maybe I can learn something."

"Still corny." I shook my head and nudged him away with my shoulder, but not too hard. The rowing machine killed it today. After five minutes of skimming through the pages, I noticed that the fragments were in order and the whole program started to come together.

Amit's phone rang, piercing the silence. I diligently read on. He had been right. This took my mind off things and at the same time, it made me terribly sleepy.

"Hello?" he said, not even bothering to get up. Instead, he slid his arm over the back of the couch, above my shoulders.

He muttered some things into his phone, but I could hear the high-pitched woman's voice on the other end. His mother.

"Where are you?" she asked in Gujarati.

"Work."

"*Beta*! Your Masa said you're not there. Just like you weren't there last Thursday night. What have you been doing all evening? Why are you lying to your poor mother?"

I stiffened beside him, but he didn't tense.

"I'm doing the work with a friend. She's helping me."

"*She*? Is it Kareena? *Ay, Ma* . . . sharam nathyi?"

I bit my lip, remembering how he'd proudly told his parents about my helpful comments to his work and now his mom was questioning if he had any shame.

"Yes."

"What did we tell you about her? She is not proper for you."

"*Hah, hah*," he grunted the sounds of a "yes, yes." He jumped up and went into the foyer, his voice farther away but not completely silent to my astute hearing . . . and the thin walls he didn't know about.

"I know, and I also know you've been speaking ill of her. Why would you do that? You've always been so kind and open. You're always talking about karma and kismet and whatever, and you're so devout, but the first teachings are to forgive and embrace. There's nothing about her to forgive, but there's everything to embrace."

Silence.

"And Saanvi . . . that's another problem. You don't even know how malicious and hurtful she is."

Another pause.

In a rough tone, he ended, "Yeah, we'll definitely talk about this when I get home. But it won't be tonight."

He returned to the couch and dropped down beside me, his arm draped over the back of the couch. I pretended to be engrossed in this spectacular program, in this fantasy program that seemed to take in a million variables and output medical jargon.

He thumped my lower lip, the one I was still biting on in the rising tension of his conversation. "Sorry about that," he muttered.

"Don't flick my lip then," I countered.

"I meant . . . I know you heard some of that."

"I don't want to be the source of conflict between you and your parents."

He leaned his back against the couch and slouched. "You're not. The source is their viewpoint, their attitude."

"You're going to be in so much trouble."

"They'll get over it."

"Rebel rising." I dug out a pencil and scribbled some alterations as he inched closer and read over my shoulder. His breath warmed my neck and, at the same time, chilled my skin. I shivered.

"Are you cold?" He pulled down the throw blanket from the corner of the couch and draped it over us.

"Thanks," I mumbled.

After some time, he asked, "Are you mad about my mom?"

"No," I muttered.

"Are you sure?"

"Yeah."

He cringed. "You seem a little mad."

"I'm not. I'd tell you if I were. Just trying to run through this program. It's a gigantic mess."

He poked my side. "Chaos usually is."

"Like you had numerical diarrhea splatter on the page."

"What the heck?" He laughed.

"Like this right here? It's gibberish. Seriously, did a baby monkey steal your pencil and go to town, or what?"

He went for the notebook. "If you're going to demean me . . ."

I pulled away and held the notebook up. "No, you're going to listen. Did you write down every random fragment that came to mind? You don't need to use all of these."

"Fine." He got to his knees to retrieve the notebook, but I climbed to mine too.

"It's like fighting. You have an arsenal of amazing moves, but you don't have to use them all in one fight."

"Yeah, this was a mistake."

I grinned as he tried to snatch the journal, but I was way faster. "You can't cram everything into one program. This beast is novel-length, and I'm talking *Game of Thrones* length."

"You're about to get into trouble."

"You want help or not?"

"Without the degrading, preferably." He shot toward me and I leaned way back, the notebook out of reach. But now Amit had me cornered against the arm of the couch. He gripped the arm on either side of my waist, his biceps flexing beneath his green T-shirt.

"Where you gonna go now?" he asked, his voice ever deeper, a sound that rumbled through my gut in explosive bursts.

Oh, crap.

He leaned in and ever so softly kissed me. My stomach did a million flips as I kissed him back. My body relaxed into his. His chest softened into an unimaginably welcoming weight against mine.

My fingers ached to climb through his hair. My back wanted to arch into him. My tongue begged to taste his.

But nope.

Nope.

Nope.

I pulled back and gasped. "Can you type this program out?" I squeezed the notebook in between us, to have something preventing our bodies from crushing one another.

His chest spasmed with heavy breaths as he took the notebook. "I have it programmed, ready to test."

"Can you add the changes? Then run it. See if it works now."

He swallowed hard. "Yeah."

Amit sat back and pulled his laptop from his backpack. He pulled up the program as I brought my knees to my chest and covered myself from neck to toe with the throw blanket.

His face and neck were a deep shade of red as he focused on the screen.

"We can't do that," I said softly.

"I know," he replied just as softly. A smirk turned his lips. "But it's always fun."

I smiled. "Do my simplistic changes work?"

"Yeah," he breathed, as if he'd discovered something life altering.

I scrambled over to the computer to view a short glimpse of a working miracle program. The input algorithms had everything from symptoms to test results, and the program arranged them down to the cellular level. I couldn't keep up. It was . . . a diagnostic program.

Amit closed the laptop.

"Is the chaos gone?"

"Yeah," he said.

"You sound disappointed."

"I should go." He suddenly looked at me, all seriousness.

"What's wrong?"

"Um, you fixed it."

"But why do you have to leave?" I frowned.

He glanced at the computer then back at me. "Do you want me to stay? It's getting late."

"Aren't you already in trouble with your parents?"

"Are you asking me to spend the night?"

Heat rose to my cheeks and my neck. "On the couch. By yourself."

"Kareena, you removed the giant mass of unfixable programming taking up brain space."

I nodded, but not understanding.

"All that space these relentless fragments took up is empty. Leaving my brain totally defenseless to be consumed by you."

My breath hitched. Words did not come out of my mouth. My brain cells couldn't even come up with a response.

"I'm completely under your spell, and I know you don't want this, not yet. But if I stay . . ."

"Then what?"

He pushed the laptop across the couch behind him and scooted toward me, his hands on my hips. "Then there will definitely be an *us*."

Still not understanding, I asked, "Did you just come here to get me to help you? Or to get somewhere with me?"

A wounded frown crossed his features. "No. I came here to apologize and make up for what I did. I came here to . . ."

"To what?" I arched a brow. "It better be the truth—"

"To tell you that you're worth the wait. If it's after USMTO or after graduation or after the Olympics in four years. I'll wait for you."

"You don't mean—"

He stopped my words short with a passionate kiss that left me heady and my skin buzzing. He spoke against my lips, "You've been in my head since the first day you spoke to me freshman year. My thoughts have been absorbed by you since the first study session. This program was the only thing keeping you from total takeover."

"And now it's complete," I whispered.

"Now there's only you."

"Amit, I . . ." I glanced down at my knees squished between our chests.

"Need space. I know. But this time I won't screw it up and be a dick. Text me whenever you need anything, whenever you want to talk. I'll be there. I promise. And I'll text you to check in on you, okay?"

I nodded.

He slid away and put everything into his backpack. "I'll probably call you just to hear your voice too."

···< TWENTY-SIX >···

How was a girl supposed to act around a boy who had fallen for her? Amit kept his distance but texted throughout. He gave the space I needed to focus on Muay Thai but always let me know he was there for anything. He still hadn't confessed about the foundation, which was pretty cool. He didn't want to take credit. He didn't want to use it to score points.

What are you up to? he'd texted.

Punching Bob, I replied during a brief rest period, guzzling water like it was the last bottle on Earth.

Who's Bob and what did he do to you??

Bob's the punching dummy. He looked at me wrong this morning. Lol!

Sounds like he had it coming. Knock his head off.

Knocking Bob's head off was impossible, but he gave great resistance to my kicks and punches. Sparring had become the top outlet for aggression, stress, and anger. Bob got his butt kicked repeatedly. Fellow boxers intermittently fought with me in the ring in between bursts of other exercises and drills and breaks.

"You got this," Natalia said with an approving slap on my shoulder.

I shook my arms and stretched my neck, repeating her words in my head in an ongoing echo.

"Weigh-in!" Coach yelled.

I lifted my tank top to wipe my face with the hem of my shirt and froze when my one unblocked eye caught Amit in the corner. He gawked at me. Or quite possibly my now-exposed abs, with their many muscles and jutting hip bones. What did he think of that? Too muscular for a girl? Too skinny to be attractive?

Ugh. *Get out of your head, Kareena*!

I dropped my shirt and waved, drawing him out of his blushing stupor so he could wave back. I stepped onto the scale, knowing I'd be doing this in a week on tournament grounds.

"You're at one-thirty," Coach said.

"I'll pack on the calories."

"You've been packing them on, right? A pound here and there since the last weigh-in isn't good. Can't hover on the edge of your weight division."

"Yeah. Eating right with high caloric intake."

"Stressed?"

"You have no idea," I muttered. He didn't know about Papa. He knew Papa got really sick every now and then, but not how bad. He wasn't top tier level to be in on that.

"Try not to be. The fight will go as well as you determine it to. Train hard, be mentally in, keep your cool, find your balance, and you will be your best."

"Sure." Easier said than done.

"Good workout. Get some rest. Carb-load tonight."

Amit and I met halfway after Coach excused me. Being around my sweaty self should be enough to keep this boy at bay.

"What are you doing here?"

"Wanted to say hi," he replied.

"At my gym?"

"Wanted to see you in person. I wanted to support you during practice. By, uh, being hidden and quiet."

"Thanks. I definitely could not focus if I'd known you were here."

"Seeing you punch Bob reminds me how badass you are."

I laughed. Bob had it coming. "In case you want to try something, Romeo?"

"Exactly." He grinned and stuffed his hands into his pockets. "How's your dad?"

"He's much better."

"Good. I'm glad! Coming home soon?"

I softly replied, "Hope so."

"Oh," he said and frowned, genuinely disappointed.

"I should go. Gotta get some housework done."

"Need help?"

I grabbed my duffel bag and shot him a playful look over my shoulder. "Thought we agreed no more house calls?"

"Ugh, yeah. Maybe Lily can come over?"

"She has some family thing going on. Thanks, though. I'll manage a couple of loads of laundry and cleaning."

My phone beeped, muffled inside my bag. I dug it out just outside the doors to the gym on the way to my car.

Papa is coming home today!

I smiled at Mama's message and texted back:

He's better?

He is for now. There's some better news to add, tell you at home.

I bit my lower lip. What did that mean? Good news could be anything. Is Papa in remission? Is Papa cured? Did they find a cure? Did he . . . win the foundation money? I eyed Amit suspiciously, but the boy would not let on.

"Good news?" Amit asked.

I smiled because I couldn't help it. It was *wonderful* news. "Yes! My dad's coming home tonight."

"Nice! He'll see the flowers, then?"

"Yeah." I crossed my arms. "How did you know I hadn't taken them over?"

"Didn't know for sure until now."

"Huh," I muttered, shaking off the coincidence of Amit showing up to ask about Papa right as Papa was being released from the hospital. "Did you know about my dad coming home today?"

"How would I know?"

"That's not an answer."

He scratched his forehead.

My hands fell to my hips, my back straight, my game face on.

He admitted, "Yeah . . . I knew."

"How?"

"My uncle's research project."

"I thought your uncle was just taking consensus for sick people in general."

"I didn't lie. He *was* taking a consensus."

"Is that why you're here?"

"I'm here to see you because I really miss you. But, yes, also because I wanted to see your reaction about your dad getting to go home."

"I feel like you knowing this much about my dad is an invasion of privacy."

"I didn't look up his status or anything. It's work."

"So you know the status of all these medical records?"

"I know when patients get admitted and when they get better or worse past a certain range. I mean, your parents signed papers allowing my uncle's company to view that info. If it makes you feel better, you can know something that no one else does about my dad. He has this rash—"

I slapped my hand over this mouth. "Ew. No, thanks."

He laughed and mumbled behind my palm, "But it's so interesting."

My hand dropped to the car door. "Maybe after USMTO, you can have dinner with us."

"Really?"

"Yeah. Why not? I had an awkward dinner with your parents, so it's only fair that you do the same with mine."

"Except your parents really like me. I could tell. I'm very likable, you know?"

I grumbled under my breath. Darn, him. He was right.

The sun had set by the time I reached the house. After parking on the street, I hurried up the driveway and rushed through the foyer, bounding to my parents' room and forgetting to knock. Mama helped Papa down to the bed. He saw me first and smiled.

"Papa!" I beamed and bounced down beside him on the mattress.

"*Beta*, careful," Mama chided.

"Sorry." I flung my arms around Papa in the gentlest enthusiastic embrace I could manage. "You're home already!"

"Already? Been gone forever. Thought I'd never make it back to this bed."

"Eh. It's not the best mattress, to be honest." I pushed down on the pillow-top.

"Better than the hospital one. Not that I was awake long enough to complain most days."

"We should get you to my massage therapist."

"Sounds like a date."

"Speaking of dates," Mama intervened, and I winced. "How is Amit?"

Ugh, Mama. Horrible segue. "He's fine. Why do you ask?"

"He was at the hospital."

"To bring you flowers? Because the roses on the table are from him for you, Papa."

"I saw," he said. "They're bright and cheery and make the entire room smell nice. Thank him for us."

"Then what did he deliver to you?" I said, biting back the hope that the foundation had actually come through.

"His uncle did, actually. We didn't realize Amit was his assistant. Did you by chance tell him about our situation?"

"No. I mean, I told him you were sick a lot, but not the financial part. He must've learned that from the data he was gathering for the company. I had no idea he helped with a foundation until that day his uncle was talking to all of us. Amit never told me. Still hasn't. So, what happened? Did you get the money? Because I want to believe they'd help us but didn't want to get my hopes up." I wrung the edge of my shirt in anticipation.

"Negative child," Mama said with a cluck of her tongue. "It's always important to have some hope to look forward to."

"I didn't mean to sound negative. I mean, what if it doesn't happen, though? Are we putting all our hope into this?"

"No. It's just another thing to put our hope into." She took my hand in hers and beamed. "Well, the foundation *did* make a decision."

My heart pounded in my chest.

"And this cycle's recipient is Papa," she said with a crack in her voice and tears lining her eyes.

Oh, crap. I lurched toward her and Papa and hugged them both. Mama cried in my arms. I'd never seen her cry and I held her tighter, scrunching up the back of her shirt in my fist. I clenched my eyes tight and tried not to bawl. My entire body shook. It trembled from keeping in the sobs, from relief, from gratitude, from the emotions that sprang out of my parents.

Papa. Well, he was hardcore. He didn't cry with Mama, but his voice was strained when he spoke, which made me clench my eyes tighter to keep from crying. "So emotional. There. We're going to be okay. We're always going to be okay."

We had a family hugfest, a Mama cryfest, a laughterfest. The only thing that brought Mama out of her tears was Papa eventually changing the subject, no matter how much I asked about the details. I mean, how much was the foundation money for? Did it cover everything? Did it cover just this visit or our entire medical debt? How much was that debt?

But nope. In all of this surrounding Papa and the immensely huge win, he asked about me. "Why don't you tell me about training?"

I happily snuggled against his arm while Mama showered. I told Papa about everything from the girls' athletics social group to the fundraisers to me kicking butt in practice. He didn't let me stray back into the foundation talk, wouldn't give up actual numbers or other details.

"Don't worry about that. Let us worry about it, huh?"

I nodded.

"And Amit?"

"Hmm?"

Papa grinned. I'd never seen him smile because of a boy in my life. "He's a nice kid."

"Mhmm," I muttered suspiciously.

"He visited me every day at the hospital."

"He did?" I sat up.

"Yes. What a sweet kid. We should invite him for dinner one day soon." Papa yawned as his eyelids drifted closed.

I slipped out. The shower squeaked off and I snuck into my room. I lay in bed for a good half hour, wide awake, and tapped the cell phone on my chest. I had lots of words, and endless feels, for Amit right now. But how to word them all? I had no idea. Was text even an option? A phone call maybe? But would I break down and cry again in front of him?

Mama knocked on my door.

I immediately sat up, leaving my phone on the pillow. "Come in."

"Was wondering if you're going to prom?"

"Uh, no. Why would you think that? Have you been talking to Amit?"

"Amit?" she asked innocently, her voice a little higher than normal. "Why? Did he ask you to go?"

"Mama . . ." I groaned, eyeing her. She was for sure up to something. "Since when do you encourage me to date boys?"

"Not boys plural. And just one date. It's prom!"

"Prom doesn't mean anything to me."

"It means a formal dance, the only one you'll have with your friends, the last event before graduation, a high school milestone."

"Still means nothing to me. I'm just thinking about USMTO, you know?"

"Well, if you decide to go, we approve."

"It's the weekend after USMTO. I wouldn't even have time to find a dress—" I stopped myself. "Do you have a dress for me?"

She grinned, walked out of my room, and returned with a plastic-draped hanger. Mama turned on the light and laid it across my bed with such reverence, as if it were a wedding gown.

I placed my hand over the zipper before she did. "Mama! How much did this cost? You have to take it back."

She gently slapped my hand away. "Nonsense. I ordered it from Jaipur, and it was not much; much cheaper than American prom dresses. I'd been putting aside a little money every now and then for this for over a year. Besides, the foundation did something wonderful, eased our burden enough to let us enjoy this. On top of that, because I told everyone about my daughter going to the Open, the nurses all remember you, and they pitched in. I bought this, *on sale*, huh, from an already low price with a tiny fraction of that money."

My heart swelled as I remembered the conversations with the nurses about finances and write-offs and foundation grants. Wow. People in the world really did care. There *was* such a thing as paying it forward.

Mama unzipped the bag and pushed the plastic back. We both gasped, even though she'd already seen it. She studied my face for a reaction.

I'd never been into dresses or skirts. I did, however, love pink and all things that glimmered. "Okay. I'm totally in love."

I touched the intricate threading and stonework over a pistachio green and baby pink chaniya choli. I hadn't worn something this fancy in years. I hadn't worn a skirt in just as long.

"You look very nice in pista."

"It's so shiny and sparkly." God, I loved sparkles.

"I knew you'd like it!" She clapped her hands once. "Try it on."

"Oh my god," I muttered but didn't deny the excitement bubbling in my chest.

I changed in front of Mama right next to the bed. The heavy green skirt kissed the floor. Shimmering pink designs of paisleys and petals outlined in gold threading glimmered all throughout. The top was sleeveless and ended a few inches above my belly button in the traditional fashion. It was snug and glittery and displayed my abs like no one's business.

Mama draped the matching dupatta over my right shoulder and tucked one corner into the front, left side of the skirt. She grinned ear to ear, her palms pressed together at her lips.

I felt like a desi princess, even when my mom turned me to face the mirror above my dresser. Traditional clothing in a culture that I felt didn't fully accept me, in colors depicted by society as girlish accentuated by muscles that many didn't consider feminine.

"You are so beautiful. Perfect!" Mama added with a glimmer in her eye.

I twirled back and forth, mesmerized by the swish of the flowing skirt. "Now I have to go, huh?"

"You are smiling! You love it! You go if you want to go. You go with Amit if you want to go with him. Go with friends if you want to be with just friends. Live in happy moments. That's all life should be sometimes."

"And what if I break a shin at USMTO?"

"Go to prom on crutches. We can color your cast to match the dress."

"Mama . . . what if I epically fail at USMTO?"

"Then go to prom determined to try your best again next time. Prom and USMTO are two different things. If one doesn't turn out the way you want, it doesn't have to affect the other. It doesn't have to affect the rest of your senior year or your life."

"I'll think about it."

"Okay. Let us know what you decide." She kissed my forehead and slipped out of the room as I changed.

I carefully placed the garment back onto the hanger inside

the plastic bag and hung it in my closet. Lying in bed, I found myself constantly looking at the dress and imagining going to prom with Amit and friends.

Ugh. What have these people done to me? What has this boy done to me?

I couldn't get Amit out of my head, everything about him since the first day we met years ago to the insignificant and awkward run-ins to everything between getting paired up by Mrs. Callihan to tonight was crowding my emotions.

Rolling the phone over and back, my thoughts meandered toward the chaos of his beautiful mind, to the program Amit had been working on, to all the patient records he'd seen, to the fragments I'd read last night, to the glimpse of a final, working version. The miracle program to better healthcare. The one that shouldn't exist in all its complexities.

Not to mention the foundation and his part in it.

I shot up in bed and called Amit.

"Hey," he said after two rings, his baritone voice music to my ears.

"Hi." God, I loved that voice. It did crazy, funny things to my soul.

"What's up, babe?"

I made a face and wished he could see it. "Did you just call me babe?"

"Yeah. Not working?"

"Nah."

He laughed. "I'll work on it, then."

"Um, did you visit my dad in the hospital?"

"Yeah. Hope that was okay."

"It was. Every day? Even when you weren't speaking to me?"

"Yes."

I dragged my nails against the patterned lines of the sheets. "Why didn't you tell me?"

"I was being a dick, remember?"

"Constantly."

"What!"

I smiled and flipped onto my stomach. "That was sweet of you. My parents liked that you did that."

"Told you they liked me."

"Did you talk to them?"

"Just a quick hello. I didn't want to intrude. I was at the hospital anyway."

"For work?"

"Yeah, with my uncle."

"The program works?"

"Yeah. I can't believe it. It actually works. Healthcare can be more affordable for everyone with what the company is going to do with it. This will change the world, Kareena."

"Sheesh. Sound more Tony Stark-ish."

"Hey, Tony Stark and Black Widow would make a great couple."

I grinned into my phone.

"I can tell you're smiling."

"My dad wants you over for dinner, by the way."

"Called it."

"Speaking of parents, how much trouble did you get into with yours, anyway?"

"They were mad, especially when I didn't go home. I went to the office and worked on the program all night and then all day today until it worked. I was exhausted by the time I got home. My parents started yelling but I was too tired to fight. I just told them that we were going to be friends and they have to deal. And then I ended with telling them this program will change lives and you happened to be a huge part of it."

"I wasn't."

"You are. You motivated me to finish faster the moment I learned about your dad. And you helped the junky parts when others couldn't."

"I guess it's *okay* if you mention my name in your speeches and papers and in the magazines and TV interviews. Maybe even if my name went first is fine by me."

"Of course, babe."

"Still no."

"No? Okay. We gotta figure this thing out."

I laughed. "So. Anything else you wanna tell me?"

"Um. No. Why? You got something to tell me?"

I rolled my eyes. So, he was still playing this game of not telling me about the foundation. "I know you have something to tell me."

"That I'm outside?"

I jumped out of bed and pulled the curtain aside. "You are! You're breaking all the rules and my parents are home."

"Your parents love me."

"Wait outside," I said and hung up. I tossed the phone onto my bed and checked the hallway to make sure my parents' door was closed and that they were not wandering the halls.

I hurried to the front door. Oh my god. This boy was going to be the end of me. It didn't matter if my parents liked him. They would not like any boy sneaking over to my house.

I swung back the door to find Amit leaning against the tree in the front yard. "You are in so much trouble, Amit Patel."

"Why? Because I came by when I'm not supposed to? I think we already established that I do this sort of thing." He uncrossed his arms and took a step toward me.

"Are you sure there's nothing else you want to tell me?" I planted my hands on my hips. No more beating around the bush about this thing.

"Uh. Oh. What did I do?"

"The foundation," I breathed. "I know all about it."

His face turned red and his eyes went wide, as if his involvement was supposed to be a huge secret. But there weren't supposed to be secrets between us.

He opened his mouth, but there were no words for a few, long seconds. Then he rambled, "It's part of my job. Helping my uncle sort through financial files. I don't know who they are. I just pick them. But once patients sign privacy waivers, I learn more about them. We're supposed to give financial help to the most deserving people. And when I saw your dad's file . . . I mean . . ."

He threw his head back and sighed. "I wasn't trying to pry. Honest. I didn't need to know all of that about your parents' situation. I know you don't need my help. I know you told me to stay out of your family's business. Maybe I interfered a little. Maybe I crossed a line. I don't think I did—"

"Why'd you pick my dad?" I asked sharply. I had to know his reasons behind it. I had to know I was right about him.

"Um. Well. He meets all the criteria. We're supposed to get to know the candidates. And I've met him. I know him. I know his family. No one deserves to be on that list more than him."

"Did you push him to the top of the list because of me?"

"I did it for him," Amit replied without hesitation.

I let out a harsh breath, my heart beating faster and faster in my chest.

"Even if it meant you might get upset with me for knowing too much. I know finances are private. That's why I didn't tell you. Also, I didn't want you to think I did it for you. I did it because your dad is the best candidate. He deserves the help. It's the best part of my job. Even if no one knows I had anything to do with it." He swallowed hard. "I don't regret it. It was the right thing to do, Kareena."

There was a moment of silence that engulfed us. A moment of utter silence. A moment of purity.

I'd been right. Amit did what he did because it was right, because my dad deserved it. He didn't do it for me. He didn't do it to win points with me. He didn't even want me to know about it. He didn't even say how hard he'd fought for my dad, or that he pushed Papa's case so that his uncle would interview him right then and there. But he didn't have to tell me those things. I knew from others.

Amit might not have thought he was perfect, but right now? He was perfect to me.

I wasn't sure how long we'd gone without saying anything. I was sort of tripping over some intense feelings for him and trying to sort them out. He blew out a breath and opened his mouth to say something. But the next thing I knew, my arms were around his neck, pulling him toward me, my chest to his as our lips met.

TWENTY-SEVEN

"Are you ready for it?" Tanya asked with Kimmy beside her, hugging her books to her chest.

"I'm nervous. It's this weekend already," I said and lifted my trembling hand. "I'm literally shaking."

"You got this," Kimmy said. "We'll be cheering you on."

"Um, from home, right?"

"Well, we didn't have the money to rent a bus or car or anything."

I sighed out of relief.

Kimmy flicked my shoulder. "You've kept this to yourself for so long, you can't stand the idea of having friends there?"

"Sort of."

She planted a hand on her hip and Tanya clucked her tongue, adding, "That's a damn shame."

"I'd be nervous. Spectators watching is one thing, but people you know is entirely different."

"We got you something." Tanya handed me a thin envelope.

"Aw, guys. You didn't have to."

"The fundraisers went really well, but we chipped in and thought you'd like this for whenever."

I opened the envelope and grinned as I peered inside at a gift card to one of the hottest shoe stores in town. "You guys . . ."

"Don't get sappy. It's only sixty bucks, but they're having a sale right before prom and you can get some nice heels."

"Heels! I'm gonna get some new sneakers." I hugged them each as Amit approached.

He didn't break the moment, but once the girls saw him, they gave me a knowing glance and eased away.

"Study date?" Amit asked beside my locker.

"Genius programmer, aren't we past that?"

"Excuse to spend a quiet lunch with you."

"I sort of wanted to eat with Lily today."

"Blowing me off? Just kidding. It's fine. I should spend some time with Vinni and the guys."

"Thanks."

He touched my elbow, winked, and walked down the hall while I pulled out my lunch tote full of carbs and other high-calorie food. Behind it, peaking out of my backpack, was the dupatta. I didn't remember putting it in there, neatly folded into a small square. I took it, rolled it up, and clutched it behind the cover of the tote.

I spotted Rayna's glorious hair on my way to the cafeteria.

"Are you all right? Did you talk with Amit?" she asked.

"I am, and I did. Did you and Saanvi make up?"

"No. She's changed a lot over the semester, especially since this whole thing with Dev went down. I feel awful that I let things get this far."

I shrugged. "I wish you'd seen this before."

"I know. I told my parents what she'd done . . . what I let happen. And they, of course, were pissed and told her parents."

I laughed. "Don't bring desi parents into the mix."

"She's in a lot of trouble with everyone. She got put on probation with the dance team."

"Dang. That's harsh."

"Can't have that at mandir, you know?" She bit back her last word. "Sorry. I know they've done much worse to you. They should've stopped all that before. It's not the same, ya know? Things are different. People are more liberal now, more accepting and diverse."

"I guess . . ." Didn't mean all of my insecurities would just vanish into thin air.

"If you ever want to go back or attend a festivity, I'd be happy to go with you."

"You'd do that?"

"I know it's hard for you there. I saw how happy you were at Holi. I want to see that again. Of course, maybe you were happy because you practically drowned Saanvi with the water gun."

"Ha! You saw that!" I wished someone had taken a video so I had something to cherish.

"*Everyone* saw that." We walked alongside one another to the cafeteria, mixing into the moving crowd. "For the best if she's like that. I hope everything worked out with Amit. I know you like him."

"What?" I asked, trying to play it off.

She side-eyed me. "If Saanvi can see it, everyone can."

"That obvious?"

"About as obvious as how much he likes you. And I mean really, really, *really* likes you."

I blushed.

"Uh huh. See? So obvs. Are y'all going to prom together?"

"No. I wasn't planning on going."

"Why not?"

"Dances and me don't go well together."

"How do you know?"

"We were in dance group together. You should know."

"I mean school dances. It's different. Maybe a slow dance,

those are easy. Or no dances, that's even easier. Anyway, Janak asked me to prom."

"Really? I didn't know you two were a thing."

She shrugged and searched through the crowd to find him in a faraway corner talking to a few guys. "We were talking for a few weeks and then last week, he popped the question at dinner."

"Like a marriage proposal?"

She giggled. "That's what it felt like, but nothing more than a one-night commitment. I'm pretty sure. But I was hoping we could do a couples' thing. Get all dressed up in a lengha or chaniya choli."

"That sounds fun. *If* I go." I mean, I had the chaniya choli part. I just hadn't decided for sure if I wanted to go or not.

"Hasn't Amit asked you?"

"He sort of asked me. I said no, not my thing."

"It would be so much fun! The six of us."

"Six?" I asked suspiciously. "Don't tell me . . ." Not with Saanvi!

"With Lily and Jared."

"Oh! Okay, that does sound a little fun."

"A little? We gonna tear it up. Will you have time to shop? We can always do a girls' trip to Houston."

"That's cool. Shopping plus Houston traffic," I said sarcastically. Neither were fun.

She bumped into me. "Downer."

"Let me think about it."

We strolled into the cafeteria and there was Amit. On the end of a corner table with his friends facing the doorway as if he waited for me to walk in. Suddenly, there was no one else. No Rayna, no hundreds of students chatting, laughing, eating, studying, walking around, goofing off.

There was just us.

Everyone else melted into blurred faces and blurred strokes of color. My heart raced and sweat formed on my temple. Was I hallucinating? Was I actually getting ready to fight or was I about to . . .

Before I knew what was happening, my feet had taken control and walked me to *the* table. His table, where he smirked upon my stalling. His friends slowly took notice too. They gradually came in and out of focus amid the ambiguous color blob around us.

Well, this was awkward. How did one go about doing this sort of stuff?

"Hi," I said. *Smooth, real smooth*. What was wrong with me? We were just talking three minutes ago.

"Hi," he replied.

I ignored the clamminess growing on my palms and focused solely on Amit. "So, about that dance thing. We should go together."

There, fast, like pulling off a bandage.

He didn't react immediately, didn't light up or respond with a resounding, "Yes!" Would he decline? What if he did? What would he do if this situation were reversed? He'd play it off and ask me later. He'd ask again and again in a variety of ways and settings until I realized our kismet was to attend prom as a couple.

The guys looked from Amit to me and back to him.

When he didn't say anything (maybe his words of joy were caught in his throat and he needed more of that soda on his tray), I gave my tense shoulders some slack. "Just breaking my heart all over the place, Amit."

"Wait. Are you asking me to prom?"

"Guess so." Why was my heart racing? Was I sweating? Ew.

Muay Thai sweat I could take. Sweating from nerves because of talking to a guy, I could not.

"Is that how you ask a guy to prom? I was expecting a little romance or something."

I grinned. "I don't think you could handle me getting romantic."

"I mean, I've only dreamt of this moment since freshman year, and that was nothing like I'd imagined it would be. Don't girls go all out these days? With flowers and balloons and doves?"

I laughed. "Is that a yes or a no?"

He rose from the table of nodding, grinning friends to stand beside me just out of their earshot. "Maybe."

"Maybe? Are you making me get flowers and balloons and doves? Because I will romance the crap out of a promposal."

He laughed. "No. Although . . . wait . . . maybe I do want to get romanced."

I playfully hit his arm. "Amit?"

"I'll go with you on one condition."

"Which is what?"

"I want you to wear whatever you want and I'll match. No questions asked."

"Did you think I'd wear something that I didn't want to wear?"

He twisted his lips in an adorable way. "You want to wear a sparkly gown or a sleeveless sequined dress with a slit up the side? I mean, you'd look great in anything, to be honest."

"I wasn't planning on a *traditional* prom dress."

"What are you going to wear?"

"I'm thinking jeans and boots. Basically, what I'm wearing right now."

He glanced me over with appreciative, lingering eyes. "Well, every Texan should own a cowboy hat and I've been meaning to get one. You think white or black Stetson?"

I laughed. "I'm planning on wearing a chaniya choli."

"Really?" he arched his brows in disbelief.

"Yep. Why not? We can rock the heck out of our culture at an American prom in the heart of the South. And don't act like you didn't talk to my mom about this already."

"Caught red-handed. I had to ask her permission first."

I chewed on the inside of my cheek, imagining a very nervous Amit asking my parents for permission to take me on a date. "That is probably the cutest thing I've ever heard you say."

"So she approved?"

"Don't act like you don't know my parents already adore you, asking you to dinner and getting me a dress for prom."

"You're wearing it?"

I nodded.

He narrowed his eyes. "What color are we talking?"

"Pink. Duh."

"I don't have anything pink, woman."

"And pista." I grinned big.

"You're killing me." His head fell back at the mere thought of trying to find something pink and pistachio to match me.

"What?" I tugged on his collar. "I think you'd look super-hot in a pista sherwani. And since you offered to match me in whatever I wear . . . no backsies."

I pulled out the pistachio green shawl lined in baby pink from behind my tote and handed it to him. "You can match colors with my dupatta. Think of it as a sneak peek."

He held it with respect. "Challenge accepted. Be prepared for the evening of your life."

"I have no doubts." I glanced at his friends, who tried to

look away, but not in time. "Are we going solo or in a group? Are your friends going?"

"Maybe Vinni."

Vinni offered a wave that turned into a thumbs-up.

"What are you thinking?" Amit asked me.

"Rayna wants to group with her date, Janak. Lily won the auction bid for a date with Jared. Turns out, both couples have been crushing on each other all semester and neither ever said a word."

"Sounds like a romantic comedy waiting to be written."

"Maybe we can go together or share the same table?"

He thought about it for a second before admitting, "Sounds like fun. But honestly, I'd love to not share you. At least some alone time in the car ride over and back."

"It's a date."

He raised a sharp brow. "Is this our first official date?"

"Hmm. I guess so. Sanctioned by at least one half of the parental units."

"The other half will come around. Well, better get cracking on finding a matching sherwani. *Pista* . . ." He shook his head.

TWENTY-EIGHT

USMTO had *finally* arrived. The principal, teachers, and Kimmy and friends had sent me off with positive vibes, hugs, and high fives after school yesterday. My phone alarm went off at 4:30 a.m., but I was already wide awake, ready to go, and literally shaking in my kicks.

I paced the foyer and texted Lily, who managed to wake up this early just for me.

Ugh! Wish I could come! My parents still won't let up on the car thing. AZ is too far for me to drive to or fly to, blah, blah blah.

It's fine, girl! You're there in spirit. I'd told her a dozen times not to worry about being there. Besides, it would make me nervous.

Be your best and no matter what happens, we're all SO proud of you! XOXO!!

I sent half a dozen heart and kissy emojis in response as Mama changed in between jobs.

Amit had also texted. *I miss you already.*

I gushed and replied to him. *That's so corny.*

Wish I could be there.

Parents still got you under lockdown?

Yeah. Bout to break out.

I laughed out loud, imagining him literally busting through his window. *Don't. Be chill. It's fine, anyway. Lily and my parents can't go. No one is going all the way to AZ for this.*

And that sucks. We should ALL be there.

Circumstantial, dude.

Is dude your new love word for me? Like babe?

LOL. Sure.

I can't stand not being there for this.

My brain tingled with all the feels. *Shut up. It's fine. I'd be more nervous anyway.*

So if I showed up, all Bonnie and Clyde having rebelled against the parents, it would throw you off?

Don't tell me you're plotting this already?

I wouldn't make it in time to get a room tonight, anyway. Knock 'em out!

I grinned and texted back with kissy emojis.

"Ready?" Papa asked, slowly making his way down the hallway.

"Yeah," I breathed.

"Nervous?"

"Oh, yeah."

He patted my shoulder. "Don't be. Let this be like any other fight. Get in their head, wear them down, take advantage of their weaknesses. And don't even let the thought of failure get to you. There is no failure here. If you lose the first fight in the first round, it's okay because you fought at USMTO."

I hugged him hard. "I wish you and Mama could be there."

He rubbed my back. "Live the dream for us, beta. You just fighting there makes us proud."

"Thank you, Papa. Are you feeling okay today?"

He pulled back and nodded. "Oh, yeah. Slowly recovering. And knowing my baby is going to punch someone out makes me even happier."

I laughed. "Not something you hear every day. Let me

know if you need anything or if anything happens around here, okay? I can come home right away if you need me to."

"No. You won't hear anything from us except cheering. Stay focused."

"Okay."

Mama walked toward us. "You ready?"

"Yes. Coach should be here in five minutes."

"You remember what I always say, huh?"

I couldn't help but cheese. "My Mama said *knock you out*."

We laughed so hard as she hugged me. "My beta is going to knock them all out."

A car pulled into the driveway, the headlights shining right into the foyer. That would be Coach. I swung my duffel bag full of equipment over my shoulder and clutched the handle of my luggage with the opposite hand. "And I'm off!"

The arena was intense on check-in day. It was way bigger than any of my little fights back in Texas, larger than life in fact. The AC blew hard and cold through the vents. Small crowds filled the stadium seating and others grouped together for their respective divisions.

Coach checked in first to get his badge and checklist all taken care of. Then he walked me to my line. We checked in with ID. I provided all my equipment and clothing for approval on use. People scrutinized every part of me, and fellow competitors turned up their frostiness factors. It was a mental game to psyche me out, but I wasn't having it. I was a good . . . no . . . a *freaking great* fighter. I could hold my own and always had. I could throw down and knock down and that wasn't going to end just because I was fighting national competitors.

After handing off my doctor-signed blood test results and peeing in a cup for my drug and pregnancy test, I stripped down to my shorts and tank top for a weigh-in. I closed my eyes and prayed to the stars that I stayed within weight limit.

"One-thirty-three," the man in front of me announced and documented on his tablet.

Yes. I'd gained three pounds and stayed as far away from a disqualifying below one-thirty as possible.

Exhausted from the travel and long lines of check-ins, I couldn't wait to get to my hotel room. A nice, spacious room with two queen size beds. One had been for my parents in the slightest chance either could come.

After showering, and full of excitement, I called them and chatted for a few minutes.

"No questions or conversation about Papa or the foundation," Mama chided.

"You win. Talk to you tomorrow after my first fight."

I logged into the girls' athletics social group and announced my safe arrival and having passed all preliminary qualifications.

Made my weight, my equipment passed, and no pregnancy or blood-borne pathogens. Yay!

That earned an onslaught of comments and likes.

Lily, Amit, Kimmy, Tanya, and Rayna offered a few texts of support while I lay in bed and floated onward to sleep.

Oh, crap. The arena was a billion times more intimidating on day one of the Open when spectators packed the stadium and the rings filled with fearsome competitors. Coach and I came early to check out a few fights in the next age group up: adult females eighteen and older. Talk about fierce! They were what I had to look forward to, which might've scared a nonfighter but put the fire in my bones.

I couldn't wait to spar with the likes of them, to have my skill pushed to the next level, to actually become like them.

The first few fighters were good, really good, but nothing that made me want to crawl out of my skin and right on out of here.

"Those are novice, first-time fighters within their own groups," Coach said.

"Like everyone else, right?"

"You're exceptional. You're going to be in the Underdog division, the Open Class. You'll be fighting fighters above your level."

"Uh, what?"

"That's what Class A is. I thought you were clear on this. It's how we'll get you noticed by the federation. You can annihilate your Novice Class easily. But you can kill in the Open Class. Open Class means ten bouts, instead of the Novice three. Three at Novice level won't do your skill justice or get you noticed."

"All right."

"You got this."

"I do."

Partway through the morning, Coach walked me to the stadium floor and to the ring on the left. My red Muay Thai shorts with a blue stripe down the side were shiny and new and grazed my upper thigh. A matching red cotton tank top, courtesy of USMTO, hugged my torso. Coach carried my duffel bag and dropped it by the man in charge who orchestrated the fights and told us where to go and when. His name was Steve.

Steve introduced the ring doctor, the referee, and the timekeeper. He checked our gear again and had to approve our garments. We all knew the dress code: Muay Thai shorts, USMTO tank tops, hair pulled back with nothing that could hit or fly off, no glasses, no jewelry, nothing more than gear and an armband. We all passed.

I stood among some of the best female fighters in my age and weight range. They looked extra badass and I wondered if they looked at me the same way. Coach called me the underdog, so maybe they mistook that for being overconfident or underestimated.

These girls had muscles bigger than mine, determined grills, and came in all shades. Some seemed nice and cheerful, others stoic and hard, but I knew they would all bring their A-game into the ring.

Steve demanded our attention with a single look. "Listen up. You have read the rules and know the rules, but you will hear them again. This is Class A, Juniors Girls Lightweight Division. You will each have up to ten bouts and points at the end to determine ranking. We have a computerized random selection system to pair everyone in their bouts. No byes this year. The timekeeper will give you a ten-second warning before ringing the gong to start a fight. He will then ring the gong to end the round. You will break and comply. You will fight three one-and-a-half minute rounds with a one-minute rest period in between. You will touch gloves before the fight to show your respect, any time after that is at your own risk.

"During a down count, the standing competitor must retreat to their corner. After a bout, you must retreat to your corner and immediately remove your gloves. Your gloves were given to you by us, and anyone wearing their own will be disqualified. You are at the command of the referee. You will listen when he dictates stop, box, and break. Failure to do so will deduct points or disqualify you.

"If any part of your body aside from your feet touch the floor, or if you hang off the ropes or go outside of the ropes or go unconscious, you have to the count of ten to get back in the fight or you will lose. This is considered a knockout and your opponent will gain all ten points and a win, and you will get zero for that bout. If you are downed and reach the eight-second count three times, you are TKO, technical knockout, and will lose all points, giving your opponent the full ten points and a win.

"At any time, you or your coach may forfeit. The ring doctor is standing by for assistance, and if she deems you unhealthy or too injured or a danger to your opponent, she can end your bout. Any questions?"

We all shook our heads.

"Everyone understand and agree?"

We all verbally complied with a unanimous, "Yes!"

"All right. First up . . ." Steve looked to the timekeeper, who ran through the computerized random selection.

My heart pounded and my pulse raged. But I was not the first to fight. That was the worst, to wait, but meanwhile I studied my could-be future opponents to the letter. Dang, they were spectacular.

"Get out of your head," Coach muttered beside me.

I nodded and pushed out the negativity. "I got this."

My name came up for the third fight. The system paired me with a muscular redhead who might as well have had a gold grill the way she was mean-mugging me. She knew she had me.

All right. Pleasantries aside. We supported one another as Muay Thai fighters. We encouraged one another as female athletes. But right now? We were in the zone and the game was on.

In my corner, Coach double-checked my ankle guards, shin guards, elbow pads, headgear, and the regulation bandages wrapped around my fists while I secured my mouthguard. The henna from the fundraiser was a dull burnt orange on my knuckles. It reminded me of all the girls who were with me in spirit.

Coach then helped with the gloves USMTO provided, the twelve-ounce ones in accordance to my weight division.

"Make this count," Coach said.

I nodded, dragged a huge breath through flared nostrils, and curled my upper lip over my mouthguard like I imagined rappers often did in their videos to look hardcore. I didn't know how it made me look in this moment, but it sure made me *feel* hardcore.

The timekeeper gave the ten-second warning, during which the referee signaled for us to meet in the center and touch gloves. But this chick had a I'ma-kill-you look swimming in her eyes.

The gong rang and the referee swiped his hand down between us and yelled, "Box!"

My pulse raged through every vein and I was sweating before my first kick. I'd always been afraid of getting punched or hit too hard. This girl came at me at full force. She jostled me with the first punch, and I stumbled back a step.

Good. The first hit was out of the way. My body remembered what it was like to get punched that hard, and now it dove into full-on fight mode.

She got her points in, but Mama's voice rang in my head. She told me to knock her out. And I went for it. Hitting, punching, blocking, striking, grunting, and maybe there was a warrior cry or two in there.

I had her against the ropes and adrenaline surged so hard through me, I almost blacked out. I kept her in place and went at it, her face covered in red, in her own blood, until the referee came over and yelled in my ear, "Break!"

Dang. I hadn't even heard the gong. I immediately went to my corner and sat down. Coach wiped my brow and face and squirted water into my mouth that I swished and spat out into a container.

"You're doing good, kid, but that was the first round. You've got two more. Pace yourself."

Pacing was for my little ten-year-old self who was still scared and timid and small. I was bigger now, meaner, harder, determined. I had prizes waiting for me at the end of this thing and this redhead wasn't going to get anything up on me.

And so went rounds two and three, the same way. She wasn't easy to corner, but once locked in, she was easy to control.

At the end of the day, with some bouts lasting for what seemed like an eternity and others so fast they made my head spin, I sat hunched beside Coach as Steve tallied our scores.

I was sweaty and gross and smelly and exhausted, and all my muscles screamed. They demanded Icy Hot and a massage, and they demanded it now. Not to mention my stomach growled for food and water, and my brain wanted a bed to pass out in.

"Kareena Thakkar . . ."

I sat up straight.

"Making all ten points in each bout qualifies you for the semifinals."

"Yes!" Coach slapped my back and I flinched. "Sorry, sorry!"

"I made it to the next level of torture?"

"Congratulations, kiddo. You deserve some rest. We've got

a big day tomorrow, yeah? They're going to bring more than just their A-game."

"If I can even walk."

"You'll do it. Wake up a little early for a massage and go for a walk to loosen up the muscles. You've got a massage appointment in an hour."

"I do?"

"Yes. You need it."

"Oh, okay."

"I'll see you for dinner? We can go over strategy and eliminate anything that might have you worried."

"Okay. Dinner at six?"

"Yes."

"Thanks, Coach."

He stood with me and gave me a quick, light hug. "Amazing work today. You should be proud."

"Thank you. Can't wait to tell my parents!" I called over my shoulder as I jogged, albeit slowly, up the stadium steps, stopping just short of a small crowd of grinning, familiar faces.

"Can't wait to tell your parents what?" Mama's voice boomed though the tablet in Amit's hands.

"What? What are you guys doing here?" I gasped as my brain tried to process the rogue group.

Amit, Lily, Rayna, Jared, Kimmy, Tanya, and Vinni all beamed down at me as Mama continued to wave on the tablet.

Lily squealed and bounded down the steps to meet me with a huge hug, followed by, yep, a group hug. We were really doing a group hug in the middle of a Muay Thai tournament with me as the sticky center.

"What are you guys even doing here?"

"Did you think we wouldn't come?" Tanya asked.

"Uh, yeah. I did think that. You all said you couldn't make

it, and I even said that was good because knowing you were here would make me nervous."

"Well, we're here. Be happy about it."

"I am!" I looked to Amit. "What about your parents?"

"I'm here for you and your parents." He handed me the tablet. "They got to see your fights. In high def. You were beyond awesome."

Mama and Papa blew kisses through the screen and asked, "What were you going to tell us?"

"I made it to the semifinals. They're tomorrow!"

"Congratulations, beta! We knew you would do good!" Papa said.

"Are you hurt? I saw you take some bad hits," Mama added.

"Nah. Can't hurt stone."

"That's my girl! Can't wait to see your fights tomorrow. Remember what I always say!"

I laughed. "My mama said knock you out!"

"Girl, they were screaming and cheering louder than all of us combined," Tanya said. "They're adorable."

"I believe it!" I blew them kisses. "I'll call you later!" I handed the tablet back to Amit, who stepped back and talked to them for another minute before hanging up.

"We recorded the fights too," Kimmy said.

"Oh! Awesome! Can I see? I need to study the ones who made it to the semifinals."

"Pro-level. *Love it.*"

···❮ TWENTY-NINE ❯···

So that night there were eight teenagers standing around my double queen bed hotel room. This could go bad in a lot of ways.

"Are you sure there are no more rooms available?" Rayna asked.

"Yeah. I've been checking for days," Amit replied.

"Days? How long have you been plotting this?" I asked.

He smirked. "Days."

"We can stay farther away," Kimmy suggested.

"Closest available hotel is a twenty-minute drive. Convention and conference season, they said," Amit answered.

"It'll have to do," Kimmy said.

"There's only two rooms available and they won't fit all of us," he told her.

Kimmy groaned. "Bad planning . . ."

He shrugged. "Hey, I offered to drive, not to set everyone up in a hotel."

"Yeah, yeah."

Amit shook his head and continued to look through his phone. "And also the rooms aren't available until tomorrow."

"Well," I intervened. "You guys will have to stay here, I guess."

"We can't. You have to get rest," Lily said.

"Y'all have to be quiet, then. And not tell anyone, especially my coach."

"We won't all fit."

"Sure we will. Two people per bed, two people on the pull-out couch, and two on the floor. Y'all decide. I'm going to sleep." I walked to the bathroom to change into sweatpants and a T-shirt, having showered right after the fights, before the massage, and now feeling relaxed and full from dinner. And once I slathered on this Icy Hot, I'd smell like a nostril-opening dream.

When I returned, everyone had picked their sleeping spots. Once everyone changed, we were in bed by nine. Awesome.

Kimmy and Tanya took the pull-out couch. Vinni and Jared took the floor. That left one boy and three girls. Rayna and Lily grinned apologetically and hopped beneath the covers in the second bed while I groaned and faced Amit.

"Seriously?" I asked.

"Don't ask us to move, we're already half-asleep after that long drive," Kimmy muttered.

"This feels like a set-up," I said.

"I concur," Amit added.

"Like you mind . . ."

He lifted the covers for me to crawl in first. Then Amit got into bed and we pulled the covers to our necks.

"This doesn't leave this room, right guys?" I asked aloud.

"Right!" everyone called back.

The truth was, we were all drained senseless and there was enough room in this bed to have a narrow pillow buddy in between us. Nothing would happen.

Another truth was Amit and I shared a *bed*. And what sane girl could just relax and fall asleep knowing such a thing? This girl definitely couldn't. After what seemed like forever and the room gradually filled with light snoring and otherwise desolate silence, I turned to Amit and whispered, "Do your parents know you're here?"

He didn't answer, but I knew deep down that he wasn't asleep. I poked him. He didn't budge. I poked harder and aimed for his armpit. He squirmed and grabbed my hand, in the process dragging me a few inches closer to him.

"They know I left to see this," he whispered back, his minty, warm breath touching my skin.

"They're mad, huh? You went rogue."

"Yeah."

"You're going to be in so much trouble."

"Oh, well." We watched each other in the dark for a moment.

"Don't get into trouble because of me."

"Totally worth it."

"Seriously. I don't want to be the reason there's issues between y'all."

He shrugged. "I see it as taking a stand. I wouldn't miss this for anything."

"Did you ask my parents before you came?"

"Yeah. They approved, especially when I offered to video call them in so they can see you fight live and to send them the videos that Kimmy took."

I smiled. Oh, boy. My parents really, *really* liked Amit. "How did everyone fit in your car?"

"I took my mom's SUV."

I stifled a guffaw. "Oh, my god. You are in serious trouble."

"Worth it. You were a total Black Widow in the ring."

"Thanks. But tomorrow, you guys stay out of sight so I don't get nervous."

"We'll be incognito for sure."

I rested my hand on the pillow in between our faces. After a moment, Amit covered my hand with his.

"Are we falling asleep like this?" he asked.

"You mean all romantic in the middle of a room filled with our BFFs?"

"Just like class, huh? By the way, you smell intoxicating." He grinned.

"Nothing like opening up your sinuses for a restful sleep."

I'd woken up before anyone else and went to slip out of bed. Unfortunately, the guys were on the floor and I didn't feel comfortable walking over them. So I decided to crawl over Amit, which didn't go over any better.

"Sorry," I muttered, accidentally kneeing him somewhere that hopefully wasn't too sensitive.

"Aw," he groaned, his hands on my hips to move me back to his side. "What are you doing?"

"I have to go," I whispered, leaning over him and pushing past the strength of his hands.

"What time is it?"

"Six."

"It's still early. Stay in bed for another half hour."

I pressed my palms into the pillow beneath his head and straddled him.

"Or right there is fine too . . ."

I leaned into him and said, "Dude. I'm about to throw down in the ring today. Do you want to get a beatdown too?"

He lifted his hands to the side in defeat. "I forfeit. What are you doing? Running? Gym? Studying opponents?"

"All of the above."

"Can I join you? Tell me how to help. I'm a great counter."

"Thanks, but I need alone time to meditate and focus." I kissed him quickly. "Remember, y'all stay out of my sight. I don't want to know you're there."

"Promise. Knock 'em out."

I crawled out of bed and did my business in the bathroom and changed into regular workout clothes, braiding my hair to keep it in place for the rest of the day. Then I took my phone and earbuds and went downstairs for breakfast in a ridiculously busy cafeteria. I played a few of the fights while stuffing my face with nutrition that needed to last until after the fights. I studied the girls who advanced alongside me. They were my competitors, and, for two more days, my greatest adversaries, but they were also fighters to be admired. Their techniques were precision, viper paced.

After gleaning what I could from the recordings, I went on a walk through the busy streets to loosen up. The songs playing through my earbuds were lyrical, mellow, uplifting, easy to relax to and meditate through. After stretches and practice kicks and squats and upper cuts, I went in for another massage, this time much lighter. The meditation continued, my energy harnessed and focused in a dimly lit room filled with the glow of candles and aromatherapy oils.

Returning to my floor, I found a quiet nook and replayed the recorded fights, and this time studied my own techniques. My brain divided and compartmentalized all the moves, both theirs and mine, and fit them together. If they came at me this way, which ways could I react for the most efficient strikes or take-downs, and with little exhaustion on my part? The judges gave points based on quality of hits, level of defense, and Muay

Thai skill, but also deducted based on levels of exhaustion, amount of bruising and injury, and blocked strikes.

I studied hard, in-depth. But I had to admit that studying Muay Thai was better than calculus any day!

My thoughts wandered toward Amit, and not in a crushing vibe sort of way. He had an arsenal of programming fragments lined up, individually strong and impressive, but useless if not placed in the right arrangement. It was the same for my skill. My arsenal was strong, but it had to pair beautifully with what the opponent brought in order to shine.

At 8:30 a.m., I returned to the hotel room to find everyone awake and taking turns in the bathroom.

Lily banged on the door. "She's back. Hurry up!"

Within two minutes, Kimmy popped out and I had enough privacy to change into my day two Muay Thai black shorts with a red stripe and a matching top. I triple checked my duffel bag for all the necessary gear and called back on my way out, "I don't want to see any of y'all there!"

"Take them out!" they chanted in return.

On the stadium floor, Coach grasped my shoulders and pressed his forehead to mine. "You rested?"

"Yes."

"Limber?"

"Yes."

"Aching?"

"Yes."

"Hurting?"

"No."

"Ate this morning but not full now?"

"Yes."

"Studied their moves? Meditated?"

"Yes."

"Feel the power of all the fighters who brought you here, all of those at your gym, of the spirit of your trainer and those before you, of those who molded even the smallest of your techniques. Feel them in your blood, in your bones, in your soul. You represent all of them, all of us."

I nodded as he ended in a whisper, "Now take these girls out."

With those final words, I closed my eyes and felt the heat and strength of my sport climb through me. I did not come to play. I came to fight. I came to win.

"Kareena Thakkar," Steve announced from the computerized random selection of those few names left.

I didn't keep an account of the names of my opponents. I liked it better that way. They couldn't be thought of as girls with lives working for similar things, girls deserving of the prize, but rather rivals seen by their strengths and weaknesses.

My opponent and I walked to the center of the ring and touched gloves. Her arms were bruised, and she harbored the slightest limp on her right side. From our fight yesterday and her other fights, she had a mean upper cut and a kick like a slab of concrete.

The gong rang. One-and-a-half-minute increments never felt longer when being in the ring with someone like Upper-Cut. She got me twice, nearly jostling the teeth out of my jaw and brought tears to my eyes. Not crybaby tears, but automatic tears.

I stumbled back, almost touching the ropes. The crowd went wild but quickly muffled into white noise. Everything beyond the ring blurred. I'd entered the zone. My head pounded with the rush of my pulse. Adrenaline spiked through the roof, making my movements fast, my feet nimble, my strikes like Thor's hammer. I imagined lightning and thunder exploding, blinding Upper-Cut with every hit. It didn't matter if this was all in my head. I couldn't be stopped.

During the breaks, I soaked up every second of rest, but it wasn't enough. My body screamed and we went at it again. She blocked my moves with efficiency, and I blocked hers just as well. I couldn't get to her right side, but I was able to pound those forearms when she blocked. Her bruises worsened.

We'd exhausted one another in the third round, and I saw myself in her. Rivers of sweat cascading down her face, arms, and legs. Bruises galore darkening her brown skin. Swelling developing beneath those bruises. Bellowing muscles beneath all the injuries. Broken skin, droplets of blood. Hot air escaping in hard, rigid breaths desperate for oxygen.

We went at it again but ended up clinching. I couldn't take her down. She couldn't take me down. We tied when the gong rang and the referee yelled in our ears, "Break!"

We immediately went to our corners and plopped down on the stools as our coaches removed our gloves, our eyes swirling flares, intent on each other.

In that moment, we knew. We knew we'd fight again. We knew the other would make it to the finals. We knew our arch nemesis in this Open, the one to beat, the one to fear, the one to study, the one head I had to get into.

She'd gained the full ten points in our bout, but since she won by a small margin, I stayed close on her heels at nine points.

My second fighter lost her edge later that morning during our bout. She'd been brutally hurt from her recent fights and it was unfair to give the final blow when the work had been done for me. But I took the win. I called her Roundhouse Kick because she had a surprise move that could've thrown me into the ropes if my nimbleness and blocks hadn't stopped her. And if she wasn't holding back because of whatever aches and injuries we'd driven into her yesterday.

I watched the other fighters from the bench, absolutely depleted, and consciously reminded myself not to lean to the left, my more wounded side, or slouch to let on how tired or hurt I was. There could be no indication of my weaknesses.

I waited as they tallied our scores. Held my breath as Steve called out who would advance. He called *my* name. My heart nearly stopped dead in my throat. I'd made it to the finals?

Coach grinned and slapped my shoulder. I didn't flinch. We both did that intentionally, I told myself. No fear, no pain.

"Way to go kiddo!"

The crowd behind us roared, engaged with the results.

Then I looked at her, Upper-Cut. Steve had called her name too. Syla. We locked eyes on one another. All I heard after that were the distant cheers, and in the forefront, my heavy breaths and the pulse behind my ears.

Syla was who I came for.

THIRTY

We were in the middle of the final bout and nothing else mattered.

They called me the girl on fire and Syla, aka Upper-Cut, was in scorching range. My nerves lit up like an Indian house at Diwali. My throat and mouth were parched desert dry, my legs heavy, my insides gooey.

Coach's words rang in my thoughts. "Get out of your head."

She had a weakened right side and forearms so bruised they swelled up. Her legs were weaker than mine, although her giant biceps lent to furious punches.

We tapped gloves and retreated to our corners. The gong sounded, drowning out my raging pulse and reigned over the roaring crowds. The first hit was always the hardest, so we got that out of the way within the first ten seconds.

We went hit for hit, block for block. We were where we'd been the last two times we fought, and if they were an indication of anything, that meant we would nearly tie. But there were no ties here. She always beat me by one point. A one-point divergence meant the difference between first and second place, between the prize money and a commemorative medal. One point could be the gap between being a USMTO participant and a US world champ, a future Muay Thai Olympian.

One point was too much to gamble.

Upper-Cut came with her signature move and I blocked. Her force hit like a concrete swing. My feet scraped the floor as the impact pushed me back. My back almost brushed the ropes.

This was not how I would go down. I harnessed all of my energy—all the anger and insecurities from the past and present, the hopes for Papa and what winning could pay for and lead to. It grew into a ball of whirling power that turned into an insurmountable, uncontrolled vortex.

I was the girl on fire. And what was fire if not unpredictable?

I would not win this bout with my usual moves. I'd seen from the recordings what nearly took out Upper-Cut, and I went for it. All gamble, all-precision rage.

The flying knee. She went for another punch. I ducked and swung up followed by a closely followed knee. My fist dug into her bruised forearm block, which left her midsection exposed, fully susceptible to the flying knee. Into her right, weakened side.

She went down. Her shin hit the floor, throwing her off balance. Her palm touched the ground.

The referee appeared, yelling, "Stop!"

I had to go to my corner, my feet constantly moving, bouncing as he bent down in front of my opponent and, with each number, cut his hand through the air as a visual count coupled with a verbal one so that no matter if she were loopy or dazed, it was clear to her, to me, to the crowds and judges.

He made it to eight and she shoved herself up. He asked, "You okay?"

She nodded and growled.

He signaled me back to the middle and we started over.

We did the same dance again, but she braced herself for my knee.

The gong rang.

The referee yelled, “Break!”

We disengaged from the tight, immovable clinching and went to our corners. I didn’t hear a word Coach spat into my ear. I swished the water he offered, allowed him to wipe away my sweat and blood, but kept my eyes on her. She winced ever so slightly when her coach dabbed her right side. She would protect that side with everything she had now.

Good.

The gong sounded and we sprang to our feet. She came at me with her best upper body moves. I swung low and to the side and pounded into her left side. When she went to block, I went for the right, one strike after another, faster than a viper, harder than a boulder.

Renewed by a surge of intense energy, I twirled to the side, ending behind her, coercing her to spin around. Spinning to face me forced disorientation, lagging, and surprise on her part. I swung. My gloved fist punched her in the center of her face. Blood sprouted from her busted lip and nose and brow.

She fell back. Her butt hit the floor, but she bounced up. She squatted, one palm on her face, the other hovering over the floor.

The referee stopped the fight and I went to my corner, pacing. *Stay down.*

Again, he made it to the eight-second count. She rose. I approached.

“Box!”

There was no time to waste. She knew it. No matter where I went, she blocked, followed by a pounding. Her elbow struck the side of my throat and I went back. Then she kicked me in the gut, and I thought I was done for. The ropes scratched my back like the ravenous tentacles of a kraken trying to drag me into the depths of no return.

My back muscles cried out in pain and wanted to sink into the ropes, to sit down, to stop this madness. Every breath killed, sent shooting pain through my chest and ribs, front and back.

I clung to the ropes for seven seconds. I shook my head and forced my feet to walk forward. There was no rest, no extra second.

Absolutely all energy drained from my being in a cyclone of death. On the edge of helplessness, of weakness, and for the briefest of moments I imagined that maybe Papa felt this way every time he went into the harsh grip of sickness.

I begged him to fight through it. I could hear his voice, shouting from some faraway tablet, for me to fight through this too.

Against the odds, against what my body wanted and needed, I shoved everything into a corner and went full force. I'd have nothing more to give after this. Absolutely, undeniably nothing. Even if I lost, my parents, my coach, my fellow fighters, my classmates, and *myself*, we all knew I had put my heart, soul, sweat, blood, and tears into this.

But that was not enough. I would not settle. Could not lose without collapsing, without giving more than my everything, without being knocked out. If I lost, *that* was the only way Upper-Cut would take me out.

But not today. I sucked it up, took in a quick breath as if it were my last, and went all in.

Mama had said to knock you out, remember?

I went for a flying roundhouse, for the strength and maneuver that I wasn't sure I could pull off. Neither one of us saw it coming, striking her left, bruised-to-black arm. She hung off the ropes. Another eight-second count.

She got up but immediately fell to her knees.

She had hit me *hard*. Motha-freaking hard. But I hit back even harder.

Three eight-second counts meant a TKO. I had her.

But she didn't get back up, which meant a *solid* KO.

The referee called it as my entire body went up in adrenaline-soaked flames.

"Knockout!"

The crowd roared so loud that I flinched. They might've actually ruptured my eardrums.

The referee took my wrist and lifted my hand above my head, sending a shooting pain down my arm. But I didn't care. I barely registered what had just happened.

He declared me the winner of the fight! I won the prize. I had *won*.

Me! Kareena Thakkar. The girl who kept her passion a near secret for fear of negativity. The girl who had once been so concerned and devastated by the unsolicited opinions of others. She really was the girl on fire. She really was a champion fighter. She really was everything her coach and friends and parents had told her she was.

I glanced around, finally seeing the crowd for what it was. Nearly a thousand people were here, and in the front, tucked away in the corner so I couldn't see unless I searched long and hard, was my support team. They waved and cheered and hollered. Amit held up his tablet, a small thing from this far away, but undoubtedly displaying a pair of proud parents.

After the formalities and allowing Coach to remove my gloves and headgear and wiping off new blood (mainly Upper-Cut's), I hugged Coach as my support team came hurtling across the stadium to embrace me.

I took in all the congratulations and kisses to the cheek

and held the tablet in my hand. I could barely hear my parents over the noise, but they cried, and I tried my hardest not to.

Coach took the tablet to talk to them, to show them a few things, and I honed in on Amit as he broke through the crowd surrounding me and pulled me out.

"You did it! That was amazing! Oh my god!"

I couldn't help myself, still dressed in my guards and the regulation bandages wrapped around my fists, sore and sweaty and bloody and gross as heck. When he went in for a hug, I swung my arms around him and hoisted myself onto his waist. I ignored the excruciating pain, fought the inclination to wince, as he followed suit and picked me up. I planted a big ole kiss on his lips, sweat and all.

"Best kiss of my life," he half spoke, half chuckled against my mouth.

I rubbed my sweaty cheek all over his face.

He laughed. "Is that supposed to be a turn-off? Cuz I gotta say, I really love it."

"Ew. You love my sweat?"

"No. I just love you."

We both froze. Okay, so the baddest of the bad junior division chicks who'd just finished the biggest fight of her life was now straddling a boy in the middle of a packed stadium and neither could move.

"Uh, what?" *Smooth, Kareena . . . real smooth.*

He pursed his lips and lowered me to the ground as our friends engulfed us and tore us out of the moment.

THIRTY-ONE

Sitting on an airplane for several hours without moving and then having to get up and walk was killer. But every sprain and bruise and scrape felt like it was worth a few grand. Probably because they were.

Coach's wife and kids picked us up at the airport, full of smiles and adorable handmade signs that read, "Welcome home!" "#1 champ!" "Best fighter!" "Best coach!" "Best dad!" surrounded by drawings of boxing gloves and trophies studded in pink glitter.

My quiet section of street was packed to the main road with cars. My house glowed with colorful fairy lights strung outside in the evening like Christmas had become best friends with Diwali and threw a house party.

I wasn't far off.

"What the heck," I muttered and emerged from the car. There had been one spot left open right behind my car in the driveway.

Mama swung back the door before I reached for the doorknob and embraced me so hard the bruises roared back to life.

"What is all this?" I squeaked.

"Congratulations!" everyone yelled and chanted, "Mama said knock you out, uh, Mama said knock you out, uh."

"I take it y'all know the story, then?" I laughed.

Amit and friends were here, having left last night ahead of us. A bunch of girls from the athletics social group hollered, guys from school, the principal, my teachers, and the parents of Lily, Rayna, and Amit.

I didn't want to look at his parents until I realized *they* should be the awkward ones, not me. They were in *my* house now. But the fact they were here meant they had changed their minds. I no longer cared. If they didn't like me for me, it did not matter one ounce. I was the best me possible, and the best me didn't have room for negativity.

I laughed and cheesed and showed off my medal and ate a bunch of ice cream cake and pizza (finally!) and rejoiced in all the love and support and appreciation and results from a decade of hard work. Nothing could beat this moment.

Amit slid his fingers down my wrist and interlocked them with mine. His parents noticed but didn't say anything, at least, not about that.

His mother confessed, "It was wrong to judge you for being a fighter. We thought that meant you were less of a lady, less of a good influence on our son. It's the opposite."

"So, it's not because we're going to be friends anyway? Or because I excelled in a way that brings prestige? What if I had failed? Or was average?"

She shook her head. "That's not it. We didn't know that you'd won something this big until we arrived. Amit asked us to come because your parents were throwing a party for you. He didn't really explain the significance of your fight. Or that you'd won. Or that you had such exuberant support. We came because he asked us to. Amit has never been troublesome, and he's been getting into a lot of trouble over you."

I scowled. I still did not want to be the cause of any rifts between a boy and his parents.

She went on, "That told us how strongly he feels about you, how adamant he is about us being wrong. Amit has always been levelheaded, so this rebellious thing made us rethink what was going on here. We came here to get to know you, to truly get to know you, and see your parents again."

"Well, that's up to them. Not you."

"Fair enough."

"Thank you for coming."

"Enjoy the cake!" Amit said and pulled me away through the masses and into the hallway and down to my room.

"What are you doing?" I asked when he closed the door.

He stuffed his hands into his pockets and gave an adorable shrug. "I don't really know."

I rubbed my arm and looked down. "Um . . . did you really tell me that you love me yesterday?"

"Heard that, huh?" he asked softly.

"Did you mean it or was it in the moment?"

"Both. I wanted to tell you the last time I was inside your house when you slapped my program into working mode. Got scared, I guess."

"Of what?"

"That you'd freak out or push me away or tell me you'd never feel the same. I mean, I'm still scared right now that you'll say and or do any or all of those. So, I'm going to go back to the party before you have a chance."

He escaped into the hallway before I could even react.

THIRTY-TWO

My parents took *all* the pictures, giggling and gushing at my bedroom door.

"Please don't be like this when Amit gets here." I groaned.

"We're leaving in a few minutes," Papa said.

"Why?"

"Foundation things."

I beamed but asked, "They couldn't wait until the day after prom?"

"Oh, so now you want to go and have parents take pictures of you and your date and friends?"

I kissed his cheek. "Nah. This is much better. How long will you be there?"

"A few hours. We'll be available on our phone. Have fun. Take pictures for us. Stay out of trouble, huh?"

"Of course. See you tonight."

I walked them out and returned to my room, sat in front of my mirror, and watched Lily through the reflection as I retouched my lipstick.

Lily was so stunning that my eyes couldn't take it. It was like looking at the intensity of the sun, so powerful and consuming, but not being able to turn away. Even if you knew continuing to look would burn your retinas.

She wore a powder blue, strapless gown lined with jewels

that hugged her chest and waist in a corset style. The gown flared out at her hips into a flowing skirt that kissed her toes. Diamond-like gems sparkled in her tiara, chandelier earrings, necklace, and lone bracelet. But the best thing was hands down her natural hair. It was thick and coarse and spun up in an elegant French twist dotted with glimmering spangles.

"Didn't I tell you that your natural hair is pretty?"

"Yeah, yeah . . . hold still." She stuck her tongue out at me in the reflection of the mirror in front of us.

Lily stood behind me and fixed the last of my hair. Long, elegant curls and twists flowed over my shoulders and down to my waist. Amit had only seen my hair down once. When he stole away into the night to see me, I'd been in bed with damp hair down. The night that he kissed me so passionately that I almost imploded.

I fixed my bangles, a dozen on each wrist in baby pink, pistachio green, and gold to match my outfit and hopefully match Amit.

"Don't slouch," Lily said, perched on the edge of my bed.

I straightened up and pulled my shoulders back.

"*Dayum.*" She whistled to reiterate. "Did I ever mention how sexy Indian clothes are? Can't believe you don't wear them more often."

"To where? School or the gym? Cuz I don't think either place would let me walk up in there like this." I twisted my lips to the side.

"What's wrong? You look *hot*. And I mean Texas sun smoldering, make a guy want to take his clothes off kinda hot."

I laughed. "What even?"

"Seriously. What now? I know that look."

"I've accepted my bony bones and chicken legs, but these abs? I mean, they look perfectly fine under clothes, and in shorts and a sports bra for weigh-ins, or maybe even in a two-piece bathing suit if I ever dared . . . but in shimmering formal wear?"

I twisted one way then another and watched my stomach muscles constrict and loosen even with the simplest of words or breaths. "Doesn't it look weird?"

"Are you saying you don't feel girl enough to wear that *and* have an athletic body?"

"Well, when you say it like that, it sounds dumb."

"That's because it is dumb."

"I don't usually see girls with six-pack abs wearing formal wear."

"Let me ask you this: Do skinny girls wear these outfits?"

"Yes."

"Do big girls wear them?"

"Yes."

"Little girls?"

"Yes."

"Women?"

"Yes."

"Old grannies?"

"Not usually."

"Women older than our moms, then?"

"Yes."

"So, basically all females of all shapes and all sizes are meant to wear this?"

"Yes."

"Then what's the problem?"

I sighed. "There's no problem."

"Why does this still bother you?"

"It's so engrained that it's not that easy to let it go. But it's not as crippling as before. More of a fleeting thought that I had to say out loud to realize how stupid it is."

"Huge step forward. I'm proud of you."

The doorbell chimed and Lily jumped to her feet. "I'll get it! Must be Jared!"

Women who modeled chaniya cholis had flat abs, true, but they weren't ripped. Like, you never saw definition as stark as what I saw in the mirror.

I slouched, which made the contrast look a little less obvious, but my shoulders looked bad. I could wear the dupatta the way Mama had draped it over and across so that it hid my stomach. Ah, forget it. I was an athlete. Heck, I looked pretty good. I straightened back up and twisted to the side, glancing up at the corner of the mirror. I gasped and turned.

Amit stood at the doorway, his hand raised as if to knock on the wall, his other hand clutching my dupatta. His jaw barely hung onto its hinges, his eyes wide and gaping and staring right at me. Right at these abs that probably didn't go with this dress. But, holy heck, he matched the pista in my dress perfectly.

Amit Patel was decked out in a sleek, long-sleeved pistachio and gold brocade sherwani with matching pants, a gold and pista shawl draped over his shoulders. And he looked damn good, like an Indian runway model. The fabric hugged his upper body just right, enhancing his torso. And that hair, that glorious, GQ, always perfect hair was gelled into place just the way I loved it.

For a minute, we stared at each other, unable to utter enough strings of grunts to make up coherent words.

"What? Do I look—"

"Nice, uh, beyond words," he stuttered, dragging his eyes up from my exposed midsection to my eyes, forcing me to yank my gaze away from those amazing arms. I mean . . . lord! Did he even look at himself before he left his house! Who in the world thought it was okay to walk around looking that fine?

"I look okay, right?"

He took a few steps toward me. "Okay is not the right word to describe what I'm seeing."

"Then what is?"

"Gorgeous. Beautiful."

"Thank you. You look amazing. I knew pista would be a great color on you."

"Thanks. Uh, we should go," he ended abruptly.

I lifted my chaniya and hurried around him, slamming my bedroom door closed. He slowly turned to me. Surprise etched his features. "No, say what you gotta say."

He didn't make a move to step forward. "We don't need to be here."

"Why? I'd honestly like to know what you think before I leave the house."

"Are you self-conscious in a chaniya choli?"

"Not as bad as I thought. I'm owning it. But if you think different, Amit, we gotta get a few things straight."

"You don't want to know what I'm thinking."

"Now it'll bother me all night, so let's get it out of the way."

He glanced at the bed before returning to me. "I think if I don't get out of your bedroom, we're going to be in some serious trouble."

I swallowed, my body sweltering hot.

"Your parents aren't home, because if they were, they'd be in the living room with me waiting on you. Lily and Jared are outside. That means we're alone in your house, alone in your bedroom, and you're wearing this looking . . . sexier than anyone I've seen. *Ever*. So if you don't open the door, Kareena Thakkar, we're about to get into some trouble."

"Oh? What kind of trouble?"

His gaze lingered on my mouth. "Things I shouldn't be thinking about doing."

"Like what?" I stepped closer.

He closed the gap, his chest flush against mine. He lifted my chin with the crook of his finger, leaned down, and gently bit my lower lip. Pulling back a mere half inch, he said, "What did I tell you about biting your lip?"

I gasped. Yep, I shouldn't have baited him because the butterflies in my stomach went from pleasant flutter to raging horde. And I really, really, *really* liked it.

His hand landed on my waist, on the exposed skin between the chaniya and the sleeveless midriff-baring blouse. His thumb grazed my hip then slid over my abs. "I really love these," he muttered and leaned down to kiss me again.

"Well, I really love this," I countered, smoothing my hand over the front of his sherwani. And before I thought any further on my next words, because then I'd just chicken out, I confessed, "But probably not as much as I love you."

"Are you saying that in the moment or do you mean it?"

"Both."

Bam! A bang at the door startled us both and I jumped.

"Kareena!" Lily yelled on the other side. "We're leaving!"

"We better leave too," I said, my voice trembling.

"Yeah . . ." Amit draped my dupatta over my left shoulder so that it hung down to my knee, partially covering my midsection.

I turned to the door, but Amit wrapped his arm around my shoulders so that my back hit his chest. He muttered in my ear, "Wait, tell me what you just said. Just in case I didn't hear you right the first time."

I turned my head and scrunched my shoulder up to keep

our mouths from locking and missing prom altogether. "I love you, Amit Patel."

He grinned, and we finally went on our way. No matter the coolness outside, or the chill of the car AC or the ballroom, I couldn't stop shivering.

"Are you cold? Sucky thing about a sherwani is that it doesn't have a jacket," Amit said as we walked through the bustling foyer where the prom committee greeted everyone with a sparkly gift bag.

"There's Vinni. Do you want to say hi?" I asked.

"Yeah. Want to come?"

"Be right over," I said, but watched Saanvi saunter out of the shadows behind Amit and toward me. Amit hadn't seen her when he walked off.

She grimaced the instant she stopped in front of me, glancing over my outfit with disgust.

"Are you that mad that I'm here with Amit? You don't even like him like that."

"I'm just in awe that you think you could pull off a chaniya choli." She sneered, as if the two of us couldn't wear similar outfits. But the truth was, there were at least four other Indian girls here rocking this style. I was athletic, Saanvi trim and elegant, Rayna tall and curvaceous, Vicki plump and stunning, Samsha short and dazzling, but we were all gorgeous in our own way.

"What's your problem?"

"You. What is all this?" She gestured to my midriff. "That's disgusting."

"What? Being healthy and muscular?"

"You look like a man. It's gross."

"It's called being active and working out. Muscles happen to be a nice by-product."

"You should cover up before you embarrass—"

"Oh. My. *Gawd.* Do you even hear yourself?"

She glared at me, stunned speechless.

"How can you stand the sound of your own voice? It's *so* annoying."

She huffed and opened her mouth to snap back, but I kept on, "How do your parents not rip their ears off? Your mouth is constantly running with garbage and that's all people see when you come their way. This giant rubbish truck spewing toxicity at everyone it passes in hopes of spreading your negativity. But don't you ever get tired? Tired of running that trash mouth? Tired of the bad junk dragging you down? Or is that why you gotta spread it around? To make people as miserable as you?"

She opened her mouth again, fury in her eyes, but I snapped my fingers shut in her face. "I'm not done. If you're unhappy, wallow in your misery cuz that's your problem. As for me? I'm living my best life and not thinking twice about you."

Her eyes flickered to something behind me, but I didn't even care. I was on a motha-freaking roll. "So go on now. I've got no craps left to give. Take your ugly cynicism far away from me and rot in it. Because you can try as hard as you want to infect me with your pessimism, but guess what? I'm uninfected. I'm even . . . uninfectable. Is that a word?"

"It is now," Amit said from behind me.

"Immune," Saanvi corrected, although her voice was half the force it had been.

"Nah. I like my word better. It makes me happy. Bye misery, I don't want your company." Then I pivoted on my heels, hooked arms with my pista-clad date, and strode off.

"How's Vinni? Enjoying himself?" I asked casually.

"Um, yep. What was that all about?"

"Didn't hear all of that?"

"Some of the last couple of sentences, but it's loud in here. Was she bugging you?"

"No need to let her ruin our evening. I took care of it."

The moment Kimmy and Tanya saw us from across the room, they swept across the dance floor and squealed. "Look at your Indian hotness!" Kimmy said.

"And those abs, girlfriend!" Tanya added, although her dress had three slits cut sideways across her stomach and waist that displayed her four-pack.

One by one, all the female athletes from the social group approached, surrounding us. It didn't take long before I noticed a common theme in all of our dresses. No matter if we wore a chaniya choli, a Cinderella gown, or a sleek cocktail dress, we all showed muscle. Some showed off defined abs, others cut biceps and triceps, sculpted shoulders, and toned thighs. And some athletes weren't muscular or trim, and they were beautiful too.

I grinned. "Beauty and power, ladies. Y'all looking mighty good!"

"Feeling strong whether on the field or in a dress," Tanya concurred.

"And looking like hotness whether kicking butt or getting our dance on," Sheree added.

Oh, lord. It just now hit me. Prom equated to dancing. And I did not dance.

Amit held out a hand and I shook my head.

"Not one dance?" He pouted.

"I don't move that way."

"It's a slow dance." He took my hands and led me to the middle of the dance floor as our friends hollered. That just made dancing worse.

His hands settled on my waist, burning right through my

skin. "Move with me. You don't have to sway or have any rhythm." He laughed.

I glanced at our feet, but of course mine were hidden beneath the ball-gown-like skirt. "Am I doing it right?"

He spun me once and reined me back in, our chests crushed against each other as I gasped.

"Looking pretty right to me."

EPILOGUE

Papa stayed in remission over the next month with no signs of relapse. The foundation had, in fact, erased all his medical debt! Mama had bawled so hard that night after prom when she came home and told me the news. I, of course, ugly cried with her. Every day since felt like a breeze, like a time long ago, before hospital visits.

Graduation rounded the corner. In two weeks, Amit would give his speech as Sir Valedictorian. And, although I hadn't heard anything from the federation, I wasn't sorely disappointed. Things were just fine, and I could live with an Open win and a father back on track, not to mention a seriously adorable boyfriend. Oh, lord. I had a boyfriend! Eek! And my parents sanctioned it? What!

Today, there were no trips to the doctors or training or double shifts for Mama or work for Amit. Today, we finally had that family dinner. Guess his parents weren't toting the now-that-she-has-prestige-to-back-her-unorthodox-sport-she-must-be-acceptable theory. They seemed interested in getting to know us again, and Mama had already told them if they ever did what they did to me again, they'd get it from her.

Mama didn't play.

Amit's parents totally took that in stride and invited us to join the upcoming summer festivities.

While the parental units were in the kitchen catching up

over glasses of sweet sun-iced tea, Amit, Lily, and I sat on the floor of the living room trying to decide which movie to watch.

My cell beeped with a text from Coach.

What are you up to, kiddo?

Just having dinner with parents and friends at the house. Why? What's up?

He didn't reply and I didn't think much of it. He checked in on me every couple of days. I'd taken a break since winning the title, and by break, I meant I only went to the gym every other day, no fighting, just weight machines.

The doorbell rang a short while later, just as we decided to go with a superhero movie, featuring, you guessed it, Black Widow.

"Probably Rayna!" I jumped to my feet, elated to have her over after so very long. My parents had missed her too.

I swung back the door to face Coach instead. He grinned in a super dopey way and held a folded letter in his hands.

"Coach! Come in. What are you doing here?" But my brain already knew the answer. He only ever showed up with a letter or email in hand for something big.

He walked into the foyer as Amit and Lily stood and the parents emerged from the adjacent room. We all knew what this was about, but that didn't make me any less anxious.

He handed me the letter. "Don't you check your mail or emails?"

"Not in the past three hours." I'd all but given up.

I opened the letter with shaking hands and silently read. Everyone hushed as they approached the foyer. My hearing went blank except for a slight ring of blood rushing faster and harder in my ears. My blood rampaged through my body and the veins in my throat pulsated as if they wished to be their own sentient entities.

"Well? What does it say?" Mama asked, drying her hands with a towel.

With trembling lips, I replied, "The federation invited me to try out for the US World Championships Team, and . . . and . . . the Olympics approved Muay Thai to be included in the next Summer Olympics. They're inviting me to try out for both!"

The last words hadn't even flown out of my mouth when everyone rushed me with hugs and ear-pounding cheers.

Coach cackled and slapped my shoulder. At least this time it didn't hurt.

"Looks like we gotta start training again! Didn't ya miss it, yeah?"

In all truth, yeah, I'd missed it. But there was nothing on this giant green ball that would tear me away from the "art of eight limbs." Those other countries I was about to fight? They didn't stand a chance.

To all the Upper-Cuts, Roundhouse Kicks, and Flying Knees . . . Kareena Thakkar was coming for y'all. And she would wear pink . . . the most badass color in all of Muay Thai.

ACKNOWLEDGMENTS

Publishing a book requires a lot more than writing all the words. *The Knockout* wouldn't have gotten this far without my effervescent agent, Katelyn Detweiler, who plucked this book out of the slush pile and loved it as much as I do. Thank you for your guidance and dedication and helping Kareena find a good home. Your positivity and humor are always just what I need.

I'd like to thank the entire team at Flux for all the hard work that goes on behind the scenes. Many thanks to my editor, Kelsy Thompson, and Mari Kesselring for seeing the value and story in *The Knockout*, for supporting Kareena and Amit, and not shoving this book into a corner as "just another sports story" or "just another Indian book." I greatly appreciate all of your hard work, dedication, and excitement.

Personal support is always important in anything we set out to do, and not everyone has a team of advocates behind them, which is why I treasure my small but mighty circle of authors (who never gave up on me when I almost gave up on myself), friends (who still get excited when I bombard them with shiny new ideas), and family (who doesn't harass me (as much) on choosing my creative side). I'm grateful for my husband who stands by my side as I journey through writing and publishing. If you didn't know, I have the best brother in the world. Seriously. He has unconditional love and respect even for something that others in the community may not quite understand. My younger cousins are now readers because they can see themselves in my characters, and that is something that I will always treasure. Thanks for cheering me on and devouring all of my stories and demanding more.

Right now, I'm at a writing retreat (in a very creepy Victorian mansion) with several amazing writers who deserve a shout out. Marissa Meyer, Lish McBride, and Rori Shay have been there since the beginning. Many thanks to Alexa Donne, Kendare Blake, Alyssa Colman, and Jessica Brody for all of your shared wisdom and creative energy.

I write stories because they come to me at all hours, at all times. I love words and creating, and there is a deep satisfaction that comes with completing a manuscript where everything fits seamlessly together. I write for myself, but as soon as the story comes together, I want to share that story with others. And now I can. Being able to share Kareena's story, taken from my own experiences, is a very personal thing. This is a proud moment where I can look back at how far I've come; all the trials and tribulations that were overcome in achieving the precious goal of being able to share my story with others. I hope you have enjoyed Kareena's journey as much as I have enjoyed journeying with her.